THE END OF THE VIRUS WAS JUST THE BEGINNING

DELIRIUM

ALEXANDER
FISHER

CRANTHORPE
MILLNER
PUBLISHERS

First published by Cranthorpe Millner Publishers (2023)

ISBN 978-1-80378-124-2 (Paperback)

www.cranthorpemillner.com

Cranthorpe Millner Publishers

To Sylvia

CHAPTER 1

The old clock in Prague broke at eleven, as a distant building burned. Anton Kratochvíl stood near Charles Bridge under street light and moon. He made his violin sing, then squeal when he saw a body on the ground.

'Dead?' Anton said. 'At least you don't have to worry about the cost of living.'

He scratched his greying stubble. That he himself wasn't dead he owed to solid drinking and not giving a damn.

'Oh God! Oh God!' someone cried out.

'What's he got to do with it?' he said as a crow cawed.

He plucked the violin strings idly as he gazed at the scene in front of him. Shattered glass from shop windows was strewn, pale firelight flickering on its shards. Mobile phones, bent chairs, torn leaflets, a broken 'Thai Massage' sign and a shoe were scattered among other rubbish. Battered cars were covered in graffiti and money lay untouched. In a door frame, a slumped and ragged figure snored loudly. The smell of burning plastic was in the air. In the distance at Malostranské Square, silhouettes of figures stood round a fire.

Anton thrust out his arms, beaming. 'What a divine disaster! What a glory of chaos!' He brought the violin to his neck and played a sad tune. 'No.' He stopped. 'No, no more of that, dear Prague. Out of your houses! Sing. Dance. Joy.'

A man holding a computer keyboard leaned out of a window. 'Mr President, you owe me a refund!' he shouted.

Anton spun round to the man. 'Forget all that. Get out here and dance!'

The man spat and threw the keyboard down in disgust, then withdrew from the window.

'No more gloom. No more of the bitter herb. Prague, rise up

and prance about. Drinking the cup of life!'

A dog standing perfectly still stared at him. Putting down the violin and bow on the ground, Anton took off the instrument case strapped to his back and pulled out a bottle of brandy that was inside it. He replaced it with the violin and bow, then slung the case over his leather jacket and took a swig. Cackling echoed from a side street. He extended the bottle to the dog, but it only gazed.

'More for me then.'

Two masked and gloved figures carrying a body came out of a side street. They turned towards the fire. A piano played, then what sounded like gunfire from the other side of the river. On the bridge he saw a ghoulish figure in a yellow hazmat suit coming his way.

'Is that you, Doctor? Is it you… it is. Thank God. You've got to save me from all these pessimists.' He took another swig of brandy.

There were angry shouts from the bridge. The yellow-suited figure ran. A gang of about five chased. As they neared, he briefly saw in the visor the determined face of the doctor. She dashed past and down the narrow alley on the left. The gang followed. Anton gaped at the figures disappearing. He lurched clumsily after and almost hit a drunk, who was zigzagging in the alley, then narrowly avoided a body on the footpath. The gang turned left on Saská, a second alley. He chased them until they sprinted past a small car park illuminated by one of the streetlamps on Charles Bridge. As they disappeared round a corner, he had to stop near the overflowing concrete rubbish bin to catch his breath. Something yellow moved under a parked van. He peered. She put her index finger to her visor in a gesture for silence.

'That won't be easy, Doctor,' he said wryly.

He hid behind the rubbish bin. Soon the only sound was that of a woman from a nearby window gently sobbing. On the side of the building opposite, a single word had been painted: Justice.

The sound of running footsteps got louder as the gang

2

returned. They spoke in punchy voices, shouting at each other. Anton slowly unscrewed the cap of the brandy bottle as the gang charged up the alley. He drank.

'I think they like you,' Anton said.

The doctor emerged from under the van and looked up the street.

'In here,' she said, pointing to the building opposite with its broken door hanging on its hinge. She and Anton went inside what used to be a restaurant. The dining area was in near total darkness and the only light came from the single streetlamp. Anton hit the corner of a table with his knee as they clattered through the chaos of upended chairs and tangled tablecloths, until they entered the kitchen. The doctor took out a torch from her backpack and shone it around. He caught a glimpse of his reflection in a shard of glass from an oven: long, greying brown hair to his shoulders; a thick nose; intense brown eyes; a keen, passionate face. Rather handsome, he thought.

She tried the light switch – nothing happened.

'Friends of yours?' he said.

She pointed the torch at him.

'The little girl I was treating in their family died,' she said, her voice muffled through the visor. 'They think it was my fault.' She panned the kitchen with the torch. There were streaks of blood on the floor amid broken crockery. She flashed the torch back at Anton. 'Where's your mask?'

'I lost it,' he said.

'How?'

'I don't know.'

'Why aren't you at home?'

He raised the bottle. 'I needed spiritual medicine.'

'Are you crazy? Do you want to get infected?'

He shrugged. 'Don't worry about me, Doctor. I lead a charmed life. If it comes, I've practised my swansong and I'm ready to play it. Live fully or not at all, doc.'

She pointed the torch along the kitchen shelves and stopped

3

at a box of gloves.

'Put them on,' she ordered.

'Do they really make a difference?' he said, but when he got no answer, he put the bottle on a table and followed her instructions.

'Any rash?' she asked. 'Fever? Dizziness? Mental disorder?'

Anton roared with laughter. He tried to put the gloves on but they were too small. His stocky hands could go no further. He held them up to show her.

'Doctor, have you noticed any mental *order* lately?' He pulled the glove hard and his fingers burst through. 'Chaos is the word.'

She pointed her torch at his neck as though examining him. He drank again.

'Listen,' she said, 'the army will leave tomorrow. I'm getting patients out of the city.'

'Leave Prague?'

'There's no hope for them or us if we stay after the army's gone.'

'Leave? Well... yes! Yes. *Bravissima.* Yes, yes... leave. It's time for a change. It's time for—'

'No more drinking.'

'Doctor!' he said in mock hurt. 'I always keep a straight bow. You can rely on me. You can—'

'Come on!'

'Don't worry. I won't let you down. I'll...'

But the doctor had put her gloved hand on the door to the restaurant and was through it.

'Now,' she yelled from the dining room.

He smirked and drank.

*

A piano played as they turned left out of Saská and, coming to a little square with a single streetlamp, Anton looked at the open

4

window where the music came from. A woman screamed and the pianist banged the piano in angry dissonance. The doctor and Anton hurried across the square. In the ground floor window of the Japanese embassy, a woman was sitting with a candle in front of a mirror putting mascara on her lips. There were large spots on her neck.

They went up Lázeňská and stopped by the Statue of Angels. A rat scurried across the road.

'What is it?' Anton said.

'I don't know,' the doctor replied.

Torchlights shone and Anton heard slamming doors and angry shouts. They hid by the corner of the building. Out of the archway of a little church behind them, a man called out to Anton.

'Psst!' A short man with a respirator stepped out of the shadows. 'Boss. Hey, boss, you want some hilaricos powder? It's real.'

'No thanks,' Anton said quietly, 'I prefer snake oil.'

'Boss, trust me,' the man said in a low voice. 'Take this and you'll have no more plague. I could trade it for jewellery, gold, food. What you got?'

'A friendly personality,' Anton said as the sound of angry shouts from the crowd got closer.

'Boss, this is the real stuff.'

'But the fake stuff's cheaper.'

'I'll give you special friend price. It's good, from Chile.'

'Really? Pity, I had my heart set on the Peruvian garbage.'

Suddenly a window shattered and the crowd cheered. Anton peered and saw them disappear into an apartment building.

'Boss,' the man continued, 'you know why they tried to ban this stuff?'

'Because it doesn't work.'

'No, because they don't want people to be cured. They made the plague 'cause there were too many of us.'

'Oh? I thought it was because of the lizard people.'

'Come on,' the doctor said and rounded the corner to the

wooden door of a cafe. She tried to open it. Locked. 'Mikuláš! Mikuláš! It's Eliška. Doctor Korbova. Open the door!'

They waited but there was no response. Someone approached from the shadow of an alley on the other side of the road.

'Mikuláš, open up!' Eliška banged on the door. 'We need to go. The army are—'

The figure strode into the lamplight.

'Mikuláš! You're here. Get what you need. We have to leave Prague.'

He shook his head.

'Mikuláš, we must. After tomorrow, it won't—'

'No!'

Anton saw the red spots on his neck.

'Mikuláš,' the doctor said again.

'No. I listened to you… but my son…'

He strode away. She appealed but Mikuláš broke into a run. The doctor chased her patient.

'Boss, boss. You got a smoke? I'll throw in a couple of rolls of toilet paper.' The small man held Anton's arm.

Anton tore away from the little man, then scurried after the doctor. He followed them up the little lane of Prokopská.

'Leave me alone,' Mikuláš shouted.

Anton fell over some scattered restaurant trays on the street. He flailed among the plastic cutlery and wet napkins. Scrambling to his feet, he narrowly avoided the upturned cash register and the rubbish bins that lay on their sides. The sour odour of their splayed contents struck him. He saw the doctor run into a lit building and barrelled forward to see that it was a pub. Entering, he looked around wildly. There were a few people there. The doctor ran into a back room and called for Mikuláš.

The barman was staring into space.

'You're open,' Anton said in surprise.

The barman looked slowly at Anton with dead, glassy eyes.

'I'm not closed,' he said with indifference.

In a dim corner were two old men playing cards. Anton

brought the brandy bottle to his lips, but discovered he was holding only a broken bottleneck. He threw it to the side and flinched when he saw a figure slumped in another corner.

'He refuses to go,' the barman said.

'But... he's dead,' Anton replied, incredulous.

'That's why he refuses to go.' The barman picked up a glass to polish.

'Doesn't it bother you?'

'It's all one to me.'

'Mikuláš, I only want to help,' the doctor yelled from the back room.

'You have beer?' Anton said.

'I have, and when there isn't any, I won't have.'

Anton put his hand deep in his pocket for something to give in exchange, but all he pulled out was a dirtied face mask.

'Ha – oh, but I don't have any ration stickers,' Anton said.

'No one has... and there are no rations. It's all one to me.' He began pouring a beer.

In another corner, an old woman was snoring with her face planted on the table. A full pint of beer stood in her hand.

'I guess she's had enough.'

'That's her first.'

Greedily, Anton took the drink and swallowed half. Then he slammed it down on the bar and pointed to the last corner, where a body lay spreadeagled on the floor.

'That one's not moving either.'

'He never did much when he was alive,' the barman said.

Anton drank the rest and gestured for another.

'Two's as good as one,' the barman mumbled.

Anton suddenly stood back from the bar. 'Are you infected?'

'If I have the virus, I am. If I don't, I'm not.'

Anton took the pint glass, touching it only with the latex of his broken glove. As he drank, the elderly card-playing gentlemen began softly singing: '*Firemen, what have you done, that you let the beer, beer brewery burn?*'

Eliška returned from the back room. 'He refuses to come.'

'You tried, Doctor,' Anton said, finishing off the second pint. 'You can't help someone who doesn't want to be helped.'

She glanced round and went to the two slumped bodies, then to the old woman snoring.

'Stay away from these bodies,' Eliška said to the barman.

'Not going near them is just as good.'

Anton proffered his empty glass with a hopeful look. The barman took it.

'Come on,' the doctor said sharply.

'Just—'

'Come on,' she shouted.

Anton conceded, and turned to the barman. 'We must go. I have nothing to give you.'

'Just as well. There's nothing I want.'

Anton frowned, then followed the doctor to the door.

CHAPTER 2

The streetlamps went out. Doctor Eliška Korbova turned on her torch and saw a pile of rubbish with half a pink bicycle on top of it. Next to it was a body with a sardonic smile on its face. They had visited two of her patients already, but the first one had run away, while the second had gone mad and attacked, calling her an Alsatian.

A nearby church bell tolled, but its sound was dissonant, as if two bells had been struck out of key and time. It wasn't the first time she'd been mistaken for a dog. Or a giant potato. Hallucination was one of the symptoms.

They walked in silence along the empty Karmelitská Street. She still believed the situation could have been saved. Even after the fall of the government and the president fleeing with forty million koruna, five mistresses and a pet albatross, she still had faith. And sure enough, in came the army. Confidence restored, she could ignore her half-sister's plea telling her to leave Prague and come up to Otočka, a village free and secure from the virus.

But now that the army was abandoning the city, there was nothing to do but leave with as many patients as possible. Only, so far, she had not been able to catch any.

She pointed her torch at a stationary tram, lonely on its tracks. Suddenly a band of rhesus monkeys bounded out of a parked van, screeching. She recoiled as they jumped and skipped up the road, no doubt escaped from the zoo or let out. She recovered and shone the light at the tram and saw Anton by the door. When she drew near, there was someone sitting inside.

An old man looked out of the window, whimpering.

'Where is…' the man said scratchily with a pleading, boy-like voice. 'Such a long time… no time. Something happened. She's gone, isn't she, Čenek?'

9

'I'm not Čenek,' Anton said.

'Aneta's gone. I can't find Rudolph.'

Eliška took out a spray bottle from her backpack and gave it to Anton.

'Spray my gloves with chlorine.'

He did, then held the torch. She examined the man, feeling his pulse and asking him questions. There was no temperature, nor were there any red marks and his heartbeat was normal. No pallor, no wheezing, no convulsions.

'Did you see her, Čenek?' the old man asked in a rising hopeful tone.

Anton shook his head. 'You can come with us, if you want.'

'My patients first,' Eliška said.

'They keep disappearing, doc. We gotta start taking somebody.'

'Aneta,' the man called through the broken window of the tram. He raised his hand up; then it fell. 'That wasn't her, was it, Čenek?'

'Come with us, friend,' Anton said. 'There's nothing here but a sleepwalk into darkness. We must go. We must.' Passion agitated his voice.

The old man looked up at him.

'We're leaving Prague and going to a village that's free from the virus,' Eliška said. 'Do you understand?'

'I couldn't,' the man said after a puzzled look. 'Aneta's making dumplings. She doesn't like it if I'm late for dinner.'

'Who is she?' Eliška said, trying to understand.

'Is she at home?' Anton said.

The man looked down. 'I don't know.'

'Then come. Come.' Anton began singing operatically, '*Andiam! Andiam!*' He stretched out his hand and beamed. 'Let's go. *Partiam, ben mio, da qui.*'

'We're going to a village. Leaving Prague. Do you understand?' Eliška said but the man stared as Anton sang.

'To the cinema?' the man said.

10

'Yes. *Vedi, non è lontano.* Let us take our chances.'

'Will Rudolph be there?' the man asked.

'Uh… sure. Yes. Yes. Rudolph, Aneta, everyone. Only, *vieni.*'

The man nodded. 'Then we should take the tram? Oh, here it is.'

'Not this one, *mio bene,* it's… it's the wrong number. Look, I see another coming. Quick. You don't want to be late for Aneta.'

'No!' He got up quickly. 'That woman's the devil if I'm late.'

'Let me help you.' Anton offered his hand.

'No,' Eliška snapped, 'it isn't clean. Take my hand.' It trembled in her grasp. 'Where's your wife? Where do you live?'

The man didn't answer.

'Don't worry, Doctor. He'll remember.'

'Oh…' the old man said, then stopped before the last step. 'What happened? Something happened.'

'*Andiam,* my friend. Never mind about it. *Il Commendatore!* Yes, you are like the Commendatore.'

The man stood on the ground. 'Which way is it, Čenek?'

'This way. This way,' Anton said, glowing.

Eliška led the way. She didn't want to take the man away from his wife, but instinct said she was dead. It was the fallen look in his eyes. She had seen it before, again and again. It would be near impossible to find anyone, even if they were still alive.

'What's your name?' Eliška asked.

'Mmm?' the man said.

'Your name?' Eliška repeated.

'Are you with the council?'

'No, Pops, what's your name?' Anton said.

'You know my name, Čenek. It's Artur.'

They turned down Říční, a dark narrow street leading towards the river. There were sounds of mumbling voices and of water dripping. At the end of the street was the flickering light of a fire. A dog squealed. There was a hard tapping of shoes coming from

11

the side alley.

'My friend, where do you live?' Anton asked Artur.

The old man shook his head. The crisp shuffle and swivel of shoe grew nearer.

'Do you remember, Čenek?' Artur said.

'I'm not Čenek, Commendatore.'

From the alley appeared the grey outline of a person, then a disappointed sigh. Eliška swung the torch to a woman wearing thick lipstick.

'Hey, lover, fancy something?' the woman said.

'Sorry,' Anton said, 'I don't want to get infected.' He stretched backwards with arms wide, as laughter burst out of him.

'What's your problem?' she said, scowling.

'I don't have any money.'

'What about that?' She pointed to the violin.

'This? I can't. You see, I'm married to my violin. And you know… she's highly strung.'

'Is that supposed to be funny?'

'Yes.' He had to stretch a hand to the cobbles to stop himself folding into the gutter.

'What about you, lover?' she asked Artur. 'You want some sugar? Don't let the pandemic stop you.'

'Do you have any eggs?' Artur said.

Anton pushed his hands on his thighs to stay on his feet. The woman retreated, muttering curses. Eliška pointed the torch at Anton, wondering if he was infected or whether this was his usual whimsy. They had been neighbours for two years and she'd met him only to complain about the late-night violin practice. All the same, she would keep an eye on both for signs of infection. She saw the building she was looking for and paced towards it. Beside the door was a stack of public information leaflets that were meant to have been distributed. Her torch caught something written on the wall in blue paint: THIS MESSAGE HAS NOTHING TO SAY.

Suddenly glass shattered and a chair came flying out of a

window. It clattered on the street and a man began shouting from the second floor.

'You bastards! You bastards!' A toaster flew out and hit the street.

She stood back and looked up at the window. 'Please, I have a patient to see here. I'm a doctor.'

'You! You are the worst. Doctors! Do nothing liars. Death in yellow. But not if I kill you first.' He disappeared from the window.

Anton stood near Eliška. 'Doctor, I don't think he's going to let you.'

The man reappeared, this time with a set of knives. 'Time for your surgery,' he shouted and began to throw them at Eliška.

She backed away as a knife clanged near her foot.

'Doctor, let's go,' Anton said.

The man raged; another knife hit the ground.

'Go,' she urged Anton and Artur. The man screamed, a shrill, inhuman sound. She ran as the man's shriek whipped her nerves. A primitive fear took hold of her and she outpaced the other two without realising. She turned down a side street, forgetting about Anton. Narrowly dodging a pile of rat-happy rubbish, she went down a small path that led to a park. There were several fires with people gathered round them. She surrendered to a nervous madness and rushed up to the first of the fires.

'Listen. Listen,' she shouted, but her voice was faint through the visor. 'You must leave Prague.' They gaped at her in silence. 'Go into the countryside… go! You must believe me. You must go. The army are leaving. Go!' She stooped forward to catch her breath. But it was hot and humid inside the suit. Why was it so hard? Why couldn't they understand? Were they all infected? She stepped back and knocked her elbow against a tree and spun round. Beyond it, more impassive faces near a fire. 'Go,' she uttered as sweat poured down her face.

They didn't. They're all mad, she thought.

'Anton,' she murmured and looked. But he wasn't there.

13

She ran out of the other end of the park and turned down a short path that led towards the river. There was a light coming from the corner of a building. Passing it, she stopped and leant back against the wall. She closed her eyes. Images flashed – patients screaming and yanking their needles out; hysterical family members howling; doctors fighting with people; laughter; drunk cardiologists; fear and anger. Fear and anger.

She slid down the wall and bowed her head.

CHAPTER 3

Anton stood on the street. He had lost Artur as well as the doctor. A sharp cackle tore the air behind him, making him flinch and turn. Shadows slunk away. Something ran down Říční towards him, and then the figure darted into a side street. It didn't have a yellow suit on.

'What do I do now? I could do nothing.'

A peal of laughter came from up Říční.

'Yes, that's right, laugh. Laugh.' Even before the crisis, it seemed to him that tragedy was an island surrounded by an ocean of comedy.

He bustled up Říční, then down the first side street. As he came to a corner, which branched into another narrow street on the left, a fire was burning. But there was no one near it. He wondered whether to continue and loop round to the far side of the park or go left and try to find the old man.

'Brother, what you got?' a voice said and Anton wheeled round. It came from behind a shrub. Of course, talking trees, he thought, what else? But soon a figure emerged, a tall man with a crowbar in his hand. He stepped forward into the light of the fire. He had a broad face with a thick, furrowed brow and a widow's peak. The white t-shirt he wore was too small and his firm muscles showed through. He had grey eyes and a malevolent expression. Despite the menace, Anton chuckled.

'What's funny?' The man's voice was gruff.

'Your shirt's too small,' Anton said.

'Brother, I ain't for fooling around,' the man said icily.

'Oh, I don't mind it.' Anton pulled down his hole-ridden mask.

The man eyed Anton sternly. 'You got the bug?'

Anton shook his head. 'Just a violin. Any booze? No? Well,

not likely to find any after tomorrow.'

'What you mean?'

'Well, if I were you, I'd leave the city. The army will vanish in the morning. And when that happens, it'll be curtains I reckon.'

'Leaving?'

'Yes. We're trying to get out. There's a village free of the virus that the doctor knows about.'

'Free of the bug?'

'So they say. But what I've figured is pretty much everything is opposite to what people say.'

'Hold it, pal.' The man stepped round the fire but kept his distance from Anton. He eyed him up. 'These ain't fool lies, are they?'

'Umm? Well, are they lies? I don't know. But if you stay here, see for yourself. I'm pretty sure, *La Traviata* has been cancelled.'

The man clicked his tongue.

'But look, have you seen an old man pass by? I can't find him.'

'You mean a crazy old bald fool?'

'You saw him?'

With the crowbar, he pointed to the side street. Anton hurried up.

'Artur!' Anton came round the corner and shouted again. He heard a whimper. It came from a hedge on one side. 'Artur? Commendatore! There you are. *Andiam, mio bene.*' He looked into the hedge and saw Artur on his knees arched forward. 'What are you doing?'

'Oh,' he moaned.

'Ah, *Mi trema un poco il cor.* Come. Get out of the bushes.'

'Čenek, is that you?'

'Let's go.'

'I can't find her, Čenek.'

'Dry your tears.'

'I just tried the supermarket; she's not there. Maybe she's at

16

the butcher's.'

'For God's sake at least get out of the bushes. *Fretta. Fretta. Andiam.*' Anton put his hand into the bush and coaxed Artur out of the 'supermarket'. Artur staggered through a little break in the shrubs and emerged, stooped. They began to walk and the tall man followed. Anton thought that his jeans were far too tight for him. They were silent for a while until Artur spoke cheerily.

'Is it Tuesday, Čenek?'

'Sure.'

They came out of the side street and were back on Říční.

'Good,' Artur said, 'on Tuesday they have a discount... I think. Rudolf knows. The pension clicks in on Monday, but not if it's a bank holiday, then it won't click in until Wednesday. But if Wednesday is a bank holiday, then it won't click in until Friday. Still, if it's Easter, it won't click in until the Thursday after. And if it doesn't click in the following week, it will come double in a fortnight.'

As they went back down towards the river, there was an erratic torchlight shining out of one of the windows and strafing this way and that. When the flashing light exposed, behind one of the little windows to his left, a dead eye, Anton hurried Artur. The exposed dead eye kept a vigil on the street.

'They've been fixing the water a long time, haven't they?'

'Mmm?' Anton said, and was seized by the thought that the dead eye blinked.

'Power too. Is the flood still going? Do you think the pension will have clicked in today?' Arthur tapped Anton's arm.

'Commendatore! What do you remember of the last half year? Surely, you know there was a virus?'

'Flu? I got a shot for that last year... I think.'

'Not flu, Pops. A deadly virus. Amazonian Blood Fever. You don't remember?'

'Did I leave the tap on?'

'Don't worry about that, Pops.'

'Have they fixed the phones yet? Do you think they'll have

17

some cheese? That's two stamps, isn't it?'

Anton saw that the tall man was still following, so he stopped and asked what he was doing.

'Here's the deal, pal,' the man said. 'I'm leaving this circus town anyway. If these ain't lies about this village, then I'm set on joining you.' He had a cool determination, as if it was a done thing.

Anton looked intensely. 'No.'

'What do you mean "no"?' the man said and rested the crowbar on Anton's shoulder so that the end of the claw pressed into the back of his neck.

'I mean…' The claw pressed deeper. 'I mean, yes. Oh yes, yes. Why not? The more the merrier. Andiam. The doctor will understand. Yes. Yes. But…'

'But what?' the man said.

'What if you're infected?'

'What if I ain't?'

'Rudolf lost his job… budget cuts…' Artur said.

'What if the old man's got the bug?' the man said. 'What if you have? And even if you got it, there ain't much point in staying anyway, is there? You don't seem too bothered.'

Anton shrugged. 'I knew someone who worried about the price of milk. Now that there is no milk, he doesn't worry anymore.'

The man clicked his tongue and waited.

Anton smiled wryly. 'I suppose you'd just follow if I said "no" anyway.'

The man threw away the crowbar with a clang. 'You just keep your distance, pal.'

'All right, all right,' Anton said.

'What are they showing at the cinema, Čenek? Not a French comedy, is it?' Artur said.

'No, Pops, not a comedy.' Anton saw the tall man's powerful scowl.

They took a side street until they eventually entered the park.

The figures standing solemn and quiet around the fires puzzled Anton. He strode near one fire and asked them if they had seen the doctor. There was no reply. He paced to the next one and asked them, but again the same response. They were like wooden totems glowing in the firelight. Anton came up close to them, too close. They retreated, even though they wore masks.

'So you're alive, after all,' Anton said. Yet they regarded him with dour looks. 'But just tell me if a doctor in a yellow suit came back this way.'

They said nothing.

'Forget these bums,' the tall man said to Anton. 'You're looking for your doctor, ain't you?'

'Yes! But this… this is beyond the pale.'

'You're a bit crazy.'

'They're the crazy ones. Why don't you go bury yourselves?' Anton shouted at them. 'You're all the living dead!'

Lights shone from the trees further up.

'Eliška!' Anton shouted at their steady, unhurried gleams. He darted towards them. 'Eliška!' He got closer but saw at first someone wearing a long cassock and an old respirator with the cartridge below the chin. A metal crucifix glistened on his chest. The figure carried a suitcase. Behind the priest were several people with torches in a procession. A man pushed a shopping trolley which carried a slumped body; he wore a similar respirator to the priest's, two great black eyes glaring like a giant fly. He passed Anton. Then, a figure with a dead body in a wheelbarrow proceeded with a grimace of utter confusion. Another body came in a wheelchair, pushed by one with a scarf wrapped round his face. Then, a woman with a pushchair and a dead man in it, his feet tied to the footrest to stop them from dragging. A garlanded street market cart followed, pulled by a lean man with a mask worn under the chin. The suitcase fell out of the priest's grip and, onto the concrete path, hundreds of Czech crown banknotes spilled out and into the wind. The priest desperately tried to gather the money back into the suitcase.

19

Anton peeled away from this parade. Something collided with him. It was Artur.

'Is that you, Čenek?' Artur said.

'Yes.' Anton held the old man by the shoulders. 'And the only way out is the doctor. She knows the way.'

'What happened to the electricity?'

'Something put out the lights. Something terrible. But we must turn them back on. We must shine. Now more than ever.'

CHAPTER 4

Eliška opened her eyes to the moon. At first the night sky looked cool and calm until she felt her own hot breathing stifling her. She tried to wrench off the headpiece to her suit when a smiling face under a bald head heaved into view. He held a paintbrush and moved a little, side to side. Something dripped off the brush and landed on her visor. It dripped again.

'You o... o... o-o o-o-o-OK? You o... o-OK?' a voice said.

She let go of her headpiece. A dream, she thought.

'You... ca-ca-ca-can grrrrrr-get up now.' The paint dripped again on her visor.

She closed her eyes yet felt the wetness of her sweat and the ache in her body. She opened them; the man's face persisted in a way a dream wouldn't. He touched her visor, trying to clean the dripped paint on it. She shuddered and pushed his hand away.

'Don't touch me!' She scrambled backwards and quickly got to her feet.

'P... p-p-p-please.'

'Get away!'

'I... I was just tr... tr... tr-tr-trying to clean yur-yur-yur... your face.'

He was a big, broad-shouldered man. She glanced round her: river, buildings, man, a candle burning beside a wall.

'I'm s-s-s-s-s...ah... sor-ra...sor-ra... sor-sorry about your f-f-f-f-face. Are... you o-o-o-okay? Wa-wa-wait... d-d-d-d-don't forget your tor... tor... tor... torch.' He pointed the paintbrush to the light lying on the ground. It was in between them but she kept her focus on him. He walked towards the wall and hunched over its burning candle. She picked up the torch and pointed it at him as he dabbed the paintbrush on the wall, which had drawings on it. He began to hum.

21

'Do you feel sick?' she said.

His hairy arms and white shirt were spattered with paint. He wore a loose necklace of rusted nails and seashells. With small doddery movements he painted. She could see no signs of infection on him and turned the light on the drawings.

'D-d-d-do *you* f-f-f-feel bett-t-t-t-er?'

'What are these?'

'I s-s-see them. I see th-th-them.'

On the wall were three painted images.

'But what are they?'

'P-pp-ppp-ppa-I see them.'

She examined the paintings once again. Simple figures, childish: a skeleton holding an hourglass, a queen holding a flower and a third unfinished painting, which had what looked like a river with a snake coming out of it. They transfixed her, as if reaching into some deep past.

'Leave Prague,' she said. 'Tomorrow the army will leave. There's a village, with no Delirium. Come with us. Join us.'

'They will be. They'll b-b-b-be. Wha-wha-what I see. I see.'

'Don't you understand what will happen?'

He hummed again with a noticeable tune and rocked slightly side to side as he dabbed the wall.

'Come with us.'

He kept humming.

'There's no hope here if you stay. I know you understand. I know you realise that if you stay here after the army have gone, food will run out. You will starve. You do understand it?'

Something flapped by the river. She shone her light; someone was standing there with a paper beating in the wind. She walked closer and stood by a girl holding a paper in an injured hand.

'You're hurt. I'm a doctor,' Eliška said. 'What's your name?' Eliška stood a little in front of the girl to get a look at her face and neck. There were no spots, but her eyes drooped and her mouth hung open. Eliška took out the disinfectant.

'Are you alone?'

Eliška flashed the light in her eyes; there was a faint twitch. The girl looked about fifteen.

'I know you can hear me. There is nothing seriously wrong with you. Where do you live?'

Nothing, except her stupefied face. Maybe pain will wake her, Eliška thought. She undid the bottle of iodine and poured liberally on the wound. The girl's arm twitched; then her mouth closed. She blinked.

'Where's your home?'

The girl grimaced. Eliška understood. Everyone gone.

'Come with us. We're going somewhere safe. To a village.'

The girl looked up with a face of complete naïvety, like a puppy wondering where the food is.

'I mean it when I say that if you stay here, it will only be worse. Try to walk.'

The girl made a demented smile like a clown and gestured her hand with the paper in it, urging the doctor to look at it. The doctor read:

Pražáks Organise!
Martial law is a trick for power.
Martial law is the play of an unknown hand
Grasping for TYRANNY.
Martial law is will to POWER.
It is the end it seeks.

Pražáks RESIST!
The Blood Fever will soon cool and go,
But what about our RIGHTS?
Are they to disappear into the clutch
Of a never-seen general?

Are we to lay down our ancient freedoms for SAFETY?
And who shall shield us
When, without our liberty, our guardians

23

Become our tyrants?

Pražáks, honest, hard Pražáks,
STRIKE before it is too late.
Before the army makes cuts to the ration as officers swim in caviar.
STAND UP against the truffle-eating generals and their secret cellars.
STAND TOGETHER. For soldiers cannot fight a virus.
Only a people can.
MARCH.
Or else don't march.

BETTER THE FREEDOM OF DEATH THAN THE DEATH OF FREEDOM

Join with the students in our struggle at Certovka Park on the 27th at 6 p.m.

'Golden One! Doctor! There you are,' a voice cried. 'Is it you, Doctor? Is it you? It is you. It is. Why did you run off? What happened? If we're going to get out of this mess, we got to do better. But I'm glad to see you.'

Anton excitedly continued asking questions without letting her answer. She saw Artur, then saw a third.

'Who are you?' she asked.

'You going to that village?' the tall man said, curtly.

'Are you sick?' she said.

'I ain't got the bug, if that's what you mean.'

'We're going, but you're not.' Eliška looked at Anton.

'Come on, Doctor,' Anton said. 'At this rate we won't get anyone. Besides, I didn't invite him. He insisted. And he helped me find Artur.'

She looked him over. Something wasn't right.

'What if I don't take no for an answer,' the tall man said.

'He didn't take my "no",' Anton said.

The man's lips curled angrily. She was about to say 'no' again but realised they might need strong people like him for the journey. And though he looked as gentle as a shark, she accepted the need. This was to be an exodus of many. They couldn't be refusing people just because they looked violent.

'Well…' she said. 'But he's coming too.' She pointed to the wall, but the man with the paintbrush was no longer there.

The tall man shrugged. 'All right.'

CHAPTER 5

'We need more patients, that's why,' Eliška said to the tall man, whose name was Viktor. They were walking up Tržiště road towards the hospital, alone. There was no point getting either Anton or the girl to climb the hill to the hospital.

'I'd rather have a gun,' Viktor said in a gruff voice.

'What do you want a gun for?' She stopped and turned the torch on his angry, mean face.

'Lot of crazy types now. You ain't seen them?' He pushed the light out of his eyes. 'Weirdos. Screwballs. Nutcases.'

'Never mind a gun,' she said and continued up the hill, but there was something sinister in his voice. Viktor clicked his tongue and eventually followed. They passed the abandoned American Embassy, still flying the flag, though grey in the moonlight. On Vlašská, they came into view of the hospital.

'Why are the lights out?' she said. 'The generator was always used during power cuts.' She hurried to a side door and expected a noisy ward. Instead, there was silence, emptiness. Viktor stood behind.

She shouted some names of doctors and went down the corridor, repeating her calls. Nothing. She shone the light on a door near the pharmacy. She tried the handle; it was locked.

'I need to get in there.'

'Got a bank card? Hairpin? No?' he said, then took a running charge at the door. The door gave way at the first go.

She pointed the torch at the shelves and took some medicines.

'Which one cures the bug?' he said.

'What do you mean? Cure? No, there's no cure.'

'You mean, you get it and you're done?'

How can he not know? she thought. 'Your chances are better if you treat the symptoms. Now take a box of those and a box of these and put them in that bag.'

'That's some odds at least.'

'Follow me.'

She brought him to the stairs, then up to the third floor. Gurneys stood at angles and drip stands lay on the floor among scattered stethoscopes and phials. A cardboard cut-out of a smiling nurse had a dozen or so needles sticking into it.

'Ain't no one here,' Viktor said.

'How is it possible?' she murmured, then heard a muffled struggle. She rushed towards it and found someone tied up to a gurney with sheets. It was Sister Karla, one of the nurses. There were suction cups from an EKG machine on her hair and an oxygen mask had been put on her right ear. Paddles from a defibrillator were tied to her hands.

'What the hell?' Viktor said.

Eliška took the stuffed towel out of her mouth.

'Is that you, Doctor?' the nurse said and, when Viktor untied her hands, she took off the suction cups.

'What happened?' Eliška said.

'They tied me up.'

'Who?'

'The patients.'

'Patients? Where's everyone?'

'Gone,' the nurse said. 'When the soldiers left, everyone was scared. We tried to start the generator, but there was no fuel. They panicked. The patients who could move, escaped. Some of them even started attacking us.'

'And the doctors?'

'Everyone left. Don't blame them. They tried. In God's grace we tried.'

Eliška looked at the window; there was a red-orange glow coming from across the river, a building on fire. The nurse stood up and crossed herself. 'The noises, Doctor... God have mercy.'

'There must still be someone left.'

'There could be.'

They made a running sweep of the hospital and Eliška found six frightened patients in hospital gowns huddled together.

'It's OK. I'm a doctor,' she said and explained everything. At first they hesitated, but then agreed to go with her.

The nurse went to the storage room to get them proper clothes. But the room had already been raided – all but one shoe remained. Viktor found a sports jacket in the waiting room. Eliška went to the windowless ICU. It felt like entering a cave. As she panned the light around, there was something almost ritualistic about the way the bodies lying on their beds were arranged – symmetrically bunched, six on one side, six on the other, a pile of get-well-soon cards on the floor.

'Did Doctor Božík euthanise these patients?' she asked the nurse.

'We were all present at Calvary, Doctor.'

Eliška sighed. 'We'll need food,' she said and made her way towards the kitchens. She barrelled through the doors of the main kitchen but was not alone. Her torch momentarily cut out. A man stood eating, clearly visible beside the pale moonlit glow of the aluminium. She whacked her torch and, at the sight of the light, he put his hand on the pile of ready-made food cartons stacked on the bench.

'They're mine!'

Eliška stepped closer. She explained everything and noticed several empty cartons tossed on the floor.

'No,' the man said.

'We need that food.'

'All this food is mine.'

'We need it. There are other people.'

'They're stupid people. Lunatics. This place is full of sick people. The food should only be for the strong and sane, like me. I could buy this hospital.'

She tried to take the cartons regardless, but the man grabbed her by the throat and pushed her against the steel refrigerator.

'You won't take them,' he shouted. Despite the bulkiness of

the visor, she felt his hands clench round her neck. She dropped the torch, yet could still see the elemental rage in his face and felt it in his hands. She tried to prise his hands but struggled to breathe. Then suddenly, his hands were no longer round her neck. They had been wrenched away, spun away. She recovered to watch Viktor calmly pull the man away and then, with a thick fist, punch him effortlessly. The man fell on the floor, knocked out.

'You all right?' Viktor said as she regained her breath. 'Pah. What an idiot!'

She picked up the torch and it lighted on Viktor's face with its heavy, scowling brow.

'Thank you,' she said.

'Never mind it. Jesus, the pig would have eaten them all. Nothing makes my blood boil more than dudes like that.'

She regained her composure and got Viktor and the nurse to pack the cartons. There were bottles of water on a bench and she told Viktor to take some. She shone the light on the man on the floor.

'Forget it, doc. He ain't worth it.'

'I can't just leave him like that.'

'Doc, he tried to eat it all and then choke you out. And your tacky little moon suit ain't a shield.'

'All the same, leave him one.'

'Honestly, Doc, you ought to wise up. Guys like that ought to be thrown in a pit of scorpions.'

She insisted, however.

'Take it you son-of-a-bitch,' he said and tossed it on his chest.

Eliška searched the kitchens for anything else, but there was nothing.

'Let's go,' she said.

They were back out into the corridor where the six patients were waiting. For the first time she considered them, now noticing that some of them were totally bald.

'Sister, do you know the records of these patients?'

The nurse at first tried not to say anything, but finally admitted, 'oncology.' Eliška felt the ground beneath her feet sink. Cancer patients! That meant chemotherapy, radiotherapy, surgery. All impossible. She fell back against the wall. It was like the wind was knocked out of her. She felt eyes looking at her as she sighed.

CHAPTER 6

The old man, Artur, had dozed and was leaning back against a railing. The girl sat watching the raging flames. Anton stood on Mánesův Bridge and a tear fell down his cracked cheek as he played the violin. It was the Rudolfinum, the concert hall, that was burning. He had played there many times and it was his favourite. Mahler, Beethoven, Mozart, Dvořák, Verdi. The Rudolfinum, he thought. The world.

He was playing the first violin part of Beethoven's cavatina of the op. 130 quartet. *This* was the end of civilisation. The house of music, like a temple, was collapsing before his eyes to the blind philistinism of fire. Not just the building, but all the music that had been played in it. It was like the sudden felling of a forest that nature had taken thousands of years to create – in a second, gone forever. He felt like his heart, too, was burning and pouring out like the crackling embers and sighing smoke. He played and was sure this was the true dirge of the whole catastrophe. This sanctuary of the sublime deserved a chorus of thousands, not his lone fiddle. Orange flames gushed out of gaping wounds. It roared in monotone, the drab unchanging note of pointless entropy.

Anton stopped playing. 'And we were due to play there tonight,' he said, sighing.

Unconsciously, he walked across the bridge. The road glimmered red. He looked away and soon his feet took him away from heat. At last, a strong voice began to penetrate. A declaiming voice. Anton drew closer and looked up. There was a small crowd of people and a man standing on a bench in the little park by the river. The sound of the man's punching words was clear.

'Repent! Repent! Repent!' the man said. The orange light

from the fire made his face look wild. 'Repent! Ye have not kept his covenant and have gone whoring after lucre. Your greed *has* befouled the air with poison that has reeked *even* unto the nose of the LORD. His house, the once clean earth, your greed has polluted. Ye have desecrated the green valleys, defiled the rivers and oceans, cut the trees, burned the oil. Ye have littered His creation with plastic, which *is* Satan's toy. Sinners, repent.' He said the last in a hopeful tone.

'Where did the virus come from? From the clean waters? From the pure sky? From the crisp mountaintops? No! It came from the spoilers of deep forests, whose hands were guided by Satan. Ye have erred, and He *is* wroth. Repent and *seek* absolution.' The man shook his fist and looked severely at each of them. Then he looked as if he was addressing Anton personally.

'Ye have worshipped the Golden Calf. Ye have served Mammon and not the LORD whose house is ruined.' Then he spoke softly to the crowd. 'Only repent, for He will strike the sinner who is proud, but forgive the penitent.' Now loudly, 'Ye have put your faith in the merchants of Satan who seduced you with tales of peace and prosperity. They told you to *buy and dispose* because it would *end all* poverty. But all the time, a gangrene was growing on His earth. Ye were bewitched by Satan's soft murmurings who told you to consume and you forgot to honour the LORD. The sleeping angels *are awoken* and their wrath is endless.

'Sinners repent! Satan's siren song has ruined us. Ye laughed at *the righteous*, but where is your laughter now? Ye have lain with the snake. Did ye not read His word?

For now I will stretch out my hands,
That I may smite thee and thy people
With pestilence; and thou shalt be cut off
From the earth!

Sinners repent. The judgement of the LORD has come. Prepare ye.

A third part of thee shall die with the pestilence,
And with famine shall they be consumed in the midst of thee:
And a third part shall fall by the sword round about thee;
And I will scatter a third part into all the winds,
And I will draw out the sword after them.

Oh sinners, ye *paved* the world with tar and concrete that has strangled His creation. He has sent pestilence for your sins. Beg for His mercy and ye may *be saved*. For the vision of the prophets *is* real. And the trumpet *shall* sound. The fire shall burn and the sky shall fill with serpents. Pestilence, War, Famine and Death shall ride unstopped. It shall rain stones; the rivers will turn black as the wrath of the LORD is poured out. A miasma will cover the land as the grand whore sits on top of the Behemoth. Titans with swords and cloaks of burnished gold, surrounded in flames, shall battle. The seven-horned he-goat will make the earth quake. Thunder shall rend the air *even* unto the ear of the *last man*. And he will blindly fall into the bottomless pit. Flesh be dung, blood be dust. Look around you. Look! Babylon has fallen! Babylon is no more. And though *there come* a hundred years of rain and wind, in vain will it clean man's defilement. My sinners, repent.' He said the last wistfully. 'Ye have set loose Leviathan and the Red Dragon, whose tail sweeps away the stars. Repent! For I have prayed for deliverance, and lo, like Job I too am afflicted.'

At this point the preacher opened his shirt to reveal on his neck and chest the spots and rash, which seemed to burn in the light of the fire. The small crowd fled in all directions, but Anton remained.

'Repent! Repent! Repent!' The preacher said manically.

Anton watched and listened and felt a depressing emptiness. Then he smiled wryly. We are playing second fiddle to a microbe, he thought.

33

'Repent!' The preacher screamed despairingly, then fell to his knees and planted his head on the ground. 'Repent.'

Anton sat down on the kerb and placed the violin between his legs. He looked at the fire for a while, then sighed. 'Without music,' he began, 'without thinking, passion, joy and wonder; without imagination, which shoots like starlight in a darkness, this jostling ape we call man is no better than a microbe.'

As the preacher was praying, Anton looked into the gutter and smiled.

CHAPTER 7

'Christ, Doc, that's patting the snake with bare feet. I'd say we've enough. We could ditch the old man,' Viktor said.

'Nobody asked you here. And if it wasn't for the fact that you are carrying supplies, I wouldn't have you with us.'

Viktor clicked his tongue again. They turned left on Malostranské and into the square where human remains lay in the ashes of an old fire.

'Do you know how to get to this place?' he asked, as they went down Letenská. 'We could jack an army truck, maybe,' he said. 'We could find a gun or a couple of bazookas, maybe. But if we ain't got no clue where we're going...'

Four hundred, she thought. Why not? Proper organisation, that's what was needed. Just figure out the details. Several trucks. They could negotiate with the army. Yes, several—

A piercing scream rang out.

'Why can't these freaks keep it quiet,' Viktor said.

'Come on!' Eliška said impatiently.

'Doc, look. This whole thing is looking more and more like a dice roll. I'm telling you, if we at least had a gun, we could even the odds.'

'You can leave if you want,' she said, then strode ahead.

'Crazy bitch,' Viktor murmured.

She outpaced them. A thousand, yes, a thousand. Break it into groups. Put people in charge of the groups. Separate the groups to keep infection rates low. We need a megaphone. Spread information and organise. Teams. Anton can take three hundred. The nurse, three hundred. The rest for me. Tight organisation. Food, clothes, medicines, transport and unjustified optimism.

They came to Malostranské metro station; just ahead was Mánesův Bridge and the fire. She saw the girl and Artur.

'Who's that?' Artur awoke as the nurse shook him.

'Can you get up?' Eliška said to the girl. She nodded. In the distance, the lights of the army trucks moved across Charles Bridge. If they were going to get trucks, they would have to hurry, she thought.

'What's your name?'

'Sofie,' the girl said.

'Sofie, do you know why you are here?'

'Because I'm in a dream.'

'I wish it was,' Eliška said, but a soft smile crept over Sofie's face, so Eliška let it alone.

'What happened to Violin Man?' Viktor asked.

The question went unanswered as a sustained yelling, getting louder, was coming straight for them. Eliška pointed the torch and saw a man running towards them. He was naked and was waving his hands wildly. They all stood back as the man screamed that he had seven fires burning him from inside. Eliška gripped the torch tightly. The man was almost at them when he swung to the railing and, in a swift motion, leapt on it and over it, plunging down to the river. They all went to the side and looked down. The man bobbed up and began swimming. Perhaps they did need a gun, she thought.

'Come on,' she said.

She took them across the bridge. It was Artur who picked up the violin bow off the ground. The others watched the Rudolfinum glowing orange, a slight touch of pink reflecting on the stones. Anton was staring at the fire. He held some kind of poster in his free hand, which he showed her. It had been drawn by a street cartoonist and had a grotesque caricature of a raven with a human head. Dripping from its feet were spiked drops, viruses. Below, the drops poured like rain on a field where people ran hysterically. Where a drop had touched someone there wasn't a fleshed-out person, but a laughing skeleton. In the bottom right foreground was a protective bubble, in which was the president, sleeping soundly in a warm bed. In the background of the field was a cracked church bell on its side. Eliška snatched the card and threw it away.

'What about that van?' Viktor said, urgently pointing to a parked van not far off. 'I say we jump it with what we got. It'll be a squeeze. It ain't no good getting anymore. We want to avoid army on the road, don't we? Then we should go and go now.'

'No,' Eliška said. 'More. Hundreds. Thousands.'

'Thousands! How you gonna get thousands out. Surely we ain't walking out?'

'Why not?'

'Walking out into Christ knows what without even a gun. Man… and thousands? You'd have to jack a train for that.'

It could be done, she thought. They could go to the train station. Teams divided into hundreds, equally spaced on a train. It's only organisation. Would need a train driver, someone who knows points. Is there a station near Otočka? Enough Diesel?

She got them all moving. Anton was particularly slow and fell back to Artur, who was not the quickest. When he saw Anton, he offered him the bow.

'Do you play the violin?'

Anton was overjoyed. 'Commendatore! You found it. You found it.'

'Eh?' Artur said, but Anton had taken the bow and began playing a capriccio like a child who was sad but is thrown some toy and forgets it all in play. They cut across the grass in front of the heat of the fire. Then Eliška led them right onto Široká Street. The light of the burning building cast a long way down the street. There ought to have been soldiers, but instead dogs prowled.

On the left was the synagogue with its small graveyard. Eliška noticed something in red paint on the wall. Shining the torchlight, she saw some words which had streaked: IT WAS THE JEWS WHO DONE IT.

Below it was a Star of David inside a spiked circle, imitating the image of a virus. The others saw it in turn. Finally, when Anton saw it, he shrugged.

'Ehh. What do you expect? We get blamed for everything.'

They continued. Viktor walked beside Anton.

'Listen, brother,' Viktor said quietly, 'I don't like it. And I ain't one for fooling around. She wants thousands. We're twelve already. It's enough. What say we two split off on our own. We'll need a gun.'

'Brother,' Anton said, smiling, 'I know the doctor. She knows what she's doing.'

'Is that a fact?'

'Yes. You just have to trust her.'

'Trust?' Viktor clicked his tongue. 'Damn crazy.'

CHAPTER 8

'The stove isn't working,' Artur mumbled. 'I'll have to get, what are they called... she could use Rudolf's electric... then she'll make me wear woollen socks... the itchy ones... good for circulation, she said... the itchy ones... valve? A valve?'

Eliška turned when she saw a light coming from a souvenir shop. She entered. Several candles were placed around the shop, which was full of Bohemian crystal, amulets, charms, astrological charts, tables of alchemical symbols, posters with Tibetan mandalas and other things. Hanging above the checkout counter was a giant plaque of the representation of *Om*. There was some writing on the wall in what looked like Sanskrit. Eliška's attention was drawn to a circle of women, who had gathered round several candles, which were themselves circled round a font of water. The women wore loose-fitting gypsy clothing. They were dancing in the circle, holding hands. Incense burned in the corner. Eliška spoke hurriedly to them. Perhaps they didn't at first understand. She repeated it slower. One of them broke from the circle and stood near Eliška.

'Why should we leave Prague?' one woman said in a soothing yet sententious voice. 'We don't believe there is a virus. Rather, a psychological phenomenon. A disturbance in energy. The chakras are blocked by a cosmic neurosis. We are cleansing the poison that has choked all the love. We chant and dance as the eagle and the buffalo, free by the mountain rivers.'

'But the army will leave tomorrow,' Eliška said. The woman, without missing a beat, smiled serenely.

'What you see is not what you see.'

'But—'

'Scientists have a theory,' said another woman, 'but that's only one point of view. Another is that there is no such thing as a virus. If there's trouble, it's because there's a tsunami in the universal waves. Only love repairs the broken frequency. By Mars, Venus and Saturn, and by the three lightnings and the river, we seek to heal the world. Om.'

'Om,' chanted the others in the circle.

'Om,' chanted the first woman.

'Don't waste your time on these nut jobs. Let them eat their crystals,' Viktor said.

She tried once again, but the woman only put her hands together in prayer and raised them to her forehead, bowing slightly and smiling, possibly to convey humility. Eliška looked at the others in the circle; they had done the same.

'Om,' chanted the others.

'Om,' chanted the first woman.

Eliška left. Next to the old synagogue was an alley. Was that the way to Františku Hospital? She couldn't recall even though she knew Prague very well. In any case she strode down the alley and assumed they were following. She got to the steps leading up to Rue de Paris – a strange boulevard it looked. Most of the windows of the high-class clothes shops, jewellers and luxuries, were smashed and a great deal of their contents had been vomited onto the road. Mannequins, many with missing limbs, filled the street, their attire sullied and some graffitied. Handbags and clothes had been thrown. She shone the torch and it lit up something white in the middle of the road. A toilet seat. Next to it an empty suitcase, in which a cat's green eyes reflected. A lot of boxes that had been flattened. People were talking as she walked out onto the middle of the street. She spun round at the approach of the others.

'Put the water and food in that suitcase,' she said to Viktor and flashed her torch at the cat. She saw the nurse trundling out the patients from the alley. Anton, Artur and Sofie followed. But something was wrong. 'Didn't we have six?'

'Yes, Doctor, I don't know what happened. I went back to the souvenir shop and searched, but one of them is gone.'

Eliška ran back down the alley towards the old synagogue. She got back to Maiselova where the souvenir shop was. She panned the torch but there was no one. She growled and ran back down the alley and back up the stairs to the Rue de Paris. 'Karla… and Anton… go into these clothing shops and find any clothes that could be useful.' Then she gathered her breath and spoke to the patients. 'If you want to go, go. But if you're with us, stick close.' They all looked frightened, except one. 'Follow me.' Eliška strode down towards the sounds of the voices. They passed a little park on the left. It sounded like a crowd, Eliška thought. Lights flickered. She turned off her torch and came to the place. It was a square and there was a large gathering. A hundred or so. They were using old oil lanterns for light. In the middle of the square was a large army tent, which was being used as a ration point. There was tension in the crowd, their voices strained and anxious. She must convince them, she thought.

The patients arrived and so did Viktor, wheeling the suitcase.

'We can avoid them by going left down this street,' Viktor said.

'No, they could join us. Then I must go to the hospital.'

'You're insane. What if they got the bug?'

But she had already advanced towards the people. They began to hush seeing the yellow suit of authority approach. She saw a raised concrete square to one side, in which was a garden that had long gone to weed. The crowd parted and she walked through the middle. She got to the raised square and climbed on it. They gathered in closer, their faces eager for answers. She tried to remain calm. She tried to slow down. It was like a sauna inside her suit. She undid the fittings one by one. Slowly she pulled off the headpiece; it made a sucking sound as cooler air rushed in. Someone brought a lantern closer. Her face had a sheen of sweat. Her ginger hair was loose and soaked; so was the undershirt. Her lips were cracked. Her blue eyes were bloodshot and looked manic.

'I have important information. I'm a doctor. Tomorrow the

41

army will leave Prague. The city will be abandoned. I am organising as many people as I can to go north to a village called Otočka. It's free from the virus. If we plan it properly, we could get thousands safely there.'

'Liar,' someone shouted. 'More lies.'

'They just don't want to give us our ration,' said another. They all began to yell.

'Listen to me,' Eliška said, 'listen. The army—'

'Our ration was due today. Where is our ration?'

'That's what I'm trying to tell you. There aren't going to be any more rations.'

'She just wants us to leave so the army don't have to give us the ration.'

'Yes,' said another, 'I say we stay right here and wait for the ration.' There was a chorus of agreement.

'Listen to me,' she said. 'There'll be no more rations. I'm speaking the truth. I'm not the army.'

'It's another trick. Always lying.'

'You must believe me.' She began to feel faint.

At the back of the crowd, Anton and the nurse had come and stood near the patients and Viktor.

'All right, pal, I'm splitting. She's lost it. You coming?' he said to Anton, who grasped Viktor's arm.

'They'll kill her,' Anton said.

'They look ready to.'

'You can't leave her.'

'I intend to live, Violin Man.'

The crowd menaced: 'Murderers! Incompetents.'

'Where's the vaccine? They told us there was a vaccine. Where is it?' said another.

'Yes, they did lie,' Eliška said a little breathless. 'But I'm telling the truth. We just need to plan and we can make it.'

There was a clattering as the crowd rushed forward. They dragged her down off the concrete square. They were too crowded to lay any blows, though she got one in the ribs. Anton rushed forward through the thick crowd. Yet it suddenly broke up when a gunshot rang out of one of the buildings around the square. The crowd scurried away to all corners. There was another shot, and the crowd ran into the cover of side streets and buildings. Anton ran forward towards the sprawled figure of Eliška. A drunken voice bellowed from a third-storey balcony window.

'Shut up! Shut up! God damn people. Shut up.' A candle burned on the window ledge, by which a portly man, wearing a police uniform with his shirt unbuttoned and hair awry, was swaying and grunting. He waved the gun that was in his hand.

'Go away. Stop your complaining. You want to report something? You can kiss my ass.' The cop shot again into the air and whooped. 'No, no I can't find your sister... she's having a plague party. No, I can't arrest him, no more judges. Your car was stolen? Lucky thief! You lost your son? Why don't you have a plague party... no, I don't know why your wife stabbed your child. It was sick. She's sick. You're sick. We're all sick.' He paused briefly in his litany to drink from a bottle of liquor.

'No, we can't stop the looting... we can't do anything. And you lie. They lie. They say, "I'm not sick" and the sergeant says "lock 'em up, he's not sick". But he is. He's just come from a plague party. 'Cause it's a party.'

He leant on the window frame. He had marks on his neck and chest. He made a wild cry, a sound of injustice. He raised the gun again to shoot at the sky but knocked his hand against the window frame, sending the gun falling to the ground. Viktor ran forward and crouched behind the raised concrete square. The policeman drank deep from the bottle and began to sob. He brought his hands to his face. Viktor darted out from the cover of the concrete and to the pavement where the gun had fallen. He took it quickly and dashed back, but he needn't have been so careful. The policeman did not notice.

'All right,' Viktor said to Anton, 'you take the doc. Run to that corner.'

43

Anton nodded. 'Does this mean you're sticking with us?'

'Nice try, Violin Man. I'm out of it. Now I got a gun. Good luck to you, pal.'

Eliška was slightly dazed but largely unhurt. The policeman was now weeping noisily.

'All right, ready?' Viktor said. Anton and Eliška prepared to run. Viktor aimed the gun at the policeman.

'Go!'

They ran to the corner of the building on Rue de Paris. The policeman didn' notice the yellow suit. They made it round the corner where the nurse, Sofie and Artur were. There was only one patient left. Eliška put her headgear back on.

'Where are the rest?' she said.

'They ran. I couldn't stop them.'

'We must find them.'

'Doctor, I don't think it's…' the nurse said, but to the doctor's back, who was pacing up the street. Viktor went the opposite way towards the river and out of sight.

Eliška stopped and tried to think but felt dizzy. She staggered back a little, then thought she saw someone in a shop. It was not a patient but a mannequin. Its face looked momentarily like a skull wearing a surgical mask. Then its long skeleton arms rose with gloved hands. She looked away.

'No. No,' she uttered. Lights swirled. Objects blurred. She pointed her torch. There was nothing there except a dismembered mannequin lying on the road. But there was something moving in the distance. She paced ahead. Or thought she did. Her torch stopped. Or she thought it did. She ran towards the motion. There were several black handbags and belts in a wavy line that seemed to animate and slither. She stepped back and hit the torch. It shone. Or she thought it did. She hurried then stopped at an alleyway where she saw a patient running down. She shrieked when she felt something grab her arm. It was a mannequin. It briefly looked like Anton. Then the face became indistinct. On the mannequin's head sat a crown and around its body it wore the

44

gold-laced garb of a mediaeval king. It held a sword in one hand and was bowing.

The mannequin took the crown off its head and let it fall where it then shattered to dust. A scarf fell from its neck and turned into a snake that started eating the golden dust. She stamped her foot; these are not real things, she thought. Hallucinations. She felt as though she was on fire.

'Help!' she said. The mannequin's hand grasped her shoulder again but had turned into Anton. She pushed it away and hid behind a car. Her head felt like it was scorching. She watched another mannequin jump on something. It seemed like a pile of hospital equipment and PPE. Then arrayed opposite was what looked like a firing squad of mannequins all holding assault weapons. They were wearing masks and gloves. At a shout, they started shooting the pile, which began to rip and then to sag. One of them looked at her and turned into a skeleton. It was wearing sunglasses. It lowered them and waved. She ran. There was a small park on the left, which she raced into, steadying herself next to a statue with its slumped head. She tried to breathe calmly. She told herself again that they were hallucinations. Yet they *were* real. There seemed no way to reach out, through into the place where one knew the difference.

'No one listened to me either. I had no end of trouble with that stiff-necked lot.' It was a soothing voice, but forlorn. She looked up. It was coming from the statue, though the form itself did not move. It was a statue of Moses. 'I should have just let Pharaoh keep them.'

She stepped back into the shrubs and a swooning darkness overcame her.

CHAPTER 9

A bright light shone in her eyes. She heard a dull mechanical sound and straightened up as the thudding sound disappeared. As she doddered along the Rue de Paris towards the river, the strange mechanical sound returned and grew louder. Suddenly it rushed near and burst above her as the chopping, shuddering pulse of a helicopter. Its lights flashed the sides of buildings and the empty square. She ran.

The helicopter passed and was replaced by another mechanical sound. Behind her a military truck was coming down the road, crashing through the detritus. The helicopter reappeared above her and bore its powerful lights. She stopped, momentarily blinded. The wind held her back as she strove to push forward. She held her arm up to shield her eyes and jerked as if trying to swipe the helicopter away. No, it was not a hallucination, and it would not let her pass.

'Move,' she said, breathless.

She pushed forward again; it didn't move, but a truck drove by, startling her. But it wasn't just one. There was a convoy of army trucks driving down Rue de Paris. In the gaps as each truck passed, she saw the burning Rudolfinum. Then as one of the trucks passed, she thought she saw in the gap a skinny horse and skeleton. Then the next truck came, and the horse was closer and wearing a surgical mask and gloves on its hooves. In the next gap, the horse came closer still. After the next truck, the horse was flying towards her until the next truck swiped it away. Eliška staggered towards the river. Up ahead the trucks were turning right at the end of Rue de Paris.

'Cowards,' she shouted.

She dragged her heavy, aching feet to the corner of the road, opposite which was the river. Standing on the corner, she looked up to see that one of the trucks was open at the back and had nothing in it. Why were the trucks empty? They could use them, put people in them, to Otočka. The next one, however, had smiling skeletons throwing their face masks and gloves at her. From behind the hotel burst the helicopter, like a banging drum and cymbal crash. The truck horns sounded like trumpets; the engines, church organs; the breaking windows of the hotel, screeching violins. She tore forward to the road; she wanted to cross it to get to the river, but the convoy was driving too close together. She waited for a gap. There were fires – the two statues of Victory on the bridge nearby. She felt the earth closing in, the sky weighing down and buckling her knees. It was sucking out the air. The hot air of burnt rubber and pungent sweat. She had a chill and shiver. 'Cross the road,' she implored herself. She took one step, but a horse-drawn cortège stopped her. A skeleton on it threw an hourglass on the pavement where it shattered into a thousand pieces – its sands cast. Then the convoy passed, and she stepped onto the road.

'Stop! Eliška stop,' voices behind her screamed.

She saw stars and breathed deep. In fact, the convoy was still going, and she had almost walked into a passing truck, but the one remaining patient grasped her arm and pulled her back. The truck growled like a bear. Eliška clutched her abdomen where she felt a shooting pain. No, she thought, I will not yield. And she broke away from the patient's grasp and lurched onto the road. This time, the convoy had really passed. It felt to her as though the world was moving up and down – crashing. Sirens. Fire. Choking. She got to the steps on the other side of the road that led down to the river promenade. She grasped the handrail and buckled; objects swirled. Trees, stairs, arms, river. The steps seemed to be rising. She turned – patients, many patients. She looked up through the fogged visor at the passing helicopter, thudding. There it passed and left the moon resting large in the darkness. She closed her eyes and saw the huge football field that was covered in white tents, with their patients and drip stands and

47

nurses. Patients in hospital gowns were walking like robots. Then the white tents shrank and turned darker. And darker, until they tightened into black pupae, thousands wriggling in the long grass.

'Doctor! Doctor!'

The city was dying too. All the cities of the earth were dying. Falling away, melting. Burning. Feverish. Infected. Strangled. Convulsing. Losing consciousness.

They ripped off her headgear. She was flapping her head side to side and swooning. Her hair glistened in the torchlight. They grasped her. She stopped struggling and became limp.

'No!' She stood up. She would not accept it and lie down. But she started to convulse. They held her and tried to soothe her as she went into seizure. Anton unzipped the front to give her air. Her torch fell from her hand; its light showed her collarbone covered in red spots. She started foaming at the mouth.

Viktor clicked his tongue.

CHAPTER 10

'God damn it,' Viktor said. 'What the hell are you people doing?'

The nurse took off Eliška's yellow suit and told the others to stand back. Eliška had several tremors and then lost consciousness.

'I can't escape you people. She's got the bug, hasn't she?' He stood back so as to avoid being close to her.

'Her pulse is weak,' the nurse said. 'I need somewhere to set up a drip.'

'Well, you ain't bringing her on this boat.'

The nurse ordered Anton to take Eliška's feet, while she took her arms.

'God damn it, I'm taking this boat – no you can't bring her on.'

The nurse insisted. Viktor took out his gun. The bald patient moved forward and put her hand on his arm. A silent battle followed. Not defiance in her eyes but fearlessness. The drone of the helicopter receded. Viktor clicked his tongue, lowered the gun and moved out of the way.

'I couldn't get it started anyway,' he said as Anton and the nurse carried her onto the boat. The bald patient then took the torch and lit the way. It was a small tourist boat. On part of the deck was an awning and seats. Forward of the boat was a small cabin sitting room. They brought her into it, first going down some wooden steps and then laying her on one of the sofas.

'I'll stay with her,' the nurse said to Anton. 'Take off your gloves and let me spray your hands. Then close the door as you leave.'

Viktor paced on the deck. All the other boats were gone; probably this one was spared because it wouldn't start. Viktor was startled when he saw a shadowy figure near the stern of the

49

boat. He pulled out the gun.

'Who are you?' he shouted.

The figure did nothing.

'She's in the cabin room,' Anton said, coming up and shutting the door.

'Is that a fact?' Viktor said, still looking aft. 'Well, you can keep her. I'm out of it. I ain't going to stay and get her bug.' He turned to leave, but the bald patient held his arm. He put his large hands to her neck. 'You have no idea—'

'Viktor, what's the point?' Anton said.

'That is an excellent question,' a voice said from the stern of the boat, the shadowy figure. Viktor let go of the patient and marched aft, past the tables and chairs that were fixed in the middle of the deck. Part of the stern was not covered by the awning and the figure stood there. The bald patient pointed the torch. There was a tall man, with a lean, angular, skeletal face. His raven hair was straight, his nose long and sharp with small wheel glasses resting on its bridge. Despite the season, he wore a long black coat, black trousers, black boots. He opened his arms, and one could imagine a dark angel opening its pitch-black wings.

'Who the hell are you!' Viktor said.

'Nobody,' he said shifting his glasses, which framed his black icy eyes. 'And it doesn't matter. To travel would be pointless. That's why I want to do it.'

'Christ. Another nutcase.'

'What a lot of noise is made! What a lot of things are produced and yet in the end it means... Well, I shan't say what it means. Chaos, anarchy, fragmentation,' the man said. Viktor marched away.

'I can get the boat started,' the man said. Viktor stopped. 'Though naturally it doesn't matter. I had the idea too, of using the boat. Up the river to go nowhere, where there is nothing.'

Viktor grabbed the man by his coat collar, whose eyes became large in his wheel glasses. 'Damn it, I'm going to put your carcass with the fish unless it starts talking sense. Can you start this boat or not?'

'I can.'

'Then do it.'

'Not if I can't be on it.'

'Forget it, pal. This is my boat.'

'Viktor, come on, why don't you?' Anton said. 'How're you going to get anywhere if you can't start it. Look, if the guy can start it, I'd say he gets a ticket.'

Viktor let the man go and clicked his tongue. 'God damn nuthouse.' He pocketed the gun. 'All right, but only because I don't want to meet any whack jobs on the road. It's still the best way. But the doc stays in that cabin and if she dies, then we leave her there, with that nurse. And, God damn it, it's my boat.'

'So much noise,' the tall man said.

'Well, come on. You said you can get this thing started.'

The man reset his glasses on his nose.

'Under that bridge, there's a battery in a pushchair. I was bringing it here when I saw you jump onto the boat.'

Viktor charged off in search of the battery that would start the boat. The tall man approached Anton. But the bald patient gestured that they all keep their distance. The tall man stopped and took out of his pocket a handkerchief, and, taking off his glasses, he began to polish them.

'Well,' he began, 'it doesn't really matter, though. I'm not infected but the virus is just information. Made from a history that probably never existed. Now surely, *that* is no basis for a reality. There must be something more total. How can we say we understand anything when we can't even figure out a virus?' He seemed indifferent to the tension. He readjusted his glasses. The bald patient sat down and Anton, too, slumped down on a seat.

'I believe this is all illusion,' the man said waving his hand to the city. Anton wondered if greater and greater insanity was part of the new reality.

'We talk of right and wrong,' the man continued. 'Is the virus right? Are we wrong? Or is the virus wrong because it has a life? Are we right thinking the virus is wrong to have a life?'

Anton rested his chin on his hand, too exhausted to care.

'These questions are meaningless. We cannot know anything in a changing universe because what we know changes.'

Anton rubbed his face and sighed.

'Therefore, we don't know anything. That leads only one way. It's really quite simple.'

Racing down the street with a pushchair, Viktor turned onto the gangway, passing Sofie and Artur who were still standing on the promenade. On deck, he picked up the battery and slammed it on the table next to the tall man.

'This way,' the black-coated man said, and showed Viktor to the engine room down the steps to the stern and then through a door. There was some cursing, shouting, loud clangs and clicking of tongues as they tried to replace the battery.

'I need light,' Viktor shouted.

The bald patient came and pointed the torch quickly.

'That's it,' Viktor said. Soon after, he came out on the stern and climbed the stairs to the deck and paced to the wheel. He turned the key; the engine started. Slapping the dash, he laughed and whooped.

'Whoo. God damn. All right. Freedom!'

Anton shuffled round the table in the centre towards Viktor, flicked some switches and a series of lights came on that illuminated the deck. Viktor went on the gangway to pick up the plastic bag of food cartons that the nurse had been carrying. He got the things on the boat, then turned to Sofie and Artur, who looked confused and scared.

'If you're coming, get your damn asses on,' he said. Sofie ran on board. 'Well, hurry up, old man.'

'What's happening? 'Artur asked.

'We're taking you to the grave. So, if you're coming, get your wrinkled skeleton aboard.' Artur stared until Viktor herded him on; then he unmoored the boat.

'Čenek, are we going to the cinema?' Artur said when he saw Anton.

'No, Commendatore.'

Artur paused. 'I'm scared.'

'Don't worry.'

But the old man's sunken eyes looked helpless.

Viktor unhooked the gangway, then went to the wheel. 'All right. All right.' He turned the wheel and applied power. The boat began to inch out into the clear river. 'Whoo!'

They began to drift free. Soon, they were clear of the land and Viktor applied more power. Despite Viktor's whoops and celebrations, the others were silent. They were drawn to the stern and there stood like zombies. The moon hung large over the bobbing buildings and Anton could see the pale light of the Rudolfinum. The black trees on the riverbank seemed to droop. The buildings in silhouette were like grand and ghostly tombstones to an emptying city. Only the moon, touching the pinnacle of the St Vitus's Cathedral on the hill had any light, any life. They were drawing away from the city which looked as though life was draining out of it. Now Viktor was silent. The tall man in the long coat pulled out a little notebook and pencil from his pocket and wrote.

'How?' Anton uttered.

They were now looking at an artefact. Millenia of human life here would cease at this terminus. The world's cities were becoming great mausolea.

Somewhere a bell tolled.

CHAPTER 11

Among the calm green hills of Bohemia, the River Elbe glistened beneath the clear July sky. In the middle of an empty road that skirted it, Šimon walked slowly. The ten-year-old boy's clothes on his slight frame were grubby, as were his shoes. He looked up, dark bags showing round his sad light-brown eyes. He had a grey bruise on his freckled cheek.

He was searching for canned food since everything else had spoiled. Up ahead were a couple of buildings and he hid among some trees in order to watch. He had learnt it was better to watch a place for a time to make sure there were no people there. He waited, then approached the house when he thought it was safe. As he got close, he saw through the open door that the house had been ransacked. Treading down the hallway hesitantly, he peered into the living room. No one. He went to the kitchen. All the cupboards were open and mostly empty; their contents had been thrown onto the floor where much of it was broken. The fridge was open and empty. He closed it and saw, on the front, a child's drawing – a golden sun, a green tree, a happy stick-figure family. He traced its elements with his fingertips.

He went upstairs stealthily – there could always be someone sleeping. Checking each room, he made sure there was no one. He came to the main bedroom. All empty. All lonely. He looked out the window. There was the river, but there were no people at all. He sat on the edge of the bed. Utterly abandoned, he looked at his shoes; his small mouth was downturned. His mother had left him with his aunt, two months ago. But she never returned. Then his aunt left to find food and said she would be back in two days. She, too, did not return, and he had no choice but to leave.

He brought his sleeve across his eyes and sniffed. He lay back on the bed and idly watched the lace curtain shifting slightly in the breeze. *Don't be afraid. Be brave!* His mother's sure voice spoke in his head. He pictured her and took courage. But soon, sleep overcame him.

After he woke, he went to the window. Still no one. On the other side of the river was Germany, but that meant little. There was a canoe moored on the Czech side. Would it be worth going across? he thought. He let that idea rest and instead went into one of the children's rooms with its bright colours and collection of dolls in one corner. On the floor was a fluorescent green backpack. From his pocket, he took out a tin opener, spoon and lighter and put them in the backpack. In the bottom, he saw a small packet. He opened it with dirty hands and blackened fingernails and pulled out some peanuts. He ate half. On the table he found some miniature teacups with peanuts in them. They were all mouldy. He cleaned off the mould as best he could and ate.

In the living room, there was a folded blanket on the sofa which he stuffed into the backpack. He sat and looked at the smashed television set, his face lit from the side by the sun. Tendrils of brown, auburn hair hung over his forehead. His eyebrows were naturally higher in the middle and gave him a helpless look.

He remembered that it was hunger that had driven him out of his house after his aunt hadn't returned. He had gone to the shops and entered one and had seen it was empty. He was about to go when he thought to look under the shelves. There, he had found some tins, but was crestfallen when he saw they were dog food. Still, he took them back home. He forced himself to eat them all. He would rather have gone hungry if it had meant he could be with his mother. But she didn't return. Still he waited. He moaned quietly, in his sleep, hoping. He dreamt of her coming and gathering him up in her arms.

Getting up from the sofa in the empty house, he took off the cushions to see if there was anything underneath. There was a bent teaspoon and a bar of squashed chocolate, which he put in the backpack. In the kitchen, he checked more thoroughly. Between the pantry and the wall, he saw something and thrust a hand in the gap. He felt a plastic wrapper and pinched it to draw it out. It was a half-used packet of spaghetti covered in dust. He slapped most of the dust off, took out some strands and began to crunch. Half of it got stuck in his teeth. He put the rest in the backpack. On one of the benches was an empty bottle of olive oil. He turned it upside down above his mouth and one or two drops came out. He licked the bottle neck clean.

He was once more on the road and further up were some larger buildings, one of which was a Swiss cottage style hotel. Before them was a small grocery shop. He came to its broken glass doors. As expected, all the shelves were bare. He knew, though, that it didn't mean empty. He went inside and, behind the counter, found a packet of chewing gum. At the empty fridges, he bent down low and looked under. There was a rectangular tin on its side. His eyes widened. He made a long arm, stretching with fingertips to draw it nearer. When he pulled it out, he saw it was a can of spam. Elated, he sat down, opened it and, without fuss, began to eat. Soon, he leant back against the fridge and, feeling king-like, dozed.

He was awoken later by the unmistakable sound of a motorbike hurtling past the road. He got up and ran to the door, but the motorbike had already gone. He heard its sound fade so he knew it was real. He went to pick up his backpack, then stood in the middle of the road looking in the direction it had gone. The steep tree-covered hills rose in all directions on either side of the shining river. In its stillness, the scene was like a painting. He wondered where the motorbike was going. He hadn't seen anyone driving cars in days. Was there somewhere people could go?

He watched the hotel for a long time and finally went to the front door. The outdoor furniture was covered in green mould and, as he passed into the grimy reception area, there was a damp smell like an old dishcloth. He nearly kicked a full bucket of brackish water as he pushed through the double doors into the dim dining room, which had all its curtains closed. One of the tables had a pair of candles on it. He opened his backpack and put the candles in. Just as he was closing it, he heard a burst of laughter coming from upstairs. His heart beat quickly and his lips twitched. He crept to the doors and quietly opened them. There were several masculine voices, then another burst of laughter. Not everyone was bad, he thought as he drifted towards the staircase. They might help him. They might give him food. They might look after him. He put his foot on the first step. But they might hurt him. Their words didn't make sense, yet their voices seemed playful and the more they spoke, the hungrier he felt. He decided to go up, but the jelly feeling grew in his knees as he climbed. He recalled the last time he tried to ask someone for help – a woman on the road. But she ran away from him, shouting that there was nothing she could do.

He stood for a moment. They sounded like young men's voices, but not Czech. It wasn't English either, which he had been learning. He took another wobbly step up the stairs. Then another.

'Powinniśmy to zrobić w kuchni, robisz bałagan,' one of the voices said.

Šimon reached the first floor, his heart thumping. He crept down the corridor towards the room where the sounds came from. He hoped they were good people. He stepped closer and his lips became numb and dry. What if they didn't understand with their strange language?

'Popatrz! Jestem królikiem. Wszystko co robię to podskakiwanie.' They laughed.

This heartened Šimon but he raised a shaking hand to the door, touching it with his fingertips. They felt like they were sending electricity tingling through him. More laughter. He withdrew his hand. He tried to silence his panting breath. A loud crash of a falling metal bowl made him jump.

'Gówno!'

'Jak możesz być tak opóźniony?'

Their voices didn't sound threatening; he pressed the door. The door slowly opened wider. He peered and saw the men had their backs to him and were sitting at a table. Šimon's attention was drawn to a pair of dead grey rabbits on the floor. They had a haunting, still expression. One of the men at the table held a rabbit that they were skinning and put it to his face as if to imitate it.

Šimon gasped. They turned to him.

'To dzieciak.'

Šimon ran. They hollered but he flew down the stairs, almost falling. He sprinted out of the hotel and to a path that led into the woods. He thought he heard them shouting again and urged himself to run quicker. The path wended up a hill. It dipped a little, then rose again. It turned and there was a small wooden bridge over a creek. On the other side the path forked into two. He stopped and looked behind, catching his breath. His hand slid across the bark of a large oak as he slumped and waited. From time to time, he peered round the tree, but the more he looked the more he knew they weren't following.

After waiting a while, he stepped out from the tree and went to where the paths forked. He looked down both and up at a signpost. He contemplated the two signs, then walked in the direction of one. It had a single word: Otočka.

CHAPTER 12

Otočka was like any small village in Bohemia – a pub, church and river. Cows and sheep lazily grazed and, on one of the fields, a widowed grandma was pulling up carrots. She stopped to smack the dust off her trousers, then looked up at the distant escarpment to the south, where the noon-day sun hazed. She was a little stocky old woman with a red headscarf, flower-patterned vest and keen movements. It had changed a lot since the army had arrived. She surveyed the hundred or so green army tents, then a part of the five square miles of barbed wire fence surrounding the village.

To her right, soldiers were cutting trees and building houses. A small number of soldiers were building a mill in the river. One of them held a book and was reading a pictorial history of mills for clues on how they should be made. They'd got several books after the colonel had sent a section to a library. She looked past them to see some villagers feeding pigs and ducks; others were setting rabbit traps. Another was fixing a roof. Another, building a smokehouse. The eggs had already been gathered. The cows had been milked by machine as, incredibly, the village still had electricity.

She waved at a grey-haired man on the east side of the river as he guided a horse into a stable behind his house. He had a large garden there, with a profusion of vegetables, flowers and fruit trees. In the field where she stood was also a variety of greens and roots. Normally only wheat and barley grew in the fields, but they'd had the good sense to plant a mixture of seeds at the beginning of the crisis. After coming back outside, the grey-haired man carried a trowel. A Labrador followed him past the washing swaying on a line. A small white cloud drifted along the rich blue sky.

Some soldiers lay about, resting from the work. There was no hurry. She looked to the colourful meadow, south of the bridge. Bees danced around the dandelion and bellflower. Dragonflies darted this way and that over the gentle river. A robin sang its liquid and soothing notes. Opposite the meadow and under a pine tree, a soldier was lying down with his hands behind his head, looking up to the sky through the branches. A pair of doves flew away over a man fishing on the stone bridge. He reeled excitedly. The fish had gone under the bridge, and he had to lower the rod so as not to have the line chafe the stone. A pike perhaps, or a catfish, she thought. Or maybe an eel. He had the air of a man hauling a big one. As he reeled it to the surface, he brought it onto the bridge. It was a branch. He threw the rod on the bridge and cursed. A thrush with a cheerful song consoled him.

Warm wind tussled the foxgloves and poppies as a white butterfly slowly fanned its wings on a fencepost. A bumble bee made a head of lavender bend near the sun-sparkled water. Then soldiers laughed as a great big man with wild ginger hair chased a goat that had escaped. He was trying to grab the trailing rope, but the goat outpaced him. The man shouted as the goat ran across the bridge, trampling on the fishing rod. The ginger-moustached man hollered again, but the goat jumped away and towards a field on the east side of the river. The man tripped and fell into the long grass. The goat slowed and began eating the grass. The grandma laughed. Nothing at all seemed to bother her. The thought of a deadly pandemic only caused her to wonder if it affected cow's milk. It did not.

She bustled over to a woman and a man sitting on one of the benches in the green near the church. The woman on the bench wore a blue dress and was heavily pregnant.

'Coo coo, my chickens,' the grandma beamed with her generous green eyes.

'Granny Petra,' the man said, 'do you have any dandelion wine?'

'Never mind that.' She turned to the woman. 'Is he taking

good care of you, duckling?'

'The best,' she said.

'I hope so. Here you are, sweet. Rabbit stew.' She gave the man a container. He looked up with a mischievous smile.

'Is your stew the best?' he said.

'What a thing! Of course it is.' She had light eyebrows and some of her greying hair fringed the headscarf. Her hands had plenty of liver spots. 'Did the colonel find any lentils?'

'I don't think so.'

'If I had lentils… pepper, beef stock…' In the distance, she saw an army truck leaving. Probably for a scrounge, she thought.

'Thank you for the stew,' the pregnant woman said.

'Nonsense. It's good for the little gosling. Giving you any trouble?'

'Not much.'

'Good. Anyway, I got my flour and my butter making.'

'Ah Granny, I've heard… that Štěpánka makes better butter than you,' the man said cheekily.

'Nonsense. She doesn't shake it enough.'

'But your wine is better.'

'Planning a spree, eh? You just keep trapping rabbits and forget about sprees. Did you hear what that girl Helena is up to?' Granny Petra shook her head. 'It's beyond me, it really is. I heard it from Štěpánka.' She leant in and spoke a little quieter. 'She's hooked up with *two* soldiers. Two! I don't know what it's all about. Really, I don't. *And* each soldier knows about it. It's beyond me. I always knew she was a vixen, that one.'

'It's not the first time,' the pregnant woman said.

'No, I know. I *know*. But those boys are so stupid. Nice boys and all. And how will they feel when she gets bored of them and throws them under the bus? Heartbroken soldiers… with guns. But, Natalie, do you think she cares? Not a bit of it. Spoilt.'

'Maybe they've arranged it all like that.' Natalie rubbed her large belly. Granny Petra huffed.

'Arranged? What a thing! What a thing! I don't get it. No, I'm telling you she's after something. And those nice boys.' She shook her head. 'No, I'm Cinderella if she proves true.' She paused. 'What's so funny?'

'Granny P, you're a miracle,' the man said. 'We could be melting in a volcano or drowning in a flood and your only worry would be gossip.'

'Eh? What are you talking about? You think the virus is the only thing to worry about? There'll be trouble enough with that one, Marek. Believe me.'

A smirk puffed his angular cheek. Marek's dark-blue eyes narrowed. 'Ah but, Granny, are you sure you're not just stirring things up here? Why not leave be?'

She regarded him suspiciously. 'Leave be? It'll be trouble – that's why. If you think leaving be ever did good, you ought to retire… I tell you what though, if it goes on like this, I'm going to need a drop of dandelion wine myself!'

'Then you *are* brewing some.'

'Well, well, lamb.' She turned cheerfully to Natalie. 'Prayer and rabbit stew, that's all you need. Prayer and rabbit stew. Ah, it looks like he's finally caught something.' She pointed to the fisherman. 'I told him I'd try pickling one. Got to go through the sergeant. The colonel's done the right thing keeping an eye on what we catch.' She turned to Marek with faux sternness. 'Now listen, my feather. You look after my cherub here. I can't be doing with dramas at my age.'

'There are no dramas, Granny,' Marek said with his long fingers trying to hide a smirk.

'Ooh,' she sighed, 'I hope not. But *that* girl. God, I'd like to pickle her.'

'Granny, honestly, the only drama is what we could make.'

'And isn't she fast on the way to it?'

'Don't you think you're exaggerating, just a little. I mean look at us. We could've been swept away by the virus. Instead, the colonel came, and we've got… well, I don't want to say paradise but… I mean what harm is in it? She's different.'

Petra stared impassively. 'You just watch yourself.'

'Me?' he smirked. 'Granny P, I think you're jealous.'

'Oh.' She slapped his shoulder as he laughed. 'What a thing. What a thing!' She stopped shaking her head when two villagers approached, returning from a forage in the hills to the north. As they neared, a pheasant, startled by its own stupidity, flapped ridiculously into the air. The bird cackled and crashed into the branches of a tall white elm.

'Should we bother giving the duty sergeant the nettle?' one of the foragers said. In his hand was a bucket of bilberries.

'Let's see what he says. I doubt he'll want to ration nettle,' the other said.

'Can we really eat it?'

'The book says boil it.'

'What do you reckon, Granny P? Could you hide it in one of your stews?'

'You just give me those bilberries, duck. You can keep the nettle.'

'What's this one?' Marek pointed to a plant one of them was holding.

'That's chickweed.'

'What do you do with it?'

'Eat it.'

'Thanks.'

Petra was surprised at how many bilberries there were. The foragers continued on and crossed the bridge.

Natalie stood. 'I will take this home,' she said, holding the stew. 'Thanks, Granny.'

'Nonsense, chick. I only wish I could make more.'

Natalie left, but heading towards Petra was the villager with the orange moustache who had chased the goat.

'That goat's perfect for you, Luděk,' Petra said.

He scowled. 'I prefer pigs.'

'So long as the colonel doesn't take them,' Marek said.

'Don't worry about that, Marek. It was her who got that litter of Landrace that were going wild. And she got that vinegar and flour at that factory. And the salt,' the ginger-haired Luděk said confidently.

Petra nodded in agreement. She remembered how they'd almost run out of salt, a crisis in itself. But the colonel never panicked. Petra doubted, until the truck had come in packed full of the stuff. Then she praised the event as a kind of miracle and looked in wonder at the colonel, who merely nodded.

'No tobacco though,' Marek said.

'And she put the fence on the far side of the lake,' Luděk said, 'to protect the fresh water. She's thought it all through.'

'It'll be a tight thing 'til harvest,' Marek said.

'Pah. You know she started tranquillising doe and buck from outside the fence and bringing it in?' Luděk said.

'It's easy to believe you two are brothers the way you argue,' Petra said.

Luděk huffed. 'Ah, Granny, he can just never believe things will be fine. Look, without the colonel it would've been a disaster. They're eating each other outside the fence. We've got it good. Except... well, we could slaughter a pig. I mean we've waited long enough. We could have a roast.'

'You'll probably get your pig the same day I get my cigarettes,' Marek said. 'If she can find vinegar, there's got to be some tobacco floating about.'

'My boar is on his last legs. We could easily have a little roast.'

'Fat chance. She locked up all Tibor's booze too,' Marek said.

'You'll survive.'

Petra wondered when the last time was they had a roast. She couldn't remember. The man fishing on the bridge cursed loudly after hauling up another branch.

'She found all those dishcloths, but not a single cigarette,' Marek said. He took out his own packet, only one left. He twiddled it for a moment, then put it back. He pulled out a twig and began to chew it.

'You're only nervous because you've got a baby on the way. Here comes something now,' Luděk said.

A truck drove up to a gravelled square on the west side of the river. There was a small car park where several other trucks were parked. It stopped and soldiers poured out and opened the back of its camouflaged canvas roof. The three of them crossed the bridge, passing the man fishing, and approached the truck. The soldiers started taking sacks out.

'What is it?' Petra said to the sergeant.

'Corn grain. Found a silo. Piles of the stuff. We could have got more but we had no more room.'

Luděk laughed heartily and slapped his brother's back. 'You see. Duck, hen, hog feed. Piles of the stuff. Beautiful. Here's your harvest. Like I told you; she's onto it.' His eyes shone.

'Had a bit of trouble in the hills,' the sergeant said. 'No big deal; once they saw our guns they ran. There were a few with guns, but they didn't try anything.'

'Beautiful.' Luděk smiled and shook his brother, who winced from it. The soldiers began taking it to one of the barns. Luděk and Marek took up a sack each as well.

'Sergeant,' Marek said, 'what's the chance of finding any tobacco?'

'I know what you're saying. But you should just forget it. Unless there's some seed. And even then, I wouldn't know it if I had it in my hand. All those seeds look the same to me.'

'Stop complaining,' Luděk said. 'It's beautiful.'

Granny Petra smiled and, hearing a chaffinch with its laughing call, agreed that indeed it was beautiful.

65

CHAPTER 13

Šimon brushed the twigs out of his hair. The cut on his forehead stung when he touched it. He thought of returning to the hotel but hadn't the courage. His aunt had said that people were eating people. It was the dead eyes of the rabbits he was most afraid of.

He walked listlessly on, dragging his feet. Sometimes he tripped on a tree root; sometimes he stumbled. His steps shortened as the path rose. Eventually, he came to the top of a steep dip. Wooden steps had been cut into the descent. He looked with glossy, vacant eyes. He thought he heard the faint sound of his mother's voice. Then the full force of the memory of the last time he saw her returned.

'But I want to go with you,' he'd told his mother as she was leaving.

'You must stay here,' she'd said.

'Let me come with you.'

'No.'

'Please—'

'You must be brave. You're a smart boy. Now you must be strong.'

'Why can't—'

'You must try,' she said, putting on a Roman face. But to Šimon, it seemed angry.

'Mama.' His lips quivered as his voice croaked. He grasped her hand. 'Don't leave me.' He put his arms around her. 'What happened, Mama? What did I do?'

'Nothing,' she said and stroked his hair. 'Nobody did anything.' A tear glistened on her face. 'I'm coming back, Šimon. I am. But I have to go for a while.'

He heaved. 'Mama... don't...'

She tenderly drew his chin up with its tortured, tearful face.

'I'll come back. The virus isn't the only thing… Stop, Šimon, please stop. I can't bear all this suffering. I can't bear it. It's a mess but we must try.' She thrust him back. He stayed on his feet and put his shaking hand on the edge of a chair just to hold something solid.

'Can't I go with you?' His eyebrows rose in hope.

'Šimon, please don't… don't, hate me. I'm doing this for you. I'm sick. I need help. Then I can help you.'

'I'll make you better. Don't go. I'll look after you.'

'Oh…' She clasped him. 'My boy… I'm sorry… but you must grow up. And it must be now.'

She went quickly to the door and picked up her bag. He ran after but his aunt held him. His mother looked back.

'Šimon,' she whispered and quickly left.

He reached out. But she was gone.

*

Looking down as he walked, the path came to a steep hill between several large boulders. He looked up the mossy path and saw a guide rope. He held it as he climbed the uneven steps. He slipped now and then because everything felt heavy. Normally for him such a thing would be easy. He had nearly reached the top when he heard a hacking, rasping cough. It was followed by a series of curses. Šimon crept to the top and peered. The path led towards a creek and close to it a man sat on a fallen branch. Beside him was a large shopping bag. The man had his back to the creek so Šimon could see his face. The man's shoes didn't match. As he coughed again, he put his hand in the shopping bag and pulled out a tin. He took a knife from the bag and set the tin on the branch. He tried to open it with the knife, stabbing, wrenching and cursing. He might be friendly if he helped him, Šimon thought. The boy took off his backpack and pulled out the tin opener. He trod slowly down the path and made sure the tin opener was visible in his hand. At Šimon's footstep, the old man instantly looked up and clutched the tin to his chest. His nervous eyes were among the chaos of grey hair above and on his face.

'What do you want?' the old man said gruffly.

Šimon stopped. He seized up and didn't exactly know what to say. He waited for the man to speak again. The man had a grim, desperate look.

'Huh?' His voice was sharp. Šimon extended his hand with the tin opener in it. 'What's that? What you want?'

'Open the…' Šimon said.

'Speak up!'

'A tin opener…'

The old man eyed the object wearily. He put the tin he was trying to open back in the shopping bag, then stood up clutching the bag. 'What do you want?'

'I want to—'

'How many are you? Where are the others?'

Šimon shook his head. 'Only me.'

'Alone?'

Šimon nodded slowly, keeping his eyes on the man.

'Don't believe it.' The man spat as he spoke. He looked around to see if anyone was hiding. 'Don't come near me. You'll say you don't have it and it'll be a lie.' The man pointed the knife at Šimon. The boy's mouth opened but he could say nothing. The man stepped sideways and kept the knife between him and Šimon. 'I don't care if you don't have the plague. You're not getting any of my stash.' The man waved his knife. Šimon stepped forward, gesturing with the tin opener as if it spoke for him. 'Find someone else!'

'But you can open the tins,' Šimon said.

'And then you'll want some? Isn't it? No! No one's stealing it *this* time.' The man quickly shuffled. Šimon waited a little, then followed the man, who spun round with a savage look thrusting the knife menacingly.

'I'm sorry. Have you seen my aunt?' Šimon said and searched into the old man's eyes for understanding. He stepped a little closer. 'Please, I just want to find her. I don't want anything else.'

The old man waited. Then he put the knife into the hand holding the shopping bag. He stepped a little closer to Šimon.

The boy smiled nervously. 'I've only got a tin opener and a knife. But I could help you. Please tell me if you've seen her.'

The old man nodded, then lurched forward and snatched the tin opener and shuffled quickly away. 'You're not taking my stash,' the old man shouted. 'No, not this time. No. No. No.'

Šimon ran after but did not approach too close.

The old man turned and put the knife into his free hand. 'Don't think I won't use it!'

Šimon stepped back, frightened by the fierce whites of the old man's eyes. He looked down at the knife.

'What are you waiting for, boy?'

Šimon looked up with large round eyes. Slowly he brought his hands together, his fingertips touching his chin.

'All right,' the man said. He put the knife into his other hand. Still staring at the man's face, Šimon didn't at first see that he'd pulled out one of the tins from the bag, the one he'd tried to open. He offered it to Šimon. 'If I give you this, will you leave me alone?'

'But—'

'Yes?'

'I just want to find her.'

'How the hell should I know? She's probably dead. Or she abandoned you. Or she's mad. Or worse. Now, boy, are you going to take the tin and leave me alone or not?'

'It's not true.'

'Don't believe it then. You'll see. You'll go mad too. There's no choice.'

'It's not true. She's not dead!'

'Last chance, boy. Take the tin. And by God if I ever see you again, I'll use the knife. Will you take it?'

Šimon shook his head as it sunk. The man put the tin back in the bag and held the knife in his free hand. Šimon looked up and a large tear rolled down his cheek. 'Please, help me. I promise I won't eat any of your food.' He extended his fingers slowly. He hesitated, then drew them back. The old man marched away. 'Please… wait.' But the old man did not. Šimon's hand fell.

He looked at the ground and the emptiness grew. His eyes quivered. It wasn't true. She wouldn't abandon me. She wouldn't do that. She wouldn't.
But a feeling told him she had. That she was gone, and forever. That he was totally alone. Šimon's top teeth lightly pressed his bottom lip; two tears dribbled down either side of his nose from his narrowed eyes. Where? Where had everyone gone? Where are they?

For some time, he walked aimlessly among the sounds of creaking trees. He rubbed his dark-ringed eyes when the woods thinned out and the path cut through a grassy field. There, he saw a rusted and ivy-strangled wire fence. And an odd sight, an old abandoned green truck. It was missing doors and windows and much of it was rusting. There was grass growing on the front seats. It had not been moved in years. The orange setting sunlight drenched the cabin. He felt as empty as the truck. As dead.·

He remembered the screams in his town at the beginning. The hopeless anguish. Everywhere wailing in bootless prayer. But to whom? To what? To the stars?

But as the weeks passed, the screams died away until they were replaced by a horrible quiet. No friends, no family, only emptiness.

He looked up suddenly with a fierce expression. In his heart he made a curse. It was a condemnation of a wicked God. A delirious God. An obscene and vile deity. They had screamed for help, and he, *He*, remained silent and base. He did not answer prayers. He did not save lives. He could not bring mothers home. As far as Šimon was concerned there may as well be no God. He could not accept such a cruel thing in the world. A God who was laughing, if nothing else.

Pushing the thoughts away, he looked down at earth and the

70

orange light on the grass soothed. A completely still fox was watching, its white crest prominent. Šimon stepped forward; it twitched nervously, then darted across the small field to a thicket, slinking through a hole in the fence. Šimon followed, just to see where it had gone. He looked over a little dilapidated fence. Beyond it was a small but dense wood, which was full of dark green ferns and ivy-hugged trunks. Sunbeams shone weakly through the canopy. There was a little ditch of inky water. Šimon saw the fox through the ferns, its bouncy trot lulling the eye. It went over a small rise in the ground. The boy squeezed himself between a break in the thicket and pressed down on the chicken wire to lever himself over. Soon he was walking through the ferns in the fox's direction. He came to the rise. There, he saw a small cottage. It had low-hanging thatched eaves and thick black wood with thin white lime in between, typical in Bohemia. The garden had long since gone to weed and the white door was ajar. The ivy had snaked onto the greening thatch. This house had died long ago and not because of the pandemic.

Šimon leapt over a small ditch and trudged through the long grass and then along a gravel path. The cottage door was mossy, its paint had mostly flaked off. He opened it and expected the scent of decay, of rot, of dirt and rust, of a cloistered and darkly growing mould exuding a bitter sulphur. Instead, it was clean.

Someone was living here.

And he saw her. She sat on a wooden bench. There was a set of rosary beads at the base. He walked down the corridor to the statuette of Mother Mary, with her face looking gracefully down from its white cowl. Her rosy cheeks, her mantle, her rich blue lapis lazuli seemed alive. She stared at her hands, brought together in benediction and gazing on gentleness. Was he dreaming? But did she speak? The cherry lips did not move, but did she say, 'there's always hope'? There was no voice, surely. He bit his lower lip. The ethereal and lulling voice spoke again, though the statuette was motionless. 'Don't be afraid, Šimon,' it seemed to say.

71

'Where are you?' he said almost in a whisper. He waited but there was no reply. He looked down.

'Where hope is,' it murmured. He looked up.

'Where?' he said desperately.

'In your heart,' the voice barely whispered.

'Don't go!'

But the statuette was silent.

He grasped the ceramic legs tightly. Between her fingers someone had put a rose which had not wilted. His fingertips traced the ceramic folds of her robe to her hands and touched the stem of the flower. Leaning at the front of the statuette was a small postcard image of her. He took it.

The door slammed and echoed throughout the empty cottage, startling Šimon. He spun round and saw the flapping door in the wind begin to slow and stop. He went over and closed it firmly. Feeling sleepy, he slowly lay down on the wooden floor and brought the image of the Madonna close to his face. He tiredly brushed the dust off it, but his eyes drooped and soon he fell asleep.

He felt the bright image of a memory come alive: he is at a beach with his mother, somewhere in another country. He is running through the shallow water on a warm day. He turns to his mother and squints from the sun. She is wearing her bathing suit and pointing to the ocean. He shakes his head, too cold. She makes a face. It's not cold, she says. She dives straight in and under. He comes closer; he cannot see her. Then she bursts through the water, glistening, drops shooting off her. She launches herself at him. She has got him and drags him into the water. He screams. The water isn't cold. He emerges and immediately puts his arms around her neck. She whirls him about, then floats him on his back, supporting him. Keep yourself straight and put your arms out wide and look up, she says. He does, and his ears go under the water. He hears his own breath as he looks up at the blue dome of the world. Then her face comes, she takes her hands away and he is floating and looking with pride into his mother's eyes. He drifts. He does not realise, after a time, that he is only gazing at the sky. It is wonderful. Such loneliness ought to make him afraid, but it doesn't, because nothing is out of step. He could drift and drift and drift. But soon he breaks with it and stands in the water. His mother is on her towel on the sand wearing her large ridiculous hat. She waves to him. He races out of the water. She is laughing as he runs through the sheen of the wet sand, before going through the stickiness of the dry. He stretches out his arms and embraces her as her hat falls off. He holds her tight, tighter than she is used to. The sun hugs them, too, in its warmth. He plants his nose deep in her neck. He is smiling as he kisses her cheek and rests his head on her shoulders.

*

The door slammed again, and he woke suddenly. He rubbed his eyes and realised it was night. He could hear rustling and wind blowing and felt a sudden horror of the dark. He fumbled in his bag and took out a candle. Lighting it, the flame soothed as did the image of the Madonna. He went into the living room and set the candle on the table. He ate the rest of the peanuts and the bar of chocolate, to which he made a sour face, but finished nonetheless. Lastly, he took out the uncooked spaghetti, without enthusiasm, to eat it. He took one of the spaghetti noodles and first wet it with his mouth, dipping it in the saltshaker that was on the table. At length Šimon tired and could eat no more. He dozed and drifted off until the door banged again, and he knocked over the candle, putting it out. In the sudden darkness, he shot to his feet and looked to the pale moon at the window.

'Help,' he said through shivering breath. Long shadows of leaves and branches jerked wildly across the ceiling as the wind rattled the cottage. He stood at the window; outside were the grim silhouettes of tall menacing trees, lurching in the wind. The moon only gave enough light to cast shadows, which wanted to choke him, to drag him under and smother him. He felt forces or ghosts in the woods close in and his chest tightened. He doubled over, strangling arms squeezing him. He rushed, gasping, to the table and reached for the lighter, but it fell out of his hands. He half kicked it then picked it up. His hands so shook that he couldn't get his thumb to spin the flint. Holding it with both hands at arm's length, he flicked the lighter many times until the candle lit. He dropped the lighter as the little candle flickered and glowed with its soothing balm. All the long shadows withdrew and it opened up the vice within. He wrapped his arms around himself and gazed at the candle until it hurt his eyes. He rubbed one of his elbows. He remembered the Madonna and pulled the perforated image out of his pocket. He lit another candle and set the image of Mary up against the saltshaker.

She was beautiful and kind. Then he slowly noticed something. She looked just like his mother.

CHAPTER 14

Under the glaring army lights in the night, Granny Petra bustled over the bridge.

Automatic gunfire blasted. She was used to the occasional single shot of a hunt, but this series of long pulses was a soldier's weapon. And it was new. People emerged from houses and tents. Soldiers came out pointing to the south near the escarpment and shouted. One of the captains ordered several soldiers to get their weapons and run in the direction of the sound. Some villagers cringed when another burst of gunfire echoed. More armed soldiers ran. Petra was unflustered; she was sure the colonel could manage it. But Štěpánka, another grandma, scurried up to Petra.

'What's going on?' Štěpánka trembled and her head turned at the sound of another burst. 'What's happening?'

'Nothing,' Petra said, calm. Another volley of gunfire set several villagers rushing back into their houses. Štěpánka clasped her chest.

'They're coming,' Štěpánka said. 'They're coming to kill us. I knew it. I knew it wouldn't last. I told you it wouldn't last. It was just a dream to think we could beat it. Now they have come, thousands of refugees, rapists and cannibals. Did we think we could hold out? Ha ha. How stupid!'

'Pull yourself together! It'll just be one or two people.'

'No. No, they've come. Thousands. Petra, I don't want to be eaten.'

'Shut up. No one's eating anyone.'

'We should run. We should run, Petra. I can feel they're coming.'

Štěpánka clutched herself shivering and moaning, then seized Petra, who stretched her hand back and, with full force, slapped her friend hard across the face. The old woman reeled back, then steadied herself and glowered at Petra.

'You can forget about panicking.' Petra straightened her headscarf. 'I won't let you.'

An air-raid siren quickly sounded, its pitch rose, sustained and fell. It had been installed high on a tree as a warning system. The villagers had been well schooled about what to do. Petra moved quickly, linking arms with Štěpánka and walking towards the church. Soon the villagers crowded in and the lights were turned on. Soldiers bustled in and took up positions at the windows and doors. Marek aided the pregnant Natalie and calmly sat down on a pew. A little girl skipped in with not a care in the world; her mother, however, seemed frantic. The man who was fishing entered, still holding his fishing rod and a bucket of fish. The old grey-haired man came in holding an old Panama hat. From snatches of conversation of the soldiers, Petra gathered that some people had jumped the fence; that the patrols had caught them; that there was a skirmish. Possibly the invaders were armed.

Finally, all the villagers were in the church and the air-raid siren wound down to nothing. It was a long wait until a group of people entered the church and conversation stopped. In the middle of this group was a striking person. She wore military fatigues, which were a tight fit. She wasn't fat, rather muscular, stout and stocky. She climbed the steps to the altar and stood akimbo. Her arms, shoulders and thighs were taut and her stance had authority and certainty. She had a large bosom, a high flat forehead, flared nose and a wart in the middle of her thick, angry eyebrows. Her lips tended downwards and her eyes were piercing, shining pure black under their sharply angled brows. They looked as though they could see through everything and arrive at the basic facts. Branching out of this head was jet-black hair, shining and curly, and it hung unfettered to the shoulder. At first look, she seemed frightening. But to Petra and many of the other villagers, she was the most reassuring presence since the crisis. Even the most skittish sighed in relief. Everyone's eyes were on this person, the colonel, as she stood in front of the altar. She could not help having a severe expression. In the silence the colonel eyed everyone personally, settling finally on Petra, who sensed that the commanding officer had everything in hand.

'There was a group of people who tried to pass the fence,' the colonel spoke with a resonant voice. 'Our soldiers at first shot into the air, to scare them. Many of them ran. But, unfortunately, several were so desperate that they tried to climb the fence. Two of them died. I say this with no pride. Our soldiers did their duty.' High behind her was the crucifix of a drooping, sighing Jesus. 'We must protect ourselves. If we stay calm and keep our eyes open, we will stand.'

The colonel looked from face to face until Štěpánka raised a hand and quickly withdrew it.

'No,' the colonel said, 'speak. Speak.'

'Could we build a safe house?' Štěpánka said. 'With strong doors.'

The colonel smiled wryly. 'There are many things we must do. We need to learn how to forge iron, make bricks, blow glass, weave, loom, make furniture and we need to know how to cultivate, make wine, thresh wheat and do many things by hand. The electricity will stop one day and quite soon. We must be prepared. If we work well, we'll thrive. But there's much work to do.'

'Did they have any weapons?' one of the villagers said.

'No. But I know what you're thinking. Let's be clear, the virus is as powerful as a weapon. More so. Think what would happen if someone infected got inside. We don't shoot the unarmed, but anyone who has the virus is armed. We cannot afford to take the risk.'

The colonel paused as if waiting for another question. It came from the ginger-moustached Luděk.

'Colonel,' he said, 'the fence could be tunnelled under. Or cut. A desperate person could get in.'

77

'Yes,' Štěpánka said suddenly. 'Thousands, tunnelling like rabbits. We're not safe. Not—'

Petra pinched Štěpánka's hand and the anxious woman did not say anything more. The colonel's smile was disarming and calming.

'That's why we have sentries patrolling the fence. They are our best defence.' The colonel stood easy. 'Now, return home. Don't worry. Tonight there will be a double guard. I don't expect they will try again. And if they do, we'll be ready. Every possibility has been considered.' She then looked at everyone directly in the eyes and made her way down the aisle. The officers followed her as she left the church. Petra helped Štěpánka to her feet and looked at the relief on the faces of the villagers as they chatted. Štěpánka nattered about dangers and fears. Petra ignored her because she realised someone was missing. She followed the others as they drifted out of the church and Štěpánka eventually went home. Petra went round behind the church and saw the back of a figure standing in the shadow of a tree. Light from a window touched his short curly hair. Something cracked by his foot, a cat pawing about the leaves. He kicked the ground to scare it off and held a nearby branch with one hand. She heard him mumbling, then strode noisily towards him.

He spun round to face her. He was thin, wiry, with thick lips, which were downturned. He had a twitchy, neurotic energy especially in his dark brown eyes. His face was disapproving. His clothes were neat, shirt tucked into trousers, and he held himself stiffly.

'What are you doing here, Zarviš,' Petra said.

'You surprised me.'

'Why weren't you inside?'

'I heard what the colonel said.' His lips twitched. 'Everything's under control.' He looked through the window. The pupils of his eyes were like pinheads, and they trembled.

She waited for him to speak but he didn't. She found her own tongue tied.

He turned to her suddenly. 'But what if she wants to get rid of us?'

Petra was taken aback at the suggestion.

'She could easily throw us out. Too many mouths to feed,' Zarviš said.

'She wouldn't do that.'

'How do you know?'

'She wouldn't,' Petra said, though on occasion she had thought of it.

Zarviš was about to say something but checked himself. He looked in through the window of the church. 'If they keep having to shoot at people trying to get in, they'll eventually run out of bullets. Then they wouldn't be able to stop anyone.' His fingers spread as he pressed his hand on the window, casting bars of shadow on his face.

She shook her head. 'Let's hope it never comes to that.'

'Oh, I agree.' He looked into the darkness of the woods. 'But you never know. Anything can happen.'

'It won't. You and Štěpánka. Worry and worry.'

He smirked.

'But why were you standing out here?' Petra said.

'She's not the person we believe she is.'

'Sorry?'

'She's not—' He clenched his fist, then opened it wide.

Petra had always tried to understand Zarviš, but there was something about him that she found incomprehensible. She couldn't help feeling pity. It seemed to her that this grown man, though young, was still living under the shadow of his dead mother.

'Goodnight.' He looked at her with an exaggerated grin.

'Zarviš, what did you mean with—'

But he had already vanished with a quick short gait.

CHAPTER 15

'Golden One,' Anton said.

He watched through the porthole as he stood between the cabin and the gunwale. The masked and gloved nurse applied a wet cloth to Eliška's brow. Despite the dirty windows, he could still see, by the flush of the dawn light, a red rash on her neck. She was sleeping, but now and then her face twitched.

'Physician… heal thyself,' he said softly.

The boat coasted along the river. Occasionally, he saw some desperate-looking people on land shouting amongst the quiet of abandoned cars and empty streets. He took out the violin and idly plucked. It cheered him. He started playing nothing in particular. Then a familiar motif arrived, which bled into the jaunty rondo of Beethoven's violin concerto. It was an awakening, quiet at first, almost afraid to express the joy it wanted to. But then it shouted freedom! With gusto he played the long strides. No more despair. Ideas came all at once to his romancing brain. Years of playing had given him a passionate imagination. In it he was soaring over broad summer landscapes under the glory of the sun. He closed his eyes and his overflowing playing, spiritually drunk, in triumph exalted. The music of life proclaimed itself.

He finished with a flourish. Wild and excited, he lowered the violin, half expecting applause and the conductor to bow. But when he turned, the first thing he saw was the dour face of the tall spectacled man in black, whose name was František and who'd been a professor in Prague. Anton could see the music had no effect on him. The nurse, meanwhile, had been banging on the window to get him to stop making such a racket. František took off his wheel glasses and began to wipe them with a handkerchief. When he put them back on, he looked in at the scene in the cabin.

'She's alive,' František said monotone.

'Yes, and she'll live, Professor. I won't take no for an answer. She'll emerge from her tomb whole and perfect.'

'It doesn't look like it,' the raven-haired professor said, matter of fact.

'What are you talking about? Of course she'll survive. She'll pull through.'

'Sounds like blind faith. It looks like she won't live.'

'Heartless.'

'But it's interesting. Yes, I am heartless. What I want to know as she closes in on oblivion, is what passes through her mind.'

'No. Nature's working to heal her. And it will succeed.' Anton waved wildly for emphasis.

'In the end, it won't matter. Only nothing matters.'

'Stop, Professor. I can't believe people like you are possible. I bet you don't listen to music.'

'That's correct. Except as a subject of pointlessness.' He looked down through the window to the doctor. 'It's like this: one is non-existent for a longer time than one exists. Non-existence is an absolutely stable state compared to existence. Which then is more true, infinite stability or temporal change?'

Anton burst into loud laughter. The nurse again banged on the window for quiet.

'I don't see what's so amusing.'

'*Il professore*, step down from the lectern; the students have gone home. I can't get angry at you, you're too absurd.'

'Not at all. Words themselves can be interpreted many ways, full of doubt and multiplicity. Only nothing is true. Things are fake. I am looking at her because she is close to *that* reality. The infinite. Why do you play in tune rather than out of it? There's no more truth in harmony than dissonance. Only silence is true.'

'You're tedious. Enough, Professor, no, not another word.'

František looked back into the cabin and stayed silent. The engines of the boat throttled back and the boat altered course.

'Violin Man,' Viktor shouted, 'take the rope. We're gonna

81

make a stop.'

Anton put the violin away and took the rope as the boat slowed towards a wooden jetty, though not slowly enough as they bumped into the side. Anton tied it off on the posts and Viktor cut the engine. They both stood on the jetty. There were no signs of people, just some boat sheds nearby.

'All right then. Just you and me. Food, tools, fuel, anything useful,' Viktor said and scanned the view, squinting with heavy creases on his forehead.

'One minute,' Anton said and darted back on the boat. Viktor knotted his brow. Anton came back with the violin case slung over his back.

'What the bloody hell's that good for?'

'I don't feel right without it.'

The bald patient stepped off the boat.

'Not you,' Viktor said, 'stay with them.'

But she gestured to the boat sheds and pointed to her temple. Then she pointed to the road and tapped her forehead with her index finger. Anton wondered if her muteness was physical or not.

'What's she going on about?' Viktor said.

'Maybe she knows this place. Do you know?' Anton said and she nodded with exaggeration.

'All right then,' Viktor said. 'Let's go.'

She led them down the road. It wound a corner and into an open expanse of fields. Large in the distance on the right were two idle cooling towers, a ghostly monument to an era very recently ended. Up ahead was a small town. There was a great deal of rubbish piled up and broken glass strewn about. Papers flapped in the wind. A smell of silage and burnt wood hung thick in the air. Despite the lack of people, they donned masks and came to a junction with some shops. As they crossed into the high street, it soon became clear that the most violated, smashed, revenged upon and torn building was the bank. On the other side of the street was the supermarket, which they went towards.

82

Viktor took out his gun, then called out inside the front entrance. If there was anyone, there was no sign of them. They entered the dim space, the only light coming from the street-side windows. Anton saw empty shelves, yet they still went through every aisle and the stockroom carefully. But everything had been taken. Anton made a hopeful pass through the liquor section but there was not a drop. At the checkouts, all the tills had been jacked open. Viktor checked the tobacco shelf – empty. The only thing that had remained untouched was the newspaper stand. On it was one of the national papers with a picture of Amazonian River Fever. There was a graphic in purple and green colours of a spiked ball. It had been superimposed over an image of the earth, whose edges were just visible. The headline read: THIS IS OUR WORLD. The newspaper was dated 23rd April, over two months old.

They left quietly and stood on the street. Anton's eyes, then his feet, were drawn to the pub. He looked in through the window and was surprised when he saw a half-empty bottle standing on the bar. He made for the door, but Viktor held him back.

'Wait. There's something funny here,' Viktor said.

'What is it?'

'It's tidy.'

He took out the gun, sneaked down the corridor and entered the pub. Anton followed and was about to touch the bottle on the bar.

'Wait a second,' Viktor said. 'Why would there be half left?'

Anton hesitated, wondering if it really mattered, then grabbed it anyway. The doors of the kitchen burst open and bearing down on them was a knife-wielding man, screaming.

'Thieves! You won't take anymore. Bastard thieves!'

Viktor aimed the gun. The man stopped immediately on seeing the weapon.

'Stay there, pal, keep it easy,' Viktor said. 'Sit!'

The man had determined eyes but eventually the knife clattered to the ground and he sat at the table next to him. He hung his head.

'They took everything. There's nothing left to take,' the man said, dejected, then looked up at Anton eyeing the bottle. 'Go on, take it. I've nothing left.' Anton picked up the bottle, put his mask aside, drank but then put it back down.

'No, it's yours. I think you need it,' Anton said.

The man looked at him awhile then started laughing. 'The best part of it is that I just paid off the mortgage on this place. Debt free.' He laughed with despair. Anton took the bottle and placed it on the table in front of the man. When the man had exhausted himself, he wiped away the tears and took the bottle, drinking deep.

'What happened in this town?' Anton asked. Viktor sat down at another table and put the gun on it.

'We had everything,' the man said, bleary-eyed. 'This place was always full. We were all friends. There was a routine. Why wouldn't we think it would go on like it had always done? There'd been viruses before and we'd been fine. SARS, Swine Flu, Covid-19. But this… I don't know why this one was worse than any other. Half the town got infected. Deliveries stopped. I heard they all went to Prague. Those people that were my friends robbed me, took everything, even what was in the cellar. I don't blame them. Fear. On the street you normally hear people talking and laughing; then it became only screaming. And then nothing. Don't go inside those houses.' He took another swig and wiped his mouth.

'How long did the army last here?' Viktor said.

'Army? No, there was no army here.'

'No army?' Anton said in surprise.

'Not sure what they could have done anyway. Shoot people, I suppose.'

'Anyone else here?' Viktor asked.

'No, they all left.'

'Why'd you stay?'

'Where would I go? And why would any other town be

different to this one? There's nowhere to go and no reason to go there.'

'But there's nothing here.'

'There's nothing anywhere,' the man said.

Viktor eyed him intently, then he slowly put a hand on the gun. 'You're a liar.' Viktor picked up the gun and aimed at the man.

'What do you mean?' The man reeled back.

'What are you doing, Viktor?' Anton said.

'Cool it, Violin Man. I know when someone's lying. I know when someone's hiding something.' He turned to the man. 'All right, pal, here's the deal. We need food, diesel, supplies. We don't need everything. We're only passing. We'll leave you plenty; don't worry.'

'But I've nothing. I don't know what I'll do in a couple of days.'

'I ain't for fooling.' Viktor stood up.

'You can see my kitchen, my cellar. They took everything.'

'You're a terrible liar. You've got plenty.'

'Viktor!' Anton said.

'I'm telling you the truth,' the man said.

Viktor swiped the bottle off the table, sending it crashing to the floor. Anton gasped. 'Where is it? No more lies,' Viktor shouted.

'I swear I've nothing.'

'Viktor, stop this,' Anton said.

'You're a liar. If you had nothing to hide, why'd you come running at us with a knife?' At this the man fell silent. 'All right, pal, if you tell us, we won't take it all.'

'I've nothing.'

'What's it going to be? I'll find it either way.'

'All gone—'

'Viktor,' Anton said.

'You're seconds away,' Viktor said.

'All—'

'You two can look away if you don't want to see this.'

'Gone,' the man said.

'Time's up.'

'Wait, wait. I'll show you... I'll show you,' he said, and Viktor lowered the gun. He stood up and looked like a man defeated. Anton was dumbstruck, but Viktor and the bald patient followed the man into the kitchen. Anton watched the double doors flap before he too followed. He entered a door at the end into what was a little office. The man had just pulled back a bookshelf full of cookbooks and tax returns to reveal a rough-hewn hole in the wall. He lit a candle that was nearby and stepped into that hole. The bald patient and Anton stayed outside, peering in. It seemed to be under a staircase and the space was crammed with tins, packets, boxes. The man put down the candle and opened one of the boxes. In it were basic ingredients for a restaurant – flour, sugar, salt, pasta.'

'You did all right,' Viktor said.

'Please, don't take it all.'

'Are you kidding? We'd need a damn truck for this lot.' Viktor took a can and read the label. 'Chopped tomatoes.' He put it down and picked up another. 'Confit of Duck. What the hell is a confit?' He picked up a sealed packet. 'Sauerkraut. All right.' He put the gun behind his belt and opened a box, took out all the flour and started packing various packets and tins. He saw a carton of cigarettes and put it in also.

'Viktor, it isn't right,' Anton said.

Viktor finished packing and tried to give it to Anton, who refused to hold it. 'Take it.'

'No.'

'Take the damn box!'

'I'm not a thief. I won't take from him,' Anton said.

'You want to survive? Or you want to starve. Huh? Then take the bastard thing. Ain't no bloody way to pay for it anyhow.' Instead, the bald patient reached out and took it. 'That's right, girl. You know how it is.' Viktor packed another box.

'No more,' Anton said.

'We need more.'

'Stop.'

Viktor did stop but only to pace out of the hole and grab Anton by the collar and push him against the back of the bookshelf.

'Listen to me, Violin Man. I'm gonna survive and I don't give a flying flustered whore who gets in my way. I'll walk all over them. So you better get used to stealing, because either you have it or you don't. And I'm gonna have it. And if you don't like it, go find another world. But don't try to stop me. You have no idea who I am.' Viktor let him go and went back into the hole. Anton slowly readjusted himself. Viktor packed another box and began a third. Things had in another way moved beyond normal, Anton thought. Viktor finished the third box and now stood outside. The man carried out the candle and put it out.

'I'm sorry,' Anton said to him.

'Why? If it had been the other way round, I'd have done the same.'

'Make the front look like a mess, and next time someone comes, don't come charging out,' Viktor said to the man, who nodded.

'You'll need this.' The man offered a tin opener.

'Come with us,' Anton said.

'No. This is my home.'

'We'd better go,' Viktor said. 'I don't want to leave the boat too long at the dock.'

'I wish there was something we could give you.' Anton said.

'It is what it is.' The man shrugged.

Viktor put a box in Anton's hands. All three had a box each.

'Thank you,' Anton said to the man.

*

Viktor was upbeat as they walked past the empty houses.

'What a win! I knew the guy was lying. Not a bad day's work, eh, Violin? The thing with people like that is you just got to scare them a little bit. Then they open up. Nice work on finding the place. I knew you'd be useful.'

Anton was silent. Sometime later Viktor spoke again.

'Get over it. This is the reality now. We won, he lost. Ain't no one who's innocent. Never was. I don't give a damn if you sulk. Look, I like you, Violin Man; you're crazy and crazy people are lucky. But the way I see it, those who'll survive are those who have weapons and are prepared to use them.'

'And would you've?' Anton asked testily. Now it was Viktor who said nothing. They continued in silence and soon reached the boat sheds. The chains with the padlocks on them had already been broken and the doors were open. Holding the gun in one hand, Viktor entered. Inside there were several canoes stacked up on shelves along the walls. There was a mess of tools, workbenches and pieces of wood. There was a small speedboat and two engines on a rack.

'Start looking. Usually a red container,' Viktor said and they spread out. He opened the caps to the engine of a boat and looked inside, but it was bone dry. Anton searched a messy pile of wood in one corner. The bald patient found a lighter on a bench. Next to it was a plastic bottle containing a clear liquid. Viktor came over and opened it to sniff.

'Turpentine.' He took it, then searched another place. The bald patient noticed next to it, though, was a notebook and a pen. This she opened and she scratched the pen until it worked. She took both. Anton was opening drawers, some of which were stiff and required force. Inside many of the drawers was a chaos of screws, nails and odds and ends. The thought of depriving the man of his food still rankled with him, but he put that all aside when he opened the next drawer. To his wonder there was a quart bottle of vodka and he took it without hesitation. He told himself, there was no one here for it to belong to anyway and put it in the inside pocket of his leather jacket. No sense letting Viktor know,

88

he thought.

The bald patient clapped her hands. Anton and Viktor went over and saw what she was pointing at. Behind an oil drum, a red nozzle could be seen. Viktor quickly cleared the way and reached down to take it. He brought up a large, heavy red container and put it on the bench. He opened it and sniffed, then stood back with a grim, disappointed face. Then he suddenly smiled.

'All right. We're set.'

CHAPTER 16

'Who are you?' a nasally voice said.

Šimon sprung to his feet and wheeled round. Bright morning light sparkled off the silver top of the saltshaker near the candle. He saw a tall man holding a branch with two hands. The man moved forward and Šimon, shocked by the suddenness of the figure, retreated.

'What are you doing in my house?' the man said. 'I found this house before you. It's my ah—' He rested the branch on the table and took the spaghetti packet in his gloved hands. He pulled down his patchy hemp face mask and pushed several noodles up so that he could eat without directly touching the packet. He was gangly, wearing sandals and shorts. He had fine sandy hair and tufts of chest hair on his olive skin grew over the collar of his singlet.

'No Parmesan, I suppose? Feta? I haven't eaten. I was so hungry yesterday I even ate meat.'

'Please, don't eat it all,' Šimon said.

'Sharing's good. You don't want to be greedy. You don't want to be like *them*.' He said the last sarcastically while bobbing his head. He saw the saltshaker, picked it up and started sprinkling salt on the spaghetti, getting most of it on the table.

'Don't do it that way.'

'It's not my fault. They're to blame. I mean the virus wouldn't exist if they hadn't sailed into Iraq and stolen the oil.' He rolled his eyes. 'I mean they created the virus with all their corporations and gun boats. I mean, seriously, did anyone really think they would help *us*? Ha. I mean, did anyone really expect Big Pharma to save the world? Please. I mean you reap what you sow. I mean, I don't think we should really be surprised. I mean, a virus was overdue what with their trade deals and toys with lead, which of course was all fake news for more greed. Take, take, take. This is just blowback. '

'Don't eat it all!'

'The one per cent could have stopped it if it wasn't for their country club poker games. "Ooh let's just walk into this country. Then throw them an onion and say we fed them."' He cocked his head. '"We can do whatever we want because we're the patriarchal puppet masters. We're going to build a megamall and take over your export of pistachios." But you know what, they weren't gods. Now everyone's starving. It's easy to share when your stomach's full, but when it's empty… You have any more?'

'You ate it all,' Šimon said. The man started looking in Šimon's bag. 'Hey!' Šimon snatched the bag away.

'You're behaving just like them. I mean, if they had listened to us, none of this would've happened.' He looked down his nose at the boy. 'You're hiding something, aren't you?'

'I don't have any food left.'

'You're lying. If they hadn't lied, we'd be safe in our houses.'

'I'm not lying.'

'You're being greedy.'

'I'm not,' Šimon said feebly.

The man snatched the bag and upturned it, emptying everything on the ground, but there was no food. He dropped the bag. 'I mean, they made a giant monster and lost control of it. And you're one of them. I mean, *really?*' The man sighed theatrically. 'I mean, because of all their arrogance, it's finished. I mean, where have you hidden the food? Because sharing is good. No? Well, and you looked so innocent. You just never know people, though,' he said on a rising, sententious note, bobbing his head again.

Šimon sniffed and wiped his eyes. But he decided that it was not worth crying about and forced himself to overcome the tears. The man kept talking but, to Šimon, it was all a series of unfocused sounds. Instead, he looked at the pattern of the blanket on the floor and waited for the man to stop talking, but he didn't.

Šimon gathered his things into his bag. He went to the table to pick up the image. The gangly man retreated but did not stop talking.

'They were too big to fail. Now they're too small to stand up. I mean, they're the ones who... Oh, are you going? You know I would give you some food, but I haven't got any. But if you are going past the "terrorist" camp, try and get some food and bring it back here. I would do it myself, but I'm not welcome there. You'll bring it back, won't you?'

Šimon left and passed through the garden. He heard the gangly man say something but was already walking down the little path to the driveway. Soon he was in the woods amongst fern and poplar. After a while, he came to a dip, past a series of elm trees. He was soon going up a little hill again, but stopped when he saw a fence. It was barbed up the top and quite firmly secured at the bottom. He wondered why it was there and what was on the other side.

He retreated and crouched behind a bush at the sound of footsteps. A soldier holding a large gun walked along the other side of the fence. Šimon breathed through his mouth and with supreme effort tried not to make a sound. The soldier continued along the fence and was soon walking away from the boy. When he was a good distance away, Šimon sat and gave a sigh of relief, but immediately heard voices and footsteps. He got on his knees and watched a man walk towards the fence on the far side. The man scanned the woods, then whistled. A moment later there was an answering call coming from some distance and more footsteps. There were more whistles and soon armed men appeared, not in soldier's uniform. They weren't in any kind of hurry and Šimon's attention was drawn to the one at the front. He was a large man with a fat face, double chin and wearing a Tyrolean hat. His gun was slung over his shoulder. He had a ridiculous, self-satisfied grin. The man inside the fence made gestures to hurry them up and soon the hat wearing man stood close to the fence.

'Quickly, the soldier will come back in ten minutes.'

'What's the story, Zarviš? Is she going to take all the deer?'

'I'm afraid so,' Zarviš said, his mouth twitched. He tucked into his trousers a corner of his shirt that had come out.

'You've got to stop her.'

'I can't.'

'You've got to. How are we going to survive without deer?'

'I sympathise,' Zarviš said, passing wiry fingers through his short curly hair. 'She does know about you lot. But she wants all the deer inside.'

'Tell me one thing. Do you think she needs all those deer?' the hatted man said.

Zarviš considered for a time. 'No. I don't think so. I think we could survive without. I think the colonel isn't the person everyone thinks she is.'

'We just need a few doe and buck. At least wait a season, the fawns are out.'

'I've tried to tell her. But all she said was it's not her concern.'

'We're not going anywhere.'

'I knew you'd say that,' Zarviš said.

'There must be a compromise?'

Zarviš shook his head.

'Well, we've got guns too,' the hatted man said.

'She doesn't care. Our leader is one of those upon whom the world projects its idealism, but, in reality, would steal food from a baby.'

'If she ever came to our camp, or any of her soldiers, I'd blaze all guns. I don't care. I grew up in Otočka. Granny P knows me. The army can't take all the deer. They can't.'

'I wouldn't blame you if you did go all guns. You know what happened yesterday?'

'Yes, I know.'

'Maybe...' Zarviš said, then winced and shook his head.

'Maybe what?'

'No, it's just. Well, the thing is, I know that tomorrow there will be a forage for more deer.'

'What!'

'One truck, around six soldiers. The thing is, I think army people understand a compromise when they see a show of force… What I mean is could you take on half a dozen soldiers?'

'You mean there's half a dozen coming for more deer?'

'Yes. Could you take on half a dozen?'

'Zarviš, I don't care if there are sixty – that truck isn't going back with a single hoof.'

'It's going out tomorrow morning.'

'Where? Where's it coming? You must know where.'

'It will pass the fork in the road. They'll probably park somewhere near the verge. If attacked, they'll call for backup. So what I think is you strike quick, take the guns and ammunition on the truck and retreat several miles. You'll only have the advantage if you do it quick. Wait five days before coming back.'

'Yes! Yes. What do you say, boys? It's time we stopped her. Enough is enough.'

'Do it, Jarek. We've got to,' said one of the men.

'Right. We will. We'll set a trap, at the fork.'

'Good. Good,' said Zarviš, smiling. 'Quick, you better go before the soldier comes back. Remember, tomorrow morning by the fork in the road.'

'You're a good man, Zarviš.'

'Go, and good luck.'

They wasted no time hanging around for the sentry to come back and were away. Šimon didn't understand what any of it meant, except that they looked like hunters. The sight of their guns shook him. But he was too hungry to do anything else but wait till there was a good distance, then stealthily follow them. Perhaps they were from the 'terrorist' camp the gangly man was talking about. He moved carefully, avoiding noisy ground and followed their voices. The ferns thinned out and soon he passed broad oaks. Šimon had to hide from time to time. Eventually, he saw a fire and tents as the hunters approached some people sitting on logs. There were several roughshod bivouacs. Two covered deer carcasses with their hooves sticking out hung on a tree branch. Further ahead was a lookout that had been built before the crisis. Hanging on it was a stag's head, its eyes and skin shrunken. Šimon stopped behind a tree. There were three women sitting on a log who seemed woebegone and bitter. Their hands were busy. One was washing something in a bucket; another was cutting meat; the third was stirring a pot. Out of one of the tents came a young woman, who bounded over and leant in to see what the other women were doing. When one of them scowled at her, she turned away laughing. Šimon watched as she opened the pot that was on the fire and smiled at its bubbling contents. The young woman then slunk over to the Tyrolean hatted man and clutched his arms.

'You could go round to the carcasses and cut some; then you can share it with me,' a voice behind Šimon said.

The boy turned round and saw the gangly man crouching. He tensed with anger.

'You're much smaller, so it's no problem. Unless you want it all for yourself. That's it, isn't it? You're greedy. You should be kind to others.'

Šimon ignored the gangly man, who continued talking, and looked at the camp. The young woman looked kind and he thought he could ask her. Standing up slowly, he tried to master his fear. He stepped towards the camp without attempting to hide himself.

'Are you crazy?' said the gangly man in a low voice.

Šimon first attracted the attention of a hunter, who shouted at him to stop and raised his gun. The others did the same. The old women stopped what they were doing and the hatted man, clearly the leader, came and huffed.

'What's this? Who are you?'

Šimon saw the array of barrels pointed at him and froze.

'What do you want?' the hatted man said again.

Šimon looked at the young woman and found his voice. 'Help

95

me... I...' He pointed, but so much of what he wanted to say choked him. 'Just a little food.'

'No welfare state here.'

'Jarek, he's just a boy. You can't send him away,' the young woman said.

'Please? I can work,' Šimon said.

'No.'

'Jarek!' the young woman said.

'Honey, we can't have any more.'

'He's a kid. Look at him. God knows how he survived,' she said.

'No!'

One of the old women looked severely down at Šimon.

'Have we not enough to look after, that we want one more? More to do, more to worry about and less food. Even if he's not infected, he'll need feeding. And who's going to do it? Us, of course,' she said with an almost Victorian austerity.

'I had three healthy boys,' another of the old women said without any expression. 'They grew up, had children. All probably died.'

The young woman's jaw dropped at the perfunctory words.

The first woman started up again. 'Don't you be so shocked – we've all lost. Grandchildren, too.' But the woman in the middle of the other two began crying.

'Now look what you've done. You know how sensitive she is,' said the first woman.

'I just can't believe she would talk about her own family like that,' the young woman said.

'Past is past,' the first woman said, 'and we don't need any reminders and we don't need any more to feed.'

The second woman began wailing.

'The boy'll probably die,' said the third.

'And he'll eat plenty of venison before he does it too,' the first said.

'I hate you,' the young woman screamed.

96

'Only work gets you through,' the first woman said stiffly, as if in that lay all virtue.

'Jarek, you will help him,' the young woman said.

'I certainly won't,' he said.

'You certainly will.'

'Honey, it's not worth it. Why do you care anyway?'

She looked over at him and said in a low voice. 'But he's a child.'

'We've got to be practical.'

'If you say no, I will never speak to you again,' she said.

'Sugar—'

'Sugar me no sugar!'

'Honey—'

'Don't honey me.'

'That child couldn't lift a twig,' said the first woman, stiff and haughty. 'He can barely hold himself. Stop crying! Your tears are wasted,' she said to the second woman. 'If you're silly, you die. That's all there is to it. Jarek, send the boy away; we've enough here.'

'Jarek...' The young woman tugged his hand and coyly pouted.

'OK. OK. He can stay for a little—'

They turned suddenly at something thudding to the ground. The gangly man looked sheepishly over the deer carcass he'd just wholesale tried to plunder. His hand was still holding one of the hooves. All the guns trained on him and Jarek flew into a fit of rage. He took one of the hunter's guns and started shooting. The gangly man ran, screaming.

'You hyena. Sneak! Thief! You come here again, and I won't miss.' Jarek turned pink from shouting. The gangly man ran out of sight. Jarek paced back to where Šimon was. 'So that was the plan! You distract us while your friend steals our food.'

'No,' Šimon said desperately.

'You wanted to steal from us.'

'No.'

97

Jarek picked up a fallen branch. 'You thought you could cheat us.'

'No,' Šimon said with a long plaintiff note.

Jarek threw the branch at him, but it missed.

'You shitty little brat,' he shouted and his eyelids twitched on his red face. Šimon clutched both hands in front of his chest in fright. Jarek strode forward and slapped Šimon hard.

The boy touched his stinging cheeks. 'I wasn't…'

Jarek went back and picked up his gun.

'Go! Go! Please go,' the young woman screamed. 'He'll shoot you.'

Šimon was still until a shot rang out. He ran only when another shot cracked. Then he flew with a speed he didn't know he had, not looking back. He hurtled out of sight of the camp and down a small slope where he almost fell as he came to the bottom. He found a path and kept along it for a while before he tripped on a jutting root. Pain jarred his head and his grazed hands burned. He lay prone with tightly closed eyes, his top teeth pressed into his bottom lip as he put trembling fingers to his smarting ear. He winced – a wave of agony rushed in. When he breathed out, he uttered a squealing moan. With stiff lips and hurt with injustice, he angrily hit the earth. He couldn't take it anymore. He'd had enough. No one was going to help him. No one.

He put his face on the ground and cried.

CHAPTER 17

By night-time, the only light came from the boat, anchored in the middle of the river. Anton looked into the dim cabin where Eliška ached and writhed. She opened her eyes slightly; the nurse cleared the sweat from her brow and applied a wet cloth to her forehead. She winced then tossed. Anton felt her struggle, like being choked. Or drowning – swirling motion, pushing her down. He felt her striving to the surface above the frothing, billowing sea. The virus is twisting and mad, heaving and churning like a raging ocean. Up, Doctor, even if the sucking water is tearing everything apart.

Her knuckles whitened as she groaned and arched her back.

Rise, Doctor.

She howled.

He felt as though lighting flared before his soul, a flash in a glorious darkness. Doctor, fight! The world will sink us unless we have the will. It rushes down on us, as the sea sucks us from below; we cannot rise. We are in the hurricane. But up. Up!

She slumped back and became still. Anton feared the worst and pressed his face against the window. She suddenly clutched her stomach and was sick on the floor. Opening her eyes and panting, she looked up at the small cabin windows. Then she was sick again. The nurse wiped her mouth.

'That's good, Doctor. Cough out the sea. Breathe,' Anton said.

She leant back as the nurse gently straightened her legs and dabbed her head with the cloth. The nurse turned to Anton and František, gazing in through the cabin window. She made a reassuring gesture.

That's it Golden One, safe on land. Rest. Peace. I will play to you – like Orpheus – I will play. Anton opened the violin case and put the violin to his shoulder. Slowly, thoughtfully, he began. It was a transcription of Mozart's Clarinet Concerto in A major. He took the airy clarinet line. Sleep, Golden One, rest. It's like the rocking cradle; the summer's playful air tickling the lace curtains. The happy smell of cut grass drifts. She's baking something sweet with ginger. A monarch is fanning itself on the wisteria. You bounce off the swing and run barefoot up the path. Doctor, you can't fight the tragedy. You can only heal. Let her heal you.

He lowered the violin and Viktor yawned. Anton looked in through the window and saw she was resting.

On deck, the bald patient was writing in the notebook she had taken from the boat shed. She got up and gave her notebook to Anton. Earlier she'd written in it that her name was Iva and that it was radiation for her throat cancer that damaged her voice. Anton read now what she wrote.

She will make it.

Anton nodded. 'Yes, I know. She will.'

'Looks like she's done for,' Viktor said casually as he smoked. 'What we'll do when she croaks is keep the nurse and the body in the cabin until we get to Otočka. Then the nurse can get off later.'

Anton frowned, then walked towards the stern.

'Come on, pal. You still sour about pinching that guy's food? Get over it.'

Iva sat down at the table and wrote in the notebook, which she gave to Viktor to read.

We may need her.

'Need her?' He sniggered.

Even you may need her.

'No one needs anyone.'

Anton climbed down the steps to the small lower deck and found Sofie, hugging her knees. He sat beside her and instead of the violin to console her, he brought out the quart bottle of vodka. He'd drunk half of it already. She shook her head, but he

100

persisted. She drank and winced.

'More,' he said, 'more.' She drank more. 'Come on girl, drink.' He looked at the moon and its reflections on the water. She drank more and they were silent for a while. Finally, Anton sighed. 'Everyone's an orphan now.'

Sofie looked at the moon with glossy eyes and Anton pressed the bout of the violin to his forehead with a greater force the longer the silence lasted. Then he leant back against the wall of the engine room and held the violin to his chest. 'No one knows what happened. We are blind! A whirlwind has come and thrown us around and away from everyone. You're looking towards Prague hoping it's all a desperate dream. It seems so. But we understand nothing. We say they're there, when we mean they were there. People like Viktor say we should understand the new reality. But how can we? The tornado blinds us. There's one thing sure. One appalling certainty. We'll never again see anyone we knew. We're utterly broken from them and into our own separate new world.'

Sofie screamed and threw the bottle into the river. She clenched her fists and hit her head. Anton grappled to stop her. Her tears flowed. He put his arm around her, and she lent her head on his shoulder. He lent his head on the girl's as she moaned. He felt her trembling and made a wry face to the moon. They had survived, but for what? To what kind of life?

'Yes,' he said slowly, 'we're on our own.'

Out of the corner of his eye he saw torchlight appear from the riverbank. The light disappeared, then flashed again. He turned to it only now wondering what it was. It panned across the boat. He heard Viktor spin round on the deck and his returning torchlight streamed on the water to expose a group of rough looking, long-haired people on the riverbank. Foremost was a man mounted on a horse. One of their number shone the torch at Anton, who squinted. The light went away and when Sofie saw the grim assembly of a dozen or so, she jumped up screaming. Anton got to his feet and tried to stop her, but she clambered up the steps to the upper deck and found a dark corner. Anton went up and crouched by Viktor who was kneeling behind the railing with his gun aimed at the gang. Nothing moved except the strafing torchlight.

'What do you want?' Viktor shouted. But they didn't reply. 'Then keep staring, nut jobs,' he muttered.

Viktor handed the torch to Anton to point. Someone moved towards the horse-mounted man. It was a woman, barefoot and cradling something.

'I'm armed,' Viktor shouted, yet the woman stepped into the river. 'What do you want?' he shouted again.

She went up to her knees and brought what she was holding down to the water. Anton focused the light. It was an infant wrapped in a blanket. Viktor lowered his gun. Anton stood up but couldn't see her face under her long hair. She held the infant for a time, then her hands gently put the bundle on the water. The baby floated for a moment before it slowly sank.

The gang began to drift back into the woods, the man on the horse leaving last. Only the woman stood there, staring at the spot where the body had sunk. She looked up and Anton felt a chill.

'We'll keep a watch tonight, in case they come back,' Viktor said.

Anton turned off the torch. 'No, they won't come back. No one's coming back.'

CHAPTER 18

Petra knocked and the door was answered by a young woman.

'Mum's with Ludmila,' the woman said.

'No, it's you I want to see, Helena,' Petra said.

The woman smiled, kittenish. She had long blonde hair, dark-blue eyes and thin lips under a pointed nose. She was very skinny. She invited Petra in and into the dining room. Petra was expecting to find her alone, but there were two soldiers sitting at the table. On the table were some plates of cold meat. Helena sat back down at the head of the table, so the soldiers flanked her, and with a gesture of her bony fingers, she invited Petra to sit at the opposite end. Petra refused and stood somewhat imperiously. Helena grinned and Petra looked at the two soldiers and then at the guns leaning against the wall. She felt embarrassed at first, but then saw Helena's furtive grin.

'What's the matter, Granny?'

'You know what the matter is.'

'You mean these two? Granny, you're so old-fashioned.'

'This isn't a game.'

'Oh, Granny, we're all very happy.' She picked up a small joint of lamb and nibbled at it.

'You don't know what you're playing with.'

'Granny, I'm an adult and I can do whatever I want. And if it wasn't for the virus, I'd have left already and you'd have nothing to complain about.'

'But you are here. And this makes problems. Jealousies.'

'Jealousy! Jealous? Are you jealous?' she said to the soldiers. They chuckled. 'I'm very open about it, Granny. There's no jealousy.'

'There isn't now. But in time…'

'Come on, Granny P, that's all old style.'

'How we behave matters.'

'Oh please, how's my little bit of fun going to make any difference? I don't hurt anyone. I follow the rules. There's no problem.'

'But is it true? Is it true that you… you, give yourself to any soldier?' At this the soldiers burst into laughter.

Helena flushed pink. 'It's none of your business!'

Petra threw her hands up in the air. 'I don't understand what's happening anymore. You think it's just a little bit of fun.'

'I don't need permission from anyone.'

'You're selfish!'

'Selfish? We're prisoners in this village. Boys are the only freedom I've got. And if you don't like it, that's too bad.'

Petra huffed but, with supreme effort, composed herself and took a more conciliatory tone. 'What happened to you, duckling? You used to be a good girl.'

'I'm still good, Granny. Aren't I, boys?' They nodded.

'Helena, there's nothing wrong with a boyfriend. One!'

'Granny… why can't you just leave it alone. Let me be,' she said, frowning.

'Ooh, you're a slut.'

Helena burst out laughing. 'Oh, Granny. You just want everyone to pray and be pure.'

'It's not that. I don't want any problems in the village.'

'And who's making them?' Helena said gravely.

'There are people dying.'

'Oh come on, Granny P. I've heard it again and again and again. "We should count our blessings." "We're the lucky ones." "Thousands are dying – we should be grateful." Blah-de-de-blah de-blah.'

'You think you can do what you please. But you don't know what you are doing. Doesn't it bother you?'

'Of course it bothers me. I don't want people to die. But honestly, Granny, does that mean I have to live like a virgin? Should I spend all my time feeling sorry for those on the outside?

Why shouldn't I enjoy myself? And, Granny, why shouldn't they?' She pointed to the soldiers. 'You say jealousy with guns is dangerous – what about soldiers without love?'

'Love? You call it love?'

'I do, Granny P.'

'I don't want to hear any more.' Petra raised her hands to her ears.

Helena smirked. 'How about it, Granny? I could get a soldier for you, if you want. I could get a couple. They wouldn't mind the older woman you know?'

'Stop it.'

'Would you like a tall one?'

Petra grimaced.

'Or a nice short one?'

Petra shrieked and rushed to the door. Helena and the soldiers laughed expansively. 'Silly old bat,' Helena said as Petra left and paced onto the road. She charged towards the bridge where the tall man who was always fishing stood. She went past him and crossed the bridge towards the grey-haired old man building a beehive near the willow by the river. He wore his Panama hat as he hammered a nail. She bustled over. Two little girls were playing with the wet-nosed Labrador. The girls had fashioned garlands of myrtle, daisy, lavender, ivy and buttercup on their heads and the smaller girl skipped over to Petra and slipped her hand in hers.

'Hello, Granny P. Hynek is building a house,' the smaller, blonde-haired girl who was about five said.

'Is that right, duckling?'

'Mmm, but it's too small.'

'But it's a beehive, gosling. It's supposed to be small.'

'Mmm, OK.' The girl bounded over to the dog.

The old man pushed his battered old Panama hat up a little and looked at Petra.

'You know where I've just been, Hynek?' Petra said to the old man.

'Helena.'

'Ooh, that girl. Am I the only one who thinks it's too much?'

'Interfering is often worse.'

'Oh, I agree, Hynek. And if the girl were in Prague, would I go all the way there to tell her what I thought? I'm not her mother. But here, we've got to learn to get along with soldiers. She thinks she can do whatever she wants and that it won't cause trouble.'

Hynek looked at the river. 'If you feel so deeply about it, then there must be something to it, mustn't there?'

'That's right,' she said as the little blonde-haired girl came bouncing back and, taking her hand, swung it back and forth. Petra looked at the sedge bobbing by the river and nodded.

'Granny?' the girl said.

'Yes, Nada,' Petra said.

'Is something bad going to happen?'

'Nothing bad is going to happen. Why do you think that?'

'I don't know.' Nada giggled.

'Are you being tricky again?'

'Maybe.'

'Hmm. We had a bit of a scare yesterday, didn't we? But everything's good now.'

'I wasn't scared. But Mummy was.'

'All mummies worry.' Petra smiled weakly.

'And grannies?'

'Grannies too.'

'Hynek?' little Nada said.

'Yes, Nada.'

'Will there be lots of bees?'

'I hope so. But first we have to finish the beehive.'

'Can we help?' the older girl with long mousy hair asked.

'Yes. Can you hold this piece of wood?'

'Let me do it. I want to,' Nada said.

'You can both hold it, ducklings,' Petra said.

'It's OK, she can hold it,' the older girl said.

The old man began hammering as Nada held the other end of

106

the wood.

'Hynek?' Nada said.

'Yes?'

'How many flowers will you put inside?'

'Flowers?'

'Yeah, 'cause bees like flowers. I just saw a fat one.' She pointed and dropped the end of the wood she was holding.

'Nada!' the older girl said, picking up the wood and holding it herself. Hynek smiled and then put a nail in so it didn't need to be held.

'It's a good home for the bees, isn't it?' little Nada said.

'Yes, Nada.'

''Cause if it isn't, they won't come.'

'Ha. You're right.'

'Have to go to mama bee's house and ask her.'

'Don't be stupid,' the older girl said. 'You don't need to ask bees for honey.'

'Do. 'Cause bee bit me, Ana. And Mummy says it was 'cause I wasn't nice. So you got to ask nicely questions.'

'And what questions are you going to ask?' Ana said.

'Mama bee, do you want a rose? 'Cause rose is biggest.'

Ana huffed.

'OK, Ana,' Petra said. 'It won't hurt to put a rose in it.' She smiled, but the older girl seemed to see right through it and frowned. Something else was bothering her, Petra thought.

Hynek smiled. 'Ha, all right girls, good things take time. We're making a good home, not a quick one. Let's leave it for today.'

'I can hold the wood, Hynek,' Nada said.

'But Nada, slow and steady wins the race.'

The little girl began to flap her arms and dance around the beehive.

'What are you doing?' Hynek asked.

'I'm a bee looking at Hynek's house.'

'Oh, and will you live here?'

107

Nada stopped, cocked her head and pouted. 'Mmm. Only if you make it purple.'

'Why purple?' Hynek said.

'It's my favourite colour,' Nada said.

'OK. Close your eyes and pretend it's purple.'

'OK.'

'Ana,' whispered Hynek, 'say it's purple.'

But Ana seemed suddenly distracted.

'Ana,' Petra said, 'what's wrong?'

Petra turned to where Ana was looking. Some soldiers were carrying a man as though dead on a stretcher. They suddenly dropped him into the river and laughed heartily as he sprung to his feet, confused.

'Do you think the virus will come here?' Ana said, deadpan.

'No, gosling, no. You have nothing to worry about,' Petra said quickly, smiling over her hesitation. But the thought had crossed her mind many times and it was in her prayers. She had no answer if it were to come.

'Are you afraid, Ana?' Hynek said.

The girl looked down.

'Even if it came, we would find a way. Everything will be all right.'

'I'm not afraid,' Nada said, bouncing back from the beehive.

'Oh, and why not?' Petra said.

''Cause...' She twirled left and right, then fiddled with the hem of her dress.

'Mmm? Because?'

''Cause I'll stamp on it,' she said with pertinacious certainty.

'You will, eh?'

'Stomp. Stomp. Bye-bye, bug.' She demonstrated.

'You can't just stamp on it,' the older girl said cynically.

'I can. And then I'll say "go away virus". And it will go away. 'Cause virus is scared.'

'You know what?' Hynek said. 'If I were the virus, I would fly away from you too.'

'I know.' Nada smiled and twirled. 'Then Mummy would scream at it. And it would fly away, over there.' She pointed a little crooked finger in the direction of the escarpment.

*

'Zarviš, what is it?'

'Colonel, umm. Well, it's probably nothing.'

'What?'

'Well, this morning I heard Marek and Tibor talking and saying that *it* was going to happen. Tibor replied that he hoped it would work.'

The colonel looked at her officers, then at Zarviš. 'What were they talking about?'

'I'm sorry, Colonel, for bothering you. It's probably some surprise or something. And I only heard the end of it.'

'But you felt it necessary to tell me? You seem to think it means something else.'

'I don't honestly know. Colonel, I'm sorry.'

'They might be planning to steal some eggs or something. Isn't that what you said they wanted to do before? Make a secret stash,' said a burly and grinning officer.

'That could be it,' Zarviš said.

'But tell me what you suspect,' the colonel said. 'You're a villager. What do you think?'

'They could do anything. Hide things. Or maybe they're worried you'll kick them out. They're smart, or maybe I'm just being paranoid. I don't sleep well. I have these headaches. Ah, there's nothing in it, Colonel. I'm sorry. It's just some stupid—'

Gunshots blasted. A series of single bursts followed by automatic fire. There was a brief pause, then more resonant shots, which now became sustained. The colonel calmly rose and went to the radio and put a call on the frequency. There was no reply.

'It's coming from the south,' she said to the officers. There was a reply from the sergeant on sentry duty in that quarter.

109

'Colonel, it's coming from beyond the fence,' the radio said.

'It could be the party we sent out for the deer,' she said. 'Captain Nebojsa, take a section and see what's going on.'

He acknowledged the order and left. There were desperate calls for backup coming now on the radio. The colonel asked for the situation and the reply was that they were under attack, but unsure of numbers.

'Where?' she said.

'At the fork in the road; they're behind trees,' came the reply.

'Hold them. Nebojsa is coming. How many are there?' she said. But there was no answer.

'Captain Železný, take a section as well. Anyone crazy enough to take us on must have some strength.'

'Yes, Colonel,' the burly man acknowledged and left.

The corners of Zarviš's mouth rose slightly and twitched. The colonel turned her shining dark eyes on him and he frowned. A call came in from the radio.

'We'll talk about it later, Zarviš,' she said to him and answered the call. He nodded and strode out with his short gait.

He burst into his house next door with a look of mad eagerness and rushed to the desk in his bedroom. He was trembling as he scrambled to find a pen and some paper. On the floor were scattered several pieces of paper with frenzied writing on them. On the walls of his room were pinned several film posters: Fritz Lang's *Metropolis* – a female figure rising stern out of a high-rise building, her eyes hypnotic. Another was the 1928 film *La Passion de Jeanne D'arc* – Joan surrounded by flames as sinister clergy look on. Over his bed was Vsevolod Pudovkin's *Mother* – the face of a determined mother clutching a flag with resolve above a line of soldiers, their guns firing.

He pushed aside the film script with his name on it and grasped the pen underneath. He breathed quickly and leant forward. He began to write and read aloud at the same time: 'I am Zarviš Olejník. I am writing this chronicle for you in the future, to show you the history of what happened here. Not the virus. But our history, which has started today. Colonel Vendula Korbova built a wall and made a paradise. She saved us. And today we have taken the first step. A humble one in a small village. Bandits attacked us and we were besieged. Killers, thieves, infecteds, hundreds of them. They climbed the wall; they tunnelled under. A number of our soldiers were killed – defenders of civilisation and culture. Brave soldiers such as Jindřich, Dalibor, Ignác and Věroslav. They died fighting the murderous gangs who have no pity for life. But she, Colonel Vendula Korbova, calmly organised our defence. And through her, and only by her, did we prevail and protect humanity against barbarism.' He glanced at the poster of *Mother* with her far-seeing eyes. 'We are free to start building something new. Free from the concatenation' – he stopped to scribble out and rewrite the word – 'free from the chain of the past. She has given us the chance to write our destiny. We cannot leave it to events because there is no justice in the universe. It's up to us to make it.'

He panted through his wide-open mouth. Another burst of gunfire made him jerk his head up. More gunfire. He gasped. He looked down and wrote.

'But the colonel is not just saving this little village. She is offering her hand to those beyond the wall. Helping them to follow our example. She knows that there needn't be just one Otočka, but thousands.'

The slow whir of the air-raid siren began. He blinked rapidly and tightened and loosened his grip repeatedly on the corner of the paper. Water dripped out of his mouth onto the page. He snapped his face up and stared with a transfixed expression – breathless. He groaned. Then wrote.

'She is as a beacon, drawing everyone into it, calling people. From the shores of the Aegean to the Bavarian Alps; from the snows of Lapland to the islands of the Adriatic; from the beaches of the Atlantic to the Romanian forests, she is saying: "Don't despair. There's a way!" Along abandoned roads and old bridges, in empty fields and car parks, desperate refugees gather, no idea what to do. "Don't let the crow's wing cloud out the sun", she says to them, "don't sink into the inky tar of hopelessness. There is a way. Follow". Her voice is like an archaic trumpet call summoning humanity, and with a single purpose. Towards Otočka. Towards a new beginning. Towards a New Way.'

CHAPTER 19

The boat chugged along the river. Viktor was at the helm while Anton kept towards the stern. He idly plucked the strings to a pop tune he had heard somewhere but didn't know the name.

'That's a nice tune, Čenek,' Artur said.

'Ah, Commendatore,' Anton sighed. 'It's bad. I looked in this morning. The doctor hasn't improved.'

'You know it has occurred to me,' František said, 'that the virus believes in nothing also.'

'Not now, Professor.'

'It wants to reproduce, naturally, but that's only so it can consider nothingness from the point of view of things. The only truth is in nothing. It is uniform and supra-form.'

'No more,' Anton said vacantly, casting a long eye on the flowing water.

'I think the virus is our desire.'

'Enough! You're not real. You're a caricature. You're a comedian who never laughs. I'm not in the mood.'

'Buddha's so-called enlightenment was in fact a total benightedness. Everything, nothing, nowhere, everywhere, equal at all points and angles. The only problem is that nothing cannot be. We are rooted in being and can only get intimations of nothing. The virus is closer to nothing than we are, so it knows more.'

'Please,' Anton said.

'Why do you doubt it? We used to have God as the ultimate. There was a time when it was forbidden to think beyond him. But we are now free to pursue nothing. God was only the pretender, an imposter. But once he was killed, nothing became supreme. Not-a-thing stood in the way. Consequently, things don't matter; nothing matters.'

'Word-clever, that's all you are, Professor.' Anton smiled wryly. 'And you think everyone else is a fool.'

The professor took off his glasses to clean. Anton looked at the far riverbank. There was a large yellow marquee inside a park. The sound of the engine had signalled their presence to some people who now appeared. There were about ten, long-haired, grave-looking men and women beside the smoke of a fire. One of them started throwing stones at the boat. Another of them plunged into the water and started swimming towards it, without any chance of catching up. They started shouting. Then one of them held up a dismembered human leg and brandished it like a club.

'It cannot be.' Anton rose, shaking his head with an open mouth.

'Why are you so surprised?' František said.

'Have we fallen so far?' He turned to František. 'In the middle of Europe?'

'The place doesn't matter.'

'I can't believe it.' Anton clutched the violin.

'Why do you clasp your violin? Do you think music will help you?'

'Yes, I do.' He looked down at the violin. 'Music is the universal hero.'

'Nonsense, you would sooner burn your violin for warmth than believe all that. When you're starving, you'd sell your own mother for a sausage.'

'There's no point talking to you.' Anton strode forward, putting the violin on the table as he did so.

The swimmer turned back as the boat continued out of reach. Anton looked into the cabin, where the nurse was holding the doctor's hand. She looked down at the patient with devotion. Anton pressed his face against the glass of the porthole.

'Golden One,' he uttered, 'help us. Before all's forgotten, before we fall completely. Rise and help us.' He looked skyward and beat his fist on the cabin. 'We're clasping at the edge of a pit.' He slumped and planted his face on the deck.

Viktor clicked his tongue.

Soon, they neared a low bridge and a dam spanning half the river. There were channels on the left, which led into a lock. Viktor slowed the boat and steered it down the closest channel and the one that was nearest the platform in the middle of the river. On it was a small building which housed the control room for the lock.

'All right, Violin Man, look sharp. Get ready to tie her up,' Viktor said. 'I don't want to hang around too long. I didn't like the look of that lot back there. I want to get this sucker past it.'

Anton raised his desolate face. 'Help,' he whispered hoarsely.

The boat slowed further as it came into the chamber and Viktor idled it as it crept beside the platform. He shouted at Anton and cut the engines. The musician got up, clambered slowly onto the platform and lifelessly noosed the rope round the mooring.

'Well, this one ain't hand cranked. Hey, Professor, you come too.' Viktor jumped onto the platform. František calmly stepped onto it.

The control building had two floors. Anton looked in through the windows. It was an empty room except for a desk with buttons and levers on it. Viktor tried the steel door. It was locked. He put his shoulder to it, but it was firm. He clicked his tongue. He pulled out the gun from his waist and signalled to the other two to stand back. Then he turned away and, using the butt of the gun, smashed the window. He climbed in through the window and stood in front of a confusion of buttons and levers on the desk.

'Christ! How's this thing work?' he said and flicked the light switch, which did nothing.

'How are you going to get the boat through without electricity?' František said.

Viktor started pressing buttons and switching levers at random. 'There ain't nothing else but to get the boat through. I ain't going overland, not with all those crazies out there.'

'There could be a manual way,' František said.

'Look at the size of those gates. You'd need elephants to shift that.'

'There should be some kind of backup,' František said and climbed into the room. Viktor began reading the labels but there was nothing to suggest such a thing. After a time, he stopped, then sat down in a chair. They were all silent as he looked under the desk. But as he did so there was a noise from the floor above. He slowly drew the gun back out from his waist.

'It's probably just a cat,' František said.

Viktor put his finger to his lips and crept to the staircase, then quietly up it. Anton looked up as he heard Viktor's stalking feet cross the floor, then stop.

'All right, pal.' Viktor's voice was firm and clear. 'I know you're in the closet. I've got a gun. Come out slow and I won't shoot.'

Anton moved towards the stairs.

'Count of three, pal.'

Anton tensed.

'I ain't fooling around, pal... Come on... two... quickly... one... It's your funeral.'

Anton lurched up the stairs to see Viktor swing open the closet.

'Nothing,' Viktor said.

Anton peered into the empty closet. 'Maybe a mouse.' He looked at the fridge, then to the window, through which he saw smoke rising from the centre of the town. Viktor opened the fridge. He reeled back and aimed.

'Don't shoot! Don't shoot!' the man screamed. Anton came round and saw a lanky youth cramped in the fridge, shielding his face.

'What the hell is this?' Viktor said.

'Please.' The man had his knees up by his cheeks. He had short-cropped hair. He looked up, dumb and innocent, with blue eyes, thick lips and large pointy ears.

116

'All right, pal. Come out, all slow.'

The youth nodded and moved, but it wasn't smooth. He thrust out his long legs and knocked a knee on the side of the fridge.

'Just come out. I'm not going to talk to a man in a fridge.'

The youth did so but not before banging his head on the top of the fridge.

'You got the bug?' Viktor said. The youth shook his head. 'Yeah, but that don't mean anything.'

The young man pulled out a mask from his pocket and put it on his face.

'And that don't make any difference now. All right, here's the deal. You're going to walk out of here, go across the river and keep walking.' The young man trembled. 'Jesus, you're not gonna start crying on me. You a man or a mouse?'

'Don't worry; we won't hurt you,' Anton said.

'Hang on, how'd you get the key?' Viktor asked.

'I helped the lock keeper,' the youth said.

'Lock keeper? You mean you know how this thing works?'

'Yes but—'

'Look out the window.' Viktor pointed. The youth glanced, then shot a look back to Viktor. 'Yeah. And we need to get it through.'

'But you can't. There's no power.'

'Wrong answer, pal. Now, you're gonna help us figure it. We're going through this thing one way or the other. What are you looking at?'

The young man was looking out the window. 'I think they've seen you.'

'Who?'

'Them.' He pointed to the smoke in the centre of the town.

'Who are they?'

The youth shook his head.

'All right, forget about them and think. How we going to get the boat through? Eh? Come on, pull yourself together. Couldn't we just ram the gates with the boat?'

117

'Uhh… there's a backup battery. But I don't know if it will work.'

'If you can get this boat through, you can come with us,' Anton said.

Viktor winced.

'Isn't that right?' Anton said.

Viktor scowled, then nodded slowly. The youth's expression brightened. Then it dimmed as he looked at the gun.

'But what if you're no better,' he said.

'You gotta choose, brother, and quick. Them or us?'

The youth hesitated. He looked out the window, then back. 'All right.'

'Come on then.'

They went downstairs. The youth rushed and banged his knee on the corner of the table.

'Who's this?' František said.

'Your cat,' Viktor said. 'All right, kid, make it happen.'

The youth pressed the buttons and switches. Several lights came on, yet he frowned. He pressed a button repeatedly, but nothing was happening.

'What's going on?' Anton said.

'It's not working.'

'There's someone over there,' František said.

They all looked through the broken window. At first there was one man standing on the riverbank. Then two others joined him.

'You gotta get it working, kid.'

'It's not—'

'Keep trying,' Viktor said and he stepped through the window, holding the gun in one hand. The three figures stood like statues. Suddenly, there were a series of mechanical noises. The sluice opened and the chamber's water level began to sink. Now the figures moved. Viktor aimed the gun and they stopped.

'Hurry it up,' Viktor yelled back at the control room. 'Professor, you get on the boat and start her up. Violin Man, you

118

get ready with the rope.'

Anton followed the professor to the boat as more people appeared on the riverbank. They were only held back from the walking bridge by Viktor's threatening gun.

'How long, kid?'

'A few minutes, so long as there's enough power in the battery.'

'A few minutes!'

One of the figures began striding boldly to the walking bridge.

'Hey! Forget it, pal. I'll shoot you cold if you try it!'

The engines started and the water level in the chamber was the same as downstream. There was a grinding and whirring sound; then the gates began to open. The figure who had walked towards the bridge stopped and signalled to the opposite side of the river, where there were several more people.

'Oh, come on!' Viktor swung his gun between both sides. The gates to the chamber were opening; then the cranking sound stopped. Then the gates stopped.

'What's going on, kid?'

The youth came outside the control room. 'The battery's dead. That's it.'

'It'll have to do,' Viktor said. 'Let's go.' Viktor and the youth backed towards the boat. 'Get the ropes off, Violin.'

Anton did this and got on board. Now the figures on both sides of the bridge crept up the stairs of the walking bridge.

'All right, Professor, when I say, full throttle.'

'But it's not wide enough—'

'Now. Do it! Now!'

The propeller churned and the boat pushed forward. It hit the right gate and jarred violently to the port. Then it hit the left gate. Viktor and the youth jumped on. The boat scraped the sides of the gates as it pushed through and passed under the walking bridge. Anton looked up as the people ran to the middle of the bridge. They stopped and watched the boat push away down the river.

CHAPTER 20

Šimon sat by the Elbe and stared into ripples in the river. He didn't remember falling asleep, only waking up in the night feeling cold. The darkness and the sound of the creaking trees had frightened him. He'd wrapped himself in the blanket, lit one of the candles and placed the image of the Madonna at the foot of it. He'd fallen asleep and was only woken by the shattering sound of gunfire. He swiftly got away from the sound.

He was hungry but past bothering about it. He listlessly picked up a pebble and tossed it into the river. A dull feeling of doom surrounded him.

'Hallo,' a cheerful baritone said. *'Sprichst du Deutsch?'*

It was a man with bright blue eyes and curly light-brown hair. He had a broad smile and a youthful, gentle face. He wore a shirt and jeans, and long brown leather boots. Šimon thought of running away but hadn't the energy. The man put down the rucksack he had on his back and sat down. He placed a professional wooden bow and arrow beside the bag.

'Do you speak English?' the man said. 'You are Czech? No? You alone? So it is. Don't fear. But I speak no Czech.' His voice was calm and the English heavily accented. There was a hessian sack tied to the back of the rucksack and whatever was inside it was long. The man's forehead was wrinkled but he looked spry and youthful – in his forties.

'You don't understand, I think. You hungry?' The man made eating gestures.

After a long pause, Šimon nodded once.

'Sicherlich,' you understand. 'You're hungry I can see.' He opened the rucksack and took out a little metal tripod and then put a pan on it. He gathered some kindling and larger branches. Using a lighter with some cotton wool as tinder, he got going a

little fire under the tripod and began to feed it with small sticks. He untied the hessian bag to reveal part of a deer carcass. He began cutting.

'*Wie heißt du?* Your name is what?' He cut pieces on a part of the hessian cloth. 'I'm Karl. You?'

'Šimon,' the boy said scratchily, then looked down and stroked his elbow.

'Šimon. You are lost, I think.' Karl reached into the rucksack and pulled out a plate and a pair of forks. Šimon wondered if he was in a dream. Belatedly, he looked up and suddenly put his hands over his mouth. He had long since lost his mask and it was all he could do.

'Don't worry,' Karl said. 'We are all past that.' He put some venison fat and the cut pieces of meat into the pan, which sizzled. Šimon lowered his hands. Karl's smile was disarming.

'But,' Šimon said, 'aren't you afraid of getting infected?' His English had an American accent.

Karl's eyes widened. 'You speak English! Oh, it's good. Good. But why should I fear? Are you infected?'

'Some people said I am.'

'But are you?' Karl pushed the venison about.

'I don't think so.'

'*Folglich,* you're not. But even if we are infected, what can be done? You must eat, virus or no virus. And if I was infected, why you don't run?'

'You want me to go away?' Šimon said.

'If I am cooking you food, why I want you to go?'

'Because nobody wants to help me.'

Karl nodded and turned the venison over again. '*Vielleicht*, they are afraid. But afraid or not we must continue doing living things.'

Karl's cheerful optimism was easy. He put the pieces of venison on the plate and passed it to Šimon. The weight of the plate dispelled the last dream-like feeling and he picked up the fork and was about to bring it to his mouth, when he looked up at

Karl.

'Thank you,' Šimon said.

'Eat. Eat,' the man said. Šimon began to, slowly at first. 'You are very hungry. I will cook more.' He cut some more strips, and these went sizzling into the pan. Karl put another branch on the fire and moved the venison about the pan with the knife.

'Thank you for helping me,' Šimon said. 'Nobody else—'

'Ja-ja-ja. Eat, eat. No need to thanks.' He stirred the meat and Šimon nodded. When the boy had finished, the second lot was cooked and Karl put them onto his plate. After Šimon had eaten everything, Karl went with a metal cup to the river and scooped up a cupful of water. He gave it to Šimon, who drank it.

'That better?' Karl said.

'Thank you.'

Karl took the plate and put the pan on the ground. 'You speak English well.'

Šimon nodded. 'My mother made me.'

'I am in the debts of your mother, but tell me, what are you doing here?'

'My aunt left and didn't come back. There was no food. I tried to find her. My mother went to Prague.'

'Prague?'

Šimon nodded, then looked down. 'She wouldn't let me come with her.'

'The city is the easiest place to get disease. Why did she go there?'

'She was sick.'

Karl sighed. 'It is misery. You think it unfair?'

Šimon nodded. Then he felt a sickness in his stomach. It was a cold realisation that everyone had left him and not the other way round. He turned slowly to the river. 'I have no one,' he said quietly.

Karl sighed. 'I had to leave my mother, in Dresden. I tried to get her to come with me. I told her we must go to the forest. But she wouldn't come.'

123

'Why?' Šimon said with a tortured expression.

'It was bitterness. I tried. But she was right. She stayed not because she wanted to but because she couldn't leave. I parted knowing I was leaving her to die.'

'Why did you do it?'

'Because I knew in my belly she couldn't make it.'

'Don't say that,' Šimon said.

'And she knew it too. Only she had more courage.'

Šimon shook his head.

'I understand what it means. But she only pitied me.'

They were silent for a while.

'I think she's dead,' Šimon said finally, with a furrowed brow.

'Vielleicht. In the other hand she is here, in nature. Feeding, nurturing. And it is happiness to wander in nature.'

'I don't know what to do?' Šimon said with a faltering voice.

'No one knows. Only follow instinct. Let it lead you. I have it. You could try the army. There's a village here. I can show you. They might help you.'

'I don't want to… They were shooting.'

'It is not far. There is a gate—'

'Can't you help me?'

'Well… yes, I give you half this deer. Is it OK?'

'But… can't I… just for a while, can't I stay with you?'

'With me?'

'Help me.'

'You want to stay with me?'

Šimon nodded.

Karl tied up the hessian bag and nodded. 'Ja. OK. Sicherlich, Šimon.'

Šimon looked at Karl with gleaming eyes. 'Thank you.'

'We can stay here in nature. She is good to you if you are good to her.'

The angel of silence fell upon them, and in that quiet Šimon heard only a pine creaking and the distant knocking of a cuckoo.

'You're not going to fight the soldiers?' Šimon said finally.

Karl chuckled. '*Nein*, what have I to do with soldiers?'

'But I heard they're taking all the deer. What'll you do when they take it all?'

'I don't know about that, Šimon. But if I must move... well, my home is on my back. If there are no deer here, I wander...'

'You don't believe my mother's alive, do you?'

The German looked up with his bright eyes but said nothing. Šimon looked down.

'Karl...' Šimon looked at the burning fire. 'She's dead.'

'It can be.'

'She must be.'

'It looks impossible, but do not sorrow.'

'She's dead. She is. Why should I try to find her? I don't mind – I don't mind if she's dead. I just want to know.' He looked up.

'I am sorry.'

Šimon waited but the German said nothing else. 'Karl?' he said, yet he could not hold the tears.

'Be easy, I will help you. With all my heart, I will help you. Do not worry.'

Šimon wiped his eyes with the back of his hand.

'You are hurt,' Karl said. He went through the rucksack and pulled out a flat tin of salve. He prised it open with thumb and finger and put some on his index finger, then applied it to Šimon's cut earlobe. He put some more salve on the boy's cheeks and forehead where there were more cuts. Then on his hand. Šimon made a brief weak smile. Karl put the lid back on the tin and Šimon stared at Karl.

'Nature heals too. She even has the cure,' Karl said.

'Cure?' Šimon said, sniffing.

'And I tell you a thing, the virus has always existed. Deep in nature, in the deepest part, she has kept it. But man found it because he couldn't stop. He unloosed her grip. The virus flew out. That is pity because man was too afraid to see that in her other hand was the cure.'

125

'Why didn't they use the cure?'

'I don't know.'

Šimon looked away for a moment. 'You just made it up. There's no cure.'

'You don't understand it, vielleicht.'

'If there was a cure, they'd have used it. They'd have stopped it. They'd have used it!'

Karl faintly smiled, then tied up the hessian bag and went with the cup to the river. He crouched down by the riverside, drank and seemed to be in contemplation of the mountains on the other side of the Elbe. He brought a full cup back and poured it on the fire and sat down to wait for the tripod to cool. Šimon wiped his eyes.

'Karl?' Šimon said with a strained voice. 'Is there really a cure?'

CHAPTER 21

'There're more locks. It depends how far you're going,' the youth said as the boat slowly approached a high bridge.

'What's your name?' Viktor said.

'Radoš.'

'All right then, brother, what was the story with all those people?' Viktor said. Radoš seemed to hesitate. 'Come on, pal, ain't nothing so bad you can't tell it.'

'They're crazy.' Radoš shook his head and spoke quickly, his large jaw with its pimples jutted.

'It's a crazy world, brother,' Viktor said.

Radoš looked at one of the open boxes under the table.

'You hungry? Yeah? Violin Man, help him out.'

Anton brought the box on the table. He pulled out a couple of tins of tuna.

'So,' Viktor continued, 'what's going on around here? Give us a clue so we're not running into anything blind.'

Radoš began to eat the tuna and some biscuits. He paused when Artur came close and smiled at him.

'You look like my Rudolf. But skinnier,' Artur said.

Radoš pressed thick lips and brushed one of his large ears. 'I don't know what happened to the police.' He put down the tin. 'I helped at the fire station. There were a lot of fires. Then I helped the lock keeper. The mayor said we needed to start growing things. But people came from other towns. He tried to quarantine them, but they refused. Some of the locals started to leave. The new people blamed the mayor. Then one day, he was gone. One of the new people made himself mayor. Then it all got bad. Gangs. They killed, stole, burned, other things. The lock keeper disappeared and everyone I knew left. My parents... I don't know what happened to them. I don't know... I looked, but I was afraid.

127

I hid in the control tower.'

'All right, brother,' Viktor said, 'you can leave out the sob story; we've heard it plenty. These people, did they have guns?' Radoš shook his head. 'Good. What kind of weapons did they have?'

'Weapons? Oh... knives, I guess.'

'And these people, they've probably got no food now,' Viktor said.

'Maybe. I ran out two days ago.'

'Still, that don't mean nothing. If I'd been the mayor, I'd have cracked those bastards.'

Radoš frowned and banged his knee on the table. 'What if I'm infected? I shouldn't even be touching this. What if you're infected?'

'Relax, we're all in the soup anyway,' Anton said calmly as he opened the violin case. 'But if you're still worried, tie your sock round your face. That is... if you can stand the smell.' From a flap in the violin case, he took out a little jar of something. 'Well, any road, there's no point being cautious now. Because you see, we're all in the same boat.' He paused, then guffawed.

Viktor clicked his tongue. 'Damn fool.'

Anton began to rosin his bow.

'I remember when Rudolf was sad,' Artur said quietly, reminiscing. 'We would put a bowl of ice cream in his hands. Even if he was bawling his eyes out, he would still try to eat it. By the time he had finished, he was happy again.'

'You do remember, Commendatore.'

'He liked the swings,' Artur said but turned to the stern and seemed to be talking to himself. 'They used to have a little train that would go under a small tunnel... and soda in glass bottles... he wore his orange cap... we'd take the bus there... what was it? Ah, thirty-two I think... he didn't like the crusts on the sandwiches... a brass band in the rotunda. There was a fat man playing. He would say, "Papa, he's getting bigger". Cherry blossoms blew across the path. We bought ice cream...' He scratched his bald head. Sofie got up and ran to the lower deck at the stern, crying. Artur mumbled indistinctly to himself and occasionally gestured as if explaining something. They were all silent awhile. František took out his notebook and began writing.

'It must mean nothing if you're writing it down, Professor,' Anton said.

'What's he doing?' Radoš asked Anton, pointing to Artur.

'Trying to remember,' Anton said. 'I envy him; most people are trying to forget.'

'One more time on the merry-go-round, Papa… oh, the duck pond…'

'What's wrong with him?' Radoš asked.

'Nothing. Nothing at all,' Anton said. 'You see, Radoš, we are the élite. We are the cream of humanity, the motley best.' Anton put away the bow and little glass jar and closed the violin case. 'There's nothing at all wrong with any of us.'

'Even if he does remember, it never happened,' František said after finishing what he had written.

'Have you met the professor, Radoš? He's the most sublime of us all. A living miracle. He cannot laugh.'

'There's no point,' František said.

'Certainly not for you.'

'I'm trying to remove contradictions.'

'Good for you.'

'There was a virus!' Artur said.

Anton stood. 'You remember. Yes, yes. There was a virus. He remembers. Yes, ha ha he remembers… he remembers… fa… what's the use in that?' He sat down again.

'Why couldn't they stop the virus,' Radoš said with feeling.

'There was no way to stop it,' Anton said.

'But people didn't do what they were told. They didn't follow rules. If they—'

'If they had, it would have made no difference,' Anton said. 'Delirium would have come anyway. Rules or no rules.'

'We would go picking blackberries…' Artur mumbled.

129

'We didn't do enough,' Radoš said.

'Ho!' Anton beamed. 'That reminds me of a guy who, when the pandemic first began, chose to dedicate every moment to it. He read every news report, watched every video and added his own opinion to every online commentary. He never left his house unless he was dressed up in a yellow moon suit. Every day he fed his obsession. He bought and hoarded everything. His apartment became a fortress. Everything was doubly sanitised. He spent all day in front of his computer, panicking himself until he was exhausted. This paranoid made himself sick with fear and lost control of his thoughts. He thought he was surrounded. He lay in his midday sickbed with the laptop and twenty-four-hour news.

'Then one day a relative came who had been unable to contact him. The relative forced his way through the half a dozen locks on the door and found the paranoid, dead. And… you know what it was that finally got him? A heavy shelf had fallen on him and he had suffocated because the shelf was stuffed full of hundreds of rolls of vacuum-packed toilet paper. He had hermetically sealed every one. He had drowned in toilet paper.' Anton paused, then broke into arms wide, booming laughter.

'You made it up,' František said matter of fact as he stopped writing.

'Did that really happen?' Radoš said.

'Of course not,' František said.

Radoš stared blankly for a time, then began chuckling. František walked aft.

'Does it matter if it did or didn't? It's still true… five hundred rolls… ha. What a way… airtight…'

'And those little onions…' Artur smiled.

After a time, Viktor's stentorian voice startled them. 'On your feet! We're coming up to another lock. Get ready on the ropes, Violin Man.'

The boat slowed and they approached the open back gates of the lock. Anton went to get the rope. Viktor manoeuvred the boat along the platform and into the chamber. Soon he idled the engine

130

and the boat drifted. Anton looped the rope round the mooring and jumped on. Radoš followed and Viktor cut the engine and joined the three on the platform.

'Bloody toilet paper,' Viktor said. 'All right, kid, you're up.'

They walked towards the control tower. Trees lined both sides of the river. Spanning over the platform was a walking bridge level with the second floor of the control tower, much like the lock before. They donned masks, those that had them, and Viktor took out his gun. There was no one inside. Viktor tried the door; it was unlocked. He made a quick search of the control room and the floor above. He came back down.

'All right kid, do your stuff.'

Radoš went inside as Viktor climbed the staircase, on the outside, to the walking bridge. There was a little town to the left but no fires. To the right there was not much more than some woodland. He was about to go down the stairs again but stopped to look at something among the trees. He scowled. 'Just the wind,' he said to himself and went back down the stairs and into the control room.

'No electricity,' Radoš said.

'Ain't that a surprise. All right, kid, what's the plan?'

'There's no backup here. Look, someone's taken the battery bank. There's nothing we can do.'

'Nah. Think again.'

Radoš shook his head.

'I'm not leaving the doctor,' Anton said.

'Relax, Violin Man, the kid just needs to figure it out.'

'But there's no way. No electricity, no battery,' Radoš said.

'We're going to get this boat through.'

'How?'

'That's what your brain has gotta figure. Couldn't we just ram the gate with the boat?'

'No. You've got to shut the back gates first and get the water level down. And anyway, that boat wouldn't be strong enough.'

'What is the damn point of these things? All right, can't we hook up some ropes to the back gate?'

'They're hydraulic. Only the motors can move them.'

'So? How we do it, then?' Viktor said.

'We can't.'

'You're getting on my nerves now, kid. I don't like this "no" business.'

'But—'

'The deal was we take you along, so you'd get us through. You're not flaking out, are you?'

'No, but we need electricity. Where are we going to find it? There's no generator, no battery, no—' Radoš's eyes brightened. He gasped.

'What is it?' Anton said.

'The boat. We could connect the batteries from the boat.'

'Bravo!' Anton said.

'Will it work?' Viktor asked.

'I don't know. Probably not.'

'All right, what do we need to do?'

'Connect up the cables to the inputs here.'

'OK, pal, you and Violin Man take the light cables from the awning on the boat. Get the professor to help. And get the toolbox. I'll see what's upstairs.'

They nodded.

Viktor went upstairs. It was a fairly sparse room. He searched and found nothing but stopped to look out the window to the woodland side. His eyes narrowed. 'What's going on here?' He ran down the stairs and to the boat. Anton and Radoš were taking down the cables from the awning. 'You need to hurry it up,' Viktor said. 'Don't wait for me. As soon as you hook it all up, get it working. I need to check something.'

'What is it?' Radoš said.

'I don't know. But the quicker we're out of here, the better.'

He climbed the outside stairs to the footbridge and walked along it to the side of the river with the woods. He pulled out the gun and proceeded slowly. There were just some trees moving

132

slightly in the wind. He shook his head.

'You're seeing things, pal.'

He went down the stairs at the end of the bridge where a concrete path ran along the riverbank. The woods were close, and he stalked up to the first tree and peered round it.

'What the hell is it?'

He waited, then clicked his tongue. He began walking towards the stairs.

'What you got on that boat?' a voice said. Viktor spun round. There wasn't only one person but about a dozen, emerging from their hiding spots behind trees. Viktor aimed the gun at the one who spoke and stood foremost.

'Stay there! I ain't for fooling,' Viktor said. 'I've used this gun already. And I don't give a flapping bat's ass about the sucker who wants a hit of bullet.'

'I said, what have you got on that boat?' The one in front took a step closer to Viktor.

'Nothing for you, pal.'

'We're not your enemy. Just asking questions. Where'd you get the gun?'

'I don't care a screaming monkey's guts about your blind-ass questions. Now here's the deal. I'm pushing this boat through this thing and I'm going to be on it, without any of you.'

The man shrugged. 'All right. Fair enough. Now, where'd you get the gun?'

'From a filthy cop.'

'Do your friends have guns too?'

'Why you asking? You a cop?'

'How many people on that boat?'

'You ask too many questions.'

'Where are you going?'

'You're a cop.'

'Do your friends have guns?'

'Yeah. Yeah, they're armed to the teeth. Machine guns, hand grenades, C4. You want to leave us alone, pal.'

'Not very friendly. What have you really got on the boat?' the man said.

'Six tonnes of crack cocaine.'

'You a funny man?'

'Ain't no one laughing.'

'Where are you going?'

'You ask a lot of questions for someone with a gun aimed at him.'

'You're right. But maybe I'm past caring. Or maybe...' He smirked.

'All right, pal, what's going on? What you planning?'

'I know you got something on that boat. We're good people.'

'I don't feel like sharing.'

'Oh well, it was worth asking. You know, I had a gun too. Until someone stole it. Cop gave it to you, huh? I can see it's a cop gun.'

'You're stalling.'

'So are you. But I think you're in a mess now. Have a look.'

Viktor glanced behind. There were a dozen or so people approaching the footbridge on the opposite side.

'You rat! You dirty bastard!'

'Twenty years on the force, you learn all the tricks,' the man said.

'Dirty cop. Only a cop would play that. Bastard, I'll shoot you.'

'I wouldn't. They'll rush the boat if they hear gunshot. That's the signal.'

'Only a cop...' Viktor inched backwards. They began to inch a little closer.

'You don't like cops, do you?' the man said.

'Only a cop would set you up like that.'

'We've got a bleeding heart here, boys.'

'Don't push me, pal.'

'Why? Because you're a con? Because you're a crim? Don't look surprised. I can always tell. It's in the face. What happened?

134

You jack your way out of prison? Or was it a sympathetic warden let you all out? Let them loose. Let them free. EU regulations. Human Rights. Ooh... ooh.' He waved his hands.

'You bastard! You know nothing about me.'

'Once a con, always a con. You must have stolen that gun from a cop.'

They were still inching forward as Viktor stood on the first stair.

'Once they got you, cops never let you go,' Viktor said.

'Law is law, con.'

'And is what you're doing law?'

'Well, we're no plaster saints. But can you blame us? We have to deal with you lot all the time. Besides, there's no law anymore.'

'You're out of a job then.' Viktor backed further up the stairs. All the time they were creeping closer.

'There may be no law, but there are still cops,' the man said as his foot touched the first of the stairs. 'And this cop is going to see what's on your boat.' At this moment the engine on the boat started up.

'Yeah... and there are still cons, and cons have tricks too,' Viktor said and leapt in threes up the stairs. The dozen ran after him, hollering. This sent the gang on the opposite side running up the stairs as well. Viktor ran along the footbridge as the gang on the opposite side appeared. He ran to the middle where the stairs led down to the platform. He stood on the top step and shot the gun. He missed everyone, but both gangs at opposite ends stopped as Viktor alternately aimed the gun back and forth between the two gangs, with an intense fierce look. 'Stay there! I'll blast the sucker who tries it.' Both gangs stayed still as he aimed the gun back and forth.

In the control tower Radoš had turned pale. Anton, standing outside, seemed mesmerised by the scene on the footbridge. He drew a hand through his hair. František was on the boat standing by the wheel.

'Anton. Anton,' Viktor shouted, 'is it working?'

Anton looked inside and saw Radoš, stiff. Anton rushed into the room and began to shake the youth. 'Come on, you got to get this thing going,' Anton said, but felt Radoš trembling in his grasp.

On the walking bridge the gangs were alternately inching closer. When Viktor pointed the gun one way, the opposite gang would take a step closer.

'You better stop that.' Viktor shouted. 'Anton! How long?'

Anton implored the youth, who finally snapped into action and began pressing buttons. '*Prestissimo,* maestro,' Anton said.

'OK, OK. Here we go.' Radoš turned a key and several lights flashed and a quiet beeping sounded in the control room. 'They're closing. It's working.'

'*Bravissimo,* maestro. *Grazie. Grazie.* How long?'

'I'm not sure on this one. Minutes.'

Anton went back outside.

'I'll shoot,' Viktor shouted and both gangs stopped moving forward. 'Take that step back. Step back!' They didn't. He fired. The gangs stepped back.

'*Agitato,*' Anton said, as he went back into the control room. The back gates had shut. Radoš now pressed another button for the sluice. Immediately the water in the chamber began to drop. 'Faster. *Volante.*' Anton ran out to the boat. 'All ready?' he asked the professor, who nodded. 'As soon as that gate opens, go full throttle. Don't worry about us. We'll swim if we have to, but I want the doctor away from it.' Anton ran towards the control room, glancing at Viktor.

'All right, we won't move,' shouted the policeman on the bridge. 'We won't.'

'You ain't gonna,' Viktor shouted.

'But something's got to give. 'Cause there's no way you can get that boat through.'

'Maybe you're right,' Viktor said, 'but I got a gun, and I don't mind shooting a cop or two.'

In the control room Anton kept asking Radoš how long.

'Not long. The water is almost level. All right, you can loosen the moorings. The chamber is almost level.'

Anton ran outside and back to the boat and unmoored, so it was now free in the chamber. 'All right, Professor, just hit the throttle as soon as the gates open,' Anton said.

'What about him?' František pointed at Viktor.

'I don't know,' Anton said and ran back but stopped when he looked up.

'Get that bloody boat through,' Viktor shouted from the bridge.

The gangs had crept forward again. Viktor took a step back, momentarily, then forward. But this didn't deter the gangs. Viktor waved the gun back and forth.

'Prestissimo, prestissimo,' Anton said as he stumbled in the control room and Radoš held his finger over a button. 'Quickly. Quickly.'

A green light flashed.

'Now.' Radoš pushed the button. The gates began to open.

'Bravo, maestro! Bravo. Come on.'

They both ran outside. František had eased the boat to the gate, but it was too far in the middle of the chamber for them to get on it.

On the bridge the policeman was cursing. 'It's not possible! Come on, boys, else this one's going to get away.'

Viktor fired the gun again and they stopped. It took the gangs a few seconds to realise that Viktor was running down the stairs.

Radoš and Anton were balancing on top of the platform side gate as it was opening. František moved the boat a little closer to it. Radoš jumped first and landed clumsily across the bow. Then Anton.

On the stairs Viktor had reached the first floor. The gangs had reached the staircase itself and were racing down. Viktor saw that the middle part of the boat had passed the gates. He hurtled down the stairs, the gangs rushing in mad pursuit. Viktor came to the bottom of the stairs and the platform, and spun round to the direction of the boat. The stern was about to leave the chamber and he ran, then stopped. But Anton shouted and he bolted towards the gates. The first of the gang got to the platform as Viktor sprinted onto the opening gate. When he got to the end, he launched himself. The gang scampered along the platform as he flew through the air and thumped awkwardly on the lower deck at the stern. The engine suddenly roared. He turned back to the platform and aimed his gun. One of them jumped but landed a few feet short of the boat and in the wash. As the boat powered forward, the man in the water made no attempt to swim to the boat, nor did anyone else jump in. Viktor panted. But the despairing and forlorn policeman and his gang stood on the edge of the platform.

Viktor smiled as he shook his gun at them.

CHAPTER 22

Slowly the bodies of six soldiers arrived in a column on the shoulders of their comrades. The villagers gathered to see the awful procession. There was a heavy quiet. The sombre line headed past the trucks. Petra shuffled along the still crowd of onlookers. She stopped when the colonel looked at her. The colonel's dark eyes shone brutally, and Petra felt them, like rods of cold steel going through her. The unhurried step of the soldiers thickened the silence. Petra bowed and crossed herself. When she looked up, a shiver. One of the pale dead looked like her son.

The column moved towards the colonel, who stood outside the cave that lay at the end of the road. The clothes of the dead soldiers had stained red; one of them had an arm saturated in blood. Without words, the procession reached the mouth of the cave where they arrayed themselves three by three. The colonel saluted the dead, each one. Then stepped to their side and turned to the onlookers. She was stately and dignified while the rest seemed forlorn. But Petra recognised grief. Maternal grief.

The colonel stood at the front of the column. She signalled to a sergeant, who shrieked something incomprehensible, yet was a command. The colonel slowly marched down the side road past the cave and towards the field, where fresh graves had been dug. The cortège followed.

They disappeared and murmurs from some villagers joined the wind.

Petra saw Zarviš walk on to the road. He had a desperate, pale expression and seemed to search for something down the road where the dead had come. Petra followed his gaze but there was nothing. He turned and stumbled, almost tripping over himself towards the side road where he peered at the back of the procession. Zarviš looked at Petra; she felt the jitteriness in his eyes and saw the twitchiness in his lips. She had a pang of shame. Even she had said bad things about him: 'Oedipus.' 'Mad goat.' She shook her head. It didn't matter that the others had said worse: 'When's he going to marry his mother?' But now it seemed so stupid, she thought. She prayed. Not just forgiveness for herself, but for everyone.

Some of the villagers were talking. Zarviš walked towards them, then seemed to hesitate, as though thinking of something. But he smirked and continued. Petra went over.

'They've got guns now. They've got guns!' Štěpánka said. 'This is worse than we thought. It's one thing for them to try to get in with just knives or something. But they had guns. That's different. And there'll be more. More. Hundreds of thousands!'

'Nonsense,' Luděk said, 'why should there be anymore? And who except the army would have so many weapons?' His ginger hair bounced with his sudden turn of head.

'They must have stolen them from the army,' Štěpánka, the nervous grandma, replied.

'This is the second time. The word must be spreading about Otočka,' Marek said.

'Poor souls,' Petra said and saw Zarviš, looking down.

'But it's madness,' Luděk declared, 'to try and take on three-hundred-odd trained soldiers. It's suicide.'

'But how many of them were there?' the tall fisherman said.

'I heard from one of the soldiers there were about a dozen,' Luděk replied. 'It's totally insane.' He scratched his ginger moustache.

'There will be more. And more!' Štěpánka glanced between each one with a terrified look.

'And they couldn't have been amateurs. Six dead,' Marek said and pulled out his packet with the one remaining cigarette. He twiddled it in his fingers before putting it back into his pocket.

'You see! You see! It's not good; it's only a matter of time,' Štěpánka said, nervously tittering. She stopped and grimaced. 'Probably soldiers themselves.' She looked close to weeping.

'It makes no sense,' Luděk said.

'Maybe they thought they had a chance,' the fisherman said, raising his thick eyebrows above his dark eyes.

'More like they had no option, Tibor,' Marek stated. 'They've probably got nothing to lose.'

'Whoever they were, they're dead now. Who attacks us, loses. The colonel knows what she's doing,' Luděk said.

'We've been dreaming,' Štěpánka cried. 'We've had it good too long and now it's going to crumble.'

'Nothing bad'll happen,' Luděk said.

'Colonel's pretty upset,' Marek said.

'For the moment.'

'But what do you think she'll do now?' Tibor, the fisherman, asked.

'What can she do?' Marek replied. 'She's going to be more cautious about sending out foraging expeditions.'

'That would mean less ration,' Zarviš said with a clear voice. They all turned to him, and he paused for a long time, as if for dramatic effect. 'If she can't go out so often, she'll have to lessen our ration. Or...' He shook his head.

'Or what? 'Tibor said, his thick eyebrows squeezed in a frown.

Zarviš sighed. 'It's...' he said in a quieter voice. 'You know how my house is next to the colonel's. This morning I heard her with one of the captains. Maybe they were just joking but I heard her say that if worst came to worst, she would only feed the soldiers. She would reduce our ration to nothing if there wasn't enough. Though she would at least give us the option of leaving.'

They were silent a while.

'It must be a joke.' Tibor smiled.

'It would never happen. The colonel needs us. What do soldiers know about farming?' Luděk said.

'They have been learning from us. They probably know it all. They won't need us,' Marek replied.

'Nonsense,' Petra said, 'she would never do that.'

'You see. You see!' Štěpánka, wide-eyed, said. 'That's it. Our goose is cooked. It's only a matter of time before we're thrown out of the gate. And then what?'

'Marek's right,' Zarviš said. 'I think actually the colonel is really afraid.'

'Afraid?' Luděk said.

'Yes. Think of it from her point of view. She's a soldier, an officer. Army people don't believe in chance. Or at least not in taking a chance where they don't have the advantage. This attack must have taken her by surprise, otherwise she would have sent out three trucks. That she only sent out one meant she thought an armed ambush was impossible. But the attackers did have guns.'

'That's all true,' Luděk said, 'but she won't be afraid.'

'I also heard her mention a curfew.'

'Curfew? Ha.'

'Curfew?' Marek said, more measured.

'That's what I heard,' Zarviš said.

'That's too much,' Marek said.

'It's not so strange. Especially if there could be an attack at night.'

'Night?' Štěpánka said. 'That's how they'll do it. The refugees will come and murder us in our beds.'

'That's enough!' Petra pointed her finger at her friend as a warning.

'It would be strange,' Marek said.

'So what? A curfew is not unusual for the army.' Luděk responded dismissively.

'But for whose safety, hers or ours?' Zarviš said. 'I mean we're certain she would defend the soldiers. But would she defend us, when she'd be willing to reduce our ration?'

'If she had to cut the ration, it would be the same for us and the army,' Luděk said. 'And then it would only be because she had to.'

'I hope you're right,' Zarviš said. 'I don't know. But I get the feeling that sometimes she thinks we're against her.'

142

'Against her?' Luděk said.

'We're not against her,' Petra said.

'Oh, I'm sure you're right. I'm sure,' Zarviš said and the corner of his mouth faintly twitched.

There was a pensive silence.

'Look, a curfew is standard army procedure,' Luděk said finally.

'You're probably right.' Zarviš nodded.

'I don't like it,' Marek said. 'It's weird. It would be wrong.'

'Rubbish,' Luděk said. 'I think it would be a good idea.'

'I think we should ask the colonel straight.'

'Right now?' Tibor asked.

'No, not right now,' Marek said and his dark-blue eyes widened.

'Do you know what I think?' Zarviš said.

They waited. He looked away, drawing them in, then turned back sharply.

'I think we shouldn't go rocking the boat, especially now. First of all, if you ask her if rumours are true about a curfew, she'll want to know where we heard it from. She might even figure out I was eavesdropping. Besides, if she's going to do what she's going to do, she'll tell you anyway. And what if she isn't planning to do it? Then no problem. But do we really know her? She's been here four months; she *seems* good, but that means nothing. She's the CO of three hundred armed soldiers. But the truth is she could have us lined up against the church and shot if she wanted to. And we are utterly powerless. She even took our rifles, you remember. Do we really understand our position? Should we really be so trusting in all this?'

Silence.

Štěpánka spoke first. 'He's right. He's right! We're at her mercy. What if she goes mad?'

'Oh, be quiet,' Petra said.

'Or... what if there'll only be enough food for the army?' Zarviš said. Again, they were silent. 'Look, we're not against her.

143

Quite the opposite. We champion her. If she's successful, we're successful. But what if she just realises she doesn't need us? We have no power at all. In fact, whatever she orders, we'd have to do. I suppose we could argue, but the way I see it, what would arguing do? No, in fact when you see it properly, we are hostages.'

Luděk, clearly frustrated, shook his head. 'Have you forgotten everything that she has done for us? Without her we would be like those idiots who attacked.'

'All the same I think Zarviš is right,' Marek said. 'We should be thinking of ourselves. We should—'

'We should what?'

'We could hide some of the catch. Preserve it. Keep a store, just in case. We certainly can't fight them,' Marek said.

Zarviš looked down.

'I could keep one fish out of four. They wouldn't notice,' Tibor said.

'And what if we're caught?' Luděk asked.

'We could say we're preserving it as pig feed. They don't know farming,' Marek said.

'They're not that stupid.'

'We could figure out something.'

'Can I suggest something?' Zarviš looked up with a slight smirk. 'Do nothing for the moment. I live next to the colonel. Let me keep a sharp ear. I speak with her often. Probably more than any of us. Let's wait. I'll let you know if I hear anything. And this curfew thing, leave it be for the moment. Now's not a good time. When the moment is right, I could say to her that I heard her talking about curfew and ask her if it was true. That way, it's all on me.'

'Would you do that?' Petra said.

'Of course. Why wouldn't I?' He stroked his short curly hair. 'It's just…'

'Just what? Ah… you mean about me? Forget it. The things people said never bothered me. We've all said things we'd rather

144

have not. Besides, does any of that matter now?'

'But the things about your mother,' Petra said.

His shoulders sank.

'Zarviš,' Petra said, 'I am... we're all sorry if—'

'Past doesn't matter; we're in this situation and all we got to do is help each other,' he said.

Petra regarded him as though a marvel. 'Zarviš, I don't know what to say—'

'Forget it.' Zarviš smiled. 'In any case, if I help you, I help myself as well, don't I?'

'Thank you, my duck.' Petra squeezed his hand, whose muscles were clutching and taut, skin sweaty.

'No one mention any of this. Just give our condolences for the soldiers.' He snatched his hand out of Petra's.

The villagers agreed.

CHAPTER 23

The next day, the boat was anchored in the middle of the river. Anton looked through the cabin window as morning light poured in. Eliška was still and the nurse was praying. He walked heavily to the side of the boat and looked at the smiling face of a woman advertising something on a large billboard next to a riverside road. Her torso had been ripped away, the paper still hanging. Her teeth were still bright white.

'Golden One,' he whispered.

Viktor scratched his cheeks and stood by Anton. 'All right, pal? Well, we should be there tomorrow. Kid doesn't know if there are more locks. But I think, if we get stuck at another one, we'll take our chance over land. It would mean leaving her.' Viktor pointed to the cabin.

Anton stared numbly at the billboard.

'But uh, Violin Man,' Viktor said quietly, 'about her... Iva. It's a lost cause, ain't it? It don't seem worth it to feed someone who's soon going to croak. I mean with the kid, at least he's useful.'

Viktor's voice grated.

'Christ, she don't even talk,' Viktor said.

Anton smiled wryly. 'Why not the old man?'

'What?'

'Why not the old man? Or the nurse? Or the girl, what use is she? Or me? Or you? Who deserves to be saved and who doesn't? And what good does any of it do? It's all a waste.'

Viktor clicked his tongue. 'Just remember, Violin Man, if it weren't for me, you'd all be starving to death right now.' He walked to the box and took out a tin.

It has conquered us, Anton thought. The comedy is over. He sat down and rested his head on the wooden railing.

Artur began mumbling to Anton but when 'Čenek' did not reply, he asked Sofie what the matter was. Sofie spoke to Anton and also got no reply. Iva touched Anton's shoulder, but nothing disturbed him. František took out his notebook and began writing.

'Violin Man. Hey, Violin Man!' Viktor gruffly shouted. 'Pah.'

'What's the use of all his sentimentalism?' František said, as he stopped writing. 'Or his moods. And for what? There's no point in all this feeling. All this mad passion.'

Viktor threw the empty tin in the river and took out a cigarette.

'Aneta liked the countryside...' Artur mumbled. 'Her mother had an apple tree there. Rudolf played by the river... oh, they were the days... we'd take the boat, Čenek... and in the evenings, wine... she would cheat at cards... she would tell Rudolf that when she was a little girl they did the harvest by hand, and they would sing while they did it. That was just after the war.'

'Who are you talking to?' Radoš asked.

'Rudolf would ask the farmer to ride on the tractor... he would wave at us.'

'There doesn't seem to be any problem with his memory now,' František said.

'He would sit on the farmer's lap and drive the tractor.' Artur nodded fondly.

'But what's he talking about?' Radoš asked.

'Something. And it does not matter,' František said. 'His something, your something, mankind's something. None of it matters. Look at what our ancestors have built over thousands of years. All that technology and knowledge. All that work. And what has it come to? Collapse and ruin. That millennia long apparatus was a sham. Institutionalised denial. All a hedge against fear. Man has all these devices to light up the night, but it's actually the dark that's true. And so he lies to himself. The logical position is to believe in nothing.'

147

František started writing in the silence as Sofie sat down next to Artur.

'You must have been very happy then,' she said.

'Mmm? Ah… I wasn't always a good husband,' Artur said.

'I don't believe it.'

'Oh, but she wasn't always a good wife. And Rudolf could be wild.'

'How long were you together?'

'He jumped off the roof once. Ha.'

'But it must have been many years?' Sofie said.

'He put down a mattress… but missed it and landed in the grass… didn't break a bone.' He shook his head, chuckling. 'Silly boy.'

'You must miss her,' Sofie said, but it seemed he didn't hear her.

'Do you remember the virus?' Radoš asked.

'Virus?' Artur looked down and frowned. He stroked his temple and frowned.

'Don't worry.' Sofie took his hand. 'It's OK. You didn't tell me how many years you were together.'

Artur looked up with a grimace and agitation. 'Rudolf got sick.'

'Don't worry.'

'Thirsty. A fire…'

'That's interesting.' František looked up from his writing.

'Red… hot.' Artur glanced round, scared.

'It's perfectly clear,' František said.

'Burning!' Artur stood up.

'Yes,' František said, 'it's quite obvious that the reason you can't remember is not from old age.'

'Help us!' Artur said.

Sofie got to her feet and held the old man's elbow.

'You can't remember because you had the virus,' František said.

Radoš shuffled backwards. There was a thick silence.

Artur staggered, looking half-demented. 'She didn't move... on fire... so hot...'

Sofie helped him back down onto his seat. 'Forget about it. It'll be OK.' She put her arm round him.

'You were hallucinating,' František said, matter of fact. 'It's an effect of the virus.'

'Don't think of it. Remember the apple trees,' Sofie said.

'You're right to forget. Forgetting is the answer. Those blanks are glimpses of nothing, of the absolute.'

'You didn't tell us what she looked like.'

'Aneta...' Artur lowered his hands and looked at Sofie, calmly. 'But her eyes stayed the same... just as they were at twenty.'

'And Čenek? You must have known him a long time too,' she said, pointing to the violinist with her bad hand. Artur looked at Anton and shook his head.

'That's not Čenek.'

'But you call him Čenek.'

Artur looked closer. 'No... Čenek is bald.' Artur stood and put his face close to Anton as if examining something without glasses when some were needed. Anton paid no heed. Artur stepped back and turned to Sofie. 'What's happening?' He raised his hand to his mouth and had confusion in his eyes. He reached out to Sofie. 'Irenka, where am I?' She guided him down onto the seat. 'Where's my wife?'

'It's all right,' Sofie said as Artur bowed and quietly moaned.

Iva came and put her notebook in Sofie's hand. She pointed to it, indicating she wanted Sofie to read it aloud. The girl looked in confusion as she took the book. Iva tapped the page, urging her. Finally, Sofie began to speak: 'I have a son. It's my fault he isn't here. I hope I can find him. Is he still alive? Half of me says yes. That's the half that hopes. Just a year ago, we were ordinary. When my cancer came, the first thing I thought was, who will look after the boy? He's smart but he's not strong. And then Delirium came. I went to Prague alone. But I thought I'd be able

149

to return.'

Viktor frowned.

'I cannot say his name. I cannot shout. I cannot scream and fight against all these things. I can only hope that he is surviving. Yet, if he is gone—' Here Sofie broke off and shook her head. Iva grabbed Sofie's arm and looked long into the girl's eyes. She looked back down at the book and continued: 'If he is lost… we should hope to be like him – caring and generous. If we are, I believe some good will come out of our mess.'

The writing stopped. Iva turned away trembling and brought her hands to her head. She looked at the sky. Viktor stood up and glared at Iva; it seemed as though some kind of turmoil was going on within him. Sofie looked with tortured eyes at Iva. The book slipped from her hand.

The only one who appeared unaffected was František. He looked at each one, then said in a steady, matter-of-fact voice that the doctor was dead. Iva hid her face in her hands.

Viktor looked towards the cabin, then to Iva. 'You abandoned your own kid?' he said weakly. She lowered her hands and looked him in the eye.

'All of this is a waste. Meaningless words,' František said to himself.

The only things that moved were the boat and the water.

Then suddenly, Anton gasped and screamed. He shuffled backwards, demented and with large, disbelieving eyes. He backed straight into Radoš and put his hand on the youth's shoulder to steady himself, his eyes wide and wild. He shrieked and they looked at him in astonishment. With every breath his grimace turned to wonder, then to laughter. He pointed. They all followed the line of his finger.

'Golden One!'

The cabin door was open and standing there with one arm around the nurse was Eliška, limp, dishevelled, pale and greasy. Anton tried to speak but only shook his head. The others all stood amazed. František's eyes were big in his wheel glasses. Anton

150

gripped Radoš's shoulders as the youth gaped. Iva clapped in a tearful rapture and Anton rushed forward. Viktor lurched and held Anton back and the nurse made ready with the door.

'Golden One! Golden One!' He beamed. 'Alive!' He wriggled free of Viktor and jumped on the table. 'Is it really you?'

She blinked.

'It is. It is. I knew it. I knew you would. I knew you would. I never gave up. Never. Ha. I can't stop smiling. She made it, Commendatore.' He jumped down and started dancing with the befuddled old man. He twirled him round until they both came to Sofie, where Anton embraced her, almost squeezing the life out of her. 'Alive!' He then spun Iva round, who he lifted off her feet. 'No more grief. Joy.' He kissed her bald head.

'You're a live wire, Violin Man,' Viktor said.

Anton embraced Radoš and swung him too. Anton looked again. 'Alive.' Anton lurched at František. 'Now you must dance. Yes, yes. Passion, Professor.' He kissed František on the cheek and spun him round too. The professor's eyes once again became large in the wheel glasses. 'Alive. Yes, alive. Say whatever nonsense you like, Professor. I don't mind. It's wonderful. It's—'

'Be quiet, she's still very weak. Come on, Doctor, you should lie down,' the nurse said.

'No, no. She won't fall now,' Anton said.

Nonetheless, the nurse got the doctor from the door and closed it. Anton whooped and ran to the stern with his arms stretched out wide. He shook his fist at the sky; then he remembered the billboard advertisement and turned to it.

'Lady! Yes, that's right, smile. Smile! She's alive!' He leapt to František. 'Professor, wasn't that something? Wasn't it *something*? Victory. Our first victory. Now we are getting somewhere. Really getting somewhere.'

František stepped back as Viktor chuckled.

Anton turned to Sofie. 'Those laughs, Sofie, prove it. We're

151

not cynics. We're not ideas. The volcano in the centre of our planet bursts through our hearts. The fire of life. Yes, that's it, laugh. Let it all… ha ha… let it out.' He kissed her forehead. Then he leapt on the railing, hair flying, as he held onto one of the uprights to the awning. He hooted at the riverbank and a flock of small birds took flight. Suddenly, he monkeyed himself up onto the awning.

'Get off it, you crazy son-of-a-bitch,' Viktor shouted.

But instead, he stood legs spread apart on top of the awning and he gaped up at the sky with arms outstretched. 'How does it feel?' He clenched a fist and shook it at the clear sky, laughing. 'Not this time. Not this time! Now we are in control. Now we determine our destiny.' His hair danced wildly. 'Now we are going to win. We've got fate by the throat.'

'Get down you lunatic,' Viktor yelled.

'Down? Ha! Yes. Yes! With pleasure.' He launched headfirst into the water, splashed and disappeared. They rushed to the side. It was a time before he emerged, but when he did, he was beaming.

'Alive!'

CHAPTER 24

Šimon cackled as water dripped off his washed face. He was standing near a rocky and bubbling stream as the cheerful sun danced over the tops of the spruce. Karl had been trying to catch a fish by hand, and when he had got one, he swivelled as if to throw the fish on the bank. But as he did, the fish slipped out, and the momentum unbalanced him sending him backwards into the water. Eventually, he sat up with a wistful face.

'Are you OK?' Šimon said.

Karl, soaked, nodded. 'Sicherlich, it is not the first time.' He put his hands together to wriggle them as if he were a fish. He puffed his cheeks and squirmed. He put his head under his shirt collar and, suddenly, thrust his head out. 'Ja, hallo, I'm a fish.'

Šimon went weak at the knees.

'Good, good. It is funny. Laugh.' Karl looked up. 'Sicherlich, above us blue sky, within us, freedom.'

The boy held out his hand for Karl and helped him to his feet. 'I couldn't help it.'

'No, no. It is good.' Karl sloshed onto the riverbank. He picked up the mobile phone that Šimon had found and pretended to dial a number, then held it to his head. 'Hallo... is that the dry cleaners? Mmm, I had an accident... oh, you are closed. Is it a holiday? Oh, but sicherlich, you needn't do the clean, just the dry. Oh.' He put the phone down. 'They ran out of steam.'

Šimon held a branch to steady himself.

'You are hungry?' Karl said. 'Ja, I think you must be.'

Karl took up two gutted fish that had been tied to the side of the rucksack. Using the broadside of the knife he began to scale them, then clean them in the stream. Šimon watched closely as Karl filleted the fish.

'Šimon.' Karl pointed up. 'Above us blue sky, within us,

freedom.'

Šimon looked up. Surrounded in the sun's warmth and the sounds of birdsong and the gurgling stream, he felt his whole body sighing in relief. He closed his eyes as the breeze ruffled a few strands of his hair. For a moment there was nothing to fear or panic him. He remembered what it was to be happy. Not to have to worry. Not to be alone. He opened his eyes to the glistening water. He looked at Karl, who was putting the frying pan on the little metal tripod.

'Can I help?' Šimon said.

'Mmm. We'll make a fire. Find some kindling and small branches. Dry and dead is best.'

Šimon quickly gathered sticks and branches and put them near the tripod. Karl placed some cotton wool and struck a match to it. He placed some of the kindling over it. Once the fire was going, he put a few larger ones on. Eventually, branches.

'This will help me dry up,' Karl said.

As they waited for the fire to die down, Karl looked through the rucksack and brought out the salve and gave it to Šimon. He gestured to his ears and cheeks, but the boy just looked at the tin.

'Put some on your hurt,' Karl said.

Šimon frowned. 'Thank you.'

Karl moved some of the branches as the fire burned well and he began to sing an old German song. A song of snowy alps, golden cloud banks and starry realms. He put some of the venison lard in the pan.

'Now the fish.' He picked up the fish and put it in the pan; straight away it seared. Karl used the knife to turn the fish. 'The plate,' Karl said and Šimon took it out of the rucksack. He put the fish on the plate and using two forks they ate.

'Karl?'

'Mmm?'

But Šimon only smiled.

Karl nodded and when they had finished, the German went and sat by a boulder to bask in the sun. 'Nature is sublime,' Karl said. 'It is wonder.'

As Šimon sat next to him he remembered that fish was his mother's favourite food. The boy looked mournfully at the glittering stream.

'But what is the matter, Šimon?'

The boy looked up and shook his head. 'Nothing.' He smiled briefly.

'But don't be sad. She is all around us.'

Šimon toyed with blades of grass and nodded slightly.

'Karl?'

'Mmm?'

'It won't go back to how it was, will it?'

'No, it won't.'

'We will have to live like this for the rest of our lives?'

'You don't like it?'

Šimon paused. 'I just wish Mum was here.' He pictured her cheerfully dancing to her silly music, side to side, then grabbing her son in a wild dance. He saw her face clearly as if she was really there now, on the other side of the stream from him and Karl. But she wasn't smiling or dancing anymore. And he wasn't holding her. He shook his head, yet the face persisted. He blinked and realised she was real. He shot to his feet. Across the stream someone was standing. He pointed her out to Karl, who also got to his feet. She was a grimy and miserable looking woman. She stepped towards the edge of the stream.

'Don't be afraid,' Karl said. 'Can you say it to her in Czech?'

'Can we give her something to eat?'

Karl nodded and went to the hessian bag. 'Tell her I will cook it.'

Šimon told her and that they wanted to help her. She dragged her eyes to Šimon. He felt stuck to the ground. Her empty eyes frightened him.

'Ask her if she is alone.'

Šimon relayed the question so softly that it didn't carry. Šimon said it again louder and she grinned. Karl had picked up

155

the knife to cut pieces from the deer but when she saw it, she bolted.

'Wait. Don't go,' Šimon called out. 'We won't hurt you. Please don't go.'

But her rushing footsteps faded away. Karl put down the knife and joined Šimon by the boulder.

'Why did she go?' Karl asked.

'I don't know.'

'It is fear.' Karl leant against the boulder.

'But we weren't going to hurt her. We wanted to help her.'

He shook his head as Šimon searched his face for an answer.

'Karl... Karl, she looked just like—'

'Was it?'

'No,' Šimon said scratchily. 'But did we do something wrong?'

Karl sat down. 'I think she ran because she thinks the world has become her enemy.' Šimon sat as Karl picked up a flower and examined it. 'But the world gave us birth. It can't hate us that much.' He sighed. 'Only, we must remember to see, not just to think. To see with a feeling eye. If we see nature in this way, we can overcome our fear and see her as a force of life for life. She can restore us, because she is the creator without and within. If we open up to her, there is a universe in this flower that can heal us. Her power is great because it is silent. In beauty she grows – *o Wunder!*' He gave the flower to Šimon, and Karl's eyes glistened. 'There is a cure. Everywhere. It is there, and it is here, even in this flower.'

Šimon took the flower. 'Cure?'

Karl looked at the stream.

Šimon was about to speak but he saw a tear fall down Karl's face. 'Karl... Karl, don't cry.' The boy touched his shoulder; the German shook his head.

'I'm not crying.' He wiped his face. 'Only, it is beautiful.' He beamed. 'And it's in us too. She's in us.' He looked to the treetops. 'She is strong for death has not conquered her. There's no ill she cannot cure, or destruction she cannot put back together. Sicherlich, more is possible with her than we know. She is wise, and with courage.'

Šimon was transfixed. He gazed at Karl with sparkling eyes and trembled.

'She is a mother,' Karl said.

Šimon suddenly embraced Karl.

'But what's wrong?' Karl said. 'What is it?'

Šimon slowly looked up. 'Karl…' the boy said scratchily.

Karl patted his head and nodded. 'Oh… I know. I know.'

CHAPTER 25

Flames leapt high into the night. Soldiers hurried with various items out of what was the armoury: guns, boxes of ammunition, equipment. Petra and some of the villagers watched the burning barn near the colonel, who directed the soldiers to remove a wood pile stacked next to it. The sergeant who had been on guard duty was a shambles, his uniform awry and he was sweating profusely. Everyone paused when part of the ceiling collapsed.

'We tried to douse it,' the sergeant said to the colonel.

'Where was he?' She pointed to the regular who was on guard duty with the sergeant.

The sergeant hesitated. 'I didn't think there was any harm in letting him sleep a little.'

She scowled. 'How'd it begin?'

'It was from round the back.'

'Where was he sleeping?'

'Inside.'

'So the back was unguarded?' The colonel's face was grim. The sergeant nodded to the fact reluctantly. 'You heard nothing?'

'No, Colonel.'

'Lieutenant,' the colonel shouted. The officer who was directing some of the soldiers joined the colonel and the two captains beside her. 'Detain the sergeant and the private. Take off the sergeant's stripes.'

'Yes, Colonel.'

The lieutenant led away the two disgraced soldiers down the road.

Racing out of his house and across to the blaze was Zarviš. He stood beside the colonel. 'How'd it start?' His voice was timid.

'We don't know. Perhaps it was on purpose.'

'Deliberate?' he said, surprised.

'Maybe.'

'But who?'

The colonel didn't answer him, instead turning to the villagers. 'Get everyone to the church. I will arrive there shortly.'

The villagers stared.

'Go! You too, Zarviš.'

He nodded and twitched slightly. He and the villagers left.

*

Petra hurried around, making sure everyone was in the church. When she was satisfied, she joined the villagers' worried conversations. The light of the dying blaze could be seen through the windows.

'It could've been deliberately set on fire,' Zarviš said.

'Why? Who?' Luděk asked.

'It could've been one of the soldiers. Cabin fever or something.'

'It could have been an accident,' Hynek said.

'Probably.' Zarviš nodded.

'They'll find out what the story was,' Luděk said confidently.

'But if it was deliberate,' Štěpánka said, 'then... our houses could be next.'

'Luckily it wasn't the food store, just the armoury,' Zarviš said.

'Guns!' Štěpánka exclaimed.

'We should remember that,' Zarviš said.

'What do you mean by that, duckling?' Petra asked.

'Ignore me. It's... my imagination. It cannot be true.'

'What cannot be true?' Luděk said.

Zarviš hesitated. 'Well, I was just thinking.' He lowered his voice in a conspiratorial tone. 'What if the colonel set the barn on fire herself?'

Tibor tittered.

159

'Why?' Marek said.

'To give herself an excuse to cut our ration.'

'Yes. And where does it leave us?' Štěpánka was shaking.

'Don't be ridiculous,' Luděk said. 'The colonel started it? Nah.'

'There are two hundred and fifty soldiers who are trained to obey orders,' Zarviš said. 'What if the colonel is mad? What if one of the officers goes mad? What if they're all mad? What can we do about it?'

Marek nodded.

The skinny blonde Helena caught Petra's eye. 'Well, Granny. Am I still the one rocking the boat?' she said but not with any viciousness. Petra shook her head; she had totally forgotten about it.

'You've got it wrong,' Luděk said. 'The colonel's not mad. She's done everything. If it was deliberate, it'll be some screw-loose soldier who can't handle country life. She'll have it all sorted out by tomorrow.'

'Yes. You're right,' Zarviš said with a deadening effect. Little five-year-old Nada yawned as she lay down on one of the pews.

'I just hope the colonel doesn't think it was one of us.'

This produced all kinds of exclamations and consternations, but these were silenced by the colonel, who was standing in the doorway of the church, flanked by her officers. As she walked up the aisle, the villagers gave her room to pass as soldiers poured into the church behind her. She went to the top step in front of the altar and the three captains stood beside her. Petra guessed there were forty-odd soldiers in the church. The fifty or so villagers moved into the pews. The colonel stood silent for a long time, looking from face to face.

'I want to assure you,' the colonel spoke in a clear, loud and sure voice, 'that no one was injured and nothing of value was caught in the fire. Everything was retrieved. It seems it was probably started accidentally. There was a candle.' She paused. Her stern look was unnerving.

But Petra felt relief. She saw ease on several faces, including Marek and the fisherman, Tibor. Thank God nothing was burned, she thought. She looked up at the cruciform of a doleful Jesus and prayed thanks for it not being deliberate.

The colonel continued. 'The soldiers on duty failed in their task. These things shouldn't happen, but do. We've had enough tragedy. All the same, there must be changes. From tomorrow there will be a sunset to sunrise curfew. Anyone caught outside their home during this time without permission from an officer will be detained. I'm sorry to have to do this, but it's for safety's sake. It may seem unnecessary, but we've been thinking these things over these last few days and tonight's event decided it.' She paused.

'Colonel,' Tibor said, 'I sometimes fish at night.'

'I'm sure you do. There will be exemptions, but you'll have a soldier with you. There's another thing we've been weighing up and we've decided. Since the ambush, we've had to double our guard each time we send out a truck. Given our petrol ration, the calculation means we cannot go foraging outside Otočka as often. The harvest is less than two months away and we might not have enough till then. So there's no choice but to cut our ration. By a third.'

There was an eruption of complaint.

Marek stood up. 'But if those people who ambushed the soldiers are dead, why do you need to double up now?'

'Because I don't know and you don't know if there are others out there. I won't risk my soldiers in such unknowns without proper backup.'

'What right have you to cut the ration?' one loud villager said.

'What right have you to the protection of two hundred and fifty soldiers?'

Luděk smiled, his ginger moustache stretched wide.

'Be reasonable,' she continued. 'Even with all the trucks going out, we would probably have to cut it down.'

'And will the soldiers' ration also be cut?' one villager cried with some bitterness. There were shouts of agreement and of anger.

'Of course, the soldiers will have the same as you,' she said.

There were derisory hoots.

'My wife is pregnant,' Marek said. 'If you cut her ration—'

'She counts as two people as far as I'm concerned.'

'It's already so small,' said a large villager.

'There'll be nothing at all if we don't ration it,' the colonel said.

'If you cut it anymore, we'll not be able to do any work,' another shouted. The atmosphere was degenerating quickly.

'It has to be done and that's all there is to it,' the colonel said finally. She shrugged as if to say the matter should be obvious. 'There's no choice.'

'The colonel's right. You're all being selfish,' Luděk said and began accusing them individually of their faults.

Several other villagers joined Luděk in defence of the colonel. Little Nada began moaning at the sound of all this shouting. Soon there was shoving and pushing. Still some villagers were throwing angry questions at the colonel. But the more the villagers got angry, the more sanguine she became. The inevitable moment came when a scuffle broke out. And when Luděk accused his brother of selfishness, it was then that those two began throwing punches. There were screams and other tussles. The colonel signalled the soldiers to move in and separate the belligerents. They did so but it was a time before order was restored.

'This is hard,' the colonel said. 'But these are hard times. When we can be sure of the harvest, then we can think about the ration again. When we can be sure that barns won't set fire to themselves, we won't need a curfew. And when we can be sure soldiers won't be ambushed, then you'll never again hear that siren. But I may as well tell you, that will never be. We could live here for half a century and there'd still be a crisis every season. We're better organised than nearly anywhere. But sacrifices must be made. No way out of it. If you don't understand that, you better learn quick. I've said all there is to say. Go home. Go back to bed. It's late. All this arguing won't change a thing.'

The villagers were quiet. She moved down the aisle and they made room for her and the captains. As she was about to leave the church, she turned to one of her captains and said sotto voce, 'I'm fast on my way to becoming a politician.' She raised her eyebrows and the captains smirked. They left the church, though not before Hynek had managed to stop one of the captains and get a word or two in his ear.

'Why a curfew, Captain Nebojsa?'

'Like the colonel says, Hynek.'

'There's more to it, surely.'

The captain smiled wryly then ordered his soldiers to file out. When the villagers were alone, Luděk glared at his brother and then swiftly left.

'You see. You see,' Štěpánka said neurotically. 'It's going bad.'

'Well, she doesn't mess around,' Marek said. 'Guess we've no say in it.'

'She's right though,' Tibor said.

'And so were you, Zarviš. You said she would cut the ration and put a curfew in,' Marek said.

'I only thought that might happen. That it *might*. But I tell you, I really wish that I wasn't right.'

CHAPTER 26

Anton watched the German side of the Elbe. There were steep rocky hills on both sides, and they had already passed several long-haired, dirty, gaunt and staring figures standing on the riverbank. Some called out in desperation. One or two had attempted to swim towards the boat but had to turn back. Then on the Czech side, there was what looked like a band of Gypsies laughing and whistling. They held up several dead rabbits as if trophies. The boat sailed on, past some riverside towns, eerily absent of any signs of human life. Now on the German side, they were passing a railway. On the track was a stationary train, which had been badly vandalised: its windows smashed, its doors wrenched apart. Graffiti.

The door to the cabin opened. In the frame she stood with rumpled and matted hair. She looked older and calmer, though still pale.

'You haven't missed much,' Anton said. 'But, Doctor, you know staying inside all the time… it's not good for your health.'

She smiled weakly.

'But it is good to see you, Eliška. Like Persephone rising from Hades to bring back the spring.'

She squinted at the morning light and raised her hands to shield her pale-blue eyes. 'Am I dreaming?' she said looking away from the light and lowering her hand. 'I was drowning.'

'Maybe you should rest some more,' the nurse said.

'No, I'm not delirious.' Light streamed in through the portholes behind her. 'I saw it.' Sunlight glistened white on strands of her golden hair.

'What did you see?' Anton moved to shield her eyes from the direct sunlight.

'A flower. I held it. There were many colours. And in the

164

middle, I saw an eye.'

'You were hallucinating, Doctor. It was a fever,' the nurse said.

'No, no, it was real.'

Anton raised his brows. 'A flower?'

'Different colours, shining.'

'At least sit down, Doctor,' the nurse said.

'No, I'm OK. I'm OK. It was so vivid and large. As if it was alive.'

Anton smiled. 'I missed you. It was no joy seeing you in that tomb.'

'Then it was gone,' she uttered. 'It was such a bright light. Then gone.'

The nurse touched her shoulder and gestured for her to rest but she shook her head.

'When you were sick in Prague,' Anton said, 'we found this boat. We've been on the river. Less trouble than going by road.'

'Prague,' she said, narrowing her eyes as if remembering something. 'I saw skeletons walking...'

'You were very sick, Doctor.'

Again, the nurse gestured to her to sit down.

Anton saw her look at Radoš and František. 'You're wondering who these two are?' Anton introduced them

'Is this it? No more?' she said with a pained look.

'And she is Iva.' He pointed. 'No, not the heaving masses you were hoping for. But we barely scraped through ourselves.'

She stared, then glanced at the river. 'Where are we?'

'On the Elbe. Towards Otočka. We should be there today. Oh, Doctor! There were times... even I thought you were gone. I'm so happy.'

'Otočka? In one day?'

Anton looked at the others before looking back at Eliška.

'One? Doctor, no, not one... five. Five days.'

'Five?' She turned to the nurse, who nodded. 'Five?'

'It was terrible,' the nurse said.

165

'It was a miracle,' Anton said.

'How do you feel?' asked Sofie.

She squinted to look at Sofie. 'Alive.'

Anton smiled.

'Once, I couldn't feel your pulse,' the nurse said. 'But you were still breathing.'

Eliška put her arm around the nurse. 'I was in an ocean... no, I'm well. I feel strong.'

'All the same,' the nurse said, leading Eliška back to the sofa as František quickly got out his notebook and scribbled furiously. Sofie puts some tins of food on the steps down to the cabin.

'Oh, Doctor, one thing,' Anton said. 'Did you hear my violin?'

Eliška paused and shook her head. Then she looked up suddenly in realisation and smiled. 'Oh, you mean that terrible noise?'

'Ha!' Anton said as the doctor sat down to eat. 'Ha!' He turned to František, who put his notebook away. 'She heard my noise, Professor. It was my noise that saved her. Oh, sublime noise! I was doctor to the doctor, Apollo to Asclepius. The medicine of noise. It was my noise that did it. Did you know that, Professor? Well, well, what do you say to my noise?'

František looked vacantly. 'Nothing.'

'Ha!'

Anton smiled and reached for his violin to play again when something on the German side made him stop. There was a desperate-looking family. A gang with metal pipes and branches ran out of the forest. One of them had a makeshift bow. They shouted in German, but it was clear they were yelling insults and curses. The family ran back into the woods. The one with the bow aimed at the boat but lowered it again. Soon they were past them and Anton noticed a lot of floating debris, close to the boat. Then came a bloated corpse. As it passed, he could see something in its hand. A book. But it was too far away to see which. Other things floated in the shimmering water: pieces of plastic, chairs, foam, bottles, smashed wood. A rainbow-coloured film lay on the water. The smell of oil was strong.

Iva gave her book to Anton.

I lived about twenty miles from Otočka. I must go there to find my son and my sister.

'Only twenty miles? It's nothing. You don't have to go alone. I could go with you,' he said.

If I have to, I'll go alone. I would do anything to find him.

'We will all go,' he said. Viktor clicked his tongue. Sofie also read the lines in the book and what Iva was writing.

If I have to go alone, I will.

'Nonsense. We'll all go. Is it along the river? We can go past Otočka. Why didn't you say anything before? Of course we'll help you find him, won't we, Viktor?'

But he suddenly cut the engine. 'No. We ain't gonna cut through twenty miles of country full of freaks on a mercy mission. It's too damn late.'

'What do you mean too late?' Anton said as Iva put both hands on her head. 'It's not her fault. She left the boy with her sister.'

'Then he's fine where he is,' Viktor said bitterly. 'The best thing someone can learn is how to live by himself.'

'Why are you so against it? Twenty miles isn't far.'

Iva's tears wet the page.

'It's twenty miles too far,' Viktor said.

'We could do most of it by boat.'

Viktor shook his head.

'But...'

'Nah, it's a crime, isn't it?' Viktor shouted. 'And even if he's alive, he ain't gonna forget or forgive.'

Iva was panting with a fainting look in her eye; her cheeks became pale. She put her hands on the table and grasped it. Anton came round the other side to support her. She squinted and ineffectually threw out her arm, but it flopped on the table.

'Doctor...' Anton said.

Iva fainted. He eased her against the back of the chair.

The nurse stood at the cabin door. 'Check her pulse. Two fingers on the wrist.'

Sofie took one hand and Anton the other.

'Tilt her head back. Can you hear her breathing?'

'I can't feel any beat.' He wasn't aware his fingers were pressing her palm, not her wrist.

'I can feel her pulse,' Sofie said.

'I can't hear her breathing,' Anton said.

'Lay her down. Just here, at the top of the steps,' Eliška said.

Anton took her shoulders and Radoš took her legs. They laid her down.

'Stand back.' Eliška mounted the first few steps up to the deck. They stepped back. 'You are sure you felt a pulse?' she asked Sofie, who replied confidently. 'Hold her legs up. She will come round soon. Get a blanket over her.' Eliška went back to the cabin door.

Radoš went for the blanket and Anton held Iva's legs up.

'Has she been eating?' Eliška said to Sofie.

'Not much. She's waking up,' Sofie said and Iva opened her eyes and began moving.

'Put that small box under her feet to keep them up.' Eliška said to Anton. 'Don't try to move, Iva. Just relax. The sooner we get to Otočka the better. My sister should have some medicine.'

'You ain't got to wait much longer,' Viktor said. He pointed to a jetty up ahead with a sign hanging over it from the roadside: Otočka.

CHAPTER 27

Anton helped tie the boat to the metal jetty and soon he, Viktor and Radoš were searching for a bathtub and some new clothes so that the nurse and the doctor could disinfect themselves. Iva looked weak and Sofie was persistent in trying to get her to eat. The girl had an air of maturity and hardiness. She looked older.

The three men climbed the steps of the jetty to the road. Immediately they saw a hotel that was in the style of a Swiss cottage.

'All right, let's do this as quick as possible,' Viktor said.

Viktor took out his gun just before they entered. As they crept in, Anton smelled a bucket of brackish water. He and Viktor mounted the staircase, but Radoš stood still.

'Jesus, you're not going to wet yourself, are you?' Viktor said.

'Come on. There's no one here anyway. Holiday season's over,' Anton said.

They reached the first floor and went into one of the rooms. Viktor turned the taps in the en-suite bathroom, but no water came.

'Try the drawers,' Viktor said to Anton. He did and they revealed nothing. Viktor opened the wardrobe, also nothing. They searched every room until the second to last, where Viktor found a big black suitcase gathering dust in a wardrobe. He pulled it out and flung it on the bed. Opening it produced a welcome sight: clothes, books, a carton of cigarettes in a duty-free bag, a bottle of schnapps and a small backpack.

'*Affabile. Bella,*' Anton said. 'What pearls! What pearls!'

Viktor zipped it up, and as he did so, shot a look at the door. There were sounds of voices. He crept to the door. The sounds got louder. He pulled out his gun. The voices said something in

Polish. Anton held Radoš by the shoulder because he was shaking. The youth stepped backwards, clattering into the table, which banged against the wall. But the Poles kept talking. Viktor aimed his gun at the door and Anton put his hand over Radoš's mouth. Eventually, the three voices became muffled after the sound of a door closed. Viktor gestured to the other two that they should carry the suitcase between them. Then he quickly led them out the door and silently down the corridor and stairs. Outside, they paced to the boat and put the suitcase on the jetty. The nurse stood by the gunwale and Viktor told her the situation.

'It doesn't have to be a bathtub, but anything similar,' the nurse said.

'Is it necessary? There are people there.'

'We might still infect.'

'What about the canoe?' František said while still writing something in a notebook, only stopping to point with his pencil.

'Come on,' Viktor said.

'Professor, for a nihilist, you're quite practical,' Anton said and followed Viktor and Radoš to where a canoe bobbed.

'Take the paddles out. We'll fill it with water, then bring it onto the shingle,' Viktor said and Radoš waded into the water and held the opposite end. They capsized it and dragged it onto the pebbles.

The nurse told Sofie to handle the suitcase while the others were sent up to the road. They sat with their backs to the river. Viktor had taken the cigarettes and Anton grabbed the schnapps. Eliška emerged from the boat. She was at first a little shaky but soon was walking on her own. Sofie dragged the suitcase part way along the shingle and then took out some of the clothes. The nurse took out the bottle of chlorine from Eliška's bag and poured some into the canoe.

'Take that bag out too,' Eliška said to Sofie, pointing at the backpack among the clothes.

Eliška looked into the canoe, then took her clothes off and stepped in. She submerged herself, lying backwards under the water. Her hair floated as the afternoon sun shone high.

On the verge by the road, Viktor lit a cigarette. Anton took a pull of the schnapps. Viktor kept glancing at the hotel. Iva was writing in her notebook. Anton offered the bottle around, but only Radoš took it. When he offered it to Viktor, the grey-eyed man took it but hesitated, then handed it back.

'Nah. It's a bad story,' Viktor said.

Artur was looking at Anton with a questioning look.

'What is it, Commendatore?'

'What's your name?'

'Antonín Kratochvíl, first violinist of the Prague Philharmonic, now disbanded. Mahler, Smetana, Brahms, Mozart. I am not popular with conductors, and other players. They say I'm too wild. But the public like it.'

'Anton,' the old man said to himself.

'Yes. Did you ever go to the Rudolfinum?'

'Rudolf?'

'No, Rudolfinum, the concert hall. Sadly, no more.'

'I can't find Rudolf.'

Anton drank again. Poor man. We could say the same for everyone, Anton thought. Artur began muttering something to himself. Iva pushed the notebook into Anton's hand.

I am ready. I know the way from here.

'You're not well,' Anton said. 'Wait a moment, Eliška will be done soon. Let's see what she says.'

They didn't have long to wait, and Anton was amazed as Eliška came up the steps. She moved freely and looked anew with fresh clothes, shining eyes and still-wet hair loose about her head. In her hand was the backpack from the suitcase.

'Golden One,' Anton said and looked at the others, expecting to see the same wonder. Instead, he saw fear, nervousness, worry, confusion, desperation and indifference.

'Does that box have food?' She pointed to the box at Radoš's feet. He nodded. 'Then why don't you all eat something.'

Radoš began to open tins and pass them around.

171

'Probably the village is past those hills.' She sat down beside Viktor. The tin was offered to Iva, but she stood still with a desperate look.

'Doctor,' Anton said, 'she wants to go and look for her son. She said it's twenty miles.'

'You're too weak,' the nurse said.

'Wait,' Eliška said, 'my sister has soldiers. When we get to Otočka, we can get the soldiers to look. They'll have trucks.'

Iva shook her head.

'That's right,' Viktor said, 'no sense walking it if you can truck it.'

'We could take the boat,' Anton said. 'Your town isn't far from the river, is it?'

Iva nodded.

'No,' Viktor said. 'Got enough diesel for twenty miles, more or less. We'd have to walk it back. Remember that gang?'

Iva groaned.

'All right,' Viktor said, 'I ain't against you finding him, even though it's your fault. But the doc's way is the best.'

Iva suddenly stood and paced away. They called after her. Anton chased her up quite easily and stopped her.

'We might be able to go today,' he said. 'It can't be far to Otočka. With trucks we could be there even quicker.'

She looked down the road, desperate and moaning.

'Come on.'

She shook her head.

'Please.'

She took a step away, then her shoulders drooped. Slowly he led her back to the others.

Anton saw that the nurse wasn't wearing her white wimple and her new clothes were too big – blue jeans, a branded t-shirt. She had a cap instead of her veil, seemingly, Anton thought, as a last resort to tradition. She knelt next to the others and prayed.

*

Eliška led them past an old, long-abandoned green truck as a fox darted off. Though her legs were stiff and the light still stung her eyes, she welcomed the sensations. The path took them downhill towards an open field skirted by a road. She stopped in the middle of the road, and it was a strange and surreal sight. On the field there were fifty or so small single-room holiday cabins. Silently, Viktor drew out the gun. He stalked past, aiming his gun at gaps in the rows of cabins. He gestured to the others that it was safe, and they followed. Among the cabins was a chaotic mess of things: furniture, rubbish, tools, toys, broken bicycles. Beyond the field was a great satellite dish perched on the side of the hill, bluish grey in the distance, like some Roman ruin. Cars had been abandoned on the road, many dented and missing windows. Litter danced in the wind. A child's car seat sat on the road. Next to it, a motorcycle on its side.

The field opposite to this seemed to have been a caravan park with greying wrecks of mobile homes. A rusty barbecue with one of its three legs shortened, stood obliquely. Stuck into the ground, a small toy propeller was spinning in the wind, visible by its shiny and flecked tinsel. A ripped tent's opening flapped. A broken guitar, and a moulding mattress had a plant growing in it. A face silently laughed, the party mask of a garish clown, resting on a sandbag. A shattered, pale purple plastic bucket had a foam magic wand through a hole in it – the act of a child. There were shattered pieces of timber and white cladding. Eliška's eye caught the laminated image of a woman. It was between the front of the jockey wheel handle and bulkhead of a caravan. It had been faded by the elements: a peeling lamination of a stained Queen of England, with gloved hand, waving and saintly blessing unseen proceedings. Eliška saw something gleaming in the gutter out of the corner of her eye. Shining coins had been stuck to a miniature Buddha, pasted in some act of despair… or hope.

'Future people will laugh at this.' Anton smiled and swayed. He stepped awkwardly scraping the ground with his shoe. 'It's too absurd,' he chuckled and pulled again at the bottle. Something cracked under his foot. It was a small plastic bottle. When he took his foot off, glitter flew up on the wind and spread out like a shining dust. He stared with red eyes. 'Vanity,' he uttered as the glitter scintillated into the distance.

There was a loud sneeze.

They all turned suddenly in the direction of the sound.

The sound cursed, then mumbled. Viktor darted ahead to where the sound was coming from. An old man appeared carrying a shopping bag. He continued towards the road, oblivious of Viktor and the others. He reached the road and then noticed the gun pointed at his head.

'All right, pal, just stay there,' Viktor said.

'You want to take my stash? Well, you can't take it! I won't give it.' The old man shook his plastic bag at them.

'Just don't move,' Viktor said.

'Where's the village with the army?' Eliška said.

'Soldiers?' the man said brusquely. 'Thieves. Bastards. They're not soldiers. They took my stash. Bastards! Took my stash.'

'Don't worry, we're not going to hurt you or take anything,' Eliška said.

'You stay away. You leave me alone. You're one of them.'

Viktor stepped closer. 'Listen, old man, I don't give a goddam squeaky fart about your mouldy stash. I wouldn't touch it if you gave it to me. But I ain't for fooling. So where's the village, old man. Speak or I'll give your ancient carcass something to shake about.'

Iva put her hand on Viktor's arm. He lowered the gun a little.

'Way? I'll tell you the way.' The old man presented them with a middle finger. Viktor raised the gun again, but the old man was walking off towards the caravans. Iva again delicately placed her hand on Viktor's arms, and again he lowered it.

'Would be a waste anyway,' Viktor said.

Eliška called out again with the offer of taking him to the

village, but the old man moved spryly and soon disappeared.

'Let's keep going,' Eliška said and they began walking.

'Isn't it hot in that coat?' Radoš said to František, who seemed deep in thought.

František raised his long face. 'It always seems cold to me.'

Radoš laughed.

'Hot and cold are relative and so meaningless. My circulation is chronically bad, but that doesn't mean anything. Neither does up nor down, left nor right, in nor out, forward nor backward, because all these things reverse if you hold up a mirror. And even if you try to reconcile them, bring them together in some solid determination, they cancel each other out in a giant zero. The great zero. Only of that can we be sure.'

'Stop corrupting the youth, Professor.' Anton beamed and gave the bottle to Radoš, who took it as Anton whistled and sang. Eliška stopped at a side road on the left with a sign pointing to Otočka Village. She pointed and led them down it.

'Professor, Professor, confess-sir, confess-sir. You're a lizard, a word-spewing wizard. But what are you really? What really are you?' He skipped. '*Là ci darem la mano, là mi dirai di sì,*' he sang cheerfully. '*Vedi, non è lontano*… no, you know what I think, Professor? I think this is all a front, and in fact you are secretly a Don Juan. The ladies are not safe. They're not safe!' He made a knowing look. He sang again and all the time with a ridiculous grin on his face. 'It's beautiful. It's good,' he said to no one. 'We're alive. We're still alive!' He slung an arm around Radoš's neck. 'Shout it out. Ahh! Life bursts with energy. Shout! Let it know we shall not yield it. We shall be full of fire, and the sun shall be jealous.'

Radoš blushed at being a bewildered hostage.

'Commendatore, Artur.' Anton disengaged himself from a relieved Radoš. And then wrapped shoulders with the old gentleman who for some reason was smiling. 'Sì, sì, *mio caro*. All life says "live", who are we to say "no". Think about it, all those nobodies who thought the news, money and routine was

175

life. Fools. They didn't know one must sing and jump.' He jumped and twirled Artur about.

They turned a corner and reached a wide expanse of fields. But what caught Eliška's eye straight away was the line of high fence topped with barbed wire that ran perpendicular across the fields. The road proceeded to a series of gates that were about several hundred yards away. The fields on the other side of the fence had sheep in them. At the gates immediately the sentries came to attention at the sight of nine people.

'Sober it up, Violin Man; we don't want any shooting.'

'We made it. We made it! Bella.' Anton jubilantly capered about. Viktor grabbed him.

'I said pipe down.'

'But we made it,' Anton said meekly.

'Stay here. I'll go alone and talk to them; then I'll signal to you,' Eliška said. It was agreed and, as she went alone, the soldiers trained their guns on her.

'Stop there,' one of them shouted as she neared. 'What do you want?'

'Tell the colonel that her sister is here?'

The soldier smirked. 'You look nothing like her.'

'Half-sister. Please tell her. We've come from Prague. I'm the doctor.' They looked unconvinced. 'Just tell her it's Eliška. She can come, and if I'm not her sister then she'll say so.'

They mumbled a bit, but in the end one of them spoke into a radio. Eliška looked at the soldier, whose expression was grim and distrustful.

'She's coming,' the other soldier said.

Eliška nodded. 'Do you have any sick or wounded inside?'

'Couple of soldiers shot.'

'Shot?'

'Some people ambushed a foraging party.'

'Why?' she said but the soldier shook his head. 'Are they badly hurt?'

'They'll live.'

'Why are you here? And who are these people?' the other soldier said.

'My sister asked me to come. You don't have a doctor.'

'And them?' The guard pointed over her shoulder.

'They're my friends.'

'Anyone armed?' the other soldier said.

'Yes.' The soldiers looked at each other. 'But we're not a threat.'

They seemed unconvinced. They spent the rest of the time waiting in silence. Eventually a figure appeared on the road on the other side of the fence, bobbing up and down on a horse. Eliška froze. It was her. Yes, it was. That long curly hair. That figure. Years. It had been so many years since she had last seen her. And then the colonel's message, out of the blue and only because of the crisis: 'We need you.'

The colonel rode with a straight back at a canter, her bearing stately. Eliška saw her serious, commanding expression as the horse neared. The soldiers at once stood to attention. The sight of her brought the past flooding up through her veins. The colonel stopped close and dismounted. One of the soldiers held the reins and the colonel stepped towards her with a commanding presence. Eliška could not help smiling, even tittering. The colonel remained serious and the soldier by the gate saluted. She stopped and eyed her sister for a long time through the wire of the gate. Eliška, tendrils of her untied hair trailing in the wind, shook her head in wonder.

Finally, the colonel smiled. 'You made it.'

'I made it, Vendula,' Eliška chuckled.

'I didn't think you would,' the colonel said. 'I mean the chances. Open the gates.' The colonel couldn't hide her astonishment. The barriers parted and she was about to embrace Eliška.

'Don't worry,' Eliška assured her. 'I did have it. But there's no danger now.' She grinned.

Eliška was clutched and almost smothered. Even the grim-faced soldier couldn't help smiling. When the sisters held each other by the shoulder, it was the colonel who spoke first.

'Ten years. And in such circumstances.'

'None of that matters now, Vendula,' Eliška said, admiring the sight of her sister who had changed a lot in those years.

'I'm so happy you're here, and not just because we need a doctor. It's good to see you. But you've gained some wrinkles.'

Eliška smiled. 'Are you well? How is it here?'

'Better than what you've seen out there, I'm sure. How bad is it?'

Eliška shook her head.

'Well, you made it, you—' The colonel looked at the group of people standing a few hundred yards off.

'They're with me. I tried to get more.'

'Eliška, when I said come, I meant only you.'

'They are not infected, and they saved my life. Vendula, don't tell me there's no room.'

'No, I mean no. I've got problems enough. Especially now.'

'I don't understand. We'll quarantine ourselves, if that's the problem.'

'Eliška, be reasonable. Be realistic. I've had to cut the ration already. I can't take any more. Imagine the resentment. They would blame me, not you.'

'Nine people can't be a burden, surely. And if it were fifty or a hundred, there would be a way.'

'Still the humanitarian. And still a headache. Your Red Cross ethics won't work here. Six soldiers were killed in an attack and the armoury was burned down. I can't.'

'Then you cannot take me.'

'What?'

'I mean it. They've come this far. I told them about this place. I gave them the hope of some kind of security. I'm responsible for them. How can I tell them to leave?'

The colonel looked at the group. 'What are they to you?'

'It's all of us or none of us.'

'Ach… I should have known you would do something like this.'

'Stop thinking military for once. They're people.'

The colonel smiled wryly. 'That I'll have to worry about. What about I give them a tent and steady food supply, but they stay outside?'

'All of us or none,' Eliška said.

The colonel stood akimbo, eyeing her sister and the group in turn. 'You and your bleeding heart. You may know the body, but you don't know people. Ach… fine. But understand Eliška, you and anyone can speak their minds but there's only one colonel. Also, I'm agreeing to this because they'll probably cause more problems outside than in. You said you are responsible for them?'

'Yes.'

'Good, then consider yourself an honorary lieutenant. If they cause problems, it'll come back to you.'

'I don't want to argue with you.'

'The feeling's mutual. Well, I have to say it is good to see you.'

'Me too.'

It took some time to make all the preparations. It was decided they would quarantine in Helena's house, both her and her mother were put in Marek's. There was an angry scene with Helena about it, but it was brief. Viktor was ordered to surrender his gun. He refused. Eliška was persuasive and he relented after he had a tense moment with seven soldiers and a display of their weaponry. Word spread quickly of their arrival and that of the doctor. The villagers came out to see them walk towards Helena's house. The colonel, mounted on Hynek's horse, watched from the car park.

Anton staggered near. 'We'll have a concert. We'll celebrate the arrival. Ah, the countryside. The pastorale.' He walked along with his arm around Radoš. Suddenly he stopped when he saw the colonel. He ran towards her imposing figure, stretching out his arms. He bent on one knee.

179

'Brünnhilde! *Ho jo to ho. Hei aha.* Do not ride into the flames!'

'Is that man drunk?' the colonel said.

Anton threw the empty bottle across the tarmac where it smashed to shards.

'Brünnhilde, forbear! Ride away. You Valkyrie.'

The colonel stared.

'Brünnhilde. Do not take the politicians to Valhalla,' he shouted. 'Leave the incompetents... and the journalists. The media personalities. The planners and plodders. The experts. The intelligencia. The religious. Leave the critics behind. And those who didn't understand what life is. Leave behind the know-alls, the moralists, the paranoids, the arrogant. And... and don't take those confident imaginations who laughed at how easy it would be to solve. And the businessmen who thought the money would fix it. Leave those who said, "just wear masks". Let a reign of retributive justice fall on all of them! Drop them in the sea. Throw them into calderas. Jettison them into icy lakes. Fling them into volcanoes. Let their tumbling bodies rotate balletically from the high blue sky down to the oceans and deserts. Let them scream their fear, like an untuned orchestra. Ride eagle high into the sky among the clouds and unclasp them, screeching.

'But we shall stand in Odin's hall. We who dance. We who thrive! Judge fairly, you Valkyrie. We who have done good battle.' He threw his hands wide theatrically.

The colonel, with a stern face, pointed to Helena's house. Anton was helped up by Radoš who was laughing.

'Judge fairly,' Anton uttered, barely able to stand. The nurse helped. 'Judge wisely.'

After much to and fro, the Prague group all got into Helena's house. Eliška made a search and came into the kitchen where Viktor was looking out the window to the wire fence in the distance.

'It's just one goddam prison for another,' he said beneath his breath.

Iva was sitting at the table counting her pills. Eliška touched her shoulder and she smiled briefly. She opened her notebook and wrote.

Will you help me find him?

Eliška reassured Iva and nodded. But she knew it was next to impossible.

*

At night, Hynek was sitting at his table binding reeds for a wicker chair when the lights went out. He fumbled for a match and lit a candle. Soon, candlelight began flickering in all the windows of the village.

'The power has finally gone,' he said.

Shadows crept into corners of his room that electric light had got rid of.

'The Old World has finally fallen. It will all be different now. '

CHAPTER 28

Ten days passed and there was a strange atmosphere inside Otočka. The food ration had been reduced again, now only enough for one and a half meals a day. Soldiers patrolled the night during curfew. At first several villagers thought it was ridiculous and childish. But soon they got used to it. Some of the children had dreams of long shadows with guns. Hynek spoke to the colonel to propose a council of officers and villagers that, if not able to make decisions, could at least suggest them to the colonel. In a moment of cynical pique, she replied that doubtless Hynek himself would be on this council.

'It would be up to everyone to decide who would be on the council,' he had said.

The colonel rejected the idea.

Luděk bored people with his animus towards his brother as well as his keen praise of the colonel. He even suggested that Marek may have started the fire after rumours spread that it was deliberate. Many villagers avoided him. Helena and her mother had been moved and so the only villager remaining on the west side of the river was Zarviš.

The villagers witnessed a court martial. The ex-sergeant and the private were brought into the field and sat on two chairs. Opposite, the colonel and the three captains. Standing around were the villagers and the army. The trial was summary. The accused admitted that the private was asleep at the time and that the ex-sergeant had failed to periodically check the back of the barn. The panel pronounced them guilty. The colonel sentenced them to be thrown out of Otočka. The villagers appealed to the colonel.

'No. It's a question of survival,' she said. 'What if it had been the food store?'

'But to throw them out,' Hynek said.

'They must accept it. And I want to show that no favour is given to the soldiers over the villagers. This cannot go unanswered.'

'I agree, but perhaps their punishment should be to rebuild the barn. Since they are responsible for it being burned, get them to rebuild it.'

'No. That would be like breaking a vase, knowing you can just glue it back together again.'

The villagers watched as the two soldiers were escorted, but preserving their honour, they went voluntarily. Luděk applauded. They were at least given some survival equipment.

One morning the villagers woke to find something bizarre. Beside the river, on the west side, a pole had been erected. At the top of this pole was a painted canvas, a kind of flag. On it was a red and black snake, as if flying and electrified in the shape of lightning. In the middle, a gold circle made with a loop of the snake's body, inside which was a human-like stick figure.

'I don't understand what's going on anymore,' Petra said. 'I don't understand.'

'Nasty snake,' little Nada said.

'It's made from the battalion insignia. The colonel wanted it up for the soldiers,' Zarviš said, despite the fact he himself had designed it. '"So everyone feels they are part of something", the colonel said to me.'

Another smokehouse was built. Villagers rediscovered sewing, salting and preserve making. Lots were drawn for gathering manure from septic tanks. With the usual things to be done, there was always work.

The colonel at first refused to send out a truck on a hopeless mission for a boy who might be dead. But the salt was getting low and she hadn't sent any trucks to Iva's town. She said she would risk the use of petrol and sent two trucks. It turned out to be worth it. They found plenty in building material and were able to pump some diesel out of a petrol station. They got clothes, blankets and salt in a supermarket. They did find people, who begged for help. But not the boy. When Iva was told the news, she just stared.

On the tenth day, the doors of Helena's house opened and the Prague group emerged from their quarantine. Eliška and the nurse wasted no time doing the rounds of the sick and wounded.

'Yes, yes,' Anton said, stretching out his arms, smiling and bustling about. 'This is wonderful. I've always loved the countryside. I could happily stay here the rest of my life.'

'What about the people?' Viktor said.

'I think I've been here before,' Artur said to himself.

'How can the people not be good?' Anton said. 'They're free from the virus. The crop's growing. No one's hungry. Now they've a musician who can play in the long evenings. If we can't make it here, we can't anywhere.' The tendrils of his hair danced. 'It is wonderful!' He suddenly clasped the first hapless human that was close to him – Radoš. He wheeled him round, laughing and eventually put him down.

Viktor clicked his tongue. 'What the bloody hell is that?' He pointed to the flag with the snake insignia on it.

'Who cares? We're free. Now we can really live.' Anton beamed.

CHAPTER 29

Šimon fell into a shallow dip that had been covered with branches. Karl helped him out, then moved some of the branches away.

'What is it?' Šimon said.

'Someone's dug under the fence to Otočka.'

'To get in?'

'Or to get out. But sicherlich, he must be very thin. See how small it is. I could not fit.'

Šimon helped Karl put the branches back and soon they continued along the fence towards the river. They had just walked the twenty miles back from his town, where they had gone to look for his mother. He couldn't rest with the thought that his mother may have returned, and he wasn't there. They had searched not just his house but the whole town. They saw people and hid from them, though the figures seemed weary and forlorn. But they did not find his mother. They waited several days, but she did not come. And then the army came. He and Karl hid in a closet as the soldiers searched the house. Šimon heard the footsteps of one of them tread nearer. He closed his eyes and concentrated on being still. The footfalls stopped. Šimon opened his eyes. The soldier seemed to just remain, as if wondering. Šimon heard Karl's strained breathing and his own racing heartbeat. The soldier's shoe shuffled, and Šimon couldn't stop his sudden intake of breath. He looked at Karl in panic. The shoe stopped. Šimon felt he was suffocating. He felt he was about to choke. He closed his eyes and tried to calm his pounding heart. Then the sound of footsteps faded as they left the room and descended the stairs. He breathed deep as Karl sighed.

Šimon wanted to stay and wait, but someone had stolen their deer. There was no river for fishing and more than once Karl had

185

to threaten to use the bow when strangers got too close. In the end they left the town and ended up at the camp of the Tyrolean hatted man. Šimon panicked at the thought of seeing the hunters again, but he quickly realised that there was no one there and that the camp had been abandoned. Everything was gone: deer, buckets, pots. Only the roughshod bivouacs remained.

*

They came to the riverbank that was familiar to them. Karl had left the two pieces of hazel wood as fishing rods near a rock. Šimon took out the knife and began cutting some small pieces of deer and Karl put the meat on the two hooks. They didn't have to wait long before the fish began to bite and quickly caught two. After cleaning and gutting them, they rested.

Karl sang and Šimon listened to the strange words and their lilting, diminishing yearning. The boy laid back on the grass and closed his eyes. He felt borne aloft by the relaxing notes and it was like a soft blanket under him. Pine scent drifted. The light and warmth caressed his eyelids, all gentle. A blackbird accompanied Karl as the leaves from drooping branches swayed over the daydreaming boy. Šimon remembered his mother's laughter as she chased him around the garden. He remembered her reading in her chair in the garden, the wine glass sparkling. He remembered helping her plant rose bushes. He remembered with pride watching her talk and talk and talk, making all her friends laugh as she held forth with soul and wit. And he remembered lying next to her on the grass on a picnic, talking and dreaming. The scene shimmered into the light as he opened his eyes.

He sat up. The German held the last note. Then silence.
'Karl?'
'Mmm?' He turned to Šimon.
'You won't leave me, will you?'
'No, Šimon. Why do you say that?'

186

'Because everyone leaves.'

'Don't worry. Where I go, you can come.'

Šimon's eyes gleamed. 'Karl?'

'Mmm?'

'I... well... it's just—'

The sound of several twigs breaking startled them. Two men stood, wearing soldier's fatigues. Karl quickly went for his bow and arrow.

'Don't shoot! Don't shoot,' they shouted in Czech.

They had their hands up. Karl looked puzzled at what the men were saying. Finally, Šimon translated. Karl lowered the bow and the men calmed down. They stepped closer, tentatively. Karl raised the bow again and they put their hands up.

'OK. Can we just sit down here?' they asked.

Šimon relayed the question and Karl once more lowered the bow. The men sat on a fallen tree. They looked glum. Karl asked if they were soldiers from Otočka. The answer was that they were. One of the soldiers began to relate what had happened to them. They described how they were on duty while a barn they were guarding burned down and they were thrown out as punishment.

'Do you have anything we could eat?' the ex-sergeant said.

'You are soldiers. You should know how to live in the wilderness,' Karl said.

'We found a rabbit.'

'Have you seen anyone else?' Karl asked.

As he translated, the thought occurred to Šimon to tell the soldiers about the hole under the fence.

'I don't know of any hole,' the soldier replied. 'Someone got inside? It was going to happen someday. But they've a shoot-to-kill order on anyone getting in; to stop the virus, even though there's a doctor now. We want to get back in. We'll ask one of the sentries to get a message to Captain Nebojsa.'

Karl was looking up to the mountains on the German side while they were talking. He turned and began to prepare the pan.

'Get some wood,' he told Šimon. 'We will make a fire and finish off the deer. But Šimon, tell them we are not infected. They look scared of us.'

Šimon did but the soldiers remained where they were. Then he gathered twigs and branches, happy at being useful. He sorted the smaller twigs from the larger ones and began to prepare the tinder. He took the lighter and with everything ready looked up at Karl.

'It's good,' Karl said. Šimon lit the cotton wool and it flamed immediately. 'Now the sticks, not so many. Blow it. Gently. More sticks. Now that one. Good. Now watch it.'

The little flames became larger. Šimon felt the warmth of the fire kindling a feeling of pride. Eventually, Karl put the metal tripod over the embers and began cooking. 'Is there anything else I can do?' Šimon asked.

'Wash this sack, then let it dry on the rocks there.' Karl pointed to the hessian bag that the deer was in. Šimon took it and went to the river.

Karl took the cooked meat out and put it onto the plate, which he then put on the ground. He gestured to one soldier to try a piece and he greedily ate. The other soldier now joined them and was on the point of eating when sudden footsteps made them turn. The sounds quickened and out from behind a bush a man ran at them. The three of them all stood back. Šimon saw the man and recognised him immediately: singlet, sandals, gangly.

'Stop! Stay there,' the ex-sergeant shouted.

The gangly man rushed and only stopped when the plate of food was at his feet.

'This is good,' he said and without hesitation picked the plate up and began to eat. 'Stop that!' the ex-sergeant said, but the man ignored him. The soldier picked up the bow and arrow and aimed.

The man looked up but continued blithely eating.

'I will shoot if you don't stop,' the ex-sergeant said.

The gangly man looked up, as if remembering something important. He stared, then shuddered. His eyes were bloodshot.

'Put the plate down!' the ex-sergeant said.

'I ran from bad people,' the man said with a frightened grimace. 'This isn't safe.' He tried to pick up another piece of meat, but his long fingers trembled and knocked it off the plate.

'Do you remember me?' Šimon said.

'It's not my fault,' the man said to Karl. 'They were bad people. I...' He waved his free hand in front of him, without any clear purpose. 'Can I sit down? I'm very... can I sit down?' He sat down and rubbed his right ear and stared at Šimon. 'One thousand crowns... I bought two. I didn't steal it,' he slurred. 'That's very interesting.' He shot up and lurched towards Karl, who retreated. The man stopped and picked up an object that didn't exist and held it in front of him.

'Just walk away and I won't shoot. Go on, walk,' the ex-sergeant said.

The man paid no attention. He put the object carefully on the ground and turned back to the plate of meat.

'He's going to eat it all,' the private said.

'Hey!' The ex-sergeant shook the bow menacingly. The man tried to eat but the plate wasn't in his hands.

'You won't shoot him, will you?' Šimon said to the ex-sergeant.

'They're the bad people... they're to blame.' He took a few steps towards Karl. 'They ran after me...'

Karl slowly backed away and the man looked sharply at him.

'Oh my God! Oh my God!' The man looked terrified of something. He lunged and grabbed Karl's arm. 'Help me! Help me. What's going to happen? I don't want to die.'

'Let go of him,' the ex-sergeant shouted.

'I don't deserve it. I'm good,' he said desperately. Then he turned angry. 'They won't die, will they? With their super yachts.' He looked at Šimon, whose cheeks had paled. 'You! You are disgusting.' He let go of Karl's arm and made for Šimon.

Karl grabbed his arm and held him back.

'I swear. I swear. They took everything... they stole

189

everything…' The man sweated and panted. 'Don't look at me.'

'Just slowly walk away from him.' the ex-sergeant said.

'Liars! How many of us will die? You must come with me. We're good. There's a clinic in India… Ayurvedic.'

'Leave or I will shoot,' the ex-sergeant pulled back the arrow.

'Thieves!' He rushed at Karl, seizing his arm. 'You…' He gasped for air, wide-eyed and seemed suddenly bewildered. Then he became afraid. He looked down to the arrow sticking in his lung. He looked up again with the grimace. 'I'm not sick.' He coughed blood and some of it landed on Karl's face. 'In… fect…' He coughed again.

'Karl, move away!' Šimon said and the German stepped aside. The man shuffled ineffectually after him, then changed his course. He stopped, grimaced with pain then staggered forward, gasping for breath. He remained on his feet and shuffled until he came to the river's edge. Then he looked up towards the sky and fell into the shallow of the river. The arrow stuck itself in the ground as blood flowed into the river.

For a long time, the only sound was the rushing river and fire. Šimon looked away from the body. He felt swirling nausea.

Karl gazed at the river. His face was spattered with blood.

'Mein Gott, was für ein Wahnsinn? Ich werde niemals entkommen.'

'Karl?' Šimon said on a falling note and stepped towards him.

'Don't come,' Karl shouted and rushed to the river to wash his face.

190

CHAPTER 30

Zarviš leant his head against the wall of the corridor in his house. Though it was afternoon, the corridor was gloomy and had only the little window on the front door for light.

'Now is the moment.' He turned his head to the little window. His beady eyes glowed. He sighed and stood straight on his feet. He checked his pocket for the piece of paper. It was there. Then he re-tucked his shirt and straightened his clothes. He re-tied his shoelaces making sure they were tight and neat. He smoothed his hair with his palm, nodded to himself and opened the door.

Shortly, he was standing in the colonel's living room, who was alone.

'Are they saying anything interesting?' the colonel said.

'Nothing, except about the poverty of the ration.'

'Ah... well that's an old chestnut, Zarviš. I'm glad that they prefer to speak to you than me. It seems I'm too military. Anyway, you've lived here all your life; you know what they're like.'

'Can I say something?'

'Of course, Zarviš.'

'I think' – he walked to the map on the wall – 'Colonel, can I tell you my dream?'

The colonel chuckled. 'Is it decent?'

'Colonel, it's what I dream every night. Every day. I want to tell you... I have to tell you... my deepest thoughts. I want to confess.'

The colonel stepped closer. 'A confession? What have you done? What is it?'

'First, are we totally alone?'

'Yes. Totally.'

'Second, I need you to promise not to mention this, even to

191

the officers.'

This raised her eyebrows. She made a promise, with reassurances that there were things also that she had withheld from her officers. Zarviš nodded, took a few paces towards the window, then spun round.

'Outside the fence, the world is searching for a way. No doubt there are other villages like this one, and they necessarily manage in a similar way. It's fair to say nothing can be done in cities. Only places where crops can grow are the future. Would you say that's the situation?'

'Yes.'

'And that governments and societies, as we knew them, are no more.'

'Yes.'

'And that it's places like this that are the future.'

'As far as we know, Zarviš. But who knows, maybe in America they have something different. Perhaps, nothing has changed in some Russian backwaters. But even in those cases, you're right it would be something similar. And maybe they're not as well-organised as we are. We have a trained army. They might have a gang or something.'

'So we're a model, aren't we? We're an example.'

'Yes,' she said with a long rising note, 'and?'

'Don't you see it, Colonel? Don't you understand? I'm talking about saving lives. Building. Organising.' He rushed towards the French doors with its view of the field. He pointed. 'Out there, beyond the fence, there are hundreds of farms. But no crops. The animals have gone wild. People are dying staring at empty fields. Why? Why don't they organise? They don't because they don't know how.'

'They don't have any defence.'

'That too is within their power, if they only knew *how*. All they need is knowledge.'

'Ach... Zarviš, you sound like my sister. You are leading up to a point where I have to help achieve this in some way. Yes, you can nod your head enthusiastically, but I'm not interested in saving the world. I'm only interested in this village. Within this fence, I have some control. It can be managed. Outside, I couldn't care less.'

'No, but Colonel,' Zarviš said, greatly excited, 'you don't seem to understand it. Maybe I haven't expressed myself clearly. It isn't people that we want to send out to make new villages – it is the idea, the way, the knowledge. It's like a vision that people can understand, can believe in and recreate for themselves. Do you see it, Colonel? All we have to do is create the legend of Otočka. Imagine it, like a blueprint that people can use. There could be thousands of Otočkas, a league of little states, all with our system and methods, ways that are proven to work.'

'What would be the point?'

'All of them managed by people in your image. In *your* image.'

'My image?'

'Because you're the reason why we have safety and prosperity here. You planned it. It's your way. Colonel, it's your village.'

This made the colonel pause.

But Zarviš looked unsure if he had quite hit the mark. 'A network of Otočkas, which in the long run reduces the threat to this one. Fewer people trying to ambush us because they're busy building their own Otočka. Stability.'

'How would it spread?' the colonel said.

'Images. Words. Simple words. A couple of pages. Word of mouth. It will take time. It is a long project.'

'There are practical difficulties. They would need fencing, weapons, know-how.'

'Small things are nothing, if you take care of the big ones.'

The colonel was thoughtful for a moment. 'I see. But I'm not convinced. It's pointless, Zarviš. It's crazy. It—'

'It'll cost you nothing.'

'Even so.'

'But, Colonel, a thousand Otočkas, with our flag, with your image, with our words of hope, of security. But that's not the main thing.'

'Right, now you come to it. What is the main point, Zarviš?'

'The main thing is this village.'

'I should hope so.'

'And how doubtful our chances are.'

The colonel looked puzzled. 'Doubtful?'

'I mean that, at least how I see it, we stand on shaky ground.'

'What are you talking about?'

'Old ideas. Old thoughts. Old feelings. Old plans. Old theories. Old worlds. It won't work now, will it? We don't have democracy here. You'll admit that you're opposed to it.'

'It's a question of survival. But mainly I wouldn't be able to command my soldiers if they were making decisions.'

'It's not a criticism, Colonel,' Zarviš said, chuckling. 'I say it to illustrate the point that democracy is now an old belief. Do you see what I'm getting at now?'

'Unless there is a place that decides it wants it,' the colonel said. 'And good luck to them. But that's obvious. There're lots of things we don't have now that we did. Aeroplanes, hospitals, tanks—'

'Courts, free press, law, civil government, artists, writers, free thinkers; ha, I was about to say prostitutes, but I think one of those has survived in Otočka.'

'No one expects those things to exist here.'

'But the villagers haven't accepted that Rome has fallen, have they? Look, Colonel, they don't fully realise that they're effectively living fifteen-hundred years in the past. Somewhere in their minds, even the soldiers still think it's possible to return to what was.'

At this, the colonel scowled. 'And why not? Within reason.'

'For the same reason, Colonel, that you are afraid to give up the power you have.' He smirked. 'Colonel, you needn't hold back with me. I know the reason. I know that if you really believed in democracy, you would have to abolish the post of colonel, captain, sergeant, all. But that would be chaos. On the other hand, I wonder how much you've thought about the future. Because it can't continue, can it?'

'What do you mean?'

'I mean soldiers and villagers. The colonel and the farmers. Army and civilian. Colonel, at some point the soldiers are going to have to become villagers; at some point there's going to have to be a new contract, a new system, one that respects the situation. One in which we're all Otočkans.'

Zarviš twitched. The colonel squared up with her knotted brow and powerful eyes that seemed to look through Zarviš and beyond.

They were silent for some time.

'I understand what you mean,' she said finally, 'but I'm not going to change anything unless it is necessary.'

'Oh, I agree. I only wanted to be sure you see it.'

'Mmm. Well… what would this new system be? What are the details?'

Zarviš turned to the field, smirking. He looked back, beaming. 'We must be a clear example. It's a system that's simple, clean and integrated and knows what it's about and why.' He became excited and jumpy. 'It must be strong, and the people in it, part of a single whole. Roles that are easy to understand, so that people are sure and not afraid and know what they stand for. A system that's reliable and solid. A way that has something in the centre of it to believe in, especially when there're problems, and there're always problems. That last thing is the most important.'

'Sounds like the army,' she said wryly. 'Sounds like what we have already.'

'Yes, and what was your oath when you became a soldier?'

'To defend the Czech Republic.'

'Which no longer exists.'

'And what's your point?'

'That the president, the army, the generals, nation, all that is gone, Colonel. All gone. Right now, we're drifting without an idea of what is to come. Or for who we are and what we want. Without it, things will slowly unwind because there's no object. Without a story, without a myth, without a vision there's nothing to hold onto let alone look forward to. Nothing at the core. But if you show them an image of a hopeful future and they trust you, they'll join the New Way voluntarily.'

The colonel thought for a moment. 'Still a bit short on details. You're talking ideas and beliefs.'

'Which are just as important as rations of flour and eggs.' Zarviš palmed his hair.

'Even so.'

'Colonel, we can talk details later. The important thing is you understand.'

'But give me at least some hard detail. You talk of a vision, but what vision?'

Zarviš sighed and twitched. Then he brightened and grabbed the piece of paper in his pocket. 'Colonel, this may help. It's a new oath. You've already agreed that the oath to the Czech Republic is useless. I'll read this new one:

'*I [name] do swear that I have a duty to Otočka and the New Way. I swear to work hard to make our new land stronger and healthier for the common good. I swear to uphold our rules and defend our new land. We are the privileged few who have a responsibility to work towards prosperity, security and health. I acknowledge Colonel Vendula Korbova as authority in our land. All this I swear.*'

Zarviš watched the colonel closely as she walked round the table, looking out the window, then at the maps, then at the floor.

'That's not a bad idea.' She looked up.

'You see, where it says, "our new land", that gives them something to believe in, and it makes it theirs.'

'Yes, I see it.' She grinned. 'Where did you get these ideas?'

'It is what is necessary. You do agree?'

'Certainly about the oath.'

'Oh well, that is only a draft. We can work on it.'

The colonel nodded and pouted. 'The new way?'

'The New Way, with new rules for a New World.'

'New, new, new. What is all this newness?'

Zarviš smashed his hand into his fist in excitement. He pointed his finger at the map. 'Yes, new! Because there's so much possibility in the new. We can do anything if we throw away the old, which is just a chain around us. If we break the chain, we can be free. We can make our new country the way *we* want, free of history. New.'

The colonel nodded and she too looked at the map. Her mouth formed a little smile and her eyes narrowed. Zarviš trembled and held both his hands awkwardly in front of him.

'What is the New Way?' She glanced at him.

'Yes. The New Way is hope. Light. It is our story and myth, which if spread fulfils itself. It is prosperity.' He was on the verge of further explanation, when the colonel held up her hand for him to stop. 'The captains are coming. We'll talk about this later. Later.'

'Yes, Colonel,' Zarviš said with a tortured kind of smile.

CHAPTER 31

Anton finished playing a minuet after he had played several little rondos to the soldiers. They had asked for some pop music, and he had done the best he could. He then went looking for Tibor. But when he found him, the publican had not a drop.

'How can I work in the fields? Don't they see my job is music?' he said to himself as he drifted over to the meadow where Artur was gazing with an innocent smile.

'Commendatore, shall we become farmers?'

Artur cocked his head at what he was looking at. Anton followed his eye line and saw Radoš with a young woman. He looked closer and saw the blonde hair of Helena. The two of them stood hand in hand by the river.

'I can see him blushing from here,' Anton said.

'Can you hear what they are saying?' asked Artur.

'No. But it's the old scene, Pops. At first, she'll ask boring questions: "Where are you from?", "What was it like?" And then' – he clenched his fist – 'she'll embarrass him and play it all the way. She'll laugh at him, then when he's thinking about running away, she'll apologise and be all coy. I can see that part has already been played out. She works fast that one. I know, because she tried it on me. But' – he touched the violin case on his back – 'it's music or the lady. And it's music for me.'

'So innocent…'

Anton put both hands on Artur's shoulders and waited until the old man was looking at him. 'Pops… she's a whore.'

Artur smiled. 'Rudolf married a nice girl… no she wasn't poor. Her father was an engineer… mother, a doctor.' He sighed.

'What's the matter, Pops?'

'She was pregnant.'

'Ah, Pops.' He put his arm round the old man. 'You can't

always protect the ones you love…'

Artur mumbled.

'… especially from their follies.'

'A grandchild…' Artur said.

Helena slipped her hands round Radoš.

'We have to carry on. We owe it to them. And anyway, there's no point trying to make sense of what happened.'

'Ahh…' Artur said as Helena kissed Radoš. 'The children are in love.'

Anton smiled. 'Nothing can ever stop that. Ahh, Commendatore. Let's leave them. Let's slink away. Let's take our spades and make the soil dance as we wedge the carrots out like old teeth. If the professor is ordered to collect eggs and to take notes on the futility of such an act, then we can do our part.'

'Mmm.'

'Let's go,' Anton said and linked arms with Artur, leading him towards the bridge.

'Young again…'

They crossed the bridge and turned up the road.

'Hang on, look. Ha. Quick, here, behind the tree. Shh. Shh.'

Anton brought him behind the crooked oak and put a hand on the old man's shoulder. 'It's the professor,' Anton said quietly. 'He's trying to put the world inside himself.' The tall, gaunt figure wearing a black coat stood by the entrance to the cave. Anton pulled Artur back. 'Here comes the strange one.'

The short-cropped curly haired figure paced with a jittery, little stride over to the spectacled man.

'What are you doing here?' Zarviš said to František. 'You shouldn't be here. No one can be here except with the colonel's authorisation.'

František's eyes widened. 'Did you say, "No one can enter"?'

'You must go somewhere else.'

'No one can enter…' František turned to the cave. 'Yes, that's true. The dead soldiers were taken into the cave, weren't they?'

'Why don't you go by the lake?' Zarviš huffed, and then

199

smiled. 'And then go jump in it.' He snorted and made a small, involuntary jump on the spot.

'What's he saying?' Artur whispered.

'The professor has been told to take a bath.'

'Oh...'

'There is nothing in the cave,' František said, 'and yet nothing cannot be. The question then is, what is in the cave?'

'Nothing,' Zarviš said.

'But it pulls me in.' František took a step closer and was stopped by Zarviš. 'It is the gate to a darkness that goes on forever.'

Zarviš sniggered. 'What do you hope to find, if you were allowed to go in?'

'The answer to everything. And nothing,' František said.

Zarviš snorted and laughed. Finally, he wiped his mouth. 'What are you looking for?'

'The truth,' the professor said.

'Bravo, Professor. Yes, the truth,' Anton whispered.

Zarviš steadied himself. 'There's no truth in there.'

František reseated his glasses.

'Leave. Leave,' Zarviš said. 'We are building a new world. Only believers are welcome.'

'I don't believe in anything.'

'Then leave. That's right, go.'

František turned.

'That's right, leave,' Zarviš said.

František walked.

'Leave the village, if you want. Leave the world, if you like. Go on, vanish into nothing, Professor. Ha!'

František stopped and took one last deep look at the cave. He disappeared into the woods and Zarviš went towards the colonel's house, chuckling.

'What were they talking about?' Artur said.

But Anton was lost in thought. 'Building a new world.' He repeated Zarviš's words quietly. He looked up at the snake flag. 'But whose?'

*

Iva and Viktor were sitting in a clearing by the tranquil river, opposite the meadow. Viktor read what Iva had just written in the notebook:

Stage four. Metastasised. Nine months.

She pulled out of her pocket a small plastic bottle and opened the lid. She emptied the remaining five capsules and looked up at him. She felt death in her hand.

'What does the doc say?'

Without treatment, less.

Viktor frowned. 'Don't it make you mad? If it were me, I'd be raging, smashing things. Ain't you afraid?'

I can't scream. And enough has been broken already.

'I wouldn't take it lying down.'

I told my boy to be brave. Her hand wavered.

'You told him "be brave". That's easy to say, but a boy ain't brave. He's on his own, thinking his mother abandoned him.' Viktor pulled out a cigarette, lit it and squinted at the river. Iva took the notebook; the pen hovered only for a moment.

They were about to stop people entering Prague. How could I take him with me?

She put the book on his lap. Viktor read and handed back the book without saying anything.

If I could choose now, I wouldn't go to Prague. The thought that he was abandoned because he felt his mother didn't want him, struck her as a deep ache, full of shame. What a stupid thing to do, she repeatedly thought. Turn back the clock. Turn back the clock. She pictured his face, confused and calling for her. She knotted her brows. *I've hurt him terribly.*

'Maybe he's braver than you think,' Viktor said. She took the book from Viktor and wrote again.

He is kind and likes to help others. I told him I'd be back very soon. I know he is alive. I can feel it. I know he would try to find me. But I hope he's with his aunt or someone is looking after him. Šimon, I want to find you. But I can't. She heaved and emitted a squeal. The quivering pen traced lines. *Forgive me. I didn't want to leave you. I did what I thought was right, but it was wrong. I am sorry. I am sorry. I am sorry I can't be with you. You must carry on without me. Šimon, goodbye my sweet boy. I hug you and kiss you and love you.* Tears fell. She ached not being able to put her arms around Šimon. Instead, she had the stinging pain of emptiness.

After Viktor read it, he tossed the cigarette. 'It ain't right, damn it, it ain't right! And he won't forgive you.' He looked angrily at her.

She sought forgiveness, yet there was none. She took the book slowly.

I know I did wrong. But I think you hate me because it's obvious your mother abandoned you when you were a boy. Tell me if I'm wrong. And do you think she had no reason? I know Šimon would forgive me. I know he would.

She could write no more and held her hands to her face.

Viktor read. He was stricken and turned with a fearful look to her. At length he sighed.

'No, he don't hate you,' he said quietly. 'He just wants a fair explanation.'

She closed her eyes and heard Šimon's voice. 'Mama, Mama…' She opened her eyes and looked up at the snake image flapping in the distance.

I'm sorry.

She pushed the book away and Viktor read.

'So am I,' he said. 'So am I.'

CHAPTER 32

Eliška stood by the church with Hynek. Some soldiers were building something on the west side of the river between the mill wheel and a fire pit. There were several uprights set in the ground in a rectangular shape. She pointed to the snake flag.

'What does it mean?' she said.

'I don't believe it's anything good,' Hynek said.

She looked at the snake in the shape of lightning and felt a weakness. There had been house searches, and she replayed the scenes in her mind: soldiers house-to-house in search of evidence of arson, forcing their way in, deaf to protest. Raids. She had gone to the colonel to complain but realised how feeble it was. She already knew her sister wouldn't change her mind.

'I lost my temper with her, Hynek. But it's just not right.'

The gentle old man rubbed his greying beard and ruddy face. 'The problem is she believes she can see it all and needs to decide everything.'

'She's stubborn.'

'You know what happened this morning?'

'What?' Her pale-blue eyes were keen.

'I saw them beat a soldier. I don't know what he'd done wrong. Two soldiers held him while a sergeant hit him with a stick. Next to them, the colonel was watching. I yelled for her to stop; instead, she smiled. Smiled. It made me pause. Doctor, she has done so much good. Why do that?' The snake flag snapped in the wind. Hynek looked up at it.

'She's not the person you think she is,' Eliška said.

'Then there *is* something.' Hynek took off his ailing Panama hat and raised his brow.

'No… I mean, she's always cared only about her own skin. Fortunately for us that means the village.'

'You know her best.'

'I'm not so sure. People change.'

'They do and they don't.' He patted his hat in some dusting ritual. 'The human soul is a mystery sometimes. There are some in the village who look to you.'

'Me?'

'The colonel's sister. A doctor.'

'Hardly. I mean, I can talk to her. But she doesn't listen to me. What else can I do?'

Hynek nodded. 'Nothing is certain. We must pay attention.'

'I'll speak to her again.'

Hynek was quiet until several villagers and soldiers had filed into the church. 'We should share the load.'

Eliška waited for him to explain, but when he didn't, she smiled, wryly. 'Maybe it's all luck.'

'No, Doctor. What would've been lucky is not to have had the virus at all.'

Eliška nodded, then saw the colonel and her officers cross the bridge. 'Here she comes. Let's see what this meeting is all about.'

Eliška and Hynek went inside. Soon the colonel arrived and stood in front of the altar. As with the last time, she waited and lengthened the silence before speaking.

'Some of you think,' she said, 'that it's one rule for you and another for the army. But how would we survive without you?'

She looked from face to face.

'To be honest, I don't really go in for all this town hall stuff. And it's strange for us because in a way our mission is done: secure the area, maintain food sources, forage, build. Now what?'

Blank faces.

Here she took out a piece of paper to read from. 'We need a new contract. A new way. A new sense of how we understand our place here.'

'Don't we already?' one of the villagers said.

'Yes, and this may sound like I'm making some strange speech. But what we need is unity, stability and certainty. We need certainty so we can plan; stability so our plans can work; unity so we're not against each other. I realised that we can't keep doing it the army way. Soldier and villager? No, that's wrong. We're all Otočkans. Unity means there's no difference between soldiers and villagers. This is what I mean by a new contract.'

Most of the villagers looked confused. But some, like Luděk, nodded. The colonel took out a piece of paper and began to read aloud.

'A new atmosphere. Better, more honest, open, simpler. Because we're all in this together.' Anton burst out laughing, but the colonel continued. 'We can create here a place that's a model on how to live simply, decently and without money.' Anton guffawed again. The colonel raised her voice. 'A place where we can not only survive but prosper. We can decide what we become, not merely just let things drift. How do we see Otočka in the future? The same as it is now? You get one candle a week, why not two? Three? Why should we just "make do"? Why can't we thrive?'

There were some sounds of agreement from Luděk and others. Eliška felt the excited tension in the colonel's voice.

'Colonel, you're the one who decides how many candles?' someone said.

'Because we're just surviving,' she replied. 'We only get the candles we need. But why not get the number we want? First imagine the thing, then find a way to have it. We don't have so many candles only because we don't believe we could. But there is a way.'

Hynek frowned as Luděk and some others murmured in agreement.

'If we can prosper,' she continued, 'it would be an example for others. Your actions here could save people out there. We could help them to make their own village, like ours. We could show them the way.'

'The way to have three candles a week?' a fat-faced villager said.

'And more,' she said.

There were sudden energetic shouts from Luděk and some others. Eliška saw an awakened force in their eyes.

'But,' the colonel said, 'we must first achieve the example we want to set.'

'Yes, we can!' Luděk said.

'What about trebling the ration?' she said. This had the effect of erasing the smug look of the fat-faced villager. Several of the doubtful now murmured agreement. 'Who says there's no way to have three?'

'Exactly,' Luděk said. Other villagers became encouraged. The colonel looked at Marek's pregnant wife.

'When I think of where we are going, I think of you, Natalie. Because it all comes down to this: what's going to exist for your child? What are we going to teach him? What things are important? What actions? What words? What values?'

Luděk stood and hooted; his friends joined in. Anton laughed into his hands.

'You may think,' the colonel continued, 'that it's funny. That it's not common sense. But there's a problem with that kind of thinking. Common sense condemns us to one meal a day. Surely, you're hungry for more. For better. And you won't get it by plodding along with common sense.'

'That's right,' Luděk said.

'Common sense led to the collapse. The old system fell because they weren't bold enough. They weren't brave enough.'

'Yes,' Luděk said.

She opened the paper again and read: 'The most complex, sophisticated and intricate network of systems ever in history, part of a finely adjusted global order, broke, beyond repair with who knows how many people infected and half as many dead. All done by a thing with only ten genes. An organism so simple it doesn't even have its own cell.' She paused and panned her eyes across her audience. 'If anything's too complex to defend itself against something so simple, then it's too weak to survive.

206

Nature tested it and it failed.' She folded the paper. 'What it means is we'll have to give up some old ways of thinking. But what ideas must we give up? What new ones should we take up? There's a very clear principle: whatever holds us back, we must abandon.'

Luděk clapped.

'Nothing's impossible,' the colonel said enthusiastically. 'There's nothing we can't do. What shall we write on this blank page called Otočka?' Her curly, shining black hair bounced as she moved about the unmoving captains.

Luděk rose, hooted and clapped. He sat down when Zarviš rose.

'If I understand it, Colonel,' Zarviš said, 'we'll have to give some ideas up.'

'Only the ones that stop us.'

'Ownership for example?' Zarviš said.

'What's important is to find the way to run Otočka efficiently. With the highest yields. It doesn't matter who works them or owns them.'

'I've owned the top pasture for ten years,' the fat-faced man said, reddening.

'And will you sell it in euros or dollars?' Zarviš said.

A tall villager, among all the chuckling, rose to his feet with self-assurance. 'It's all balls.' His accent was Moravian and more rural than the other villagers. 'Just grow bloody crop, milk cows, fatten sheep and pigs, crack a few eggs and bugger the rest.' He sat down with the same languid self-possession.

'And that's about it, isn't it?' The colonel smiled. 'But how much crop? How many pigs? It all sounds simple. But the answer to these questions is the difference between one meal and three. Now do you begin to see it? It's *how*. When we find how then you can bugger the rest all you like.'

This produced retributive laughter from Luděk and friends.

'Shall we try?' The colonel asked.

Luděk and friends clapped. Hynek rose and waved his tired

207

old Panama about to attract attention from the hoots coming from one side of the church. Silence eventually came and they sat down. Hynek waited beyond the silence to speak. Eliška thought he was waiting for calm also.

'You're right, Colonel, *how* is the question. Yet so many people were certain they knew the answer. How will we ever know? We err, we stumble, we laugh at our stupidities after we have the sense to make them. Man is full of serious frivolity. If you are asking how, then how is it the old system failed? If you don't know that, how will you know *what* works?'

He sat down, but Zarviš rose so quickly, he was speaking before the old man leant back.

'It was too complex!' Zarviš said with intense passion, thrusting out his fists. 'Come on! Share index this. Euro bonds that. If the Chinese weaken the Renminbi, the Iowan farmer must pay a quarter more in tax. Who can make sense of it? So a virus came out of the Amazon. And it meant the Japanese had to change their constitution. And the Pakistanis *had* to invade Kashmir. Come on! Who can explain it? Complex economies of infinite growth? But you can't have endless growth on a finite planet. The people who could have acted had their hands tied by too much information and too little understanding. So, Hynek, if you're asking how they weren't able to act, it was because there was not a single person in all the world who knew what the hell was going on.'

There were whoops and hollering of assent from Luděk and friends. Zarviš twitched and sat down. The colonel thrust out a lower lip in nodding agreement. Hynek looked like a sorry child who had forgotten his lines in a play. More than half the church clapped at Zarviš's explanation. But not little Nada, who was busy counting the flowers on her skirt.

'But if we had known how back then,' Hynek mumbled, 'it wouldn't have come to this.' The hat fell out of his hand.

'OK. OK. Listen,' the colonel said, 'I want those three meals a day. I mean, look at me; do you think I can make it on one meal a day?'

The fat-faced man giggled. She then reiterated the main points about unity and goals. She then said she had to go on a forage and so swept out of the church with the captains in train. When they had gone, Viktor, looking mildly bemused, pulled out a cigarette and lit it.

Blowing out the smoke he said, 'Well, that was some weird shit.'

Some babbled and there was a spirited conversation between Luděk and Zarviš. Little Nada started playing with her mother's fingers.

'Do you understand it, Ludmila?' Tibor asked Nada's mother.

Her blonde hair jostled as she turned to Tibor. 'She wants to figure out how to improve the village. Aren't we doing that already?'

'Are we?'

'I hope so,' Ludmila said and shrugged.

Štěpánka was busy poking Petra's knee every time she made a point. 'She knows what she's doing. She's got it worked out. She's right. But she didn't say anything about the refugees. Murderers and rapists. What if they cut the fence? What if there are just too many?'

Marek got a smoke off Viktor, then asked Radoš what he thought of the colonel's words.

'I don't really understand it,' Radoš said.

'It was like a motivational speech,' Tibor said.

The conversations continued in this way until Nada asked if she could go play now as she was quite bored.

'That's quite right, Papageno. Go and play.' Anton beamed.

'I'm not Papageno.'

'No, you're right, you're Papagena.'

'What's that?' Ana asked.

'What's a Papagena? Don't you know? A Papagena is a… Pa-Pa-Pa-Pa-Pa-Pa-Papagena!'

The girls were bewildered.

'And a Papageno?' he said. 'A Papageno is a… Pa-Pa-Pa-Pa-Pa-Pa-Papageno!'

'Ana, let's go,' Nada said.

Anton's guffaws echoed.

210

CHAPTER 33

The next day, the soldiers had finished building what turned out to be a platform. It spanned the river like a bridge. A soldier on a ladder was nailing a large square of wood to a tall timber that they had just driven into the ground next to the platform. When the soldier had finished, Eliška saw in large painted letters that it was a sign with three words, each on a separate line. The first was in red, the second in gold and the third in black.

UNITY

STABILITY

CERTAINTY

She heard some soldiers yelling. Two of them appeared from the road going east into the woods, carrying something. Soldiers from the other side of the bridge soon joined them. There were loud shouts, which roused some of the villagers from their houses, but Eliška saw straight away that what they carried was human. She ran but when she got close, knew it was a body. They put it on the grass. She knelt before the naked body and had never seen anything quite like it. Never. It was smeared with its own blood. There were several large wounds in the abdomen. Some villagers arrived and when they saw it, reeled back in revulsion. Experienced soldiers stepped back in terror. One of the villagers was promptly sick. Eliška was struggling to keep her composure. Štěpánka arrived and fell into hysterics and Hynek led her aside. Marek had ushered away the children who had followed their parents. Several more soldiers came and cringed. Some of their hands shook.

'It's Alfréd,' one of the soldiers said.

Eliška tried to raise one of the arms, but rigor had set in. The blood had been smudged and streaked as if by hand. Soon the colonel arrived. If she was shocked, she hid it all away behind furrowed brows and a stiff scowling jaw.

'Sergeant!' she said with a firm, calm voice. 'Who is it?'

The sergeant repeated the name.

'Where was he found?'

'The sentry found him by the fence, F section, Colonel.'

She looked at the villagers who had gathered. Marek held his head in despair.

'What time was he found?' she said.

'About half an hour ago,' the sentry said.

'How long has he been dead?'

Eliška didn't answer at first but then when the question was repeated, she realised it was for her.

'Four hours, at least,' Eliška said.

'Who would do such a thing?' one of the villagers said. The question became rhetorical when no one answered. Zarviš, almost tripping with his short gait, arrived. He flinched at the sight, tottered to the road and was immediately sick.

'Captain,' the colonel said, 'take two squads, do a spread search of F section. See what you can find. And, Captain, the murderer may still be there.'

'Colonel.' The captain began organising two bodies of soldiers to search. Some of the villagers looked at each other in wild horror at the mention of the word 'murderer'.

'You wouldn't say it was suicide would you, Eliška?' the colonel said.

'No.'

'Murder,' Štěpánka squealed as she held tightly onto Hynek's arm. 'I told you. I told you. They're here already. We're not safe. A murderer. I'll be next. I feel it. I feel it.' She lurched onto Marek's arm and shook her head at him in wide-eyed panic. 'We're all going to get stabbed in our beds.' She nodded frantically. 'Yes.' She attached herself to Tibor's arm. 'Murderer.' She made wild gestures at the colonel. 'They're inside. It's over.' Hynek tried to pull her away.

'This is why we have a curfew,' the colonel said. 'This is why

212

we have sentries. This is why we have the rules we have! What are you afraid of?' She looked at Ludmila, who was trembling. 'It's a dead man. Murdered. Or maybe it was *you,* who did it.'

Ludmila looked startled.

'Or was it you?' she said to Tibor. 'Or you, Marek?'

He had a sudden look of horror.

'The murderer is among us! The murderer is here,' Štěpánka yelped and staggered. 'Among us…'

Hynek led her away with soothing words.

Sofie and Anton arrived, and Petra at once whisked Sofie away. Anton stood next to Viktor, who scowled.

'And what about you?' the colonel said, stepping towards Viktor. 'My sister's people. We know nothing about you. I'm sure she didn't discriminate. You could be criminals for all we know. Killers.'

Viktor clicked his tongue.

'Well?' the colonel said.

'I ain't touched the man. I ain't even seen him before.'

Luděk glowered at Viktor.

'Who's saying you did?' the colonel said.

'What you want?' Viktor said to Luděk.

'Where were you this morning?' Luděk said.

'It ain't any of your business.'

'He isn't saying, Colonel. He isn't saying.'

'Well, we'll find out who did this.'

'Where were you?' Luděk asked Viktor again.

'Where were you, big boy?'

Luděk stiffened his lip.

'All right, Sergeant,' the colonel said, 'put it in front of the cave.'

The sergeant and two soldiers took up the body and were away. The colonel turned to the villagers.

'This crime is against all of us. I don't believe in paradise. But I do believe in order. We'll find the responsible. They'll be punished.'

The villagers were silent. But Luděk once more smirked and seemed to have a bone to pick.

'So, where were you?' he said to Viktor.

'Shut it, pal.'

'No, I won't.'

'I ain't for fooling.'

Luděk smirked. 'Just tell us where you were.'

'No.'

Iva stood between them as peacemaker and Luděk moved back a little. Some of the villagers had furtive looks.

'What about the violinist?' one of Luděk's friends asked. 'It could be him.'

Anton chuckled.

'Where were you this morning?' Luděk asked Anton.

'Oh, yes. OK. Yes, ha. I did it. But you know, this one was unusual because I usually do my murdering in the evenings. But you know… I couldn't sleep last night.'

'Colonel,' Luděk said.

'Oh, come on, how can you ask such a question?' Anton said.

'It's not a joke.'

'And why not you? 'Anton said.

'What about you?' the colonel asked František, who calmly put away his little notebook. 'Where were you this morning?'

'Nowhere,' František said.

'What do you mean?'

'Nowhere.'

Luděk rounded on František.

'This doesn't concern me,' František said.

Eliška watched the swift looks of accusation turn to the professor.

'It doesn't?' Luděk grabbed the professor's coat. 'You come into our village, eat our food and you say "this does not concern me"?'

'Leave it, pal. He had nothing to do with it,' Viktor said.

'Who asked you?'

214

'Listen, pal, he was with me all morning, so neither of us did nothing.'

'I don't believe you.'

'Stop it, Luděk,' his brother said sternly.

'You want to start something, Marek?'

'You're the one wildly accusing everybody.'

'No, just you Marek. Just you. Colonel, I think here's the arsonist and murderer.'

Marek stepped back and his cheeks went red. He took three paces and punched his brother. Luděk staggered back, then charged at Marek and they were both on the ground laying blows.

'Stop it! Stop it!' Ludmila screamed. They punched and yelled. The colonel looked on.

'It was probably a soldier,' Viktor said.

One of Luděk's friends swung at Viktor, who bent back quickly so that he got less of the hit than the full force. He retaliated swiftly and knocked the man flat on his back. There was a cacophony of shouting.

Eliška looked away and saw, at the edge of the woods, Radoš and Helena. He stroked her head and she leant on his chest. Yet he seemed even more scared.

The soldiers and villagers managed to separate Marek and Luděk. Eliška didn't at first hear the colonel until she started shouting. 'Eliška. Go and examine the body and see what you can learn.'

Eliška slowly nodded.

'As for the rest of you,' the colonel said, 'go about your work. Carry on as normal. We'll get to the bottom of this. We'll find who did it. And we'll find him quickly.'

CHAPTER 34

Šimon ran back from the river with a cup of water and poured some on Karl's forehead.

'It'll make you better.' Šimon put the cup down for him to drink but the man only stared with red eyes. The two soldiers watched impassively.

'Are you hungry, Karl? There's still some fish left.' Šimon waited but Karl only grimaced. 'Just a second.' Šimon went round so that he was facing the top of Karl's head and picked up a forked branch with the hessian bag tied tightly in the gap. He held it up and down to fan Karl with a cool breeze.

Karl clutched his stomach and howled. The soldiers sprung to their feet. Šimon shot up, dropping the fan.

'Karl, what is it?' Šimon looked at the soldiers. 'What can we do?' His voice was flurried and his heart beat hurriedly with the angst of being useless. 'Can't we do something?' he said to the soldiers and didn't notice he was speaking in English.

Karl groaned again, a desperate sound like a bear. The soldiers shook their heads.

'Karl, tell me what to do.' Šimon felt frantic at doing nothing.

Karl started to sing softly. '*Einst, o Wunder!*'

'Even with a doctor, it's bad,' the private said to the ex-sergeant.

'*Entblüt auf... entblüt... Grabe... Eine Blume—*'

'Doctor?' Šimon said.

'Forget it,' the ex-sergeant said. 'Anyway, we can't get back in. The colonel wouldn't let him.'

Karl clutched his stomach again.

'Karl, I'll get a doctor. I'll be back very soon,' Šimon said.

'No, you can't go,' the ex-sergeant said. 'The soldiers'll shoot you.'

'I'm small. They won't see me. I'll run all the way.'

'It's crazy. How will you get the doctor past the fence without the sentries seeing?'

'I don't know but I've got to go. I've got to.'

'It's pointless. There's nothing you can do. He can only help himself now. Every soldier in there will shoot you on sight.'

'I can make it.'

'No.'

'I will!' He ran. The private ran after him and very shortly caught him. Šimon struggled. 'Let me go. Let me go.'

'Šimon,' Karl shouted.

The boy stopped struggling and the soldier let him go. Šimon ran back. 'What is it, Karl?'

The man looked vaguely in the boy's direction, his eyes glassy. '*Der Asche meines Herzens…*'

'I'll get the doctor.'

'*Deutlich schimmert…*'

'Please, let me go,' Šimon said to the ex-sergeant, who had grabbed his shoulders. 'I know it's dangerous. But you've got to let me.'

'Don't you think you should stay here?' the ex-sergeant said.

'I want to, but I've got to get the doctor. I'm not afraid.'

Karl reached for the cup and slowly dragged it to his mouth; his jittery hands spilled most of it. He had a coughing fit with the little he did drink. He clutched his stomach and yelled. The soldiers turned to him. Šimon saw an opportunity and slinked away, keeping a keen eye on the soldiers. He ran and headed towards where he thought the tunnel was. The soldiers shouted and Šimon heard a sudden rustling. He came to a small clearing and hid behind a tree. The soldier's footsteps got closer, but he didn't dare look. The sounds changed direction then faded. He leant round the tree and saw the fence. He sneaked back at the sight of a soldier walking away on the other side of it. He waited and the sentry gradually disappeared. He crept up to the fence, then along until he found the hole. He shifted the branches, then squirmed under and into Otočka.

He hurried along a path until a scurrying figure, almost a flash of motion, made him halt. He breathed a sigh of relief when the figure disappeared. His eyes cut from tree to tree as his heart pounded in his ears and his lungs stung. Yet there was neither sight nor sound of anyone.

Despite flinching at the alarm call of a blackbird, he put a nervous foot forward. Assured that there was no one, he sped along the path.

Tiring, he stopped and clutched his knees to catch his breath. To his right was a slope leading down to a path. He heard lapping water and went down the slope towards the sound. At the bottom, he came to a bank of what he thought was the Elbe but was in fact a lake. He held onto a tree trunk, then spied. There was a tall man wearing a long black coat. He was facing the lake and writing something in a notebook. Šimon couldn't see any soldiers, yet he waited. The man stopped writing as though working out a thought. Šimon realised the man was no threat and stepped out onto the path.

'Hello. Hello,' he said faintly.

The man continued writing.

'Hello,' Šimon repeated louder.

The man was startled; his eyes widened in his wheel glasses.

'I need to find the doctor.'

František put away his notebook.

'Please, my friend needs the doctor.'

'Doctor?' František said.

'The doctor.'

'Doctor?'

'Please help me.' Šimon felt as if he was being studied.

'What is it?'

'He's sick.'

'The virus?'

Šimon didn't want to admit it but finally nodded.

'And is he near the end?' The professor's eyes widened. 'And

218

I guess you are infected too.'

'No, I was very careful.'

'I doubt it. And being careful doesn't stop anything, especially the end.'

Šimon tugged the professor's coat.

'There's no point to all this panic; it doesn't matter. All this drama, and to what purpose?'

The boy's large eyes looked up; around them, bruises and dirt.

'Nonetheless, though it will make no difference, I will go,' the professor said. 'All right. I'll get the doctor. You wait here. But…'

'But?'

'Does this suffering make any sense?' he said to himself.

'What?'

The professor shook his head. He pulled out his handkerchief but just held it. When Šimon appealed to him to be faster, he looked up and walked away at an unhurried pace.

It was a long anxious wait. Šimon paced nervously. The doctor would come soon, she would see Karl. And Karl would live.

But what if the doctor couldn't do anything?

He stopped. No, it would be OK.

But what if he was too late? He suddenly felt a dread, a foreboding in the pit of his stomach. Something bad was going to happen. Why wasn't there a cure? He looked up the path. No one had come. No one would come, he thought.

In the time it took, the sun weakened and reddened. He thought now and then of running into the village. But the idea of meeting a soldier persuaded him not to. At last, two figures appeared. They seemed like angels as he ran to meet them.

'Who are you?' Eliška said.

'I'll show you the way.' Šimon stepped along the path.

'But that way leads nowhere.'

'He's outside the fence.' Šimon stopped.

'Outside! You didn't tell me it was outside,' she said to

František.

'Does it matter?' František said.

'Yes, it does. How can I get outside without—'

'Please,' Šimon said.

'You came from outside?' Eliška said.

'Yes.'

'But how can I get outside that way?'

'There's a hole under the fence.'

'No, if the soldiers—'

'They won't. I know the way. No one will see you.'

'I could tell Vendula. But she'll—'

'Please.'

She considered, then nodded. 'Fine. OK. Show me. But we must be careful,' Eliška said.

Šimon began to go.

'Wait!' She turned to František. 'Don't tell anyone about this. If anyone finds out this boy got inside, I don't know what might happen. You understand?'

The professor nodded casually.

'Let's go,' she said.

Šimon ran. He looked back to see the doctor following far behind, though she was twice his size and gait. He scampered up the slope to the top path, then raced to a tree stump and waited. Why were doctors so slow?

They sped on.

'Tell me when we get close to the fence. There'll be soldiers.'

'I know.'

She nodded. 'I'm ready.'

Šimon bounded over tree roots and rabbit holes as the doctor was nowhere to be seen. He waited. Eliška came, her ponytail of ginger hair dancing.

She whispered, 'Where's the hole?'

Šimon pointed. 'I think it's over there.'

'You're not sure.'

He shook his head. He hadn't paid attention when he was

220

running towards the village. 'I don't see any soldiers,' he said.

'OK, let's go. But quietly.'

Šimon led the way but saw no hole.

'Where is it?' Eliška whispered, urgently.

'I think it's this way.' He strode left along the fence.

'Wait!'

'Here,' he said.

She rushed up to him. 'I won't fit.'

Šimon took a branch and scraped. Then he gave it to the doctor while he scraped with his fingernails.

She dug with the branch, but flinched at a sound. 'Sentries!' she said.

Šimon saw no one. He continued and went first; then, once through, urged her to follow. She scrambled into the dirt, and he pulled her arms as she emerged.

'Go,' she said.

They darted through all the way until he saw the ex-sergeant.

'Soldiers,' she gasped and clutched him.

'It's OK. These soldiers are OK.' He held up his hand at the bow-wielding ex-sergeant, who recognised him straight away. 'It's me.'

But when Eliška approached he raised his bow again.

'Don't shoot. It's the doctor. Doctor.'

The ex-sergeant put the bow down.

'He's over here,' Šimon said to Eliška. She followed him to Karl, who was looking calmer, though still with a faraway, aching look.

'Give me the bag,' she said.

'Are you bloody crazy or what? You actually went in?' the ex-sergeant said to Šimon. 'You're out of your mind. We tried to stop him,' he said to Eliška, but she ignored him.

'But he pulled it off,' the private said.

'Yeah, he pulled it off – crazy kid.'

Putting on gloves, Eliška started to examine Karl. 'How long has he been like this?'

'This morning,' the private replied.

She felt his neck. 'Where does it hurt?'

Šimon translated and Karl shook his head.

'He isn't Czech?' she said.

'He's German.'

'Stomach cramp?' she said in heavily accented English, pronouncing the 'ch' of stomach like that in church. Šimon had to repeat, but Karl was distracted by something on his left. She took his pulse as he mumbled something incoherently in German.

'Does it hurt when you breathe?' she said in Czech, no more attempting English. Šimon conveyed the meaning.

'*Tausende von Blumen...*' Karl put his hand out as if caressing something. '*schimmern...*'

She touched his belly and he flinched. 'Open my bag. Take out the box of pills there.'

Šimon quickly looked through and took out a blister of pills.

'Put two in my hand.' She put them into Karl's mouth and closed it.

'Will he be all right?' Šimon said. He knew by her hesitation that it was bad.

'I don't know. I've seen people pull through who were worse. But don't worry. He looks strong enough. You have a blanket?'

'Yes.'

'I'll put it over him,' she said. Šimon went to his bag and got it. She draped it over him. 'The medicine will soon work; then he'll feel cold.'

'OK.'

She stood up and took off the gloves and threw them in the fire.

'Doctor, can you get a message to Captain Nebojsa? He might be able to persuade the colonel to take us back in,' the ex-sergeant said.

'You are the soldiers who were thrown out?'

'Yes, and he might be able to get the colonel to take us back.'

'But he'll know I've been here—'

222

'Nebojsa won't tell. He didn't want us thrown out. He'll try to convince the colonel. He won't mention your name.'

She hesitated. 'If you're sure.'

'We must get back in. Or at least get the patrols to leave us some ration along the fence somewhere. Without the colonel knowing.'

'I'll try. But what about the boy... in case the man dies.' She whispered the last.

The ex-sergeant shrugged. 'We'll figure something.'

Eliška stood by Šimon. 'Two tablets every four hours. Plenty of water. I'll try and come back tomorrow.'

'OK. Thank you.'

'You know, he's very lucky to have a friend like you. It was quite a thing sneaking into the village.'

Šimon nodded. 'Do you need me to show you where the tunnel is?'

'No, I remember.'

CHAPTER 35

By the morning light, the army marched in columns onto the field while all the villagers stood in the middle. The flag was being held on a short wooden pole by a standard bearer. Next to him was the colonel who watched dispassionately as her troops filed in. When they had done, everyone stood in silence. Eliška had the feeling that they were drifting out into the unknown and that some innate and ineffable standard had been broken. Finally, the colonel spoke with a clear voice.

'What happened yesterday must surely make clear what we stand for. All the same, we must declare it in no uncertain terms. The person who did this crime is not an Otočkan. He's an animal and without honour. That's why I want us to take an oath to say clearly what we are for.' The colonel took out a piece of paper from her pocket and held it up. 'But I want to be clear – this is not an obligation. I want you to take this oath because you want to. Because you believe in Otočka. I'll read it:

'*I [name] swear to work towards prosperity, security and happiness. I swear to work hard to make our new land stronger and better for the common good, inside and out. I swear to uphold our rules and defend our new land. I shall work for our New Way, which is a way of peace to prosperity. Colonel Vendula Korbova and I shall always strive for Unity, Stability and Certainty.*'

Some of them nodded. Luděk and friends in particular.

'First,' the colonel continued, 'I will ask the soldiers who wish to take this oath to step forward one by one and hold the flag while they recite the oath. I will start with the officers.'

The captains were first. Captain Železný stood in front of the colonel, saluted and held the corner of the flag. The colonel then gave him the piece of paper and he read the oath slowly and loudly. Once finished, they saluted each other and the next captain repeated the exercise. Once the officers had recited the oath, and in an orderly fashion that seemed rehearsed, the soldiers came one by one to do the same. This took over an hour because every soldier took the oath. Eliška thought they were all mad. She wanted to stop it but didn't know what to do or say. When it came to the turn of the villagers, the line that formed was more than half.

Luděk looked back with proud contempt at those who hadn't joined the line. 'If you don't join this line, then you don't belong here. If you don't join this line, you should leave Otočka.'

Marek scowled.

'Aren't you doing it?' Štěpánka asked Ludmila.

'No.'

'Why?'

'Because I don't understand it.'

Viktor clicked his tongue and lit one of his vanishing stock of cigarettes as the oaths began to be taken. Luděk took the oath with a booming voice. Zarviš's was manic. Štěpánka was desperate and at the same time joyous. Luděk went over to the group who hadn't taken the oath.

'It's clear to me, one of you must have burned the barn. Probably did the murder too. Well, it makes it easier for the colonel. But if you're innocent, you better quickly join this line before it's too late. I would if I were you.'

No one joined the line.

'That is the farm Rudolf was on,' Artur said to Sofie, looking away from the oath taking. 'They had a red tractor. Yes, there's the dip there. He liked the tractor.' He raised a shrunken and bent finger. 'He could have driven it all day. You know boys, they never get tired. Shall we have a brandy, Aneta?'

'Look, there he is. Far away,' Sofie said with maturity and guile.

'I can't see him.'

'He's past the sheep. Over there.'

225

The old man looked doubtful but then brightened. Finally, when the line was finished the colonel spoke to those few who hadn't taken the oath.

'You do not believe it now. Perhaps you don't understand it. That's OK. You can take the oath anytime. Think it over. Think what it means. And when you want to take it, come to me. I want only those who want to take the oath to take it.' She smiled at Eliška. 'Now, there have to be changes.

'First – a resource commission is to be established that will take a full inventory of everything in Otočka. They will have the power to search any property. They may commandeer any property deemed in the interest of Otočka. Appeals should be made to me. However, anyone interfering in the duty of this commission will be detained.

'Second – all farm equipment, fertiliser, machines, barns, vehicles are no longer under private ownership. Instead, they now fall under the authority of the Resource Commission.

'Third – a Villagers Army is to be established and comprised of volunteers. You will get training. Those who achieve a certain standard will be given soldier duties. This is a good opportunity to be a part of the defence of your land. It is not compulsory because we only want those who join to do so of their free will.

'Fourth – in the interests of unity, there will be no more separation of duties between villager and soldier. Soldiers will begin learning how to farm, and the volunteers how to fight.

'Fifth – the house currently occupied by my sister and her friends will need to be vacated for the army. They will be moved to the church. In future, meetings will be held here in the field.' The colonel waited, but only the tall Moravian grumbled that no damn soldier was going to set foot in his house.

'Colonel,' Hynek said, 'who will be on this commission?'

'Captain Železný, Lieutenant Bílka, Sergeant Mišák, Sergeant Janoušek and two corporals.'

'No villagers?'

She shook her head.

'I thought as much.'

'Well, if that's all, this meeting is finished,' the colonel said.

Eliška couldn't bear it any longer. 'This isn't right,' she shouted. 'You have no right to take people's property.'

'Ah…' the colonel said, 'Amnesty International has arrived. I was wondering why you hadn't spoken up earlier. Well, and what's your antibiotic to Delirium? How would you run the show?'

'Not this way.'

'I see. You have every idea how not to do something, but no idea how *to* do it.'

'This is like a cult.'

'Cult? We took an oath in the army. Is the army a cult? The oath focuses minds and is a public declaration to each other, without shame, that we stand united. We just declared peace, prosperity and love for our land. You don't think that's worth anything?'

'You can't treat people like this?'

'You ought to be careful about giving lectures. I came here and acted decisively and quickly. If we did things your way, we'd all be dead now.'

The doctor was on the point of saying something desperate. But the colonel didn't wait and signalled for the army to withdraw. Eliška turned away in disgust.

*

The Resource Commission acted quickly. Eliška watched them and understood that they only visited those who hadn't pledged the oath. They went through Ludmila's house and emerged with several rugs, cushions, plates and a table. They took Nada's bicycle and Ludmila came out to protest. But the soldiers said that she could be detained if she tried to stop them. So she sat on the grass. Nada cried and pulled her jacket, but Ludmila stayed still as her daughter hit her.

227

Eliška went to Petra's house where they took pots, pans, several chairs and very clean crucifixes. But when the corporal tried to take the gold-framed photograph of her late husband, the plucky grandmother fought back. She clutched so hard that she turned pink. In the end, the captain let her keep it.

Eliška saw a similar thing at Hynek's. But as to the number of Indian curiosities he had, the Commission was at a loss. No logic was applied. The iron Shiva was left. But the wooden Vishnu taken. Incense sticks were taken, but their holders left. A half-metre porcelain Ganesh was spirited away. Yet, a ceramic orange-clad fox playing a cornet was left. Hynek bore it all with equanimity and went out into his garden and began to sweep the flagstones with a brush. Soon, a soldier came and took that away also.

'Are you hiding treasure?' the soldier said.

'Treasure?' Hynek smiled. '*Om mani padme hum.*'

'What?'

'The jewel is in the lotus.'

Rolling his eyes, the soldier went away.

*

The soldiers brought some cushions and mattresses into the church and moved pews around. There were some rooms upstairs including the priest's quarters, but most of the Prague group would have to stay in the nave.

'Why don't we go back to the boat?' Anton said. 'At least no one will move us.'

'Not me,' Radoš said.

'Why not bring her along?' Anton made a cheeky smile. 'You didn't waste time. We could travel with the boat. This village is getting too stuffy for me. And it's completely dry.'

Eliška entertained the notion as the soldiers left the church but quickly put it out of her head. Where would they go?

'You should have waited until the soldiers left before saying things like that,' Sofie said.

'Why? Because they will tell Brünnhilde? So what? You're not afraid of her, are you? She's all show.'

'She's mad,' Viktor said.

'Here's an oath for you,' Anton said. 'I swear to be a pain in the arse to any officious pest that wants to start making snake flags.'

Viktor went to the front door of the church and began pushing and pulling it.

'What are you doing?' Eliška said.

'Seeing how strong it is. If the colonel doesn't catch the murderer today, I don't want some maniac slashing my guts in the night.'

In the silence, František stepped up to the altar and took an interest in the candle stands and the chalice with its PX symbol. Anton stood beside him with a smirk.

'I thought you were only interested in nothing. What could you find here?' Anton said.

František paid no heed but looked up at the statue of human sacrifice.

'Or have you become a heretic to your heaven of nothingness?' Anton made a waving flourish of his hand.

'It's absurd,' František said. 'Ritual. Incantation. Offering.' He took the chalice in both hands. 'They hold it up, don't they?'

'Don't ask me.'

František held the chalice up in imitation of a priest. As he did so, Iva collapsed on the ground and doubled up. Her eyes were squeezed tight in convulsions of pain. Eliška rushed to her.

'Your chest?' Eliška said. Iva nodded erratically and opened her eyes so wide they bulged. The nurse crouched beside.

'Heart attack?' the nurse said.

Eliška shook her head. 'I must go to my sister. She has morphine.'

The nurse rubbed Iva's back and consoled her. Viktor watched, then turned away. Then back. Sofie held Iva's hand while Anton stood nearby, looking aimless. Iva regained breath as Eliška took her pulse. Anton got out his violin and put it to his chin but paused. Iva frowned. A tongue clicked. A lighter lit a cigarette. Feet shuffled. A pencil scratched in a notebook. Anton began to play Beethoven's Romance for violin No.1. Slow opening strains of hope. The sounds of a soft hand. A gentle touch. A light in the night of long nightmares. A mother's eyes and voice. A kiss on the forehead. Music of sighs. Music of forgiveness. Music of healing. Long, slow, calm.

'You're OK,' Eliška said. 'I'll just get some medicine.' She rushed out of the church.

After crossing the bridge, she quickly reached the guard outside the colonel's house. She began screaming at him when he would not admit her.

'You cannot see her,' the soldier insisted.

'It's nothing to do with the damn oath. I need medicine. Go inside and tell her I need a drip.'

'I can't.'

'Vendula! Vendula!'

'She cannot see you.'

Eliška grabbed him by the collar.

'Take your hands off!' the soldier shouted.

'Vendula! Vendula!'

'I warn you, I can detain you,' the soldier said with military firmness. But it wasn't needed. The smiling colonel presented herself through the opened window. Her curly locks bounced like a peruke.

'At ease soldier. It's just my hysterical sister. Eliška, ninety per cent of the village have taken the oath, so if you believe in majorities, you're not in one,' she said pleasantly.

'I need morphine. It's Iva. She's in pain.'

'Oh?' the colonel said with a rising note.

'I need the medicine. She's in agony.'

'You need it? I know all about your needs. You would call an ambulance for a broken leg. But medicine is rationed. Unless you

230

can justify why a dying woman needs pain relief, I don't think I can spare any.'

'For God's sake, she needs it.'

'What if a soldier gets shot, stabbed or maimed. Does he have to just grin and bear it because my heroine sister wasted all the medicine on a suffering that cannot be cured?'

'What if it was you?'

'Ah, the compassion! The compassion! Now I know your strategy. Save the world with a fountain of sympathy. It's fortunate for this village that I'm in charge, because if you were the decision maker, we would all perish... but painlessly. No?'

'Vendula, I'm sorry about what I said. If you want, I'll take the oath.'

'My own sister showed me up in front of all the soldiers. Not very good for confidence. I know your views, but did you have to broadcast them? Perhaps, I can just say you were adopted. No, what really bothers me is that you think there is some standard, which is inviolate. Eliška, we are doing what has to be done.'

'If you want me to take the oath, I'll do it. Whatever you want. But I need that morphine!'

'What I want you to do is to tell me that my way is the right way. That you understand what I'm doing.'

'I do. I do. You're right.'

'That was insincere; you only say it to waste medicine on what you think is a good cause. But I tell you what. I'll give you the medicine if you not only take the oath, but then in front of the entire army accept, and without any shenanigans, the official commission of lieutenant. I will officially make you lieutenant with a commission of soldiers under you. I know it's cheap nepotism, but they'll get over it. You think that's very odd. But to be honest, as a doctor, you're actually worth a captaincy.'

'OK, OK. Yes, anything. Anything. Just, I need the medicine.'

'All right. All right,' she said with a smile. 'Soldier, let the doctor enter.'

231

Eliška went inside. Zarviš was there but she went straight to the boxes along the wall, then to the ones marked with a red cross.

'Eliška, there's something I need to tell you,' the colonel said.

'Not now,' Eliška said as she found the drips.

'It's important.'

'Later.'

'It would be good if you took the oath, Doctor. You know, we're all on the same side,' Zarviš said.

Eliška did not even glance at either Zarviš or the colonel as she hurried out of the house.

*

They had moved Iva up to the priest's bedroom. She slept after Eliška had given her the morphine.

Viktor paced about.

'She'll sleep for some hours yet,' the nurse said.

He glared at the nurse but when he looked at Eliška, he seemed afraid. 'Will she be all right?'

Eliška nodded and reassured, though she knew it would only get worse. She must have failed to disguise the fact because Viktor stormed out of the room.

'What's the matter with him?' the nurse said.

Eliška slowed the drip rate. 'He's angry because this is one fight he won't win.'

The back door of the church slammed. Eliška went to the window and saw Viktor standing outside, seething.

'I didn't think he cared about anything,' the nurse said.

Eliška saw him squeeze his temples with his wrists. She had seen it before, grown men crumbling. He pulled his shirt off and threw it down in anger. Across his muscular, broad chest were several tattoos of menacing knives, skulls and dragons. The tendons bulged on his neck.

'He cares,' Eliška said. 'He has to; there's no reason to fight if he doesn't.'

232

Viktor strode away down the path towards the woods.
Eliška looked at Iva. 'And I think he has a reason.'

CHAPTER 36

'It's him. It's him,' Štěpánka said, pointing to the church.

'It's who?' Zarviš said.

'The tall one with the glasses. He's the murderer. Tell the colonel.'

'The tall one? How you know he did it?'

'Look at his eyes. You can feel it.'

'You think he did it because he looks guilty?' Zarviš said with a smirk.

'It's obvious he's hiding something,' she said with agitation. 'Oh, he's calm about it. But that's what they're like, aren't they? You expect someone strong and violent. But the murderers always turn out to be teachers or accountants. And they're not villagers, are they? Who knows what they are? Rapists and murderers. And in the church!'

Zarviš tittered. 'But why would he do it?'

'Satanic perversions.'

He guffawed.

'Who knows?' she said in perfect earnest. 'Why does he wear that coat in such hot weather? Huh? Ask yourself that. We know nothing about them. They could have eaten the flesh of man. They must have killed people to make it here. The colonel must throw them out.'

'OK, OK. I'll tell the colonel. Don't worry. Though you could be right. You know, I have a word for the ones who haven't taken the oath: *Ditherers*. And when you think about it, there's absolutely no reason why the murderer couldn't be a Ditherer.'

'Exactly. Oh, it's not safe. It's not safe. I sleep in the living room now and I make sure the soldier on watch keeps an eye on my house. I have a knife beside my pillow. Just let the rapist come. I'll be ready for him.'

'Relax, Štěpánka, I'll tell her everything. Let me go and I'll do it straight away.'

'Go. Go. The tall one. It's definitely him. You can tell. You can't hide it.'

Zarviš disentangled himself from her and cut across the bridge. He had something odd sewn onto his shirt – a carefully cut white circle of plain linen.

*

Eliška watched Zarviš go into the colonel's house. She saw also that the soldiers had finished their construction. It was a wooden platform of several square metres, which spanned the river. It seemed a surreal object because its purpose wasn't clear. Then she had a foreboding thought: could it be a scaffold? But she shook her head. It looked more like a stage. Zarviš approached the guard at the colonel's house and entered without a word. Why was it he was always allowed to see her so easily?

Then she saw who she was looking for: Captain Nebojsa.

She followed him, walking alone on the road the soldiers took to go to their sentry duties. She shadowed him until the road curved out of sight of the village. Stealthily she closed the gap then lurched at him, pulling him to the hedge along the side so that no one could see them.

The startled captain raised his fists.

'What is this? What are you doing? Doctor? Really? Really? You? First Helena, now you. I have to say, I'm surprised at you, Doctor. But why me and not some younger soldier?' He patted his sandy hair.

'Don't be stupid,' Eliška said. 'That's not the reason. Look, Captain, the oath, unity, stability, house searches… what's going on? Do you like the way things are going?'

He smiled. 'Oh, I see. I mean, I understand but the colonel has no choice. If we're to survive, we've got to do what needs to be done.'

'Do we need an oath for that?'

He shrugged. 'It's not easy to organise something in such a situation as this. You should give the colonel more credit. Look, why don't you speak to her yourself?'

'Because I can't tell her what I want to tell you.'

His eyes widened. 'Tell me what?'

'Hynek said you could be trusted.'

'Something in confidence?' He raised his eyebrows. 'I will help if I can, Doctor.'

She hesitated, but instinct urged her. 'I saw the two soldiers who were sent out. They're desperate to get back in.'

'I don't understand. How could you see them?'

'I went outside the fence.'

'Outside? Are you crazy? The sentries will shoot you as soon as look at you if they see you by the fence.'

'They want to get back in.'

'No doubt.'

'They seem to think you would help them.'

'Do they?' he said. 'But why on earth did you want to go outside?'

'Will you help them?'

He huffed and took a few steps back. 'You won't tell me what you were doing outside the fence?'

'It's not important. What matters is we don't let the village become—'

'Mad, Doctor? Mad? She's the CO.'

'I was going to say worse than the outside.'

He scratched his head. 'Maybe she overdoes it a little.'

'Then you'll try to help them?'

He sighed. 'I mean, in the end she's right. All we want is to build a home, grow food and live in peace. And she wants that too.'

Eliška waited.

'Well, OK,' he said. 'I'll try to help them, but I can't promise anything.' He smiled weakly.

'Thank you, Captain.'

'But you know, I am a soldier. Whether or not I like the CO and her orders, I'll follow them.'

'Do you think the world now needs soldiers?'

'We haven't done too badly. It's a battle, just not one against other soldiers.'

'You won't mention I told you?'

He nodded. 'I would have thought as her—'

'Sister? Forget it, Captain. That never held much for her.'

He smirked. 'I won't breathe a word.'

*

In the church, František staggered in, dazed with a chip in his right spectacle, a dirtied jacket and cuts and bruises on his face.

'What happened?' Eliška said.

'Something,' the professor said.

'Did you fall?'

'Not a fall. Some people.'

Eliška examined his face, nothing serious. 'What do you mean?'

'You didn't expound one of your theories, Professor, did you?' Anton said.

He took his glasses off and cringed. 'They think I'm the murderer.'

'Who?'

He took off his glasses. '"Come on, cannibal, pervert, vampire", they said, "confess. We know you knifed the soldier". There were five of them. They pushed me against a tree and threw my notebooks on the ground. Then hit me.' He sat down on a pew.

'Who was it?'

'It doesn't matter.'

'Who,' Eliška said, anger boiling.

'Ginger moustache.'

237

'Oh, him,' Anton said with levity. 'Knuckle draggers like him would never understand you, Professor. Not like we do.'

'I will go to Vendula,' Eliška said.

'It doesn't matter,' František said.

But Eliška was out the door. At the colonel's house the guard told her that she had gone out with two trucks for a forage. Eliška paced towards Luděk's house and banged on the door. Luděk came to the window, then closed the curtain.

'How brave! To take five people to beat up one man,' she shouted. 'Come on! Come out here!' She waited but there was no sign or sound within. 'You're a thug. Why'd you beat him up, brave man? Because it's easy?'

She kept yelling, but Luděk would not come to the door.

*

In the priest's bedroom, Viktor sat on a chair next to Iva's bed. She was sitting up with a seraphic look of contentment and felt as light as a drifting cloud.

'You ain't eating?' he said.

She shook her head and picked up the notebook.

I've been looking out the window. I think life is like those little clouds. They pass quickly and they're gone. Were they ever there?

He read this choice piece of philosophy and looked puzzled.

The morphine is making me a little silly.

'It ain't no passing cloud. It's a battle.'

What are you fighting?

'Anything. Every damn thing. It's all a fight.'

He had a grim look with creases in his brow. You cannot move, she thought, for the weight holding you down.

What was your crime?

He reeled back. 'How'd you know that? Who told you? Someone's said something.'

She put her hand on his arm and smiled.

238

No one said anything. Intuition. But I think you are still a prisoner.

He drew back as if afraid of something.

Your crime must have been terrible.

'It ain't any use thinking about it. It ain't any good.'

Free yourself. You were a criminal. You don't have to stay one.

He frowned and clicked his tongue as if trying to shrug it off. Yet she saw some great struggle going on within him. He looked wounded.

'How?' he said. 'What do I do? It ain't any bloody use. You can't fix people like me. We're past helping. We've done things... no, there ain't nothing can be done.'

She shook her head.

There is a way. What was your crime?

'I've said it a million times. Makes no difference.'

She shook her head and pointed to herself. He didn't understand the gesture, so she wrote.

You haven't said it to me.

'You... what about you?' He looked down and clenched his jaw.

She touched his cheek and felt him trembling.

Because I care.

'You care about me? Me? Ain't nothing good about me. Ain't nothing. Past helping.'

Say it. Say it. She wrote hurriedly, then gazed with a paling face.

He looked away. But she turned his head back towards her gaze. Imploring with her eyes. You must say it, she thought.

'No. It ain't no good. Too damn far and no way back. No one can help anyone.'

She pointed to the words, *Say it. Say it.* She moaned. He shook his head. She slapped the page and winced, then grasped his hand, which curled his lip. She pleaded with her glossy eyes.

He sighed heavily, looked down and with a faltering raspy

239

voice he spoke. 'I murdered someone... murdered her.' He breathed loudly. 'Life in prison.'

Nothing was said for a long time. But when she drew his chin up, she was neither afraid nor disgusted. Instead, a look of calm dignity and forgiveness. Someone who didn't come to judge but to liberate.

'Ain't you appalled?' He sunk his head into his hands and breathed deep.

She wrote and then raised his head. Beams of light streamed into the little room as a cloud passed the sun. It filled her with a new hope. It was like a charge coursing through her to the centre of the world.

There's always a way to be good again.

His reddening eyes gleamed for a moment until he shook his head. 'I did it. I was mad. I hated everything. Wanted to break it all...' He stiffened his lip. 'Ten years in prison... when the warden opened the gate, I didn't feel anything. No freedom, nothing. I didn't want to go.'

The light was soft. We must renew ourselves, she thought. We make so many mistakes and we don't want to. Failure is blessed by the sun, only we must forgive. She pointed to the last line in the book: *There's always a way to be good again.*

'How? What must I do? How can I bring her back to life?'

Let her live in the good that you will do.

'What good? What must I do? I must do something. Some work? Tell me what to do.'

Pick up the broken pieces of this world and begin to put them back together.

She saw a gentle gleam on his face and felt as though she were floating.

He took her hands gently between his. 'I will. Work. I must *do* something.' He let go of her hand.

There's much to do.

'Don't leave,' he said suddenly. 'You gotta stay. You—'

She stopped his mouth with her hand and smiled. He hung his

240

head. We are clouds, she thought again. Drifting.

'I'm sorry you couldn't find your boy.'

She looked up at the window and, in the light, appeared saintly.

There's always hope.

*

'Can you find the doctor?' Šimon startled František who was looking out at the lake. He saw the professor's bruises.

'The doctor?' František said.

'What happened?' Šimon pointed to his face.

'The marks of meaninglessness.'

Though Šimon's face was grimy and with old bruises, his light-brown eyes were hopeful. 'Can you get the doctor?'

'He's dying then?'

'He needs some more medicine. Can you ask the doctor for some?' Šimon waited. Then he stepped closer.

'I want to be left alone. If you want the doctor, go find her. It's nothing to do with me.'

Šimon looked down the path towards the village, took a few steps, then shook his head. 'Can't you go?'

'You'll just have to forget it,' František said bitterly. He took out a notebook and pencil and seemed on the point of writing something, but didn't.

Šimon lowered his head. 'What if it was your friend?' He looked up with large eyes and raised brows.

'Friend?' František said sceptically. 'What is this idea? Nobility?' His eyes were big in his glasses. 'No, it's meaningless. Only nothing is the Alpha and Omega.'

'You won't help me?'

'Ethics are not eternal.' The professor stamped his foot. 'There's not a thing in all of this to believe in. Look at all these people.' He pointed the way to the village. 'They're trying to find something to believe in. But they won't.' František took off his

241

glasses but when he sought for the handkerchief to polish them, it wasn't there. He was shaking when he put the glasses back on. The professor raised his hand again to his glasses and then down to his chest, without taking them off. His hands trembled and he seemed agitated. 'I… I do feel. But it's illusion. Your goodness is not an eternal value. It has no value.'

Šimon had a faraway look of dignified sadness.

František tried to put the notebook back into his jacket pocket, but it fell to the ground. He stretched a twitching hand to pick it up, then pulled himself upright suddenly. 'You think goodness makes suffering bearable?' he shouted. 'You believe in it. But it's not true. Goodness does not exist.' He clenched his fist tightly. He glowered and turned to the lake. Šimon stood in front of the professor, trying to meet his eyes. All he saw was the professor's contorted face.

'Won't you go?' Šimon said. He didn't understand why he wouldn't.

'You cannot believe in life,' František said, 'because all the value you have instantiated in it will vanish suddenly. All the knowledge built upon it implodes. There's no certainty in that. You cannot rely on change. You cannot say it is true. Only nothing is eternal.'

'Then I'll find her,' Šimon said.

'No!' František said with a look of surprise, as if not meaning to. 'No… I'll go.'

'Thank you.'

'Because maybe…' he said under his breath and brushed his brow with his wrist. 'Could it be true?' He gulped and sweat appeared on his brow. He took off his glasses as if to see better and stepped towards the boy. 'I sneaked into the cave.' He spluttered. 'It was like nothing. It narrowed and narrowed on the way to unknowing. But… but… I found something.' He wiped his mouth with trembling hand. 'I found some thing.' He shook his hand in the direction of the cave, squeezing his glasses. 'I found a box. Hidden. To me it doesn't matter, but to them… to you… everyone's looking for it. It would help your friend. And it is surrounded by darkness. On it is a flower. I don't believe in it. I can't believe.' He closed his eyes and shook his head. 'But if they really believe in it, why… why don't they bring it out into the open?'

The boy looked forsaken.

The professor waved his hands. He put his glasses on. He hesitated, then walked up the path. When he looked back, Šimon was stroking his own arm. František walked towards the village.

When František was out of sight, Šimon was startled by something scurrying off beyond the trees to his side. He saw the flash of a pair of legs running. He froze. But the figure had disappeared.

CHAPTER 37

The soldiers used crowbars to pry off the crucifix. They all watched as it fell. Anton pressed the bout of his violin to his forehead as soldiers took the paraphernalia: chalices, vestry garb, altar cloths. Petra punched the soldiers and tried to drag them away. The soldiers even got to the roof of the church though they struggled with the cross mounted there. Petra screamed and paced. In the end though, it fell. She shouted that she would speak to the colonel as a soldier held her back. Finally, she tottered with despair up the steps to the altar. There was a pale white outline where the cross used to be, and the dust could not reach. The boltholes appeared like stigmata. She lurched to the wall, touched it and sobbed at the removal of the image. She looked up and bent her knees.

Anton thought of playing, but couldn't decide what? Instead, he pressed his violin harder into his forehead.

The crucifix was carried across the bridge. After it, came the Ditherers – those who hadn't taken the oath. Granny Petra, who had to be dragged, was inconsolable. Viktor was taken, but Iva left. František was also marched into the field. The rest of the villagers came, some conspicuous with white circles on their chests. Then the rest of the soldiers filed in. Soon everyone was standing in the field waiting. An order was given for the Ditherers to sit down – only them.

'I haven't been in school for thirty-five years,' Anton said.

They waited.

It was a long wait.

Then the flag came down the pole. The flag bearer took and mounted it to a branch. The colonel emerged, her step clean, sure and ceremonious. First, the standard bearer mounted the platform, then stood in the back left corner. The colonel climbed on the platform and stood in the centre with folded arms, saying nothing. Radoš kept glancing round in a strange kind of panic as he held Helena. Anton noticed the colonel had clean boots, then yawned at the unnecessary formality of proceedings. He started singing about Brünnhilde. Petra stood up and staggered forward, screaming until soldiers came and sat her down. The Ditherers caused a fuss until soldiers hushed them. The colonel watched all, aloof. On her fatigues was sewn a white circle. Finally, Anton became quiet, and this solemn silence was long and tense. He stroked the wood of his violin.

'A sacrifice!' the colonel said, with a loud and sure voice. 'A sacrifice, for unity. Some of you object to the removal of the crucifix, but how will *he* help us understand each other? When I see those oath-takers, I feel sure. I can see where they stand. Take the oath! Take it. Crush out the old and rise up again in the new.' She paused and looked at her audience.

'If you serve Otočka, Otočka will save you. Put one boot firmly into the future, strong and certain. If we are to stand any chance, a great effort is required. Take the oath. Help us. Build on stone. Take the oath. If we follow the rules, the New Way will keep us safe and prosperous. Take the oath. Let us flourish! Do not be afraid to do what has to be done. Take the oath. Do not be afraid of being determined and focused. Take the oath. Don't be afraid to act. Not for me, but to make us all stronger. Take the oath. Take the oath because time is short and you are needed. We need you. Not me, us! You're essential. Take the oath. You are the rearguard.'

Anton burst out laughing. 'And you are the lunatic.' One of the soldiers came and threatened. 'It's a tiny village, but you think it's an empire.'

'If you were outside the fence,' the colonel replied, 'you wouldn't laugh. The bodies being eaten by dogs. Bodies hanging from ceilings. And always nothing left. It could have been you. It's no laughing matter.'

There were now two soldiers standing near him, towering

over him. He shook his head and traced one of the soldier's boots with his bow.

'It could have been anyone here,' she continued. 'We know there are people out there who are desperate to get in. But if we let them in, we would no longer have a village to save, no longer a place to call home. And we have a killer inside. This is no laughing matter. We are surrounded.' She paced the platform as if in thought, then suddenly turned. 'But we will survive! Rise up in Unity, Stability and Certainty! Rise up those who now want to take the oath and declare before everyone here their love for each other, and Otočka.'

She waited. It seemed as if no one would take her offer. Then three Ditherers rose, one of whom was Tibor. He trailed after the other two, then turned to Marek and seemed to wait for something. Not the barman, Anton thought. Surely, not him! Finally, Tibor went towards the platform. The flag bearer stepped to the front left corner and in formal movements lowered the flag so that his branch was horizontal, and the flag draped free in front of the three. The colonel ordered the first to hold a corner of the flag and the woman repeated the oath after the colonel.

'This is babyish,' Anton said. 'None of this will make you better people.'

Zarviš stepped towards the first Ditherer after she had taken the oath. He had in his hands some white circles. He gave her one, which she pinned to her chest. The others did the same; then they stood in a line as the army clapped. They then went to those who had taken the oath, or the *Real Otočkans*, as they had started to be called.

'You see we just became more certain,' she said. 'There are some soldiers who were on duty during our last gathering. They have agreed to take the oath now.' And at that about twenty or so soldiers repeated the oath and were given little white circles.

'However,' the colonel said, 'there's one soldier who was caught sleeping on duty. We can't let it slide. We gave him a choice: either he must leave or accept punishment. He chose the latter.' She signalled, and the soldier was summoned, flanked by two soldiers. They all mounted the steps to the platform on the west side. 'OK, sergeant.'

The Ditherers watched in anticipation as the two soldiers held the man's arms and the sergeant held up a branch. The beating was swift. The children were shielded from watching by their parents. The soldier did not make a noise as he was struck, though his face betrayed the blows. Sofie looked transfixed by the physical terror.

'It'll be the rod for your own back,' Anton shouted. He quickly felt the towering presence of the soldier standing beside him. He smiled wryly. Suddenly Otočka seemed very small and stuffy. The beating went on and on. Then what followed was clearly prepared.

'I'm sorry,' the beaten soldier said in a scratchy voice. 'I'll never do it again.'

The colonel nodded.

'Please,' he said, 'let me take the oath. I want to take the oath.'

Viktor clicked his tongue. The flag was lowered and the soldier held the corner with an unsteady hand. The colonel spoke the oath and the soldier repeated. Zarviš handed him a white circle, which the soldier pinned. The army applauded. The soldier tried to smile but could only grimace. He saluted the colonel who returned the gesture, then shook his hand, welcoming him back into the community. The soldiers cleared the platform so once again it was only the colonel and the flag bearer.

'Now we are sure of him. We don't want to throw anyone out. Now he's an Otočkan, a real Otočkan. Though there are still some who haven't taken the oath, I'm confident they will. When we're all Real Otočkans then we can... we can... we... what the hell are you mumbling? What's he saying?'

Artur was muttering.

'Stand up if you have something to say. Soldier, get that man on his feet.'

A soldier got Artur up. 'Speak up,' the colonel bellowed.

'I don't know...' Artur said.

'What don't you know?'

'Who are these people?'

'What are you talking about?'

'Wha... why am I here?' Artur said.

The colonel glared with her cavernous eyes.

'Lieutenant,' she called to one of the officers standing among the ranks. He came quickly.

'Where's Rudolf?' Artur said.

'OK, Lieutenant. This man,' the colonel said and again the action seemed rehearsed. Two soldiers came and gently escorted the old man.

'Where are you taking him?' Anton shouted. Some of the Ditherers stood in panic and the soldiers had to hold them back as Artur was taken.

'What are you doing?' Petra said, but the colonel was unmoved. The slowness of the lieutenant's step was foreboding. Marek wrestled with the soldiers until they got the better of him.

'What's happening? What is this?' Eliška said.

The lieutenant and Artur were walking towards the old oak by the river. Ludmila, holding Nada, looked fearfully at the Real Otočkans. They too seemed concerned. Except for Luděk who appeared smug. Anton tried to pass the line of soldiers, but they stopped him.

Hynek stepped towards the colonel. 'He's not going to get hurt, is he?' he said. She said nothing. 'For pity's sake, he's harmless. Colonel, I know you are a good person.'

The soldiers stood Artur behind the tree so that he was out of sight. Sofie squealed when the lieutenant took a pistol out of his holster. Helena held onto Radoš tightly. Sofie gasped when the lieutenant raised the gun. Anton tried to barge through, shouting. 'Commendatore.' He turned to the colonel. 'You're mad. You're mad!'

'Vendula stop it! Please. I'll do anything you want. Just stop this,' Eliška said. 'I'll take the oath now. I'll say it, right now.'

'We all will,' Hynek said.

Helena squeezed Radoš's hand. Štěpánka, wearing her white circle, fidgeted. Anton raged like a bull, and it took four soldiers to restrain him. Petra prayed. The colonel remained icy and unmoved. The shouting of the Ditherers became louder and louder, almost deafening until a single gunshot echoed.

Silence.

The lieutenant put his gun back in the holster and he and the two soldiers walked back to their ranks. They all gaped at the tree. It was some time before Eliška turned with a look of pure despair at her sister's shining eyes. Anton fell to his knees. Hynek took off his Panama hat and scrutinised the colonel's face as if trying to find something.

But most of those who looked at the colonel had fear in their eyes. She was resolute. Štěpánka shook. Sofie stared at the ground.

'Commendatore,' Anton said softly.

The colonel scanned the faces of the soldiers, the Real Otočkans and the Ditherers. She seemed pleased. This act had concentrated minds.

Ludmila screamed.

They turned. Artur appeared tottering out from behind the oak tree unhurt. There were gasps of incomprehension. The consternated old man doddered towards the group as the soldiers began to leave. Anton ran to meet him.

'Commendatore!'

'I want to go home,' Artur said. Anton embraced the old man.

The colonel smiled slightly under her steely eyed gaze. Then she walked down from the platform. As she went, she made a signal to the soldiers standing near the crucifix. They nodded and dragged the wooden cross onto the fire. The other soldiers added the priest's garb to the fire. Soon it was all surrounded in flame.

*

By early evening, it was still and quiet in the church. Anton was gloomy as he shuffled about absent-mindedly. Without meaning to, he ended up in the vestry. The wardrobes were empty, and the clothes pegs had no garb on them. There was a long desk with some cupboards underneath. He sat on a low stool by the window. All the paraphernalia had been taken, but there was one large candle that remained. Anton thought it slightly amusing that they had taken the symbolic but left the practical. He leant his head against the wall barely able to raise his eyes off the ground. A large emptiness welled within him. He had a vague notion of hanging himself, but couldn't be bothered. After a time, he noticed something red faintly glistening in a cupboard in the corner, whose door was ajar. At first, he didn't pay it any attention but then it persistently glistened. Instinctually he was drawn to it, and in a swift motion, he bent low and threw open the little door.

He gasped.

A dark ruby sparkle widened his eyes. Three large bottles of a red liquid. He grabbed one. Unscrewing the top of the first, he smelled it – fortified wine. He drank and was suddenly transformed. He laughed. He sipped again, stood up and put the bottle on the desk. He reeled back in wonder. Then he grabbed the next bottle, unscrewed the cap and drank. Joy! Putting it on the desk, he shuffled about, laughing; he brushed his hand through his hair. Then he tried the third bottle, the same. He wiped his smiling lips, clapped his hands and whirled round trying to find something to thank. He stopped when he saw the candle.

'Thank you.' He put his hands together. 'I don't believe but thank you.' He took another draught of the wine, which rushed down with its warm calm. The dull heaviness melted away. Enough of all this, he thought. No more. He looked at the three large bottles and beamed and shook his head in disbelief. He grabbed two bottles in sure hands and ran out of the vestry.

'Enough. No more!' he said with a booming voice. 'If there

must be suffering, there must also be joy. *Professore!* No. Now is not the time for writing.' He threw his arms wide open, and like some modern Dionysus, bore in each hand the darkened ruby of wine.

They looked puzzled.

'To hell with the colonel. Forget all her ideas. Forget about the army. No one says we have to be miserable. No one can tell us how to feel. Look, I've found wine.'

Luboš, who had been asleep, woke and wagged his tail. He trotted up to Anton.

'The dog knows it. Come on, free yourselves. I will play. You will sing and dance. Let's go out somewhere. All of you. Out. If she wants to start a tinpot dictatorship, then let's at least have our moment.'

'Now is not the time for this,' Eliška said sternly.

'Ah, Golden One! But this *is* the time. There has never been a better time to celebrate.'

'Go outside if you must drink. If you don't care about anything or anyone. Then get out,' she said bitterly.

'Oh, Golden One. I care, I do. But who knows what will happen? So let's take this time into our hands. Three big bottles of sherry and a fiddle. Why should we be miserable? Now is the time. Who'll come with me? Come on! Stand up. Let's celebrate. Who's coming? I know the dog is at least.'

Helena stood up.

'*Bravissima!* More. More.'

Radoš rose.

'Bella. The lover birds understand. Lovers always do.'

Ludmila stepped down from the altar and rushed towards the sleeping Nada and gathered her in her arms. 'Both of us will go.'

'Yes. Yes. *Andiamo Amici.* Let's have a spree. Yes. A good old-fashioned spree.' Marek stood up and asked the musician holding the wine: 'Can you play a pop song?'

'Anything. Anything. Only come. Professore, you don't have to come. If the nothing is keeping you busy, you needn't come.'

251

To Anton's amazement, however, František put his book in his pocket then stood up. '*Incredibile*. Professore. Andiam. You are welcome.'

Sofie slowly stood up and Anton rushed towards her with full encouragement. 'Yes. Yes.'

Eliška got up but went to the stairs. 'I must see Iva,' she said and went with the nurse up the stairs. Hynek was the only one who remained sitting.

'Hynek, come.'

'Not me. But you go. Enjoy yourselves. You're right. Who knows what will happen tomorrow? Or even tonight?' the greybeard said with a kind smile. Anton didn't press him, and they went out of the church.

Soon they were spiritedly pacing down the path towards the lake. Nada was skipping and Anton talking with gusto. It didn't take them long to reach the lake. They looked at the peaceful landscape.

'Drink! Drink!' Anton abruptly shouted. 'Forget the colonel. She eats iron bread. Now music.' He put down the bottle and shuffled the violin case off his back and the violin into his hands in a well-practised, elegant movement. 'Mozart. *Eine Kleine Nachtmusik.* Rondo.'

They drank and listened.

Anton stopped. 'No, no. You're not supposed to listen to music, you must move to it. OK. Not this. Another. You'll see. You'll understand.' He played the opening burst of Mozart's *Vivat Bacchus.* A sprightly tune. And Nada began to skip. The dog followed her – the only ones who hadn't drunk anything but seemed the most drunk. Then the others danced, until Anton stopped.

'No, Professore. No,' Anton said as František was writing. Anton put the bottle in his face.

'I don't want it,' František said.

'Drink!'

'No.'

'You don't want it?'

'I'll never want it. It's illusion.'

'Leave him alone,' Marek said.

'You think that when you discover nothing you will become none with it in an explosive crescendo of blah blah blah. But you won't.'

František shook his head.

'You know, I think you're the cure to the virus, Professor. I think if you were ever infected, the virus would give up out of mad despair. But let me tell you something about the animal called man. It's not a happy animal unless it suffers. It's an ironic animal. It needs... ha... it needs hope and that only comes from disaster, and most of those are self-made. If there were no problems, man would create them. Any excuse to go deep within his own nature and prove himself worthy by overcoming. How stupid-smart? How miserable-joyous? How noble-inglorious? We have joy because we shoot ourselves in the foot. Look at my lot, and what a ragtag bunch – the children of Israel. How we've suffered! How we died! What tragicomedy! But it isn't Jerusalem that's sacred; it's joy. Life has no point, only a way. A path with song, dance and love. Joy brings us together.'

'What good can you do?' František said.

'I liberate. You want to wither on the vine, but life cries out: "Live! Thrive!" Professor, writing? No, you're the mad one. Stop it. Don't write, dance!'

'Let him be,' Marek said.

'Even the professor could celebrate, if he only knew how. Fine, let the man who wants to cry to himself, do so. But we'll rise out of the common place. Shining, rising, flying. Flying.'

They tittered. Anton drank and put the violin to his neck.

'Very well. Friends. Not these sounds. Let us hear something more pleasant. *Ode to Joy*.'

He played and they started nodding. Then their feet moved. Ludmila couldn't let her daughter dance alone, so she took her hands and they moved about. Radoš and Helena followed.

253

Natalie insisted Marek dance. At first, he cut a sorry figure, but then got into it. Sofie took the other bottle and drank and danced. Natalie tried to get František to dance but he was firmly fixed to the earth and instead just observed. Anton was ecstatic as he played the chorus to the symphony.

Every creature drinks in joy
At Nature's breast;

'Now join hands,' Anton said. 'A circle. A circle. Turn! Turn!'

He played. They joined hands and made a circle but couldn't agree on a direction. They collided into laughter.

She gives us kisses and wine,

They tried again, hand in hand, moving, laughing. The music impelled them, like a *moresca*. The music of energy and motion. Freedom is joy, joy freedom.

So you, brothers, should run your course,
Joyfully, like a conquering hero.

Anton's mind raced. He imagined water rushing like a quick river, majestic in a great sunbeam. Flowing, across, down, in; all things connected. Where fear divides us, joy unites. Its magic makes enemies friends. In every chest beats the same heart; joined as equals in the universe. Our statement to that vast oblivion is that we have each other. And we shall not be afraid. Never! We will laugh and dance and shine.

He imagined the pulsing of the French horn as a signal call – an echo. The chords swelling, billowing, rising. The water is building up at a dam, pressing.

Suddenly it bursts and gushes.

Joy, beautiful spark of Divinity,
Daughter of Elysium

Anton's violin poured with rapid expression, long wondrous strides into the bright heart of the world. Man frees himself. And then helps others do the same.

All men shall become brothers,
Wherever your gentle wings shall hover.

The rushing water eases as the music slows and becomes stately.

Anton turned his eyes to the sky, the setting orb. They stopped dancing and followed Anton's lead by looking up. A communion. Out there, millions are starving, alone, hurt and afraid. Look up! Whatever may weigh you down – look up. Wherever you may tread, look up, for joy raises you to the stars; joy that lives in everyone.

Anton trod knee-deep into the lake. They all gazed in peace at the clouds of the setting sun and its golden light.

Be embraced, you millions!

This kiss is for the whole world!

CHAPTER 38

Ludmila's faltering voice broke the hush in the church. There had been another fire in the night, this time the food store. They had managed to save most of it, but as dawn broke, the accusations were wild and free and chiefly directed at the Ditherers. With a murderer and arsonist still at large, the colonel acted swiftly. The soldiers responsible for guarding the store were thrown out of Otočka without trial and Marek was detained. Eliška had argued with the colonel, but the result was the same.

'The colonel will have to do something,' Ludmila said. 'She'll do something against us. Everyone thinks it was one of us.' She darted her eyes from face to face, her blonde hair awry.

'Why would anyone do it?' Sofie said.

The question became rhetorical.

'I think we should just take the oath,' Ludmila said. 'Just get it over with. We're first in line for blame. Why are we sticking out our necks? What are we trying to prove?'

Eliška sighed. 'If you want to do it, do it. I won't. I can't. And I won't be her lieutenant either.'

Ludmila rounded on her. 'Come on. You just say some words. Who cares whether you believe it or not? I think we should take the oath. Play their game. I'm going to. I've a daughter to think about.'

'I won't,' Radoš said.

'Aren't you brave?' Ludmila said mockingly. 'But not very smart. Look, do you think Marek would have been taken if he was wearing one of those white circles? No.'

'I won't do it,' Sofie said.

'Yes, you will. Can't you see what's happening? It's going to get worse for those who don't take it. Just say the words, wear a circle.'

'No. If you did, it would mean you agree with her,' Hynek said. 'Then, anything can happen. Besides, I'm too long in the tooth for swearing anything.'

'It doesn't feel right,' Sofie said.

Ludmila burst into manic laughter.

'What about you, Helena?' Hynek said.

'I don't know. I mean we should think about it.'

'I'll take it,' Natalie said. 'Maybe it'll help Marek.'

'You must do what you think right,' Hynek said.

'What I think right is to join the crowd,' said Ludmila. 'We're powerless. You realise that the colonel could expel anyone. Why would she throw out any of the oath-takers when we are here?'

'I will speak to Captain Nebojsa,' Eliška said but not with any conviction. He hadn't been able to do anything for the two soldiers outside. Perhaps he hadn't tried.

'What good will that do?' Ludmila said.

'It couldn't do any harm.'

'Just take the oath. What's the point of holding out?'

'Because I think she is going insane.'

'All the more reason to play along with it.'

'Playing a game with a mad person is madness.'

'She's not mad,' Ludmila said. 'But you are.'

'No,' Hynek said slowly. 'Playing along only delays the trouble.'

'What trouble?' Ludmila said.

'The moment when it becomes far better to live outside the fence than inside it.'

Ludmila huffed.

'Nebojsa doesn't like what Vendula's doing,' Eliška said. 'Especially now she's thrown more soldiers out. And were they really to blame? Or is it a threat?'

'Don't you go stirring things up!' Ludmila pointed at Eliška. 'Don't make problems. You've got to think about others. What about my daughter? Huh? Why you want to kick the hornet's nest?'

'Because she's dishonest,' Eliška said. 'There are signs of psychopathy. Do you want such a person to do anything she wants with three hundred soldiers? It's becoming a tyranny.'

Ludmila laughed. 'So what! At least we have food and protection. If that's the price, then we'll just have to pay it.'

'It's a high price.'

'Oh, look how pure you are! The colonel's right. Who cares about the old ways. You think you are so brave refusing to be a lieutenant. But you're the colonel's sister. I don't give a damn if you hate her. But she won't touch you. If you cause trouble, it's bad for us. Do you think I can stand up in front of the whole village and tell the colonel she's a guileless bitch?'

'Don't be stupid,' Eliška said, incensed.

Suddenly Ludmila screamed and lunged at Eliška. Hynek ran to hold her back, but Ludmila pulled the doctor's clothes and hair. The church was full of shouting and scuffling. Radoš and Hynek managed to pry Ludmila off. They screamed at each other and then all at once the church quietened because a little voice was singing. They all turned to see Nada singing in the aisle.

Virus, virus is so bad
Virus, virus makes me sad.
If you touch me, I will cry
Virus you must go, bye-bye.

She sang again, crouching and bobbing to the song. Everyone else stood still.

*

'The great mother?' the colonel said, astonished.

'Yes,' Zarviš said, holding the paper and pen as he sat at the table.

'No. It's too strange.'

'Colonel, it isn't that they become your children or anything

258

like that. Heaven forfend! What you would be doing is playing a role that has a lot of psychological power. Something that is deep and ancient and able to reassure people without them even knowing it. The mammalian nurture instinct. Tap that and you have something wonderful and potent. Besides, it isn't *you* that would be the mother, it's the *idea* of you. It's the idea that would be doing all the work. That's why it's better if you are seen less.'

'Near impossible in a village. Or should I stay in this room?'

'We could build a house on the hill, where the sheep graze.'

'Ha.'

'At least think about it,' Zarviš said.

'I always do.'

'So shall we get back to it?' He dragged the pen down to the line that they were up to. 'Ah here it is. I want to cut this line: "we must work and fight for victory".'

'That's a good line.'

'Better to be pessimistic. Then they won't be disappointed if nothing happens. Besides, what victory? What does it look like? Are we not victorious already?'

'You wrote it.'

'Yes, but saying it to you makes me see the mistakes. Ah, and this line: "we need new words". True, we need new words, but we shouldn't say that until we have those words.'

'New words? Why?'

'Because new words and new ideas amount to the same thing. And that's the beauty of it, Colonel. They're yet to be made. That's why they're new. The future is in the mind.'

'No, no, Zarviš you must write them down; then I'll check them. The worst thing for a soldier is not knowing what's going on. Those three words are the best because they give a clear picture.'

'Yes, but we shouldn't commit to writing too much in case we become hostages to it. Besides, more is achieved by the speaker than the writer.'

'I've embraced your ideas because it's necessary. You don't

know it, but you're a good strategist.'

'OK, Colonel. Let's continue. Ah... this line, "... rumour, which is winged...". Too poetic. Better to say, "News about our success has spread and they are coming. They are surely coming". Because thousands are desperate to get in. We have seen the crumbling shell of Europe – the starved, dragging their feet, ready for anything because they've nothing left to lose. They are many, we are few. They could overwhelm us, even though without us, they too would not survive. Desperate people do not think. But we will succeed if we become like paladins of the New Way. We need those heroic virtues. That way we can stand a hundred feet tall.'

'Ha! How you talk! All right. But, Zarviš, you know it would be easier if I just kick the Ditherers out.'

'No, you mustn't do that. No, we really do need them. You see, Colonel, it shows the strength of our ideas if we are able to persuade them to take the oath. If we throw them out, we will never know how to persuade doubters. The strength of our ideas could never be tested. And it's important to find out, because in each Otočka there will be sceptics.'

'All right. Well, write it in. But do it quickly. I need time to recite it.'

*

Eliška rushed into Petra's house. She saw Artur in the bed and the sheet bloodied. Petra had tied a pillowcase to Artur's left wrist; the knife was on the floor. Eliška unbound the pillowcase and pressed the wound quickly.

'Unroll the bandage in my bag,' she told Petra. Artur followed the doctor's movements and was lucid. She felt his pulse – slow and steady. She could see that the wound oozed rather than flowed. It wasn't arterial and he hadn't gone deep enough.

'OK, put some iodine on the cotton, then put it on the wound.'

Petra did it. Eliška took the bandage and wound it round his

260

wrist. She tied it off, then put his hand on his chest. She examined his eyes and listened to his breathing. He wasn't critical.

'Artur, do you know where you are?' Eliška said.

'I don't want to be here anymore,' he said.

'Do you know who this is?' She pointed to Petra.

He turned to the side. 'I've had enough.'

'Why'd you do it, duck?' Petra said, stroking his arm.

'Wife, son, life, gone.'

'We have to keep going,' Eliška said, but he shook his head. She touched his shoulder. He slowly turned back to face her.

'You mustn't give up,' she said.

He frowned. 'Why?'

'Because you could help. Someone may need you. We need you.'

Artur looked away. 'I have nothing.'

'Try,' she said.

'Don't mock me. I'm not a child.'

'Artur, I'm serious,' Eliška said. 'A person can do much good. It's precious. It's important. You do the world wrong by taking a good person out of it.'

A smile fluttered, but he quickly shook his head. 'What can I do?'

'Live. No one knows what will happen. But something may fall to you to do. There's a battle and we need every good person. It's not true you have nothing. There is much in you yet. Will you help us?'

After a long silence, he nodded slightly.

*

Towards evening, Eliška was with all the others in the field before the platform. As before, the Ditherers were made to sit. The Real Otočkans stood to the left. Everyone who stood was now wearing a white circle. Some of them were also wearing military fatigues. Luděk in particular looked ready for a mission.

261

Anton, on the other hand, was scruffy, dishevelled and plucked at the violin idly. He yawned.

Finally, the colonel arrived, but this time she was flanked by the flag bearer and Zarviš, who mounted the platform at her side. Many whispered in surprise at this. The colonel stepped forward on the platform.

'Let's have a moment of silence and remember the soldiers who fell in the ambush. Let us also not forget the genocide of the Great Virus.'

Eliška looked at the soldiers standing around and it seemed to her there was a new kind of sternness about them. After the quiet, the colonel resumed.

'It's a thing of pride that our strength shines in our sense of purpose.' She pointed to the flag. 'We're strong because we have order, which gives us freedom. We're not leaves on a tree blowing in every direction. We can plan. We know where we stand. Follow the rules and you'll live free.' She paused. 'The freedom to work and build. Society is hard, anarchy easy. We're not just a village, but an idea. A powerful idea. We're an island against the dark seas that are rising. News of our success has surely spread, and they are coming. They are coming. We stand on a pivot between falling into the sea with them or onto sturdy land.' She paused, then resumed in a quieter voice. 'If we are sure of ourselves, we become giants. We have a heroic purpose like old knights. We are together, the same. No soldier, no villager. One.'

'Whoo!' Luděk shouted in a pink-faced rapture. Anton rubbed his bleary eyes.

'Beyond that fence,' Vendula continued, 'the silence of the machines thunders in our ears. The factories, the cars, the trains, the Old World has rusted up. But we don't need machines. We don't want them. We want us. We're all in it. Unity, Stability, Certainty. The New Way. All new. New people. New ideas. New wishes. New dreams. We decide our destiny. And you are all heroes, because you are the first. The originals. You are making the New World.' She paused for breath; her audience seemed to be gasping too.

'Unity! Stability! Certainty!' she shouted.

In response, the army shouted wildly. Then the Real Otočkans. There was a sustained period of shouting and clapping. Eliška cringed – the sounds had a psychotic menace to them. At length, the colonel gestured to Zarviš, who signalled to someone to come onto the stage.

Slowly, her little feet climbed the steps. On the last step she caught her shoe on the platform, but didn't fall. Her face blushed and her shaking feet trod to the middle of the platform. On her chest was the white circle of the oath-taker. The standard bearer stood beside, so that the flag flapped above her head. Zarviš made quick gestures of desperate encouragement. Then of painful anger. She sang a little, very scratchily, then stopped. After Zarviš's whispered appeal, a piece of crinkled paper fell out of her pocket. While pinching her fingers and shifting her eyes nervously, Ana began to sing.

The New Way leads to liberty,
The New Way built by you.
We are the children of Unity,
We decide what we do.

(Chorus)

Unity. Stability. Certainty.
Magic in our ears.
Unity, Stability, Certainty,
Banishes all our fears.

The virus was a gift.
It began the Way.
Our hearts begin to lift
Together, as we say,

(Chorus)

Oneness is our theme.
A hard rock that is true.
The New Way that we dream,
Is one with me and you.

(Chorus)

Our leader is our Way,
She keeps us from the worst.
A mother, so we say,
She always puts us first.

(Chorus)

When Ana had finished, the crowd hadn't. They sang the chorus again with its jolly, upbeat march. Some were tapping toes. They sang again and couldn't help smiling. Even Anton brought his violin to his neck, but then put it back down. The colonel stopped singing and was grim. Eventually the singing died away.

'But one of you,' she shouted, 'wants to destroy us.' She pointed surprisingly towards her right. 'One of you, Real Otočkans. One of you has mimed the oath, then broken it. Said and broken. It would be better to be a Ditherer, at least they're honest. But to break an oath, such people have no place in Otočka. And it's worse – the oath-breaker I'm talking about is the murderer.'

Panic spread through the Real Otočkans. There were hysterical murmurings. The colonel eyed the Real Otočkans. Slowly she looked from face to face.

'Yes, the murderer is among you. Hiding. But we have discovered who it is.'

Štěpánka trembled.

'Throw him out, Colonel! Execute him,' Luděk shouted nervously.

'Send the murderer out,' shrieked the fat-faced villager, in a panicked and affected avowal of innocence. 'We're with you all the way, Colonel.'

'We'll never break the oath,' shouted another.

'With your leadership, Colonel... you have found him,' said another.

'We are grateful that you came to our village, Colonel,' another said. 'Without you...'

'Unity! Stability! Certainty!' Zarviš suddenly shouted. Several echoed in reply.

'Thank you, Colonel,' someone screamed.

'We have found proof of who did it,' she said calmly. 'Soldiers, bring him here.' Three soldiers went to the Real Otočkans and pulled out Tibor. Eliška frowned in surprise. Tibor couldn't have done it, she thought.

'I did nothing,' he protested and screamed. 'Nothing. This is a mistake.'

The fat-faced villager started clapping manically; others joined in.

'You found him, Colonel! I always knew it was him,' Luděk said desperately, with a sigh of relief.

'Tibor, pah. Of course it was him,' someone shouted.

'Colonel, this man is a thief as well,' said another

'Murderer!' shouted Štěpánka. 'Arsonist. It's written on his face. Oh God!'

The other Real Otočkans started jeering and cursing the man. The soldiers brought him to the spot.

'I didn't do anything. You've made a mistake.'

'We found your knife,' Zarviš shrieked.

'I didn't do it.'

Zarviš produced the knife and showed it to the crowd. 'This is your knife.'

265

Tibor stuttered.

'Is this your knife?' the colonel asked.

His mouth was hanging low as if he didn't know what was happening.

'There's his shirt also,' she said. Zarviš produced a blood-stained shirt. 'This is definitely your shirt.'

He looked at it. 'Where?' he uttered.

'Did you hear him? He asked me where we found his shirt? Where? I'll tell you, the Resource Commission found it. Blood-stained knife and shirt. You killed the private and then kept these things out of pride. You are sick.'

Tibor turned from eye to eye that was locked on him. His mouth moved but he said nothing.

Eliška could bear it no longer. She shot to her feet. 'This doesn't prove anything.'

'I agree, Eliška,' the colonel replied. 'And it isn't for the murder that we are judging him. No, this man's crimes go deeper. Soldier, remove his white circle; he taints it.' A soldier came and tore it off and threw it down before him. 'You thought you could hide behind the white circle. Then accuse the Ditherers. But we also found this.'

Zarviš produced a box of gun cartridges.

'These were discovered in his house,' she said, 'long after we had requisitioned all the guns and ammunition. Are these yours?'

He stared. He didn't say no.

'His,' she continued. 'The same brand and gauge as the bandits who ambushed our brave soldiers. It was you who helped them. You who gave them supplies. Told them where and how the soldiers would come. But that's not all. My God this man's crimes are endless. We also found this.'

Zarviš had already descended the platform to bring a Molotov cocktail.

'Here is the arsonist,' she declared.

'He couldn't be,' Hynek said.

'This isn't the right way, Vendula,' Eliška said.

266

'We say you murdered, you set fire and you aided our enemies. Very simple question: did you do these things?'

Tibor shook his head.

'But you broke your oath. You lost your circle. How can we believe you?'

'I didn't do it,' Tibor said.

'Liar!' Luděk shouted. 'Colonel, he's always been a devious bastard.'

'No surprise!' said another.

'Is anyone else surprised?' the colonel said.

'No. He stole my wood.'

'He pinches eggs,' another said.

'Look at his face,' Štěpánka screamed. 'Of course he's guilty.'

'All right, enough,' the colonel said. 'Why don't you confess? You're guilty, whether you say it or not. You're only speechless because you can't believe we found out. It's lucky for all of us that you were discovered in time. Otherwise, what else would you have done?'

Tibor wrung his hands and stuttered. He then collapsed in a shivering heap.

'He's guilty. But you Real Otočkans, you are guilty too.'

Luděk suddenly looked panicked.

'Yes, you are, because if there was real unity among you, you would have discovered this man's crimes yourselves. You were not certain of him. Real unity is in knowing each other. Your punishment is to find out why you didn't know, and in future, make sure you do know.'

Suddenly Anton got to his feet. 'Damn it! You're giving me a headache. When does this circus end?'

'Colonel, you are right,' Luděk said, not giving Anton a chance for an answer.

'All right.' She turned to the fallen man. 'You have been found guilty. Only say the words, and you shall be healed.'

He raised his head. Eliška looked from the colonel to the flag and the knife and the hatred bearing down on the fallen man. She was shocked by the terror her sister wielded. Words failed her. The colonel quietly repeated her request.

Tibor looked up. 'Un-unity. Sta-a-a… stability. Cert-certainty,' he uttered, breathless.

'Now you are free – Unity! Stability! Certainty!'

'Unity! Stability! Certainty!' the army echoed.

The same officer who had come to take Artur now marched to Tibor and some soldiers brought him to his feet. They dragged him. It was clear they were going to the oak tree.

'Stop it. Stop it.' Eliška ran to the platform, but several soldiers held her back.

The same fearful procedure as with Artur was happening. Luděk beamed. Eliška begged the colonel and tussled with the soldiers, though she knew it was all just to scare everyone. All the same, when the lieutenant did take his gun out, there was still a collective shudder. The gun fired. The soldiers walked away from the tree. Sofie whimpered.

The colonel was ecstatic. 'Now we are closer together than ever. Now we have been united by blood. Now we are one.'

The villagers watched the tree. Eliška stopped struggling and waited, expecting the man to step out.

They waited. And waited. When the colonel left and Luděk clapped, it began to dawn on Eliška and the others. The soldiers let her go and she tottered, dumbfounded. She realised the man would never walk out from behind the tree, because he was dead.

*

Eliška followed Captain Nebojsa as he was entering Helena's old house. She barged into the living room. His face was stern.

'I know why you're here.' He didn't look surprised. 'Hynek sent you. My advice would be to take the oath. It would be better for you.'

'Maybe I will. I don't know. I'm not certain,' she said. She could read very little in his face. But the time had come and Eliška was convinced the confrontation could no longer be put off. 'Captain, I wanted to ask you a question. Would you say you have honour?'

The captain paused. 'We're not barbarians.'

'And does that honour come from a little white circle?'

He smirked. 'It doesn't stop it.'

'And if it did?'

'If.'

'Yes, if it did. What would you do?'

He nodded. 'I would do something.'

'But you would be ordered to do nothing.'

'Orders from a CO must be followed.'

'With or without honour?'

'A CO must be honourable.'

'And what if she isn't?'

He winced. 'To you she's a sister. To us she is the CO.'

'Let me ask a more pointed question. What would you do if the colonel ordered you to beat one of the children?'

The captain was taken aback. 'Doctor... what are you talking about?'

'You've got to obey orders.'

'It's...'

'Why the hesitation?'

'I would argue.'

'Insubordination. You would be detained. Besides, why would you say no? There'd be no consequences. It would be more trouble if you didn't.'

'My conscience—'

'Ah, conscience. Honour. That's all fine, but it doesn't take much to overcome that. You say you're not a barbarian. You are cultured. I see you read, and you say you've honour. But all that really means nothing if power forces you.'

'I'd refuse.'

'To obey an order?'

269

'There are times?'

'When?'

'When it's illegal.'

'No laws anymore. Colonel makes the law.'

'Conscience.'

'Ah. Again, conscience. And what would your conscience say if the colonel ordered you to rape me?'

The captain shot to his feet and retreated. Then he became angry.

'What's the matter, Captain?'

'Don't you dare say such a thing.'

'Why are you so shocked? Do you think it doesn't go on? Especially now.'

'She would never give such an order.'

'She wants to teach me a lesson. I'm a thorn. She wants to put me in my place.'

'She wouldn't.'

'As a humiliation. I don't conform. I refuse the oath. I don't believe in her ideas. I think she is going down a bad path. Is it so unlikely?'

'It's not right. I would argue with her.'

'Ha! And what if I demanded it? What if I made Vendula give such an order, as a way to humiliate *you,* to damn your pretend honour.'

'Why?'

'No consequences, Captain. There'll have to be a breeding programme anyway; the sainted colonel will pair us up. Your concubine. I couldn't stop you. I wouldn't.'

'No! No, I'm not like that.'

'Who's going to know? I won't scream. Even if I did, no one would help.'

'Get out!'

'The colonel ordered it?'

'No.'

'For God's sake the colonel has ordered it! Just get on with

270

it.'

'Doctor, I refuse.'

'You can't refuse.'

'I can't.'

'That's right; you can't refuse.'

'No, I won't do it. It would never come to that.'

'Really? It's a slippery slope. Most certainly an innocent man was shot today and most of the village believe it's a fine thing. You remember what it was like before the virus? We didn't even have capital punishment, and to condemn someone without a trial…'

'Doctor,' he said as though slightly winded, 'we… have to make a new system. The reality is much much harsher now. We've got to be firm, or it will fall apart.'

'Be firm, yes, but do you want a system where you kill on a whim? We can't have law courts and judges, but is there nothing in between?'

He gave a long sigh and scratched his stubbly chin.

'Captain,' she suddenly shouted. He jumped. 'You've been given an order.'

'I refuse it,' he said scratchily.

'Ah, then if the colonel ordered you to kill a villager, you wouldn't do it?'

'No, I wouldn't. But she has never given me a reason to disobey… it was all going so well—'

'Then you do doubt her.'

He stared. Then nodded.

That was the moment she was waiting for. She smiled. 'I thought so. I thought you were true. Don't worry; there's no such order.'

The captain pushed his hand through his sandy hair and seemed to realise he had been tested. He smirked, then nodded. 'OK, OK. But the real problem is Zarviš. He's always with her. She listens too much to what he says. He writes her speeches you know.'

271

'You think she's a good person?'

He walked to the table and picked up his cap. 'Yes.'

'Captain, listen to this. When I was seven and she was fourteen, she was arrested for beating a kid. Broken arms and legs. Really savage. There were other crimes too. When she was old enough, she joined the army.'

'I knew she was a private before becoming an officer... but I didn't know why. No, no, it's him that's the problem, not her. I've known her for years and it's never been like this.'

'Don't believe it. You think he's using her, but what if she's using him?'

The captain blinked repeatedly. 'But why?'

'What reason does she need? I had a dread she would be like this. But what can I do? Talking to her is beyond hopeless. Captain, is there a time when a CO may be removed from command because they are unfit? Insane?'

'Yes. But, generally, we would need a medical opinion to...'

Eliška smiled. 'To confirm it? Captain, she is unfit. And something has to be done. Now, something now.'

The captain looked blankly.

'If the other officers agreed,' Eliška continued, 'you could depose her and make one of you commanding officer.'

His eyes widened. 'What! Impossible. They would never agree, especially captain Železný.'

'Then what about the soldiers. What do they really think? How many of them are beginning to doubt? How many think the colonel is unfit?'

'Careful, Doctor. Be very careful.'

'But they won't all blindly follow, will they? Will they do *anything* she asks?'

'Enough, Doctor. Mutiny would make it worse. I want peace. I think the best way is still to deal with the colonel wisely and persuasively. I don't think she is what you think she is.'

'What if she does something wild?'

'You have not seen her in ten years. I can also say I know her, and I don't think you need to worry.'

'I hope you are right.'

'Doctor, there's something—'

A group of soldiers was heard passing by the house. He gestured for silence. 'You better go; it'll be curfew soon.'

'We must talk again.'

'Yes, yes, but I'll come to you.'

'OK. And, Captain, we're for the same thing, aren't we?'

He looked long at her. 'Yes. I understand you perfectly. Go.'

As she left, she glanced back and saw him curse and throw his cap into the corner.

CHAPTER 39

The next morning Eliška and Hynek waited outside the colonel's door. The soldier once more refused to admit them, but at that moment Zarviš was about to enter and he decided to ask the colonel. Eliška spurred herself for the task. Vendula let the two come into the room. She was sitting at the head of the table and invited them to sit down but they elected to remain standing.

'Zarviš said it was very important and you had to speak to me directly,' the colonel said. 'But I've a feeling I know what it is. You think the execution of that criminal was extreme? You think I should've expelled him. The simple reason is, I needed to impress on everyone that the New Way is real.'

'It was unnecessary,' Eliška said.

'Wrong, it was more than needed. The evidence was overwhelming.'

'It proved nothing.'

'If you've come to preach, I'll get these soldiers to show you the door.'

'No, Vendula,' Eliška said, striking a more conciliatory tone, 'we've not come for that, but rather to persuade.'

'Oh?'

'We're lucky in Otočka. But can we keep it?' Hynek said.

'What do you mean?' said the colonel.

'Things change and we can't expect the same as before the crisis. But those three words are just a slogan, not a rule book. If we are a state, the law should be clear.'

'The rules are clear. More will come, when they are needed,' the colonel said.

'Forgive me, Colonel, but what exactly is unity? Is the fact that we are human not unifying enough? Or is something more required?'

'Something more of course.'

'What exactly?'

'A sense of duty to each other,' Zarviš interrupted and shared a knowing look with the colonel.

'You take too much on your shoulders,' Eliška said.

'And I suppose you want to relieve me of some of it,' the colonel said.

'No. Why not a council of soldiers and villagers? They needn't have any power but to advise. You said that there should no longer be any army or villager, only Otočkan. Well, if you are not a colonel, what is your position?'

'She is like a World Mother,' Zarviš said.

Eliška was startled and couldn't say a word.

'You'll understand it in time,' Zarviš continued. 'This movement isn't just about our village.' He made an excited little jump. 'We model the New Way, codify it, then we spread it outside. We even found a printing press in a little museum. Of course, we'll need to send some soldiers out as messengers. Even through this way, we may only make one other Otočka in our lifetimes.'

'Like a virus,' Hynek said.

Zarviš smiled briefly. 'If you like.'

'Vendula, I'm pleading with you. Don't go down this path.'

'It's strange to hear you talk as though you don't want to help people on the outside.'

'Not at the cost of this village.'

'So now you're a doctor with a border.'

'Stop.'

'I won't. And if you really can't get on board, then you'll have to consider your place in this village. My duty is to the well-being.'

'Is that a threat?'

'Don't stand in my way, Eliška. If you really want to influence us, take the oath. I'll still give you a commission, even after your appalling behaviour. You'll be a part of the meetings.

You should be. I'll give you a room in this house. You'll have a section of soldiers under you. You can use the medicine as you like. What do you want? I could get it for you. Take the oath and you can have your way.'

'And if not.'

'I won't stop you leaving.'

Eliška stared, hoping, but the moment passed. 'It's my medical opinion, Vendula, that you are mentally unstable and unfit. And I say that for Zarviš too.'

The colonel exploded into a rage. 'Unfit? There would be no Otočka without me and the army. Unfit?' She drew out her pistol and aimed it at Eliška.

'Calm. Calm,' Hynek said and raised his hand to stop the colonel doing anything rash. But she seethed, her lips pressed tight, her eyes glaring deep.

'I won't be scared by you, Vendula,' Eliška said.

'Colonel, we'll go. We won't bother you anymore,' Hynek said.

But Eliška would not to be cowed. The colonel aimed the gun above Eliška's head and pulled the trigger. The shot blasted her ears.

'Get out,' the colonel said, deadpan.

Hynek gently pulled Eliška away.

'Don't forget you're not exempt from being sent to the tree too,' the colonel added.

Eliška looked back from the door; for a second she thought she saw some hope. But it disappeared. Nothing could be done.

*

'This place is sick.' Ludmila was sitting on a pew and staring into middle distance.

'It's worse out there,' Petra said with certainty. In her hand was a set of rosary beads.

'I can't take it anymore.'

276

'It's the sound of the gun that gets me.'

'It's all these speeches that I can't stand,' Anton said. 'Too many words.'

'I can't stand it anymore,' Ludmila shouted and paced towards the altar. Then she tittered and pulled her hair before screaming. 'I can't—' She collapsed into a heap.

Little Nada gaped. Eliška got to her feet to help her. Ludmila was laughing and crazed. There's no turning back, Eliška thought. From the corner of her eye, she noticed someone beckoning by the archway that led to the back door. She at once recognised the uniform. After helping Ludmila into a pew, she hurried over to Captain Nebojsa, who retreated into the corridor.

'I don't want to be seen through the windows. Make sure everyone here doesn't say a word about my being here.'

'I understand,' she said.

The captain looked worried. 'I heard what happened. I've just been to see her and told her Zarviš must be expelled. There was an argument and I lost. She listens only to him now. Do you know what she's done?'

'What?'

'She has fed the body to the pigs.'

Eliška knotted her brow.

'And I'm certain he was innocent. The whole thing was a show. And she'll only release Marek if he takes the oath, which he refuses. I came here because I woke up this morning wondering what she would do if the murderer kills again. There would have to be another execution, another victim.'

'She must be removed from power.'

'I would never convince Captain Železný. I don't know with Bradáč if he's for her or not. No, an officer's coup won't work.'

'What about the soldiers? What do they think?'

'Some of them, maybe. But that's an even worse risk. If we appeal to them, pull them to our side but misjudge them, both of us would be sent out or to the oak tree. No, Doctor, I'm afraid there may only be one option.'

277

'Kill her?'

He nodded. 'I'm sorry.'

Eliška leant against the wall and nodded slowly. 'Truth is, I've been thinking the same thing. A doctor contemplating murder! But if it must be, if there's nothing else that can be done.'

'She's your sister.'

Eliška walked to the other wall and looked down. 'Even so.'

'I thought you would be against it.'

'Maybe there are other ways. I hope there are. But if we have to do it, I agree.'

Hynek appeared in the archway and joined them. 'To kill is a terrible thing,' Hynek said.

'We may have no choice,' she said.

'It's a bad thing. When we look into the eye of someone else, we see ourselves. Part of us dies, too, in such an act.'

'But there may be no other choice,' she reiterated with more intensity.

'We should use the power we have – words. Her fight is with ideas.'

'She doesn't listen,' Eliška said.

'I'm convinced it's Zarviš. If we just get rid of Zarviš,' Nebojsa said.

'No, it *is* her,' Eliška said.

'If we tell ourselves there's always a way, it must also mean the same for the colonel too,' said Hynek.

'You told me people don't change,' Eliška replied.

'I said they do and they don't.'

She threw her arms up.

'We could get Zarviš expelled?' Nebojsa suggested.

She shook her head. 'No. It would still leave her in charge. There'll be more expelled and more for the oak tree, and us dithering about it only delays the time when we'll really have to do something. If we are going to take a risk, it must be for something that's got a ghost of a chance of working.'

Hynek scratched his beard. The captain paced about.

278

'I think you're right,' Nebojsa said. 'I think you're right. But if the attempt should fail... I'm afraid it won't just be us, but everyone in this church will probably get it.'

'Then we must be certain,' she said.

'I've a thought. Manoeuvres. I could take my company into the woods to practise ambush drills. I could even get Bradáč's company. It's about a hundred and fifty soldiers.'

'How would that help?'

'It would mean half of the army would be in the woods during any attempt.'

'Attempt?' Hynek said.

'Yes. If it fails, we could try to rally the soldiers to us,' Nebojsa said.

'We could leave,' Eliška said. 'You could take some soldiers and we could get some of the villagers together and leave. The colonel wouldn't stop us.'

'Doctor, I've been on forages outside the fence. There's no way forty or so people could survive. We've got to make this place work.'

'The captain's right. Running away only makes other problems. Worse ones. Whatever we do, it must be done in Otočka. I've been here all my life. I won't leave.'

Eliška paced about, then stopped. She slowly nodded.

*

In the priest's room, Viktor took Iva's book and read.

He got up to mischief sometimes but never gave me a reason to hate him. I know if I wasn't his mother, I would like him. I have wondered.

'Wondered? What? Why'd you stop writing?'

She took the book again.

I have looked into those large watery eyes and wondered if it wasn't a saint looking back at me.

'A saint?' He screwed his face up sceptically, then smiled.

279

He's not like other boys. His anger never had any bite. And my leaving was worse. Yes, he has a right to be angry, but I know he wouldn't be. My only wish is to die in the soft hug of his forgiveness. Let my hand clasp those tender fingers. Oh God, let me hear his voice. Let me hold him.

Viktor read and his look of disdain changed. Iva writhed and clutched the sheets, gasping. She knotted her brow and punched the bed. She leant up, tried to get up. But Viktor held her. Embraced her. Leant his cheek on hers. Kissed her. Held her head.

'She suddenly left one day,' he said.

Iva clasped him, felt his body slacken. She held him up with what strength she had. Her hand held the back of his head as his forehead weighed on her shoulder. It was heavy, and yet like sunlight.

'I was alone in the house. She never came back.'

She took his head between his hands. There were no freckles to kiss, only his wrinkled brow and the knot of grief between his eyes.

'Don't leave him on his own. Not on his own.'

She held him up, squeezed him, turned his weight upon himself and closed her eyes, and felt the thin-legged boy; saw him on his bicycle; pulled him up when he lost his balance; brushed the dusty earth off his cheeks; kissed the scratches.

'He ain't afraid,' he said. His head shot up, eyes clear. 'Because he knows she will come.'

Iva moaned.

'He ain't afraid because she's here already.'

She squeezed him with all her might.

'You didn't leave. You stayed.' His cloudy eyes teared. 'You stayed.'

She closed her eyes.

'I won't let you go. Not now.'

It *was* Šimon, she thought.

'Don't leave me.' His plangent voice was sucked into silence.

She looked up to see Eliška standing by the bed. Viktor flinched at being surprised. As he let her go, the doctor took her pulse. Viktor wiped his eyes with his sleeve.

*

Hynek opened the door and Eliška bustled in.

'Two days.'

'Two days? It's too soon.'

'Vendula won't let him do the manoeuvres tomorrow as she is planning some celebration. It has to be two days. It needs to be soon.'

Hynek had a folded square of silk in his hand and as he came to the table, he put it down. 'But to kill them?'

'It may not come to that,' she said.

'Let's hope not. And then what?'

'We'll cross that bridge when we get there.'

'You're not confident?'

'It depends so much on convincing the soldiers.'

'What's another way?'

'There's no other way.'

'No. There's always another way, only we're too ignorant and blind to see it.' He began unfolding the silk while still looking at Eliška.

'Until then, this is the best we can do.'

'Yes, I know. That's the problem.' Hynek looked down at the opened silk and covered the table with it. It was a kind of symbol of a flower.

'In two days, he will take his soldiers to the… to the…' She looked down at the flower.

'To the woods?' Hynek finished the sentence.

Eliška was transfixed by the image. 'That's incredible! It can't be!'

'What?' he said.

Eliška pointed at the flower.

281

'This?' he said. 'I found it in the attic. The Resource Commission never bothered to look there. I've had it for a long time.'

She stepped back, then looked up in fright. 'This was in my dream. This exact image.'

'Dream?'

She pointed at it again. It was a square and in the centre was a purple-petaled flower with golden beams stretching out. There were four quadrants, each with its own colour surrounding the flower, in the middle of which was a white eye. The whole was surrounded by a black border. 'When I was sick, I dreamt this. Exactly the same. The colours are the same. Everything. Top right corner, red. Bottom left, blue. Top left, yellow. Bottom right, green. What does this mean?'

Hynek scratched his beard. 'I've never quite understood it, but when I first saw it on my travels in southern India, I had to have it. It made me stop. It hung from the seller's marquee, waving in the grey-orange haze of the eastern sun. I bought it at once. But it's just a coincidence. Nothing more.'

'Why did you put it on the table just now?' The more she stared at it the more unreal it became. She touched it and the reality of it hit her at once.

'I don't know.'

They gazed at the image. Eliška felt it flood up and become alive to her. It breathed.

'Perhaps it's meant for you,' Hynek said.

She felt ghostly. 'It is light,' she uttered vacantly, not understanding what she was saying.

'What was that?' Hynek said.'

But she just stared, and they were silent.

CHAPTER 40

In the early evening of the next day, smoke rose and fat spat in several fires on the field. Some animals had been butchered, and only the army and the Real Otočkans could indulge in the feast that followed. A cheap offer was made to the Ditherers: 'Take the oath and you can have some of the feast too.'

None of them accepted.

The Resource Commission had set up a table with the last of Tibor's liquor and a strict ration was dished out. The colonel called it a celebration of victory over the Great Virus, only possible with the New Way. They ate and drank, and the noise of their lively conversations reached the church. There the Ditherers watched from windows. The whisky was being carefully poured. Zarviš had asked Anton if he would play and offered him some if he would, but he refused. Helena also watched the feast with a dour face.

Behind the platform on the west side, a curtain had been erected, behind which were some of the soldiers dressed up. When he was satisfied, and everyone had eaten, Zarviš stepped onto the platform and called for silence. Then for shouts of hoorah, which were followed by a little speech. It was more an encomium to the colonel. He went on to say that this marked day one of a new calendar: 'A new beginning.'

He mentioned *unity* many times, *stability* more still and *certainty* the most. And though it was a surprise to see Zarviš making the speech, and the colonel on the field among her troops, they warmed to it. Finally, he was pleased to announce that there would be a little entertainment, a play celebrating the occasion and acted by soldiers. The play was called *The Circle is the Heart* by Zarviš Olejník. Without adieu he left the stage and two soldiers mounted, one wearing several strips of yellow trouser on his head, representing a wig. The other, a woman soldier, wore a skirt. On their back were large white circles. The audience clapped and laughed at the sight. Then the play began.

WOMAN: I'm so happy. Today is the anniversary of the day the fence went up. The day we turned the tide on the Great Virus – Otočka Day.
MAN: I love it. It's better than Christmas. I always feel... I don't know... full of life.
WOMAN: It is the day we stopped it. We kept it out.
MAN: Happy time. Everything is just—

Man turns away overwhelmed.

WOMAN: Just simple.
MAN: We've come through the chaos and into the circle.

They pause in a moment of euphoria. Then the woman turns sharply on the man.

WOMAN: And what a disgrace you are! Don't think I've forgotten, just because it's Otočka Day. Don't think you can be so easily forgiven.
MAN: But, honey, I didn't mean to.
WOMAN: To lose your circle...
MAN: I didn't mean to. I've looked everywhere.
WOMAN: Cut from the same cloth as the colonel's!

Woman becomes tearful.

MAN: I did make a new one. It isn't the cloth that matters, it's the circle.
WOMAN: And to lose the second one! How could you do it?

[The crowd in the field groaned.]

MAN: I know I had it somewhere. I had it this morning.
WOMAN: And on Otočka Day! You're hopeless.

She turns away.

MAN: I had it this morning. I swear I did.

Man looks around the stage.

WOMAN: One of these days you're going to end up a Ditherer.
    You better find it before the colonel comes.
MAN: I will. Now think, I know I had it this morning. Definitely.
    We had breakfast. Then I chopped the wood. Then we…
    oh…

Man turns to audience with a knowing and suggestive look.

    [The audience laughed.]

*The woman turns to audience embarrassed and pulls out of her
pockets two red circles. She puts them to her cheeks imitating
blushes*

WOMAN: And after we…

She puts red circles to her cheeks again.

MAN: I don't remember.
WOMAN: But seriously. Think.

*Man and woman both look around the stage hunting for the lost
white circle. At this moment three characters appear on the
stage. They are dressed each in a separate colour and with faces
painted. Respectively they are green, blue and orange. On their*

285

heads they wear different objects. They mount the stage and begin to do somersaults, cartwheels and forward rolls. They jump and caper about.

[Some soldiers in the audience joked about the soldiers playing the roles.]

The three characters seem invisible to the man and woman on the stage. While the other two are still capering about, the orange one, whose name is Division, addresses the audience. On his head are two horns, like a devil.

DIVISION: I am Division. I split everything. First him and her; then they against them; then the good you from the real you. What you love, you must not have. What is right, must not be. I keep the river between east and west. I make categories. You go in one, she in another. I make friends angry. They won't see eye to eye. I keep the rich rich and the poor poor. I put the cat with the pigeons. I am Division. I never stop. But I have friends.

The other two are caressing the man and woman, who are still unaware of their presence and continue to look for the missing white circle. The blue figure, Instability, comes front of stage as Division now performs a little dance by standing between man and woman and pushing each apart. They cannot see the force that keeps them from each other. Instability wears a hat with waves, representing the ocean. He does not stand still.

INSTABILITY: I am Instability. I am, yet I am not. Where did your life go? Your job? Your world? I make the earth like the ocean. What you want, I pull away. You build a house, I foreclose. You have a wife, I divorce you. You have savings, I tank the market. You have a house, it was burned. Family? They left you. You walk on earth? It

286

becomes a swamp. You want to stand still? I keep you moving. You build something? It's already broken. And the future? Hope? Surely not. No way.

Instability cartwheels and twists off and caresses the woman as the green figure comes stage front. He is Uncertainty, and is wearing a green upside-down question mark for a hat. He makes some wild gestures, wide-eyes, and gibberish talk for some time. Then he speaks.

UNCERTAINTY: I am Uncertainty. It's true, isn't it, that it's up? But is it? Maybe it's down. It looks safe, then you die. How? I know, but I don't speak your language. I love to confound. What you think is good, isn't. Moral acts write law, and moral acts destroy law. One and one is two, but sometimes it isn't. You feel secure, then something happens. You are sure, then everything changes. I put fear and doubt about what you take for granted, because behind each corner, a maniac is waiting for a quick rape. There are so many horrible things that can occur. Anything could happen. You never know.

Uncertainty forward rolls and skips towards the man and begins to whisper in his ear. Division is still pushing them apart. Instability pushes the back of the woman's knees, so she loses balance.

MAN: I am hopeless.
WOMAN: Unbelievable! To lose one circle is a misfortune; but to lose two is…
MAN: It must have been when we… ah…

Woman puts red circles to face, then addresses audience.

WOMAN: Don't laugh. He's not up to much these days. Keeps

287

talking as though he's Goliath. But it's more like David with gout and asthma.

[The audience jeered and laughed at the soldier playing the man's part.]

MAN: Is that all you can think of? We've survived the worst crisis in history. We've triumphed. We've said, 'enough is enough'. There are more important things than…

Red circles. Then they continue to look for the missing white circle. Meanwhile another character mounts the stage. On his head is half of a soccer ball, coloured purple, with twigs sticking out of it uniformly. His face and neck are crayoned purple with black dots. He wears a bin liner over his back as if a cape. The man and woman equally don't perceive him. He stands foremost.

THE GREAT VIRUS: I am Amazonian River Fever. I am the Great Virus. I like people. Some people call me Delirium. Some people call me the plague. I don't care. You can call me what you like. I call myself lucky.

He turns to the man and woman.

Hello… a two-for-one. They'll infect each other all right. You know there are some bacteria who tell me: 'you shouldn't change so much'. They don't know what they're talking about. They're such snobs with their cellulose structure and their large number of genes. They think us viruses are vagabonds. But who's turned the world upside down? Who's made a revolution? Yes, the stupid, simple virus. Who's laying waste? The smallest things can have the biggest effect. Who brought down the world economy? Me. Me. Me. A mobile phone has more information than I do, but I serve myself, no one else.

288

He strides to the front of stage. He gestures to the audience to come closer and listen to his story.

No one knows much about me. Let us call it... Uncertainty.

At this, Uncertainty drifts over to the Great Virus and stands at his right side.

No one knows how to deal with me. Let us call it... Instability.

At this, Instability drifts to the Great Virus and stands at his left side.

I separate the living from the dead. Let us call it... Division.

At this, Division drifts to the Great Virus and stands behind him.

I spread like lightning. Just the idea of me sends the stock market to the deep. My name alone makes you hysterical. Simply the thought of me sends you locking your doors, as if that will do anything. I possess man because I am simple, and he is complex. I take advantage of the fact people stick together. You can put me in taboo, but I'll jump it. Just the picture of me offends you. And all this happens before I've even touched you. I've many allies: Fear, Stupidity, Panic – not to mention these three.

He indicates the three figures surrounding him.

I'm too fast for you. My advantage is I act; I do not think.

WOMAN: (*to man*) Do you see something? I feel something is
      wrong. There's something wrong.

*Uncertainty gambols over and leads man by the hand to the edge
of the left side of the platform.*

MAN: Something is wrong. How did I get here?

*Man seems confused. Instability capers over to woman and leads
her to the same brink.*

WOMAN: What's happening?

*Division, laughing and clowning and skipping about the stage,
finally joins Instability and Uncertainty. He puts his arms round
the other two and they back up stage right, ready to charge at
man and woman and push them off the stage.*

MAN: I don't know.

*At this point, another character mounts the stage. This female
soldier has several wire brush scrubbers tied to her hair, pulled
as if to imitate curls. She wears military fatigues and a large
white circle on her chest. She is Vendula.*

VENDULA: (*to the man and woman*) Otočkans! Where is your
      courage? Open your eyes.

*They turn. Vendula raises a pole with a carving of a pinecone on
the end of it.*

MAN: I'm sorry, Colonel. I don't know how but I can't find it.
      Give me some time and I will find it.
VENDULA: You're blind. Not to your white circle, but to the
      forces that circle you.

At this point Division, Uncertainty and Instability run at man and woman. Vendula bangs the butt of her staff loudly on the stage and it causes the three to separate as they run. All of them miss the man and woman and their momentum carries them over the edge of the platform and they fall into the river.

[The audience laughed and clapped.]

Then the colonel takes the Great Virus and pulls off the purple half of a soccer ball and throws it into the river.

WOMAN: Look, it's the virus!

The Great Virus, exposed, scurries around until he jumps into the river.

MAN: Look, in the river, I see Division.
WOMAN: And there goes Instability. And there, Uncertainty.
MAN: Did you see that? We saw them after you came, Colonel.
VENDULA: But why didn't you see them earlier? Where were
      your eyes then? You must always have the eye open if you
      want to keep Otočka.

She addresses the audience.

> Constant vigilance. This is the path to the New Way. If
> you're blind, you'll only see when it's too late. Keep the
> eye open. Stay awake!

[Behind the stage Zarviš chanted 'Ven-du-la! Ven-du-la!' Then the audience joined in. This went on for some minutes until it eventually died down. Luděk was the loudest.]

MAN: Yes, Colonel. Yes. I'm sorry, but we were looking for my circle. That's why we didn't see it.

VENDULA: (*to man*) And where's your circle?

Man panics.

> More important than a piece of cloth is what the circle
> means. It's no good looking for a little piece of cotton
> when Division, Instability and Uncertainty lurk. Better to
> stay alert than worry about a piece of cloth. Because it's
> the circle here that matters.

The colonel puts her hand on his heart and feels something.

> What's this?

The man takes off his jacket.

> Your shirt is inside-out.

*The man realises, then takes off his shirt. Turns it inside-out to
reveal the white circle that was touching his heart all the time.*

[There was an 'ooo' from the audience, then cheering.]

> You are a Real Otočkan. More important is the white
> circle inside. Always keep it close to your heart.

*Vendula shakes the man's hand. The woman embraces him as the
Great Virus and the three adversaries rise to the platform and all
characters take their bow. Exeunt Omnes.*

[The audience applauded playfully. After some moments there
was quiet.]

A soldier climbs onto the stage. He stands in the middle and

292

brings his hands to his eyes and scans the horizon. He shrugs and yawns.

SOLDIER: I've been looking for hours. Everyone's asleep. Some owl is making a racket. Nothing's going on. Honestly, it's quite silly. Tonight will be the same as it was last night and the night before. Nothing will happen. (*Yawns*) A quick nap. Ten minutes. Then I'll walk about.

He sits down cross-legged on the stage, bows his head and goes to sleep. Up onto the stage creeps the Great Virus, still wet. The black dots have run streaks down his purple face and neck. He swoops in silently and grabs the soldier from behind, wrapping his arms round him. The soldier wakes in panic.

THE GREAT VIRUS: No point screaming – you're done. I've waited just for this moment. You drop your guard and I pounce.

As the soldier turns to look at the Great Virus, the latter audibly exhales into his face to suggest that he is infecting the soldier. The soldier turns his head back to the audience.

SOLDIER: Help. I feel sick. I…

He goes limp. The Great Virus lays him on the stage, then stands up gloating.

THE GREAT VIRUS: He let down his guard. There is no New Way for him. Only no way.

Turns to audience and bows low, slowly taking something that he had concealed behind his back and under the bin liner cape. He returns to the vertical and shows it. It is a human skull.

Here is Death. This is what happens in a moment, if you don't watch out. Me and Death are good friends. We are close.

He brings it to his face, so they are cheek to cheek.

We never stop.

He strokes it fondly. He kisses its temple.

[Some of the silent audience looked confused. After some time, they wondered what was going on. Zarviš tapped the stage as if reminding the actor about his cue.]

He guffaws intensely. He throws the skull up in the air and catches it. Turns to the audience.

Amazing to think this was once running about and talking and dreaming. Now his role is Death. Doesn't he play it well? Look where he used to see, but now…

[Vendula looked angrily between the actor and Zarviš. The actor's cynical tone seemed unscripted.]

This skull weighs the same as a long novel. Doesn't matter which, the stories all end the same – tragically. Repeating the old mistakes, over and over again.

He walks about the stage whimsically smiling. He stops suddenly.

Is that all it is? Is life nothing more than a novel?

[Zarviš stood on the lower steps of the platform.]

But we shouldn't worry. Oh no, we're OK. We're doing

very well. We know what we're doing. The colonel's leading us into a wonderful future. One where everything will be a garden of roses.

The Great Virus pauses.

But we don't mind killing people to get there, do we! We don't mind sending them behind the tree. Or banishing them. Or feeding them rotting meat. Or starving them. Or beating them. Because when we get to the golden time, no one will suffer. It'll all be worth it.

[Luděk began to cheer and shout in agreement. He didn't seem to grasp the actor's cynicism.]

LUDĚK: Yeah! Whoo! Send them all to the tree. Banish all the Ditherers. Until we're all Real Otočkans, the New Way isn't possible.
THE GREAT VIRUS: Oh, this is not the way, friends. This is not the way at all. We're going downhill.

[Zarviš walked up the steps to the platform.]

And the colonel? She doesn't know everything. Maybe someone in a hundred years will stand here holding her skull and will touch her jaw.

Turns to skull, touches the jaw.

And they will say, 'Where are your speeches now? Your dreams? Your circles? Your visions that had roused? What? Nothing? Not a word?'

[In the silence, Zarviš quickly came up behind the actor and booted him in the back. The actor fell off the stage and onto the field; the skull flew up out of his hand and landed nearby. Vendula immediately ordered several soldiers to arrest the actor. The actor looked up innocently at Zarviš's seething face looking down. If there had been any doubts in the audience as to whether this was part of the play or not, there were no longer.]

It's only a joke.

ZARVIŠ: No one's laughing.

CHAPTER 41

The next item in the ceremony came at twilight. Forty sticks, each wrapped with cotton as flambeaux, were soaking in a large metal container full of kerosene. Soldiers had also been busy stacking wood in the middle of the field in what was to be a great bonfire. But the chief object of interest was a large effigy. It was about ten feet tall and made of various bric-à-brac that filled a basic wooden frame. It was wrapped tightly in some white plastic sheets, on which logos were stuck, painted or drawn. There were dozens and dozens of company logos and symbols from the Old World such as public information icons, scientific symbols, emojis, etc. Circling its left eye, was the alchemical symbol for Venus, and round the right, Mars. Across its painted mouth was written *Logos*. On top of its head was a large, brimmed hat, made from a black cloth round a plastic bucket. On it, painted in white, were the symbols of the three main monotheisms. Underneath, painted smaller, were the lesser religions. On one hand was the dollar symbol; on the other was the flag of the United Nations. Painted at the bottom of its left leg was an electricity pylon. On the right was an image of a combustion engine. On the crotch was a crude computer processor chip. On the reverse side, the only thing of note amongst the profusion of advertising was the end of a pipe, dripping the last oil.

Once the wood was stacked and the effigy was put on top and some fireworks placed around, Zarviš nodded to the colonel and there was quiet. He stood next to the flag bearer, and both were backlit by the cooking fires.

'Tonight, we become New People.' He looked up at the flag with a gentle face, then suddenly pointed and scowled at the effigy.

'But you! You! You are guilty of the worst crimes. You stole

297

meaning from man. You kept him from his divine purposes. You degraded his soul and turned him into a commodity. You kept him from reaching his true self. His ultimate freedom. You made him utterly mindless and dependent. But no more. Not in the New Way. No, instead we will raise man where he should be' – he looked up – 'into the sublime.' He smiled. Suddenly he looked down, pointing to the effigy. 'But you! All the crimes are on you. Now you will take them with you. Your world is over.'

The soldiers and Real Otočkans watching burst into cheers and applause. Once it had died down, Zarviš gave a signal, and a rehearsed ritual began. In the fading light, four soldiers emerged from behind the curtain with already lit flambeaux. They mounted the platform and the flag bearer moved into the centre of the platform while the four soldiers each occupied one corner. Zarviš made another signal and a soldier wearing a regiment drum walked solemnly to the space in front of the platform on the east side. He played a slow single drumbeat and four soldiers on the field took four flambeaux from the metal container. The torch-bearer stage left lowered his flambeau and the four soldiers lit theirs from it. Then they went with an even ceremonial march step, the drummer following behind, and began to make a circuit round the assembled soldiers and Real Otočkans. They returned to the platform; the drum rolled and stopped. The colonel in the meantime had mounted the platform.

'We know that in front of us is the New Way, in us the burning flames and behind us the weary thousands who see the light.'

The colonel saluted and the flag bearer shouted, 'Unity! Stability! Certainty!' The entire army and Real Otočkans repeated the same in unison. With one voice, they roared it out again, 'Unity! Stability! Certainty!' And again. And again.

*

When darkness came the drummer struck a march beat. The trees loomed eerily, and the church became a screen for long shadows of flame and man. The smell of kerosene was pungent as the smoke rose. The drum rolled and stopped; thirty-six soldiers came forward and each took the remaining flambeaux from the kerosene container. Once again, they lit them from a flame on stage. The drum started again, a solemn march, and the thirty-six formed a single line, widely spaced. The light from this made the giant effigy glimmer. They proceeded to do a circuit of everyone as before. On the wall of the church were the shadows of marching legs. They stopped. The crowd were all in flamelight. They seemed in awe of the ritual. Luděk looked up at the illumined flag, now back on the platform. He saluted and trembled as though possessed. The drummer struck a new beat, a quick march. The flambeaux bearers then marched straight to the effigy. The drummer stopped. The flag bearer on the platform, then lowered the ensign and the thirty-six at once put their torches to the wood. Soon it was alight. The flag bearer waved the flag enthusiastically in the shape of the symbol for infinity. The drummer started again; the thirty-six then marched and stood at even points round the assembled.

Shortly, the feet of the effigy were in flames.

Soon the fire had burned up all the iconography.

'We are really part of something,' a soldier said to another.

'Unity! Stability! Certainty!' Zarviš, appearing almost rabid, shouted. 'Unity! Stability! Certainty!'

The chorus echoed.

'Unity! Stability! Certainty!' Zarviš screamed at them and the fire.

'Unity! Stability! Certainty!' They chorused back as the drummer beat the syllables. The smoke billowed up and sparks shot up from the effigy as it buckled.

'The old is finished! We have done it! We have done it.' He jumped and screeched. The Real Otočkans were now given the signal to perform their part of the ceremony. At the foot of each Real Otočkan was an object that they had prepared earlier, an object representing something from the Old World. Now they lined up in single file, holding their objects and proceeded to the bonfire. The first in line was Luděk and he held a small radio. He threw it into the fire and then stood apart. Next was Štěpánka, who had a vegetable blender. As this was happening, the army began to sing the 'Song of Otočka'. The next villager tossed in a laptop. The next, a vacuum cleaner. The flambeaux waved side to side in unison. Into the fire went an electric kettle, several mobile phones, wallets, money, a microwave, several toys.

Inside the church, Anton watched from a window. Now he brought the violin to his neck to play for himself, not for those outside nor their ideas. And not a march of triumph as Zarviš wanted, but a lament. He played the Andante from Bach's Harpsichord Concerto No.4 in G major BWV 1049. Stately, melancholic, falling, even as the fireworks shot up and flashed.

Ludmila stood pale as the light of the colourful fireworks flared on her vacant face. Eliška sat, half in shadow. Hynek stood by the altar, looking down.

Beside Anton at the window, František gazed at the scene outside – firelight and green and red fireworks flashed on his chipped glasses.

'It will fail,' František said slowly. 'Time will wreak havoc on it. In a changing universe there can be no stability. Between night and day, no unity. And with life teetering before death, nothing certain. It is a whirlpool, a fever. And the little fire they hold will not light the world. Trillions of stars and the universe is still dark. All their labour and ideas are a fantasy trying to cheat nothing and conquer the night. But only nothing beats nothing. Nothing defeats all.'

Anton stopped. Someone wept.

CHAPTER 42

By morning, Karl's eyes were bloodshot. '*Die Blume,*' he uttered.

Šimon was falling asleep, with the stick for a fan still in his hand. *It would help your friend; a flower on the box* – he remembered František's words.

'*Ich sehe die Blume,*' Karl whispered.

The fan fell out of Šimon's hand as he imagined a flower on a box. He heard the ex-sergeant grunt and opened his eyes slightly to see the soldier unbutton his own shirt, rub his chest and curse. He scratched several red spots on his collar bone. Šimon heard the private's footsteps, and the ex-sergeant quickly began to button his shirt.

'He's not looking good,' the private said as he walked back from the river. The ex-sergeant quickly fumbled in his topmost button.

'There may be a chance,' the ex-sergeant said, 'if we send the boy back in for the doctor.'

Šimon shut his eyes.

'It's too risky,' the private said.

'We've no choice.'

'What can the doctor do?'

'We've run out of medicine.'

'Already?'

Šimon opened his eyes slightly, then closed them when he saw the ex-sergeant look at him.

'He's awake,' the ex-sergeant said. 'Šimon, Šimon. Wake him up.'

Šimon felt someone shaking him. He opened his eyes and saw the private.

'He's worse. You must go get the doctor,' the ex-sergeant said. 'He needs more medicine.'

Šimon understood. He looked at Karl with his glossy eyes and it seemed to the boy that the sick man approved. He got up and waited for Karl to say something. But he didn't.

'Goodbye,' Šimon whispered to him and ran. František's words came back to him. *It would help your friend. Something that everyone is looking for. Hidden. A flower.* He stopped suddenly. He realised what František meant. His eyes shone. 'The cave.'

He passed the fence and into the woods, then crossed the clearing. He kept thinking about František's words and walked without paying too much attention to where he was going. He stopped. Something wasn't right. There was no path. He looked around but didn't recognise anything.

He retraced his steps. It led him further into a part of the woods he hadn't seen before. He had a vague notion of the direction he had come from and so headed that way. It led him to a creek, which was unfamiliar. Recognising no way behind him, he decided to follow the creek. It came to a slope. As he went down it, he lost his footing and tumbled. When he rolled to the bottom, he hit something hard and cut his cheek. He rose slowly, then continued to follow the creek, which led to an open field. It was surprising to see a road, long disused and taken over by weeds and long grass. The road led to a ruined factory with a smokestack and faded red-and-white stripes. He approached. Glass, bits of brick and concrete were strewn. He went inside the hole that used to serve for a door. A section of the roof had collapsed, and inside was a scene of dark, musty and mouldy decay, heavy with the odour of damp earth. Not a single pane of glass remained intact and in places on the ground was bare earth or rotting wood at angles with bent rusty nails and electrical wire. The stucco had mostly peeled off the brick and rusted tools lay about. In one corner, shrubs had taken over. There were several old diamond-shaped metal signs half buried in the ground and moss had covered an entire windowsill. Large cobwebs, long abandoned, had turned brown. At the far end was a kind of anteroom, which was lighter as it had some white tiles on its walls.

He detected another smell, that of rotting vegetation. He heard a scurrying sound. A shuffling. Then a knocking sound.

Then coughing.

Šimon flinched when he heard a man's mumbling voice coming from the anteroom. He poised, ready to run out, but stopped himself. The man must be someone from the village, he thought. He should know the way there. Šimon's hands trembled as he held onto the brick wall. He took several decided steps away from the building until he halted. *Be brave,* his mother's voice sounded in his head. He looked back. 'He must know the way to the village.' Fortifying himself, he stepped towards the building. He breathed deep before entering and, careful to avoid the nails, trod towards the anteroom. He had to climb over a jumble of broken timbers, which creaked. The man mumbled again and Šimon gaped. He clambered down the pile and stood at the entrance and peered. It was a room that used to be toilets. The coughing started again, and Šimon shivered as he saw a man flat on his belly, crawling across the bare earth. He retreated, then heard the man hiss like a snake.

Be brave. His mother's voice sounded again.

He breathed deep, then craned his neck round the wall. The man was wearing a business suit jacket, utterly soiled over a torn yellow shirt. His jeans were dirty and greasy. His face was ruddy, dirty, oily and stubbled. His cheeks were sunken and so were his green eyes, which emitted a flashing, mad keenness. He hissed again, poked out his tongue and then growled like a dog and mewed like a cat. Then laughed. Šimon stared as the man smiled and revealed some missing teeth. Šimon wanted to retreat but his feet seemed stuck. The man wriggled again like a snake towards some floorboards at the far end of the room, then spun round and sat up cross-legged. On the floorboards by the wall were a torn blanket, plastic bags filled with faded toys, a set of Russian dolls lined up from biggest to smallest, bottles, cardboard, and a radio with a broken antenna. On some of the filthy white wall tiles above where the urinals used to be, were drawings, hieroglyphs, numbers and line graphs. Instead of urinals there were rusted pipe ends reeking of ammonia. There was no roof and flies darted about. The man grinned and put his thumb to his ear and his little finger to his mouth, imitating a phone.

'Now! Ten thousand on Hitachi. Seven thou on Tata Group. Sell the twenty-five on Xerox, they're falling, falling – are you there Dušan? Yeah, that's right, like the girls in Ibiza. Hang on I got a business call... right tell me... no I don't know what's going on with BNFP! It's all up and down, like a whore's drawers. Tell your client to ditch the twenty-five, for the moment, but keep the other in case the Hong Kong boys do a Hang Seng special... hello? Are you there? Fucking phones.' He started shaking his hand and poking it as if it were a real phone.

Šimon breathed deep and put a foot into the room. 'Do you know where the village is?' His heart pounded.

'Information? Information. She knows.' He pointed to the Russian dolls. 'Let's ask the hers.' He lurched onto the dirt and grabbed the smallest Russian doll. '*Babushka* No. 1...' He looked inside. 'Nothing.' He opened the second biggest. '*Babushka* No. 2... nothing.' Then the next. '*Babushka* No. 3... nothing... *Babushka* No. 4... nothing.' He proceeded with great solemnity to the last and biggest. 'Now this her has never failed yet. This her has never predicted it wrong.' He opened it and looked in and gasped. 'Yes, here it is. Here's the answer.' He put his hand in, then gingerly pulled it out, with his fingers pointing down. He suddenly rotated his hand with only the middle finger pointing up. He cackled and jumped around like a chimpanzee, kicking himself off the walls and straight into the dirt where he rolled about with the finger still extended.

Šimon clutched his hands to his chest and reared back in fear. 'God.'

The man laughed even louder. His foot kicked up one of the floorboards sending several Babushkas flying.

304

'There's no God, but do you want a chick? I know a girl. She's no looker. Come on, dude. What's with that innocent face?'

'There's a doctor—'

'Doctor? Doctor? Yankee Pharma? German Pharma? Nah, they never delivered!'

Šimon retreated to the corner and a rusty bolt hit him in the small of his back. He winced.

'This is rock bottom, kid.' The man slapped the ground, then dug some earth up and threw it at the urinals.

Šimon held one hand on his lower back and looked up at the blue sky. 'Oh God. He's so sick.'

'Sick? Nah dude. Market always recovers.'

Šimon looked down. 'Please, where's the village.'

'Follow the current, see the wave. And then when the time is right' – he clapped his hands making Šimon flinch – 'you strike. Predator-prey – no rules – a win's a win.' The man then took a plastic bag and emptied it on the bare earth. Out of it fell a great heap of small bones, similar to a pheasant's.

'The village—'

'The village – colonel. Ten thousand batches to the army units. Twenty euros a piece – Israelis paid sixty – good investment – Norwegian University – partly made with a flower, or some shit – opens gates – colonel, lying bitch – ah, wait.' He jumped suddenly to the wall and with an index finger scanned the line graphs and numbers, as if calculating something. He tapped the pipes of a urinal and his forehead alternately in some kind of thinking ritual, then turned to the boy.

'Yes! Buy two hundred thousand in the New Way. Then tell the boys in Singapore to pull out of the Chinese. Put money on our guy. Finance Zarviš.' He looked back at the mass of drawings and lines on the tiled wall. 'Look at it. Finally, the market's looking good – back Zarviš. Back Zarviš!'

Šimon saw a bloody knife on the ground near the bones. From another plastic bag the man pulled out the shirt and coat of some military fatigues and threw them on the ground. They had dried blood on them.

'PRE-DAT-TOR!' The man's head shook as he laughed.

Šimon steadied himself with one hand against the wall. His eyes were fixed on the blood-stained knife.

The man hissed, then leapt at Šimon, who reeled back against the wall.

'It happened like this,' the man said. 'First, pleasure – cruise ship – Bahamas – girls – party. Virus? Problem? Nah, big brains will figure it. Buy Novartis, Pfizer – government bonds – then yacht cruise – Majorca – Black Sea – cocaine – Bunga Bunga in Tuscany – lockdown? – hysteria – plummeting interest rates – a week in Bangkok. Who cares if they're not eighteen? – borders closed? No flights? Fake news – jacuzzi, Moroccan girls – dollar won't run – dollar is running? – confidence! – buy bonds. Fed'll back it – Dow, FTSE, Nikkei down? – down? – it'll come back – Barbados, jacuzzi – empty shelves? – triple lockdown? No milk? – confidence – where's it going? – I am the wave. This is money – false panic – false panic – ration card? No vodka? – wait, wait, it'll turn. It always does. Then boom time, Capri, Bermuda, Ferrari – no, it can't be falling again – quick buy gold – gold, gold, gold – I am gold – bubbly jacuzzi – no gold? ' He fell to his knees. 'No electricity? – no petrol? – no trade – no money? – no yachts, booze, girls – Dow, FTSE, Nikkei down, down, down – out – game over – lights out – market closed, ding, ding, ding – civilisation over – down to the ground – down and dirty, baby, whoo, whoo, whoo – whoo whoo.'

The man planted his face in the earth.

Šimon's eyes were closed tight as he pressed his two balled fists to the sides of his mouth. He heard strange sounds and as he slowly opened his eyes, saw the man eating dirt. He shovelled more dirt into his mouth and cackled. Šimon put his hands over his own mouth. The man shot to his feet and grabbed the knife and brandished it at Šimon. Dirt fell out of his mouth.

'You've been doing some insider trading, haven't you? Yes, you have. Yes, yes, yes, yes, yes, yes. You have. Don't deny it.

Don't deny it. Yes, yes, yes, yes, yes. You're done now. Your rates have been falling for a long time, buddy. Time to cash in your bonds.'

Šimon shook his head but the man grabbed him by the scruff of his neck.

'Starting a little syndicate? Trying to undersell? I'll teach you. I'll give you market forces!'

'Please...' Tears streamed, but the man had forced Šimon's face into the remains of a urinal. Šimon resisted but the man was too strong.

He rammed Šimon's head against the metal pipe. The boy screamed as a tooth fell out and his mouth bled. 'You broke the system!' He then thrust Šimon's face down into the bare earth. 'Broken!' The man brought Šimon's head up and shovelled dirt into his mouth. He took the knife and held it against Šimon's throat. 'Tell me why I shouldn't?'

Šimon's vision blurred. He raised his fingers to plead.

'Why shouldn't I? I've done it before.'

His fingers reached for the man's knife-bearing hand. The man swung Šimon's hand away and shook the knife. The boy drew back, his face taut with fear; his eyes begged. 'Don't hurt me.' His voice was weak.

'Why not, little boy? Why shouldn't I cut you up? Predator-prey.'

Šimon put his fingers on the man's chest as tears cleared trails down his dirty face. 'I'm sorry.' Šimon's forehead wrinkled in pain.

Šimon felt the blade press on his neck. His brows rose and lips trembled. Blood from the fallen tooth trickled down his chin, which twitched. 'I'm... scared...'

'Only prey fear.'

'God...'

The man pulled Šimon's head up sharply. The boy gasped and couldn't move.

'Fear made it all crash, boy. No fear, no crash.' The man

307

shouted the last.

Šimon slowly brought his hands together as he looked at the clouded sky. He muttered, his quivering lips were sticky from the blood.

'Spit it out,' the man shouted.

'... Cure...'

'Cure? What are you talking about?'

'Mama,' Šimon screamed.

The man hissed.

'Please' – Šimon's hands knitted together – 'I'm sorry.'

'Praying?'

'Be brave.'

'Brave? Ha!'

'I tried—'

Šimon felt the knife press. He closed his eyes. He wanted to call out, 'Mama,' but his lips couldn't move. He hung his head.

'You're a nothing, coward, little boy.'

Šimon suddenly felt as though possessed. A strange peace and calm soothed him. A tranquillity coursed through him, like a kind of spirit. He opened his eyes and gazed ahead. Everything went quiet and he felt all the light focus at a single point on the wall. He shook his head.

'No... I'm not afraid.' He slowly looked up at the man and said softly, 'I'm not afraid of you.'

The man scowled. He squeezed Šimon's neck, and though the boy winced in pain, he soon overcame it and remained sure.

'You're lying.'

'I'm not frightened of you.'

'I'm going to cut your throat.'

'I'm not afraid to die.' Šimon held his gaze. He felt the edge of the blade ease back. 'You can kill me. I'm not scared.'

The man glared. Šimon slowly pushed the man's hand away, which he did not resist. He then unhurriedly stood up and looked down at the man.

The man scowled. 'You won't scream?'

Šimon shook his head.

'Get out,' the man said in a low voice. 'Get out and take your courage with you. Get out before I kill you anyway.'

Šimon paused for a moment and turned back. What he saw barely seemed human, a shell of a man.

'Go!'

Šimon passed the door and heard the knife clatter against the tiles. He ran out of the ruined factory, weeping.

CHAPTER 43

Captain's Nebojsa and Bradáč were walking in the woods with their soldiers. Bradáč talked incessantly; Nebojsa occasionally grunted. Nebojsa stopped and looked down at his white circle.

'What's the matter?' Bradáč said.

Nebojsa looked up. 'Don't you hate these things?' He tugged the circle. 'It's not a badge.'

Bradáč smiled.

'Don't you think it mad?' Nebojsa said.

'What?'

'Don't you think sometimes the colonel is—'

'Is what?'

Nebojsa shrugged.

'What are you talking about?' Bradáč said.

'Nothing.'

'Tell me.'

Nebojsa frowned but then looked up and pointed. 'There's the hill.'

Bradáč nodded. 'Mmm, here we are.'

'I'll take the top first,' Nebojsa said.

Bradáč narrowed his eyes. 'Fine.'

On the top of the tree-lined slope were several crags that offered protection. Nebojsa ordered his soldiers to move to the top. His lieutenant walked beside him.

'Let's call it off,' Nebojsa said quietly to him.

'Bradáč with us?' the lieutenant said.

'I don't know. I don't think so. I didn't try him.'

'We've got to risk it. There'll be no better chance.'

'Maybe it'll get better. We should wait.'

'For what? When we get sent out? Putting it off only makes it harder.'

They reached the top. Nebojsa sighed.

'Captain, the only choice we have is to do something now or wait until we can't do anything.'

Nebojsa scanned the terrain.

'We can hope it won't get worse,' the lieutenant continued, 'but it's delusion. And when you think of it, to be sent out is worse than to be sent to the tree. How long will it be before that happens to officers? How many soldiers? Do you have a number, Captain? Does she?'

Nebojsa paused. 'I wish you weren't right.'

'So do I.'

Nebojsa had a faraway look. 'I wish there was another way to make her see.'

'She's blind. Unless we write down the rules and respect them, we won't—'

'She'll never do that.' Nebojsa narrowed his eyes.

'Then we'll either end up monsters, or dead.' The lieutenant held the captain's shoulder. 'We must act. '

Nebojsa turned to his officer. 'I know. I know... All right, you ready?'

'Ready.'

'All right. Here, Bradáč is coming. Get the men.'

The lieutenant went off. Nebojsa directed Bradáč and his lieutenant down the other side of the hill towards the creek, away from the main body of men. Nebojsa's lieutenant, accompanied by two soldiers, arrived. The captain rubbed his hands nervously.

'You're going to have trouble defending this side,' Bradáč said.

Nebojsa said nothing. They came to the creek and out of sight of other soldiers.

'I'd have more troops on the other side,' Bradáč said.

Nebojsa spun round with his drawn gun. His lieutenant did the same. The two soldiers quickly took Bradáč and his lieutenant's guns.

'What're you doing? We haven't started yet,' Bradáč said.

The two soldiers gagged Bradáč and the lieutenant and bound their hands. They took their guns from them.

'Over there.' Nebojsa pointed to a large boulder by the creek.

They marched their prisoners to the boulder and round the back of it. Nebojsa gave his handgun to one of the soldiers.

'Guard him,' he said, then turned to the other soldier. 'Go back to the village and bring the Ditherers here.'

The soldier acknowledged and left.

'Don't worry, Bradáč, you'll be fine. I think you know and why,' Nebojsa said and he gestured for his lieutenant to come with him back to the creek. 'Well, Mirek, this is the moment. If we don't get it right, the colonel will send us to the tree.'

'I'm with you, Captain.'

'Yes, but are they?'

'The men know the colonel's lost it. If you just show them that there's a sensible way, that her way is not the answer, they'll come round.'

'I hope you're right. Christ, you better bloody well be right.'

*

A handbell rang, and this signified that the soldiers, Real Otočkans and Ditherers were to gather in the field. Nebojsa's soldier had come to get the Ditherers to the place in the woods, but Eliška decided that it was better not to be conspicuous by absence for the colonel's meeting.

Everyone assembled and the colonel arrived with the flag bearer and Zarviš. First, they sang the song; then they all recited the oath again. The Ditherers did neither. When the colonel spoke, her voice boomed.

'You'll be wondering where half the army is. They are performing drills. We must continue to keep in practice and readiness. But though they aren't here, it doesn't mean we should delay our duty too. And it's important—'

Anton loudly tapped his violin case. Eliška whispered to him to stop but he continued. She held his arms.

'Soldier,' the colonel said to one nearby, then pointed at Anton. 'Is that man uncertain?'

The soldier stood next to Anton. 'Are you uncertain, sir?'

'I don't know,' Anton said.

'Are you uncertain?' the soldier reiterated.

'Yes, very.'

'Are you sure?'

'No, no, no. I'm not sure. I'm very uncertain.'

The soldier looked up at the colonel.

'Stabilise him,' the colonel said.

The soldier kicked the violin case out of Anton's lap and put a firm boot in his back.

'One day,' the colonel continued, 'he'll be a Real Otočkan. But we have time. Everyone must come to the circle of their own free will. Now, bring the accused.'

A pair of soldiers frog-marched the actor who had gone off script. He was brought in front of the stage as the colonel looked down on him. His circle had already been removed. Eliška felt each moment of the silence like a squeezing vice. Her palms had a sheen of sweat on them. Hurry up, she wanted to say. She desperately hoped Nebojsa had rallied his soldiers.

'Private Adamčík we think you deserve pity,' Zarviš said. 'You're a good soldier, actor, person and Otočkan. But it seems you have no pity for us. Even though you have already in a sense confessed, and in front of everyone.'

'Of what crime?' Adamčík said.

'Of all of them,' Zarviš said. 'Since all crime is against unity, all crimes are equal. What does it matter what name we give it? It's outside us, like the cannibals and barbarians that scurry about outside the fence.'

'It sounds uncertain,' Adamčík said.

'Not at all. It's *more* certain. A crime is a crime without degree.'

The private stared, po-faced.

313

'Take the Ditherers,' Zarviš continued. 'We're certain, as sure as the sun and the moon, that they'll eventually take the pledge and join us in unity. That's why we don't expel them. In fact, we can regard them as Real Otočkans in waiting – people who don't yet understand. But when the epiphany strikes, they'll come with hungry hearts and thirsty spirits to wear the white circle. They'll love the World Mother and her rock-like stability. They will, but what you did was to break that faith. That's an act of un-love. Crime is an act of un-love to each other. Or failing in your tasks is un-love. Not trying is un-love. Uncertainty is un-love. Division is un-love. Selfishness is un-love. Secret talks are all un-love. In any case, there's no point doing such things because the Mother will always find out eventually.'

The soldier laughed.

'If you're unified,' Zarviš continued, 'it isn't possible to commit a crime. The conclusion is then that you were never unified with us. You never believed.'

'That's right,' the soldier said with a sardonic smile.

'But you took the oath. You're a liar.'

'You're the liar.'

'But you do not have the circle and I do. You are guilty because you cannot be innocent. You are guilty of all crime, yet I recommend the most lenient sentence.' Zarviš turned to the colonel, who nodded. Zarviš then continued in a diplomatic tone. 'Private Adamčík, this decision was reached after careful consideration. In these difficult times, it's important that we all work together as a team to avoid division. The words we use can negatively impact our community. We all must be careful what we do and say in order to avoid unacceptable views and inappropriate behaviour. We do understand the strain these adverse conditions have put on you. But at the end of the day, you chose to undermine Unity, Stability and Certainty. Unfortunately, we have no choice but to go ahead and say that you are non-innocent.'

Soldiers advanced to flank the private, who had just stopped

314

laughing. He looked up at the colonel and smiled.

'Well done, Colonel. More lies. I'm not the first and won't be the last. How many more before it's your turn to go to the tree?' He chuckled, then shouted, 'Huh, how many? How many?'

The colonel gave the signal, and he was dragged towards the tree.

Eliška reluctantly kept her silence as the inevitable shot echoed. There was a task to do and a place to be.

*

You must help them.

'Let me stay with you,' Viktor said. The priest's room was gloomy.

They need you.

He held Iva's frail hand with the needle still in it. Her eyes were jaundiced, her cheeks shrunken and sallow.

You are no use here.

'But I want to be here with you.'

She shook her head.

I will be here when you come back.

'They don't need me. It ain't any use what they're planning to do anyway.'

Leave me. Help them. Please.

'But—'

She touched his lips.

If you do nothing, you are nothing. Go. Help them.

He hesitantly touched her cheek. 'I'll be back soon.'

Go.

*

Šimon trudged through the woods. His chin was covered in sticky blood. He came to a slope. A crow's caw made him flinch. He dried his red eyes and looked in several directions. He softly

315

moaned but finally settled on one direction, hoping it was the right way. He put an unsteady foot towards it.

*

Captain Nebojsa stood on a boulder jutting from the side of the slope. The soldiers from his company and Bradáč's had gathered.

'Captain Bradáč had to return to the village for the moment,' he said to them. He looked jittery. They waited in silence, which became uncomfortable.

'If you are sighted,' he said finally, 'you must hold your guns above your head.' Sweat trickled down his cheeks.

'Maintain your position… maintain your position and…' He clenched his fists and looked away. He gasped and the soldiers murmured. He turned back.

'Listen, there's something I must tell you. There's something I think you know that needs to be talked about.' He paused. 'When we joined the army, we knew exactly why we serve. But now we have forgotten.'

Blank faces.

'You know that if an order is a crime, you can disobey it. The killings behind the tree were crimes, which you obeyed. We all did. If it was you going to the tree, you would want your comrades to behave like soldiers. You obeyed because we officers did nothing.'

They glanced at each other with puzzled looks.

'We don't even know what we're doing. It seems easier to obey something than to think about it. If a superior is mad, should you obey, especially when she's a criminal?'

Some looked panicked.

'The colonel is sick. She must be… removed from her power. Otherwise, we are not soldiers but thugs, killers and terrorists.'

There was shock.

'Yes… yes, mutiny.'

They gaped, but the lieutenant also standing on the rock,

316

began to tear off his white circle. He slowly held it out at arm's length and let it fall to the ground. Nebojsa was momentarily breathless; then he did the same. But after the circle fell to the ground, the silence only thickened.

'To serve the colonel,' the lieutenant said, 'is to obey an insane murderer, no matter how good she was before. She has lost her commission. She is no longer a soldier. She is not a colonel.'

The only sound was the creaking of the pines.

*

Eliška and the other Ditherers followed the soldier. She was heartened to see Viktor with them. But she dreaded their chances of success and had brought her medical bag, allowing for the worst. When she arrived and saw Nebojsa on the boulder pleading with the soldiers, she felt a fresh touch of panic. And desperation.

'She knows what she's doing,' a soldier shouted.

'She's gone crazy. That Tibor for sure wasn't the murderer,' said another.

'How can you be sure?' a third said.

'Anyway, this is what she's got to do to keep things together.'

'Keep things together? What are you talking about?'

Nebojsa paced about on the boulder.

'What does Captain Bradáč think?' a soldier asked.

'Does he agree, Captain?' another soldier said.

They all turned to the captain.

'Why else would we both be here,' Nebojsa said.

'But he isn't here.'

'What if he's gone back and told the colonel?' said a soldier. This caused a brief flurry of soldiers professing support for the colonel.

'He hasn't,' Nebojsa said. Eliška realised it was slipping away. She rushed to the boulder and leapt on top.

317

'What's happening?' she asked.

'They're against it,' he whispered. 'I think we're done for.'

Eliška shook her head and turned to the soldiers. They waited; she stood tall.

'It's already too late,' she said. 'If you go back now, she'll know you have all conspired against her. Whether you have or not, doesn't even matter.'

'But what's the plan?' one soldier shouted. 'We're not going to fight, are we?'

'Half of the army is right here. My sister may be insane, but she's not stupid. If we resist her, she will agree to our terms.'

'Which are?'

'That she, Captain Železný and Zarviš be expelled from Otočka.'

'And if she doesn't agree.'

'Then… we would have no choice but to fight.'

'That's a terrible plan.'

'Disaster.'

'Captain, we're not seriously going to fight our own soldiers, are we?'

'I hope not.'

They murmured.

'The only other way is that we leave Otočka ourselves.'

This produced even greater dissent.

'Listen. Listen to me,' Eliška shouted and got their attention. 'Before I came here this morning, they had an assembly. You must have heard the shot. Private Adamčík went to the tree just for mocking the colonel. Do you think conspiracy is not as bad as mockery? And what do you think will happen to you?'

Silence.

*

The mad man with the dirty suit jacket and jeans strode from the ruined factory. He was a little hunched and sometimes leapt,

318

sometimes stopped and cackled. Occasionally, he hit a branch and swore. And all the time he was speaking manically, though there was no one there. Then he dropped something, turned abruptly and picked it up. It was an envelope.

'Goldman Sachs – Bilderberg Group – Alex Jones – Harry Potter.' He patted the blood-stained envelope several times. 'Knights Templar – state secrets – world government – downloaded – don't lose it. I have the letter. I am the letter – passed from hand-to-hand-shake – deal – seal the deal – two per cent commission, because the colonel let me into Otočka. Then she went back on her word – bitch – military bonds – interest rates up two basis points.' He patted the envelope again. 'Given to me by inside man in Brussels – two hundred and fifty a share – I am the messenger – colonel betrayed me. Should have gone on the yacht. I go in and out of Otočka for secret deals. She doesn't know – knowledge – information – I confirm the messenger is the message. I will sell it for three hundred thousand, plus commission – deal! – a hundred per cent true – confirmed – Euro News, BBC, CNN – insider info, big scoop – should have gone on the yacht, didn't see it. Why didn't you see it? – blind-spot. You're no wiz after all – shh.'

He spun round as though startled by something. He pocketed the envelope.

'The boy. He knows. If he tells, I'll get nothing – sell it to the Singapore boys – four hundred thousand – two per cent commission – or the Frankfurt boys – I am the revealer – I own the exchange – back Zarviš (pervert) – I am the triple-truth-teller (two thousand an hour) – put fifty thousand on Guatemalan bananas – they said Dušan had emptied one of my bank accounts – Tokyo bank boys – the boy knows. Gotta catch him – no one's going to undercut me – take him out – pred-a-tor – pre-da-tor – PRE-DA-TOR!'

He shook a nearby branch with both hands like a chimpanzee. Then he clenched the knife between his teeth and scurried away.

In her house, the colonel and Captain Železný were sitting at the table.

'We have to change the words,' Zarviš said. 'It will be the same thing but feel new. So you'll still be a captain; you just won't be called that.'

'Sounds like garbage to me,' Železný said.

'Only their image of you will change. The same thing but with new words. So how about New Way Management Officer?'

'Don't like it,' said the colonel.

'Does anyone else have any ideas?' Zarviš asked.

'New Way Discipline Keeper,' said Železný's lieutenant.

'Not bad. Or New Way Oneness Official,' Zarviš said.

'New Way Path Orientator,' the colonel said.

'I'm afraid not,' Zarviš said. 'That suggests that we are not on the path. But we *are* on the path. We *must* be on the path.'

'New Way Operations Assistant,' Železný's lieutenant said.

'Not bad,' Zarviš said.

'New Way Implementation Executive.'

'You seem to have a knack for this,' Zarviš said.

'New Way Unity Superintendent.'

'You have more?' the colonel said.

'New Way Happiness Engineer. New Way Certainty Processor. New Way Togetherness Supervisor.'

'New Way Defence Operative,' the orderly standing by the door said.

'New Way Maintenance Administrator,' Zarviš said.

'New Way Command Authoriser,' the orderly said.

'Of course, to us,' Zarviš said, 'nothing changes. To us the colonel is the colonel. But in the New Way League of States, she is the Mother and benefactor. And they will never meet her. So she becomes God.'

They all laughed.

'God the Mother,' Zarviš said.

'You're crazy,' Železný said.

'Well... but we do need to find a painter; we have to make many images, icons. But that's for later. What's important now is we teach the Otočkans how they must be prepared to sacrifice for the New Way.

'New Way Selflessness Professional,' Železný's lieutenant continued.

'OK, that's enough. And, Colonel, we must also figure out our curriculum for the children.

'New Way Pedagogy Programmer,' Železný's lieutenant said.

'OK,' Zarviš said.

'New Way Enlightenment Coach.'

'And we must consider a breeding programme.'

'New Way Generation Co-ordinator.'

Suddenly a soldier arrived, out of breath and hunched over. The colonel took him to task for barging in, but he said it was urgent.

'I managed to sneak away from Nebojsa and Bradáč's companies. Colonel, you must do something. They have mutinied. They are discussing how to get rid of you. They say you are mad. They want to get rid of you, Železný and Zarviš. Nebojsa wants to take command.'

They shot to their feet.

'And they all want to get rid of us?' the colonel said.

'Yes, Colonel. They must be stopped.'

'This disunity is surprising,' Zarviš said.

'Nebojsa,' Železný shouted.

'Assemble the rest of the army,' the colonel said.

*

Captain Nebojsa looked almost broken as he appealed: 'We just want the simple life, without big ideas and mad dreams. The New Way? That's all Zarviš. But she's the CO. She's responsible.'

321

'But, Captain,' said a soldier, 'what if it really does work? The New Way.'

'Is the colonel your mother? Do you want to be her children? If you think the New Way works, keep your white circles on. If not, take them off.'

Nothing happened.

Eliška realised it was a terrible miscalculation but didn't know what to say. Now it really was all over.

'Do you really want Zarviš to command?' Nebojsa said almost hysterically.

Eliška watched Nebojsa, hunched with begging eyes. The silence was heavy, but a slight smile quivered on her face. Well done, Captain, she thought. Something moved out of the corner of her eye. A soldier tore off his white circle and let it fall. The captain thanked him, trying to hide his desperation. At least one. Eliška's smile widened. Another soldier ripped off his circle and let it fall. And a third. Then a fourth. Then the white circles began to fall like snowflakes. Nebojsa wiped the sweat off his face. Yet when the circles had stopped falling, at least half of the soldiers still had theirs.

'They are all my soldiers,' Nebojsa said to Eliška, pointing to those without the circles. 'If the colonel ordered you to shoot yourself,' Nebojsa said to the soldiers, 'and it *is* an order, who here wouldn't hesitate?'

He waited.

'Really? No one? But that's the New Way.'

A soldier tore off his circle and threw it down.

'And if the colonel ordered you to shoot your closest friend, and that is an order, private, would you not hesitate?'

More took off their circles.

'Or to shoot your child? Your parents, if they were here?'

Now more circles fell until only about a dozen men kept their circles like proud confederates to a cause.

'Very well, go if you must,' he addressed the dozen who still kept the circles. 'Tell the colonel that if she resigns, she will have nothing to worry about. But if not, we are prepared to fight.'

CHAPTER 44

'Šimon,' Karl called out scratchily. He tried to raise himself, but feebly fell back. 'Šimon… *die Blume ist die Heilung.*'

Some distance away, the ex-sergeant trudged. He panted and sweated, and his neck was bright red. A gunshot rang out and he turned towards the sound.

'They'll let me in. They will. They—'

He found the fence. He clutched the wire, then staggered along it, wheezing. He stumbled until he fell into the shallow tunnel.

*

Iva managed to stand up from the bed, though she buckled and held on to the doorknob. Determined and panting, she shuffled into the corridor.

She could hear the colonel shouting in the field: 'They're Old-Wayists. And it's my sister who has done this, be in no doubt of that. She's gone, and the Ditherers too. For sure she has screamed her righteousness at them. She is their queen, Eliška the Maniac. Soldiers, we must defend ourselves. I know you don't want to fight your friends. But I know you will do your duty. Either we win or we sink. Enough. Bring the standard. Beat the drum. Let's march!'

The drum did beat.

Iva moved as fast as she could down the stairs, with one fixed thought in her mind. She staggered towards the altar, then stumbled when she reached it. Her hand grasped the edge to steady herself, but still she fell to her knees. She heard soldiers marching and began to crawl, breathing heavily. A suffocating ache tried to stop her, but she made it across to the room next to the vestry. She reached with both hands up to the doorknob.

'Give me strength.' She pulled herself up in agony.

By degrees, she got to her feet and heard the drummer's sound begin to move away. They were leaving. It wouldn't be long before they were gone. There was little time. She stumbled towards the centre of the room, then lurched with two hands out and fell upon the rope. The action pulled it down just enough for a slight knell to be made. The swing of the bell pulled her back up. Then, as the rope slackened, the bell swung the other way. She did not have to pull hard for the bell to toll a resounding peal.

Outside, the sound echoed loudly, and the colonel turned to the church. The army that was walking along the road stopped.

'You told me there was no one in the church,' the colonel said to a sergeant.

'There was no one. They had all gone.'

'Well, there is someone.'

'Just the sick woman, but she can't do anything,' said the sergeant. The bell rang again.

'She's ringing the bell,' the colonel said. 'That's nothing to worry about. That's... unless... Sergeant!'

'Colonel?'

'It's a signal. It's a bloody signal.'

'What?'

'A signal! You five, go in there now. Stop that ringing! She's signalling to them that we're coming. Go! Go! Stop that ringing. Stop it.'

Iva saw stars as she pulled the rope again and large tears fell down her gaunt face. She pulled again and smiled – each ringing sound was joy, a sudden burst of hope. The bell rang again, its knell pure and sure. She closed her eyes and clung to the rope beaming because she imagined it was Šimon.

*

Šimon stopped in the woods. The light was gloomy as clouds had thickened. But from one direction was the sound of a bell and he turned towards it. It's the village, he thought. The bell sounded again; it dragged him out of the hurt. He brightened and moved as fast as he could in the direction of the sound.

*

The bell echoed as Nebojsa's soldiers hastened into position. Some went down the hill while others took up their places behind the crags and rocks on top of the slope.

The bell stopped and everyone paused.

Then Nebojsa went to the boulder near the creek where Bradáč and his lieutenant were still tied up.

'Before I take these gags out, all your soldiers have agreed that the colonel must be replaced. It's got to be done. I hope you'll join us.' He took off the gags.

Captain Bradáč said nothing.

'I don't have time to spare. I'm going to untie you. Then you'll have to choose. Join us and command your soldiers or go to the colonel. But let your lieutenant here speak for himself.' Nebojsa untied them. 'Will you come?'

'I'm with you, Captain.' The lieutenant rose.

'Good. Bradáč?'

He sat there somewhat haughtily and refused to move.

'Fine. Come on, Lieutenant.' They all went up the slope to the crags, leaving Captain Bradáč alone.

'If they attack,' he said to Bradáč's lieutenant, 'wait until they reach within fifty feet, then fall back. Take Bradáč's soldiers to the rear. I'll do the same on my side. If we have to fight, it'll be a shoot and dash job.'

'Good luck, Captain.'

'Good luck.' Then Captain Nebojsa turned to his sergeant. 'I've got a job for you. Take several men and go back to the village. I need kerosene, a couple of torches and rope.'

'Right,' the sergeant said. 'You know, Captain, if it does come to battle, this would be the first time many of the soldiers have seen combat. And they would be fighting their own.'

'Yes, I know. And that's the worst bloody part of it.'

High above the trees came the sound of an airline jet engine. Nearby, Anton, standing with the other Ditherers on the hill, looked up at the plane – this was the first since the crisis.

'Where the hell do they think they're going?' he said wryly. 'Do they think there is somewhere to escape to?'

Several soldiers ran down the hill towards positions by the creek. This sudden flurry of action scared Helena, though Radoš held her.

'Nothing's going to happen. It'll be all right,' he said, smiling nervously.

'I have an extra pistol,' Nebojsa said to the Ditherers. 'Who here has used a gun before?' They all pointed to Viktor. 'Here, take it.'

Viktor held out his hand to take the gun. But when his fingers touched it, he quickly pulled his hand away and shook his head.

'Take it. We may be up against the wall here,' the captain said.

But Viktor looked aside. 'I ain't doing that no more. I ain't doing that. No more. No more.' He stepped backwards.

The captain tried to give the gun to Anton.

'Oh, giving it to me would be like throwing it in the lake. Unless you want the air to be shot?'

'Is there anyone?' the captain appealed to the others.

František started writing something and glancing at the gun.

'I'll take it,' Radoš said.

'You used one before?' asked the captain. Radoš shook his head and took the gun in both hands.

'Here, aim it a little lower than the target and try not to flinch. Are you sure you want it? You don't have to take it if you don't want.'

'I want it. I want it,' Radoš said with a look of bravado.

327

'All right,' the captain said and briefly explained how to use it. Radoš stood tall with square shoulders and determination as he listened to the captain.

Eliška had fixed the flower emblem that she had taken from Hynek to a branch and, at that moment, she showed it to the captain.

'Not another symbol,' the captain said.

'It's important.'

'If we do end up fighting, keep it hidden, unless you want to be a target.'

Eliška nodded. Then the captain continued to make his preparations. He stopped when the colonel and her soldiers arrived not far from the bottom of the hill.

On the colonel's side, standing next to her were Zarviš, Captain Železný, Luděk and the flag bearer.

'Železný, you take the other side. Don't engage until you hear me say on the radio.'

'Colonel,' he said and took half the soldiers round the other side of the hill.

'We should make a peace offering,' she said to Zarviš.

'You don't mean to rehabilitate them? They'll only end up a fifth column later,' Zarviš said.

'Not the officers or the Ditherers; there's no coming back for them. But I need the soldiers.'

'We could say they were infected. We could cure them.'

The colonel advanced a little with the flag bearer and shouted. Nebojsa replied. Their positions were about two hundred yards.

'Captain Nebojsa! Surrender and nothing will happen to anyone. It's a mistake. I know you didn't mean it.'

'It's not for you to request anything, Colonel.' Nebojsa shouted back. 'But if you, Zarviš and Železný give up, we'll give you a good stock of food and send you on your way. We can't continue like this. We don't want any harm, but you've lost your commission. We must change direction. The only solution is if you leave Otočka. Please, Colonel, you don't see what it's done

328

to you. No one blames you, but all the same you've got to go.'

The colonel spoke to the soldier who was next to her. 'Sergeant, take twenty men and join Železný. Tell him to form a wide vee.'

'Colonel,' he said and was off.

'Lieutenant,' she said, 'take three men, go to the village and round up any Ditherers there might be. We may find hostages useful.' Then she turned to the enemy. 'Soldiers on the hill! We won't shoot if you come down now and join us. Come down in the next ten minutes and nothing will happen. But if you stay, it's all over for you. You have ten minutes.'

On the hill Nebojsa shouted back, 'If you want to go, go. We won't shoot either.'

Eliška mounted a boulder and held the flower emblem high. 'Vendula! Vendula. You have done so much good, then burned it. You can fix it though. And we would think the best of you if you did. But it means you must go. For your sake and everyone's.'

'Doctor,' the colonel's voice strung the word out, 'it's for you to quit, for the sake of peace and stability. It's you who is making war.'

Eliška turned to the soldiers on her side. 'I don't want to fight anyone. I don't want to fight my sister. And I don't want anyone to get hurt or die. But does anyone want the New Way? If you do, go.'

After a few moments, one soldier defected. The other of Nebojsa's soldiers howled and hooted at him. Helena clutched her shirt. She looked at Radoš, then down the hill. She frowned as she looked back again at Radoš. She flinched, then bolted. Radoš called after her, but she kept running and soon reached the colonel and then ran straight into Luděk's arms, who beamed and stroked her hair.

'You chose well, Helena,' Zarviš said.

'You didn't want to be a traitor, did you?' Luděk said.

'And Radoš?' asked Zarviš.

329

Helena wiped her tears and looked at Zarviš. 'He's only a boy.'

On the hill, the youth shouted her name again and paced back and forth.

'Forget her,' Anton said.

The gun fell from Radoš's hand. He breathed short as though winded.

'It's not worth it,' Anton said.

Radoš slumped down and stared vacantly.

'You never can really know people.' Anton reached down and picked up the gun. 'Come on. This isn't the time for heartache.'

A soldier ran up from the rear side and told Nebojsa that they had spotted some of the colonel's army coming from behind.

'Where the hell is that kerosene?' he said.

At that moment there was movement below from the colonel's side. Her soldiers were beginning to dart from tree to tree. He climbed onto a boulder.

'Colonel,' he shouted, 'it's all gone wrong. But we can work it out. How about this? You stay in command, but Zarviš and Železný must go. Let's have a written agreement about rules. There's no need to fight each other.'

There was silence; then the colonel's bellowing voice broke out: 'Time's up!'

A shot was fired and flew past Nebojsa's ear. He scrambled behind a boulder as more shots were fired. The colonel's soldiers advanced. Nebojsa gave the order to open fire.

'Aim for the white circles.'

A gunshot made František jump. 'What? Do I fear to lose something?' Then as more gunshots blasted, he cowered and hid behind a tree. 'Do I fear for my life?' He held his head in his hands as more gunfire sounded. He took off his glasses. 'What's wrong with me? How can I be afraid?'

On the colonel's side at the bottom of the hill, she toyed with the radio. Shots fired on her position, and they retreated behind a large boulder.

'Colonel, it's time,' Luděk said.

'Not yet,' she said.

On Nebojsa's side, rushing along the creek was the sergeant with the rope, flambeaux and kerosene. He found the captain.

'Quick, follow me.' Nebojsa led them down to the creek. 'Put some kerosene round the base of those trees, all along the creek, and light it.'

The sergeant acknowledged and quickly got to work.

When Nebojsa got back to his lines on the hill, he rushed to his lieutenant. 'Can you hold them?'

'So far, but ammo, Captain.'

'I'll see what I can do.'

He ran past Eliška and the nurse tending to the wounded soldiers, some of them yelling in agony.

On the colonel's side, Luděk turned to the colonel. 'Now! Now! It's giving them the advantage.'

'No, they have no advantage.'

Zarviš winced at every shot and it seemed to make him paler. Colour came back to his cheeks when the two hostages, Ludmila and Nada arrived. The colonel ordered them away from the firing.

'All right. Time for Železný,' she said and ordered the attack on the radio.

On Nebojsa's side, behind him, the flames grew. The rearguard under Bradáč's lieutenant retreated to the bottom of the hill on the creek side.

'Captain, we can't stop them,' Nebojsa's lieutenant said.

Nebojsa looked behind him down the slope, then to his flanks. 'All right. We'll move now. Keep a few to slow their advance.'

The lieutenant nodded.

Nebojsa ran over to the Ditherers. 'Follow the soldiers down to the creek.'

Gunfire burst out from the rear and Bradáč's soldiers shot back.

Nebojsa ran back to his lieutenant. 'They're attacking the

rear. Time to go.' He ran amongst his troops calling for retreat.

'Help me carry the wounded,' Eliška said to some soldiers as they started falling back. The soldiers helped her and the nurse to move the casualties.

'I'll kill them,' Radoš screamed and madly stepped out from behind the cover of a rock. Shots fired past him.

Viktor pulled him back. Radoš struggled. 'Ain't you got any sense?'

The colonel's advance from the front continued. But Železný's soldiers from the rear were stopped by the fires.

'Run! This way, down this way. Run! Run,' Nebojsa shouted.

Villagers and soldiers dashed along the creek as the colonel's soldiers advanced up the hill.

'Time for us to pull back,' Nebojsa's lieutenant said to the soldiers near him. The order was spread.

'We got to go,' Viktor said to Radoš still struggling in his arms. 'Now!'

Nebojsa's covering forces began to fall back. Viktor dragged Radoš with them.

'Run!' Nebojsa shouted.

Soon, the last of Nebojsa's soldiers darted down and along the creek as the flames roared.

'Quick,' Nebojsa yelled again. He waited behind until the last soldiers had passed and made a tail of the retreating forces.

Then a bullet struck him.

CHAPTER 45

'Shots fired – man-down – 9/11 – Yankee military (Lockheed Martin, down) – all on army and gold – Goldman Sachs – bust – broken bonds – chain-smoking – fire, fire – burn the witch – colonel – bitch.'

The bald man with his flashing green eyes lurched towards a tree and crouched down. Then, from his jacket pocket he took out, one by one, five small squares of pure gold. Occasional gunshot could still be heard in the distance.

'This little one's a house in the Canaries and this little one's a brand-new Lamborghini. This little one's a bag of cocaine and this little one's a bus load of Swedish girls. And this little one... this little one... is unearned fame. You're all my sugar. Hang on! Hang on! I'm getting a call.' He put his hand in his coat pocket and pulled out an imaginary phone.

'Recession, Depression, bust-bust, talk to me... is that you London? What's the deal on your colonel? She stiffed you? So did mine... fifty kilos of C4? What'd she do? Blow up Parliament? Madness. Mine is expanding, taking over – imperial. Hang on!' He pulled the phone down and jerked his head around. Above, in the darkening sky thunder clapped. 'What's that! Somebody's here. Somebody's there.' He put the phone back to his ear. 'Did you find the boy? No? Frankfurt will know. Frankfurt? Is that you? Gotta find the boy. Gotta catch him and slice him up. He... he knows the secret. Ah, I know where he is. I know.' He put the phone down and spun round.

'PRED-A-TOR!'

*

Šimon was walking up a large hill, certain he was walking in the direction of the bell. He could hear the gunshots in the distance, now only sporadic. The thunder, however, burst out above him. The trees on the hill became fewer and fewer as he neared the top, until there were none at all. It began to rain lightly. But when he reached the grassy summit, it poured. He didn't hear anymore gunshot; he climbed on a boulder to get a clear view of the village. Then he saw it, about half a mile off. Lightning flashed and, almost immediately, thunder clapped. The heavy rain soaked him and began to wash off some of the mud and blood on his face. His hair hung over his forehead. He could see the cave. He was startled at the sound of a woman's voice. He spun round, but there was no one. He felt a chill when he heard it again – his mother's voice.

I'm here.

He looked back at the cave. 'Mama.'

Come home. The voice trailed.

'Ma...'

He waited to hear the voice again. But he knew it wouldn't speak anymore. As he climbed down from the boulder, lightning flared in the distance.

*

Eliška tended the wounded as Nebojsa's soldiers retreated just past a large clearing. She got to Nebojsa's thigh wound and patched it. It was very gloomy in the heavy rain. Some soldiers had been killed, and the others looked shocked. They had shot at people who that morning had been their friends. She surveyed the anger and heard some of them openly contemplate surrender to the colonel. The ranks tried to rally them. She could see they blamed her and that they had no conviction in what they were doing. She looked down at the wounded, one of them mortally so, and thought about surrendering herself. The soldiers raged with each other until an airhorn squealed.

'I don't want pointless death,' the colonel's voice boomed at the opposite edge of the clearing. 'Soldiers, you are safe. I know you were tricked by Eliška the Maniac. Turn your guns on her; turn your guns on your officers; force them into the clearing and you can once more enjoy the freedom of the white circle.'

No one moved.

'It's a reasonable offer. I wouldn't blame you if you took it,' Nebojsa shouted. The soldiers who had been arguing about going back to the colonel remained silent. Eliška felt smothered by the rain, like it was pushing her down. Surrender, her mind repeated. She looked at the soldiers, who had fixed their eyes on her. The wind pushed her like a swelling sea, and she hunched. A soldier angrily threw the flower symbol and it landed near, its eye staring straight into hers. She snatched it and defiantly strode out into the clearing. Her golden hair hung loose, wild and wet – she stood tall.

'Here I am!' she shouted to Vendula. 'The Maniac.'

She held the symbol tightly. Up, she thought. Rise!

'Eliška. Eliška,' a voice shouted behind her.

She turned. 'What are you doing?'

Nebojsa hobbled quickly over to her. 'I'll surrender myself,' he said. 'It'll save anymore trouble. She'll spare them if I fall on my sword.'

'How can you give up so soon?' she said.

'It's over. No more. It's enough.'

'No. There's a chance. Don't flake out now, Captain. I won't let you do it.'

He looked surprised.

'What we are doing is right. We're nothing if we lie down now.' She raised the symbol high into the air, then strode with it along the lines of the soldiers so everyone could see it. She felt a strange energy, an electricity. Lightning flashed and the flower burst into momentary fluorescence. The colonel stepped out into the clearing, the flag bearer standing by her side.

Eliška saw her. 'Vendula! Let's not fight. There is a way.' She strode closer to the colonel's line of soldiers and appealed to them. 'It's not your fault.'

'Let's smash them,' Luděk yelled and was like a hound ready to pounce.

'The white circle is making you sick,' Eliška shouted.

Zarviš seemed almost rabid. He strode along the colonel's soldiers and screamed: 'It's a lie. A lie! Only the New Way can save us. Eliška the Maniac is a witch; she is mind poison. We are close to victory. The New Way *is* the way of the future. We are so close. This day will decide it. This disgusting woman lies because she hates you and she wants to destroy our army so she can become queen.'

'No,' Eliška said calmly, 'I don't. Vendula, it's a sickness that can be cured.'

Zarviš continued to rant.

But coming from behind Nebojsa's side was a sudden chorus of yelling. There was a rush of soldiers. Nebojsa shouted for his troops not to engage. Some of the colonel's soldiers had sneaked round the back and were behind Nebojsa's soldiers. Eliška was shocked at the swiftness of the manoeuvre. Moving out from the line of advancing soldiers was Captain Bradáč. He advanced towards Nebojsa, who smiled wryly and nodded.

'I don't blame you for staying loyal to her,' Nebojsa said.

Bradáč looked at the flower symbol and glowered.

The colonel beamed.

He looked at the line of Nebojsa's soldiers, then at Nebojsa, then at the colonel. And again, at the emblem the doctor was holding. He turned to his men and with a steady hand he ripped off his own circle. He held it up so all his soldiers could see, then with a passion threw it onto the ground. Nothing seemed to move except for the rain and the flags. Nebojsa's soldiers encouraged the section of the colonel's who had been a part of Bradáč's manoeuvre to tear off their circles. Bradáč urged them also. One of them tore off his white circle and threw it onto the ground. Then another. And another. Then the rest. Some of Nebojsa's soldiers had tears.

336

'They have given up their circles,' Eliška said to the colonel's soldiers. 'Look.'

Bradáč's men and Nebojsa's shook hands and embraced as Nebojsa looked in wonder.

On the colonel's side, Zarviš, already frenetic, started shrieking.

'It's a conspiracy. A fifth column. It's the Ditherer within. Bradáč the Traitor. Colonel attack now. Attack.' He rushed to her and said quietly, 'They now have as many as us.'

'Put down your guns!' Eliška called out. 'Let's figure out a way. Start again.'

'Colonel,' Zarviš pressed, 'we got to stop the rot before it spreads.'

The colonel ordered Železný to take the left flank and his lieutenant to take the right.

'Do what your friends have done, give up the circle,' Eliška shouted to the colonel's soldiers.

'What a nasty woman,' Zarviš screeched. 'Pure evil! Liar. It's a terrible thing to lie to children. Lying is the way of the Old World. It's de-harmonisation. It's an act of the worst kind of un-love.'

Lightning flashed and Eliška saw that the colonel's face was full of a defiant malevolence, with eyes of a passionate hatred.

'I won't give up, Vendula. Hope is the cure.'

The colonel laughed. 'Greenpeace to the rescue! You are so deluded, sister. You don't know how it works. Pity, you could have been such a help.'

'Colonel, shoot her,' Zarviš said. 'I beg you. Shoot her. Shoot her!'

'You are in the way, Eliška,' the colonel said. 'Get out of the way and I won't hurt you. Only, get out of the way.'

Eliška paced closer to the colonel's soldiers. 'Soldiers, follow what you think is true. I don't have the answer. I promise nothing. Only no one can tell you for sure what is right and wrong. But you know it. Surely you know it.'

Železný soldiers attacked several of Nebojsa's. Some were killed instantly. They fired back. Nebojsa leant round the tree and fired his gun. Radoš looked reckless and desperate. He rushed towards the shots. He gripped the gun so tightly that his knuckles were white.

František looked at the colourful flower symbol, lush in the rain. 'Maybe there is…'

'Doctor, doctor,' Anton yelled. 'Come back. Get behind a tree.'

There were shots from the left as Železný's lieutenant began to attack. Radoš fired but flinched as he did, and the bullet went wide. One of Nebojsa's soldiers pulled him back down as bullets shot past. He fought the soldier's protective grip and crawled forward to hide himself behind some ferns. He looked up to a clear shot of a woman soldier near a tree, her white circle clearly visible. He aimed, resting his wrists on the muddy ground in front of him. His hands began to shake. He looked up at the symbol. When he turned back to the woman soldier, she was looking at him. Thunder roared and seemed to knock the soldier out of her daze. She swung her assault rifle at Radoš but reflexively he had already pulled the trigger. She had a look of surprise and despair as she fell. The gun dropped out of his hands. He put his head down, brought his hands to his head and shuddered as he sobbed.

Viktor helped the nurse tending to the injured. He found a soldier who was shivering and holding his knee. He put the soldier on his back and ran him to the nurse.

Eliška slowly stretched her hands out wide. The branch of the emblem slid down her grip and stopped as it touched the ground. It was a deliberate provocation to make herself as easy a target as possible.

'Don't be afraid,' she whispered to herself.

On the colonel's side, Zarviš eyed the holster on her hip. His hand twitched as he reached out to it; then just as quickly he snatched his hand back.

'Now, Colonel. Please. Shoot her. If you wait any longer it

will be lost. It'll all be lost.'

'What are you talking about?' the colonel said. 'We're winning.'

'Shoot her, please.'

Luděk was kept back by the colonel, like a dog on a leash. He held his own hunting gun. He seethed.

'Enough is enough,' he said and shot at Eliška. It grazed her right shoulder.

'Hold your fire,' the colonel raged.

He took aim again, but Helena ran at him and threw her hands at his gun. The weapon flew into the air.

On the other side, Nebojsa ordered his soldiers to press forward. Železný's retreated a little.

'Follow the soldiers,' Nebojsa said to the villagers.

The soldiers led by Železný's lieutenant advanced behind him so that everyone moved in an anti-clockwise direction.

The colonel suddenly shouted, 'What am I doing? What am I doing?' She widened her eyes. 'You're right, Zarviš. I see it now. For God's sake, shoot her. Shoot her.' She aimed with her gun and pulled the trigger. The bullet missed. She shot again and hit the doctor's right hand. Then a bullet from Nebojsa's soldiers struck the colonel's left hand sending the handgun falling. She bent down to pick the gun up, but another shot grazed her arm and she reeled back behind a tree. Eliška dropped the flag as blood reddened her hand. She stooped and gathered it up.

Viktor and Anton helped carry the wounded. Radoš pounded the earth as bullets flew. A hand touched his back.

'Rudolf. Rudolf!' Artur said, beaming.

Radoš looked up with a face of desolation.

'Come on, Rudolf, I found her. I found Mother. Come, she's over there.' Artur helped Radoš to his feet, then guided him towards the clearing. 'I'm coming, Aneta. I found Rudolf.'

Nebojsa continued to order his soldiers forward.

Železný motioned his soldiers to fall back. 'Back to the colonel's line.'

They retreated to the colonel and she ordered everyone to move towards Železný's lieutenant. Eliška remained steadfast as blood and rain dripped off her fingertips.

'Commendatore,' Anton shouted and tried to pull Artur back to the safety of the trees. But the old man stubbornly kept staggering forward with Radoš. A bullet rushed past them.

Viktor hurried to a fallen soldier and picked him up. A bullet sang past his ear. 'Nurse,' he shouted. She was running to a soldier fallen in the long grass of the clearing.

Nebojsa looked at the doctor and the villagers going into the clearing. 'No,' he said to himself. 'No.' He hobbled towards her. 'Across the clearing!' he called to his soldiers. 'Across the clearing!' Nebojsa's soldiers began running into the clearing. When shots fired in their direction, they ducked and crawled in the long grass. More of Nebojsa's and Bradáč's soldiers saw their comrades go into the clearing and followed. A bullet shot past Nebojsa's ear, knocking him off his good leg.

Viktor, still with the soldier on his back, ran over and helped the captain.

'Cease fire,' Nebojsa mumbled. 'Cease fire,' he shouted and tottered towards Eliška.

'Cease fire,' Nebojsa and Bradáč yelled. Now all the soldiers in the clearing raised their hands and were shouting for cease fire.

Železný and the colonel reached Nebojsa's original position so that Eliška's back was to them.

'Very well,' the colonel said, and she too shouted, 'Cease fire! Cease fire!'

The call was echoed.

'Wait until they surrender,' she said to Železný.

More and more soldiers rose out of the grass with their hands in the air. Quickly the chorus of 'cease fire' replaced that of gunfire. The villagers gathered round Eliška, who held the branch of the emblem close to her shoulder and looked up at the sky even though she knew the colonel was behind her in the woods. Bradáč joined them in the middle and looked weary. Now all of

Nebojsa's and Bradáč's soldiers stood in the clearing with raised hands.

Next to the colonel, Zarviš laughed and clapped.

'They're crazy to surrender. They could have won,' Železný's lieutenant said.

'Put your men in a line,' the colonel said to Železný. 'Tell them quietly to mark a soldier and when I give the order, gun them down.'

'But they're surrendering,' the lieutenant said.

Captain Železný was already zealously going about executing the order. The lieutenant protested, but in vain.

'That's right,' Zarviš said quietly, but excitedly. 'Let the grass turn red.'

By Eliška, all the soldiers in the clearing looked relieved that they didn't have to continue to fight.

'Maybe there is an eternal value...' František uttered as he looked along the line of soldiers, then ahead to the line of guns trained on them. 'Maybe there is something.'

Bradáč sighed. 'You and me are cooked,' he said to Nebojsa, who shrugged wryly.

Eliška was calm and felt in communion with something as the symbol flapped in a gust of wind. She watched the parting of the clouds in the sky. There, the sky was a light grey. Faint beams of light formed. Nebojsa glanced back, then faced the same way as Eliška. Soon other soldiers did the same until they all had their backs to the colonel.

'It's pathetic,' Zarviš said.

'Colonel,' said Železný's lieutenant, 'you're surely not going to shoot them in the back?'

'Don't be afraid,' Eliška said in an airy and gentle voice. The sunbeams shone through the broken clouds and the rain eased. She looked steadfast.

'I don't blame you,' Nebojsa said. 'It was the right thing to do. Even though we failed—'

'Shh,' she said.

Železný went through his soldier's line and told them what to do. Some of the men turned to each other with an expression as if to say, 'are we to shoot them in the back?'

Eliška felt a bright dream-like feeling. The sounds died away and it was as though, between her, the emblem and sun, no one else existed. Peace.

The colonel's soldiers were spared the dilemma, because Eliška slowly turned to face the colonel. She stepped forward, the symbol in vibrant colour. Her arm had a washed-out streak of blood down its sleeve. She stopped and slowly scanned the faces of the soldiers with their guns aimed.

'Be brave. Don't be afraid,' she said.

Behind her, the villagers turned round also. Then the rest of the soldiers faced the colonel.

The colonel's soldiers sighed at the dignity of the unarmed soldiers standing in the clearing. Some of those taking aim lowered their heads.

'Do not be afraid,' Eliška said louder, but gently. Nebojsa repeated it. So did Bradáč. Those in the middle stood firm with high chins and straight backs. 'Don't be afraid,' they all said. 'Be brave.'

'Fire!' the colonel shouted.

'Fire!' Železný shouted.

'Fire!' Zarviš shouted.

But the only sound was the rain.

'Fire!' Železný shouted again.

'Fire!' the colonel shouted once more.

But there was not a single shot.

'What's wrong?' Luděk said. 'Why aren't they shooting?'

'Fire! Fire, you bastards! Fire!' Železný raged. But the soldiers were looking only at the peaceful, bright face of the doctor. The colonel stopped and stared, too, suddenly mesmerised, as if under a spell.

One of the colonel's soldiers wept. Another one stood up slowly and threw down his gun. Another, a woman soldier, rose

342

and walked into the clearing.

'Don't be afraid,' Eliška said softly.

The soldier tore her circle off and let it fall from her hand. Then another soldier stood in the clearing and did the same. More and more stood and took off their circles and joined them in the clearing. One by one they tossed their circles away. Eliška closed her eyes in a moment of bliss. More soldiers tore off the white circles. They all had a look of relief as though just being released.

They joined the ranks of those in the clearing. The colonel watched in silent horror. Železný's lieutenant watched in awe. Železný swore at the soldiers and pulled out his gun in order to shoot but his lieutenant held his arm. Helena slowly backed away from Luděk and ran. No one noticed her disappear. Zarviš looked amazed and eyed the colonel for guidance. But she looked bewildered. Soon all the colonel's soldiers were in the clearing, their circles fallen in the grass. They all faced the colonel as the rain stopped. The light shone on them.

'It's a miracle,' Zarviš said softly and in awe. '*This* is real power... it's magic.'

Only Luděk was unmoved. He yelled at the colonel to try to snap her out of her daze.

'You did it well, sister. Bravo,' the colonel uttered slowly.

'It's over,' Zarviš said.

'Colonel! Do something,' Luděk yelled.

Železný, who had freed himself from his lieutenant, called out orders to his soldiers in the clearing to come back. They did not. He turned to the four remaining loyal soldiers standing near the colonel and ordered them to fire. The colonel countermanded the order. He rushed up to the colonel and grabbed her arm.

'Colonel, fall back. We'll make a plan. We'll figure something out. Come on.'

But the colonel was now smiling. Luděk tugged her other arm.

'We still have Ludmila and Nada,' he said.

She slowly looked at the two hostages held by two soldiers,

standing near the flag bearer. She seemed to snap out of her daydream.

'Come on then,' she shouted. 'There's still a way. Come on.' She grabbed Zarviš and he too snapped out of the enchantment. They took off: Železný, the colonel, Zarviš, Ludmila and Nada, the flag bearer, Luděk and four loyal soldiers. They ran through the woods with purpose and speed.

CHAPTER 46

The sky was lighter. The bald man with his wet suit jacket hid behind a tree and watched the feverish ex-sergeant stumble along the path in the woods. He tittered as the ex-sergeant disappeared, but swivelled round at the sound of footsteps behind him. Helena was running. He smiled and lurched from behind the tree to confront her.

'Yeah baby, let's get close.'

She shrieked.

'How about it, Helena? I'm nice and clean after this rain.'

'No. No.'

'Come on baby – Johnson & Johnson.'

'Get off.' She ran; he followed and grabbed her arm.

'What do you mean no? I've got the strength of ten men. And,' he said, holding up the knife, 'I invested in steel.'

She pulled herself away and picked up a nearby branch.

'Ooo, scary,' he hissed. 'Spicy! Baby, you're real spicy. I tell you what. Let's make a deal – seal the deal. I'll give you some gold, you give me your body – ding-dong-boom-bang – champagne – good time.'

She swung the branch.

'Ooh. Hoo hoo.' He jumped around. He pulled out the envelope and danced round her, skipping sometimes, with the knife in one hand and the envelope in the other.

'Secret – Kremlin – military – bang-boom – I'll tell you the secret if you put down the branch.'

She swung again.

'Ooh. Hoo, ya, ya. But Helena, babe, you never fought like this before.'

'Get away!'

'You know I'm a great man. I have done great things –

unbelievable – double mighty things – I'm the monopoly – I have the gold – golden boy – boy! Forgot about boy – get the boy before he goes to press – Predator – double-predator – ah! The boy! The boy.' He darted off.

'PRED-A-TOR!' His voice trailed away.

*

In the village, the colonel's group crossed the bridge. They ran to the armoury on the west of the river and took what was left. Nervous and frightened villagers emerged from their houses and murmured. Some of them said that the colonel must have had some disaster.

The colonel paced up and down near the car park, swearing to shoot anyone who was going to give up the circle. 'We must have unity. There's still a way. If we are sure we will still win. It always looks hopeless before victory.' Despite her words, their number was just eleven, two of whom were unarmed hostages.

Zarviš mumbled to himself, 'Unity, Stability, Certainty. Unity, Stability, Certainty.'

'I'll go down shooting, if it comes to it,' Železný said.

They all hushed, however, when from behind the church on the east side of the river, the flower symbol emerged, then the rest of the army. As those soldiers poured onto the field, the colonel and her group took cover behind one of the trucks. They fired and the soldiers in the field scattered to find cover.

A bullet sang past Eliška who was behind a tree. This provoked the soldier next to her to tear the emblem from her and throw it to the ground so that it wouldn't make themselves targets.

On the other side of the river, the snake flag waved proudly. The colonel became frantic and started screaming, then laughing, then screaming. She grabbed Zarviš and threw him to the ground.

'I shall not leave,' she shouted. 'The New Way only works if we believe. Believe in the victory. We'll shoot them all when we

346

win. I only want pure bloods, true and loyal. True and loyal.'

One of the colonel's soldiers threw his gun into the river. He tore off his white circle and rose, hands in the air, with the little white circle of surrender high above him. He ran towards the other side. The colonel stepped out as he passed the middle of the bridge. A bullet tore through his back. Then two. Three. And a fourth.

The colonel stood by the truck, screaming, her handgun firing, a fifth. She spun round behind the truck again and began pacing up and down. She screeched and everyone froze. It was like the sound of a crow being attacked. Ludmila and Nada, held together by rope, cried.

Zarviš repeated his mantra: 'Unity, Stability, Certainty.'

'Come on. Be men! Stand by me,' the colonel shouted.

The lieutenant who had remained loyal, appealed to her. 'Colonel.' He stood in her path. 'Surrender. They'll let us leave.'

She shot the lieutenant directly in the forehead. As he fell, there was a monkeyish burst from the east side of the river. A man screamed and cackled into the centre of the field, calling for the colonel. He ran to the river with his suit jacket flapping.

'Colonel – fat – fat – remember me?'

The colonel aimed.

'How much for the truth colonel?' He pulled out the envelope and waved it. 'I got the truth – Japs offering me a cool half-mil! – better the deal, or I break the seal – woo – woo – I got gold, baby – this little nugget gave me sadness – this little nugget gave me pain – this little nugget gave me an empty bank account – this little nugget gave me the shits – and this little—'

The colonel shot several times. The man fell with a sardonic smile onto the riverbank and died still clasping the envelope. The colonel took Nada by the collar and pointed the gun at Ludmila.

'Get into the house.' She shoved them.

The flag bearer threw down his flag and tried to cross the river. Železný shot him down. Luděk, Železný, the lieutenant and three men tried to hold off the whole army.

347

Zarviš slipped away into his own house.

There were shouts from the field for the colonel to surrender, though she had gone inside with her two hostages. Luděk answered with gunfire. Some of the soldiers near Eliška took a broad approach creeping through woods and swiftly wading through the river and to the meadow. Other soldiers gave covering fire.

Inside his house, Zarviš poured petrol on all his writings, on the curtains and film posters and on the books on the shelf. He took a match and set it on fire.

'It's all out of the box now, Mother. She failed because she was uncertain. She dithered, she lost. But the New Way isn't over. It sleeps. One day, somewhere it will awaken.'

Outside, the soldiers from the field were closing in on the trucks and Železný began to be attacked from the side. Zarviš ran outside the house, over to the where the flag was, took it and the flag bearer's pistol, and headed towards the cave. He began singing.

The New Way leads to liberty,
The New Way built by you…

He lit a ready flambeau and made a final scan of the collapsing scenery of his regime. He entered the cave with the flag.

Near the trucks Železný got hit and fell dead at the foot of the lieutenant.

The lieutenant ordered them to surrender. The men and he took off their white circles. But Luděk shook refused. With fool's bravado, he reloaded his weapon.

'Unity! Stability! Certainty! Woo yeah!' He ran out from behind the truck screaming and shooting his gun wildly, hitting nothing. He made it to the bridge before several bullets kicked up through his lungs and brought him down.

The lieutenant and the two soldiers shouted surrender and

emerged with their hands in the air. Soldiers quickly surrounded them. Eliška searched for the colonel. Some of the soldiers entered the colonel's house. Eliška followed, but she was not on the ground floor. More soldiers entered and searched the second floor and found no one. Captain Bradáč arrived and stood at the staircase to the cellar. Muffled voices could be heard below.

'I'll go, alone. I've got to talk to her,' she said.

'No.'

'I need to talk to her. If you send soldiers, it'll only provoke her.' She was determined.

Bradáč relented.

'Don't do anything until I yell for it,' she said.

'All right. Doctor, here.' He offered her a small handgun.

She shook her head and began to descend the steps to the cellar.

'Vendula. Vendula. It's Eliška. It's me. There are no soldiers. I'm not armed. Can I come down? I want to talk.' She carefully went step by step into the darkening passage. Eliška saw it would be near darkness down there so went back up to ask Bradáč for a torch. A battery torch was nearby for the purpose of going into the cellar. Eliška went back down.

'Vendula. I'm going to stop by the door and we can talk, all right?'

Outside, smoke emerged from Zarviš's house. Several soldiers started to pull down the sign with the three words on it. When they had achieved this a loud cheer went round as the rest of the army emerged into the field.

*

In the woods, Šimon studied the cave entrance from a distance. He looked at the burning house and the soldiers. He couldn't see the doctor. He began to walk towards the river and the cave. As he waded into the river, he shivered but did not take his eyes off the entrance. Climbing up the riverbank, he passed the grassy

349

clearing and neared the cave. But the darkness of it stopped him
– a malevolence. He had seen Zarviš with a gun enter it earlier
and his eyebrows arched in fear. He put out his hand, hesitated
and drew it back.

'Don't be afraid. Be brave,' he said to himself. Yet he was
looking deep into a swallowing darkness. 'It could save your
friend... everyone is looking for it.'

With a deep breath he went to the flambeaux resting nearby
and lit one, then looked into the cave with clear eyes.

With another deep breath he took one step, this for his mother.
With a straight back and a calm face, he took another step, this
for his auntie. He took another step, this one for Karl. His eyes
were sure as he took another step. And one for his friends. He
trod until the mouth of the cave embraced him.

Another step and another.

In the church, Viktor cradled Iva's shot and bloodied body in
his arms and lap as he sat on the steps to the altar. He stroked her
sunken face. There was a piece of paper clasped in her hand. He
undid it.

*Pick up the pieces of this broken world and begin to put them
back together. In this way you will love me. The world needs
people like you, Viktor.*

He clasped her head to his chest and lent his cheek on her
head. His lips stiffened; then his mouth opened and he uttered a
moan, soft yet pained. He kissed her. And resting his face on her
head, his tears touched her hair.

Outside, František stood on the bridge looking down at the
bodies near the truck. 'Am I wrong?' He took off his glasses and
looked up at the burning building. 'Could it be true? Something
great...'

On the stairs to the cellar, Eliška took another step down. She
heard things banging and shifting about. The stairs turned at a
right angle just before the door. She peered round the corner; the
door was open but there was only darkness and vague shadows
in the cellar.

350

'Vendula. Vendula. I'm alone. I won't come any closer.' She turned the torch on. The colonel darted behind some boxes with Ludmila. Eliška turned the torch off. 'Vendula, I haven't come to give you up. I just don't want you to do anything stupid.'

Feet shuffled and then a gruff voice answered: 'Once again the bleeding heart. Once more the fountain of charity wants to pardon. She wants to save the world. She can do no wrong. It's enough to make you sick.'

'Vendula, I just want to help.'

'Oh… the doctor will cure us. The world was ruined because people like you weren't sure.'

'It's not like that.'

'Denial. But I must say, little Eliška, what you did in the clearing was one hell of a performance. Hypnotised all my soldiers with your act. And all you did was stand there. It was beautiful. Well done. But it won't work. You haven't got the nous to keep it together. They'll eat you up.'

'Vendula, no one knows the way.'

'Ha. The UN special envoy of kindness. Eliška, there's only one way. You'll fail because you won't take it.'

'Vendula, give up.'

'No. You always were a righteous little bitch.'

'Vendula, please let Ludmila and Nada go.'

'It's a trick.'

'No. It's just you and me.' Eliška stepped onto the floor. There was more scuffling.

'Actually, I'm happy because I know it won't work with you in charge,' Vendula said. 'You'll oversee a highway of death.'

Eliška stepped closer. 'I haven't given up on you, Vendula.'

The colonel fired her gun. The bullet flew past Eliška and the sound punched her ears as she recoiled. She was momentarily deafened.

'Come closer, Eliška. Come in. Come in,' the colonel shouted.

Eliška took a hesitant step forward.

'Closer. Closer.'

'Let them go, Vendula.'

A second shot rattled the metal parts of the cellar and missed her. She ducked, then took two steps forward and one to the side. 'Let them go.' She crouched down.

A third shot missed. Eliška tiptoed and squatted in front of the boxes. She sneaked round to the side as the colonel shouted. She aimed the torch round where she thought the colonel was and flashed it on, momentarily blinding her. The colonel shot wildly. Eliška crouched back behind a box. Free, Ludmila darted to a corner.

'Eliška,' the colonel yelled, 'I won't shoot. Can you hear me?'

The doctor had managed to come to the end of the row of boxes. She crept round and saw that the colonel had her back to her. She turned the torch on. The colonel spun round. Eliška dropped the torch and leapt on the colonel, who fell backwards. The gun went off – the bullet struck the wall. With her good hand, Eliška grabbed Vendula's hand which held the gun. She put her whole weight onto it so that it hit the floor and the gun fell out.

'Stop, Vendula.'

The colonel tried to reach for the gun with her bad hand but couldn't. Instead, she rolled so that she was on top, but the gun was under Eliška's back.

'I should have killed you in the clearing,' the colonel said then rolled back so that they were both on their sides as they struggled. The torch shone up from their feet to show the grotesque smile on the colonel's face, which was half in shadow. She reached behind Eliška and grasped the gun. She rolled again on top of Eliška, who grabbed the colonel's hand with both of hers, pushing the gun's aim aside. Suddenly the pressure from Eliška's hands folded the colonel's wrist, so the gun pointed round to her. She tried to push it aside, but it went off. The colonel gasped as the gun fell out of her hands. She rolled off Eliška and onto her back. The doctor sat up. She felt the colonel's chest, and the

352

blood. The shot was near the heart, and it was beating erratically. Yet the look in the colonel's eye was of solid hatred. Eliška rested her hand gently on her sister's cheek. The colonel scowled and her breathing lessened. Her eyes rolled back, then she breathed her last and went limp.

Eliška stared for a long time.

'It's over.' She closed the colonel's eyes and felt relief as well as defeat and waste. Soldiers entered with torches, which showed Ludmila and Nada huddled in a corner. There was a clamouring coming from behind a door in a corner of the cellar. One of the soldiers turned a key, which was in the door's lock. The figure inside immediately put his arms over his eyes, blinded by the light. Eliška saw the man and told the soldiers not to shine their lights on Marek.

Soon, they emerged from the house, Marek covering his eyes from the light. The fire burning Zarviš's house was raging. The villagers arrived and rejoiced at seeing Eliška.

'Golden One is alive,' Anton said, and embraced her.

Natalie arrived from her house and clasped Marek; everyone looked exhausted.

But shouting erupted from the field across the river. The ex-sergeant staggered and coughed and shouted for the colonel. People retreated from the man creating a wide space round him. The ex-sergeant tried to get closer to one of them, but they retreated.

'Delirium!' someone shouted. 'He's got red marks on his neck.'

'The virus is in the village!' another shouted.

Eliška sighed and fell to her knees. The virus was in the village. She bowed her head. 'All for nothing,' she said. 'The virus is in the village.'

Šimon emerged unnoticed from the cave, carrying a plastic box. As he walked towards Eliška and the others, he raised the box.

'I found it, Doctor,' he yelled.

She didn't hear him.

'Doctor, I found it. I found it.' His face beamed though the sun made him squint. On the box which Šimon held was a flower. 'I found it, Doctor, I found it. '

Eliška finally saw him and began walking towards him. Šimon took another step, then another.

'No! You can't have it!' Zarviš shrieked from the darkness of the cave. There was a sound of scuffling feet. He squealed again and Eliška stopped. Šimon took another step, not noticing the sounds behind him. From the dark of the cave a hand emerged – in it, a gun. It fired.

Šimon took a step.

The gun blasted again.

Another step…

Another…

A…

The box dropped and Šimon collapsed.

Everyone was still. Except for Zarviš, who stood out of the cave. He gaped at the villagers with a grotesque smile. Someone ran towards him, screaming rage. With his long coat flapping, he charged at Zarviš shouting: 'Snake! Snake!'

Zarviš grimaced as František rushed at him. He raised the gun. At first, he pointed it at František, but then turned it to his own head.

'I won't be forgotten,' Zarviš said.

He cackled and pulled the trigger. When František reached him, he was on the ground, dead. But František grasped his shirt and punched him in savage madness.

Eliška rushed to Šimon and turned him onto his back. Two little streams of blood stained his shirt. She touched the wounds to his warm heart. There was no beat. She held him up; his limp head fell back; the sun glistened in his wet hair. She gently put him down. His head rested a little on its side, facing her. She sighed, then softly closed the lids to his shining eyes.

The soldiers that had arrived near Zarviš managed to peel

František away. But he continued to rage. His glasses flew off.

Hynek stood close to Eliška and bowed his head. Petra knelt beside the boy and picked up his warm hand. She looked up to Eliška as if for explanation, but the doctor looked away. Petra turned to the others who were standing around. They said nothing.

Eliška saw the box, which had kicked open. The liquid inside its vials sparkled in the sunlight. She got up and examined it: vaccines.

Anton arrived, hesitant and clutching his violin case in both hands. When he stood close to the body of the boy, he shook his head and suddenly threw the violin case into the river growling as he did so. Petra gently put Šimon's hand on his broken heart. She stood up and looked from the body to the burning house. Then she pulled off her headscarf to show a full head of grey hair. She wrung the scarf between her hands, then threw it down and began to beat her chest. Radoš and Hynek both stopped her, and she bowed her head.

František, with unkempt hair and undone shoelaces, paced dementedly up and down by the cave.

'Gone… to nothing?' He turned. 'No… it cannot be nothing.' He stopped to see the boy. Then he continued pacing. 'No!' He stopped. 'There must be a point.' He clutched his hair. He turned towards the gun. He lunged at it and threw it into the cave, then shouted after it, 'blind.' He yelled into the dark cave. He spun round. 'There must be a reason!' He ran towards the fallen boy. He bent down next to him and put his hand on his forehead. As he touched him, he gasped. He looked up at them.

'How can this be nothing?' He waited but they said nothing. He took Šimon's hand, looking closely at it. 'Nothing?' He put the hand down and touched the boy's chest. 'Nothing?' He shot up and recoiled backwards. 'Take it away.' He screamed and shook his head, walking backwards. 'Take me away from myself!' He turned and wrestled with his coat and pulled it off. He looked again at the boy and screamed, pulling his hair. 'It was my fault… I knew the vaccine was in the cave… I knew and did nothing.' He stumbled but remained upright. He ran towards the cave. 'No!' He fell to his knees. 'I am judged.'

They were all silent.

Yet one of the villagers had retrieved the violin from the river and offered it back to Anton. The musician shook his head.

Only the trickling river moved and made a sound.

CHAPTER 47

It was evening when Viktor carried Šimon across the bridge in solemn step with the rest of the villagers. The soldiers stood gloomily. Šimon was brought into the field and towards another body, which Viktor had already laid out. Šimon's slightly parted lips had paled grey-purple; his dangling fingers reached out for no one now. Something fell out of his pocket. It was the image of the Madonna.

Eliška and the nurse had tended the injured; the ex-sergeant had been isolated and given medicine. She had gone to Karl and was confident he would recover. He'd asked about Šimon, but she hadn't been able to tell him.

Viktor laid Šimon down next to Iva; the boy's pale, freckled cheeks and fair eyebrows were peaceful. His bottom lip rested a little inside his top teeth. Petra prayed as Viktor knelt next to Iva.

'I only wish we could've found your boy,' he said.

František groaned, then pulled out a notebook from his pocket and began tearing the pages out of it. He threw the notebook down and staggered towards the oak tree.

'Blind,' he said and stopped. He lunged at the base of the tree and hugged it. Then he hit his head against the tree again and again, making it bleed. Anton held and stopped him.

'I did nothing,' František said.

'It couldn't be helped,' Anton said.

'Only life matters. Only life has meaning. It is the ultimate value. I could have... I did nothing.' He rocked back and forth. A small tear fell.

All the villagers had removed their white circles and stood in silence. Even the dog was quiet.

Sofie put her arm around Ana. 'It was like an illness. But it's over now.'

Eliška took the paper that the bald man had held. It was a letter from a ministry: A final strategy – Clean Village Directive 57/1f – an army unit each to take a village … store a newly made vaccine … ten thousand villages in Europe … self-sustainable…

She let the paper fall out her hand and blow away, then went to Nebojsa.

'How could she do it?' Her eyes were angry. 'To only vaccinate the soldiers. You should've told me.'

'I'm sorry, Doctor,' Nebojsa said. 'I wanted to. I thought…'

'And the ex-sergeant?' she said.

'Not everyone… I didn't know her reason. I don't know.'

Eliška stared then sighed. 'It doesn't matter now. It's done. Only… let's not repeat it.'

The captain nodded.

Viktor held Iva's hand. He looked at the boy, then slowly took his hand and put it in hers. He reached down to Šimon's shoe and began tying up the laces. When he had finished, he held the shoe and looked up at the wheat in the distant field, drenched in sunset. He wept.

Hynek mounted the platform. He took off his hat and drew everyone's attention as he looked from face to face. 'The dead do not take hope with them; they bequeath it. Death is not the end of hope. Forgive. Believe in life. Make things grow.' He waited as though he would say more, but didn't.

Eliška looked at the plastic box at her feet, the box that Šimon had carried. She gazed at the flower on the top.

There were sudden hushed voices. Soldiers pointed to something at the edge of the field. Eliška looked and saw the emblem waving above the heads of the soldiers as it began to proceed into the centre of the field. Soldiers made way as the breeze fluttered and stretched out the flower for all to see. And then it moved towards Radoš, where it stopped. He looked at its sunbeams, its eye, its bright flower, set against the sunset. He slowly looked down at the bearer, who had scratches and cuts and a despairing face. Then she knelt; the branch of the emblem touched the ground and rested against her shoulders. She looked up at him. Her hair was awry and clung with sweat. Radoš looked at her bitterly. She raised her hand, unsure and hoping. Her lips parted but there were no words, only sad and frightened eyes. He looked away and scowled with anger. Helena mouthed the word 'please'.

He did not look at her, but at the two bodies. His frowning brow and harsh eyes were defiant, despite all the villagers looking at Helena in pity. But not him.

'Forgive me,' she uttered. Tears wet her trembling lips.

He looked up at the emblem.

'You abandoned us,' he said.

'You're right,' she said. 'You're right. Please, take this flag. I brought it for you. I brought it... take it and I will leave.' She hung her head. 'I will leave.'

He slowly looked down to her. She held the emblem out to him with bowed head. His face seemed tortured.

'Take it from me. Take it,' she said.

'No. Do not kneel... not to me.'

'Take it.'

'No...' he said, and slowly knelt in front of her and raised her tearful head. 'First, take me.' He looked into her shamed eyes, which gazed back in wonder. 'Why did you run from me?'

'Forgive me.'

He slowly put his arms round her and drew her into an embrace. She leant her head on his shoulder. As the emblem flapped above them, Petra smiled, eyes wet. Some of the soldiers had tears also.

'Only you,' Helena said.

Radoš looked up at the sky and held her tight.

Eliška looked at the wheat under the setting sun with its promise of future harvest. František stood beside her. Anton followed, holding his violin case. Chicks from a robin's nest in the oak tree chirped. Little Nada skipped over and put her ear to Natalie's belly, who looked down from the wheat to caress the girl. Nada pointed at a swarm of bees around the beehive and the flowers she had put on top of it. Her cheeks puffed in cherubic joy.

And Hynek looked down from the symbol with its eye to the waving wheat.

'It will bear witness to our future,' he said.

'As it does to this beginning. This beginning.'

BV - #0123 - 230523 - C0 - 198/129/21 - PB - 9781803781242 - Matt Lamination